D1315373

A FRACTURED TRUTH

ALSO BY CAROLINE SLATE

The House on Sprucewood Lane

A FRACTURED TRUTH

CAROLINE SLATE

ATRIA BOOKS

New York   London   Toronto   Sydney   Singapore

For Eamon
We got through all of last year—and we're here!

ACKNOWLEDGMENTS

Amy Pierpont's gifted editorial hand is in evidence throughout this book. I appreciate her more than I can say—and that includes the relentless grace with which she held my feet to the fire until we got it right. Thanks, you're a joy to work with!

Loretta Barrett is the kind of agent whose dedicated expertise is always on the job and always available. I'm grateful to be one of her writers.

My visit to Bedford Hills Women's Correctional Facility was invaluable. Many thanks to the staff for their generosity and candor.

GEORGE: *I love you, love you, love you, dear, I cross my heart it's true. Do you believe me?*

GRACIE: *I do.*

George Burns and Gracie Allen, c. 1934

JEWELRY DESIGNER
KILLS HUSBAND

By Gabriel McCail

Grace Leshansky Boudreau, the jewelry designer known profession-ally as GraceL, shot and killed her husband Paul, Manhattan prose-cutors say, in the Hudson Street loft, which until last month the couple had shared. Mr. Boudreau was a financial adviser and writer.

Police arrived on the scene at 1:30 A.M. Tuesday in response to a phone call from Grace Boudreau. At a brief press conference, NYPD Lieutenant John Classon, in charge of the case, described Ms. Boudreau as sounding calm on the phone.

When the officers arrived, Classon said, they found Ms. Boudreau sitting on the couch staring at the victim who was lying on his back on the floor maybe thirty feet in front of her. There had been a single shot, the bullet fired from about fifteen feet. No sign of a struggle.

"The victim would have died in minutes," Classon said. "The bullet hit an inch under the heart. It was either a skillful shot or, as his wife claims, 'dumb luck.'" Classon identified the weapon as a Sig Sauer .38 caliber revolver, which Ms. Boudreau claimed to have seen for the first time that night when her husband pulled it out of his coat pocket. According to Classon, police investigation shows no weapon registered to either Boudreau. He said, "Ms. Boudreau has admitted to the shooting and is in custody."

Specific circumstances surrounding the shooting are unclear, but the Boudreaus separated two weeks ago, according to friends, after an incident at the Soho art gallery opening. Other guests at the Huffman Gallery report that Grace Boudreau attacked her husband, knocking him against a large canvas on exhibit, allegedly damaging the painting and the one hanging beside it. The following day, he moved from the couple's loft to the Chelsea Hotel. He was still registered there when he died. The same day, Ms. Boudreau filed for a court order of protection to bar her "abusive" husband from entering the loft or otherwise coming within fifty feet of her. The order had not yet been issued.

Sources close to the couple called the two-year marriage, "always intense," and said that it had been "stretched to the snap point" by a series of misfortunes beginning about seven months ago with the disappearance of Ms. Boudreau's father under mysterious circumstances, and peaking with sudden, dramatic reverses in her business. The six-year-old GraceL Company produces Ms. Boudreau's striking jewelry designs, often combining precious metals with unlikely materials such as driftwood, bottle glass or industrial nails. The enterprise had been from its inception a great success but recent over-leveraging, over-commitment and late deliveries put the company in jeopardy, according to business associates. On July 16, it filed for Chapter 11 bankruptcy protection.

Grace Boudreau's father, George Leshansky, an accountant said to be a habitual gambler, disappeared last March. The story received intense media coverage at the time, most of it speculative. It was rumored that Leshansky had been slated to testify in the FBI's case against Josh Pyatt, alleged boss of a Harlem-based mob involved in loan-sharking, protection and other forms of racketeering. The FBI declined comment. To date, neither Leshansky nor his body has been found. He is presumed dead. Initial suspicion focused heavily on the Pyatt family, specifically on Josh's son, Michael, but no charges were brought.

Four days before his death, Paul Boudreau had turned thirty-two. Grace Boudreau is thirty-three.

CHAPTER ONE

OCTOBER 3, 2002

'd been charged with murder. The lawyers had pleaded it down to manslaughter. Manslaughter. The slaughter of a man: the bloody sound of it had seemed to me worse than murder, and still does.

They'd pronounced me lucky, my lawyers had: lucky that it had been Paul's gun; lucky I'd put in for the court order of protection against him even if it hadn't had time to come through; lucky that everyone knew about my monumental losses—my father, my business; lucky I had behaved erratically in public. All of this supported the claim that the killing was unpremeditated. After all, I hadn't gone out and bought a gun, but simply been swept away, provoked in my vulnerable state into the impulse to use a weapon ready at hand—Paul's weapon.

Premeditated. Swept away. Provoked. Vulnerable. Impulse: the terms with their self-important airs marched, heads high, masquerading as hard facts. Like little soldiers they'd protected my flanks. *Oh yes, one lucky lady, that's me.* But of course I was: five to twelve, out in seven, as opposed to, say, seven to fifteen, six to eighteen—life. That could be seen as luck.

3

Here I stood now in a changing room for just-released prisoners, peering at myself full-length: charcoal pants, black turtleneck sweater, shiny black shoes with small silver buckles and, unseen in the mirror but a definite presence, silken underwear—every item expensive; every item brand-new. I was unused to looking into mirrors and the experience jarred. It seemed like the reflection had dimension, life, was ready to walk away, while I was flat and without substance, a figment of my own imagination.

I'm half an inch shy of six feet. My build used to be generous like an Olympic swimmer's, skin taut over a layer of insulating flesh. But seven years in prison lost me the habit of eating much, developed the habit of exercise, lots of it, which had leaned my body out. The eyes that looked back at me were still my eyes: the color of Russian amber, yellow flecked with dark bits—tiny prehistoric fossils maybe. They are set wide, shaped by the high cheekbones beneath them into crescent moons, suggesting a smile no matter what. My nose is straight and emphatic; the chin, though small, has a jut to it, and my long, mobile mouth belongs on a comedian. The features were there, intact, but my face had changed anyway: it reminded me of a slum store shuttered for the night.

And then there was my hair. During the first two years up here in Bedford Hills, its Indian black began a leaching to white—all but a wide, off-center skunk streak that held stubbornly onto darkness. The hair hung in a fat braid to my waist. Funny, I'd always wondered whether there was Indian blood in me—hoped there was.

I glanced down at the stylish, witchy points on my shoes. The new leather felt stiff on toes used to spreading themselves in sneakers. Sheilah Donlan had arrived here early this morning, her arms filled with tissue-plumped Bergdorf shopping bags. Sheilah and I went back as far as third grade together—the only person on the outside I knew anymore. For the past half an hour she'd been bustling around me like a mother dressing her child for the first day at a new school, handing over the outfit piece by piece, talking up the provenance of each item, its particular claim to wonderfulness. Sheilah's mirror reflection stood behind mine, holding out a hand now, offering "A little blush?"

I turned to the actual Sheilah and said, "I don't know a fancier way to say thanks, but if I did I would." Sheilah said, "I'm your friend. It's what friends do. You'd do it for me. You've *done* it for me." True, I'd seen Sheilah through a booze and pills crack-up, checked her into Four Winds Hospital not so many miles from here, collected her two months later, clean and sober. But that was then. Now I seriously doubted whether I had the emotional horsepower to fuel the complicated demands of a civilian friendship, particularly one with Sheilah who gives too much and wants too much back.

I thought of Toukie and Wanda and Mercedes, lifelines during the years that are about to become the past—friendships rooted in impermanence, stripped of demands, vigorous maybe for just those reasons. Chiefly, I pictured Toukie's smart black eyes and the gold tooth that twinkles when she laughs. We'd had a special bond: two women who had killed their men.

"Thanks, Sheil. I'll just leave it at thanks for now," I said, taking the blush compact and brush, turning back to the mirror to apply it. The luxurious fabrics felt illicit against my skin as I moved, taunting in a way that I thought for a moment might make me cry. Actually, I'd have loved to cry. A big, long jag of wet sobs would've been as satisfying as . . . a comparison did not spring to mind immediately, then it did: as satisfying as a good come. The homecoming queen, Paul used to call me. But that was then too.

In these seven years I had schooled the riskier emotions with a hard hand, dressage discipline of dangerously frisky horses—something like that. I could laugh within bounds but produce not a tear; rushes of anger sparked and quickly fizzled like wet firecrackers: mad, sad, glad—all three were there but powerless. Sex? The ex-homecoming queen's urges were frozen or dried to dust—one way or another, so out of commission that going gay for the stay, as they put it up here, had not been even vaguely tempting.

Yet . . . yet, as I stood before that mirror, Sheilah watching expectantly, my insides asked for the buzz of strong feeling, the kind that bucks in the gut, races the pulses. A first day of freedom should be marked, shouldn't it, if only to prove you're alive? But no luck. I could tap no feeling other than the craving for feeling, a feeling in the second degree. Maybe this was how it would be now: a life in the second degree to pay for a death in the second degree. Laid on the line that way, it seemed only fair.

"Do you feel remorse?" they had asked. I'd said, *"Yes,"* knowing it was the answer they—the judge, the psychiatrist, the parole board—needed. The parole board didn't buy it at the first hearing, the five-year mark; they almost never did, I'd been warned, in a case like this. They'd hit me for two more years. At the second hearing the same simple *"yes"* rang truer to them.

Did it ring true to me? Does it now? Well, it was true that at the crack of the shot, the kick of the gun in my hand, Paul's body jerking back, I had hollered *"No."* I remembered clearly my finger tightening on the trigger, knowing that it was; the terrific jolt to my own body—then, his slow wilting collapse, the sounds from him, except for the very last one, drowned out by my scream. I remembered also the preceding hour, every bit of it, every word, every move, though I said I did not.

"Yes": a clear answer to their clear questions. But how could I seriously claim remorse when I knew that given the final moments to relive exactly as they'd gone, I might do exactly what I'd done?

"You feeling bad?" Sheilah asked, moving toward me. "You look a little shaky."

"No," I lied, fooling neither of us. "No, I'm good—just ready to get the hell out of here."

"The owner's a dancer on tour with some Andrew Lloyd Webber show," Sheilah said. It was maybe half an hour later and we were driving down the Hutch, The Bedford Hills Women's Correctional Facility a good five miles behind us. "Look, don't expect anything grand. It's kind of a skinny building scrunched in between two better ones—no doorman, but you said you didn't care. I signed a nine-month lease for you. That's when he'll be back."

"Sounds perfect," I said, trying to be positive despite a sense of dread beginning to rise like a fog around my heart. So this was freedom: a vast, shapeless space said to be filled with possibilities—but I could see only pieces of possibilities and even those felt beyond my reach.

"Ninety-third Street, you said, Sheil?"

"Ninety-fourth, just east of Amsterdam, remember?"

"Oh right, you told me that. And I *do* care about the doorman. I'm Goddamned relieved there isn't one. I've had enough hall monitors to last me awhile."

"Ah, Sweets. It's going to take you time to get over this." Like a cold or a car accident or a divorce. After years spent thickening my skin, I found myself suddenly skinless, too ready to be chafed by a brush against anything, even a friend's sympathy.

"How much money do I have left from the loft sale and all?" I asked. "I know you told me that too, but . . ."

"God, for someone who's made a fair amount of it, you're really hopeless about money."

Paul: "Back in Century One B.C. some smart Roman said, 'Money alone sets all the world in motion.' Ergo, the one who runs the money spins the earth. I'm pretty good at it."

Grace: "I'm not. I seem to know how to make it and how to save it. Want to feed my nest egg some growth hormones? Just tell me where to sign."

Paul: "Hmm. Let me think about that. You're my wife, may be a bad idea."

Paul had been nothing if not subtle. No rush. I reminded myself that replays like this one were hot coals, to be handled with tongs—imagery picked up in the stress-management therapy group, Tuesdays and Thursdays at four.

"Hopeless about sums up money and me," I said, back with Sheilah. "So what's the bad news?"

Her nose wrinkled with the arithmetic of my finances. "After brokers, lawyers and all, just over twenty-three thousand, except for the paintings and sculptures you wanted to keep." Just a few of the many I'd owned—mostly by artists who'd been friends of mine.

"I'd have to be flat-out broke to sell those, not that they'd be worth all that much in the world of dealers and collectors."

"Probably not. But look, you're *not* flat-out. You'll have the salary from me, at least for the short range."

We'd known each other at close range for thirty years—long enough for us both to recognize it would be no walk on the beach, me working for her. But we recognized also that for a paroled convict a solid job in waiting was worth almost any walk required, plus a kiss on the ground beneath her feet.

"I still suspect you didn't exactly need another mouth to feed," I said. "I really will try to be useful. Hey, thanks to you I am, in discharge-manual lingo, an employed woman with a domicile and bank account—a good bet to reenter society as a responsible citizen."

"Bet your ass you are! And I *didn't* invent the job. Swear. I've taken on another recruiter and a full-time research guy—who's fabulous, by the way, and I pay him a fortune. I admit it's scary, the extra expense, but I had to do it. The search business is way more complicated than it was— *much* more work, and thank God the work's coming to me. Used to be that our mandate was finding and wooing the best candidates. *Now* we practically have to do an FBI check to make sure they've been good boys and girls as well as good executives. Not all of them have, which means more recruits, more meetings. So I'm there some nights till ten, phoning and e-mailing my little heart out. What I'm saying is I need to be nicer to myself. I mean what's the good of *making* it if all you get is the chance to work harder?"

"Right." A shrink's question and Sheilah, always the student with her hand raised highest, had the right answer. But the answer in her case came with a footnote: her fingers would never really come off those details, not if she had a dozen schedulers. "E-mail," I said, "you'll have to teach me that. The Internet got big just about the time I went in. We weren't allowed to mouse around in cyberspace up there."

"You'll learn it in half a second. But look, you know and I know this isn't the kind of work you're used to, or ought to be doing in the long run." No use in recapping what I was currently used to, or in pointing out that the long run was territory as remote to me as the afterlife. "By the time the dancer gets back and wants his apartment, Gracie, you'll be . . ."

Sheilah kept talking but I didn't hear the rest. My thoughts had cut and run down a private path after "Gracie." She called me that only occasionally. With George gone, she was the only one who did. I'd been Gracie; he'd been George, never been Dad or Daddy. He was George from the time I could talk. It suited the way we were with each other. *Now say Jawge. Atta girl.* I could hear his charred voice, with its Noo Yawk dips and swells. *And you're Gracie. Gray-see. What else would a Jawge name his girl?*

Especially *this* George: when I saw George Burns on television reruns and later in the movies, the fox-faced, dapper look, as well as the hoarse vaudeville sound of him, were uncannily like my father—well, like George Leshansky might have been, given the luck and swagger to be a winner.

Burns and Allen were our household mascots, a scratchy record of their stage and radio skits on the priority list of stuff that came along each time we moved: George, the faintly gruff, exasperated but protective leader; Gracie, the adorably child-voiced dumbbell always trumping his ace, far wiser in her innocence than he. I said mascots, not models—I was no more adorable than George was protective, and wisdom was scarce in our household.

How to explain about George and me . . . we were a team, just us two. Originally, there must have been a third team member, but she was gone before my memories began. George never mentioned her, and during my earliest years there seemed nothing strange about that. By the time my curiosity began to put out shoots, George's elusiveness about anything to do with family ties was normal too. Asking became a kind of halfhearted game:

"*So who was my mom? Come on, George, did she run away or die or what?*"

"*Who do you want her to be?*"

"*A Indian warrior princess.*"

"*You got it, kid.*"

"*No, tell me, really.*"

"A seven-foot Indian warrior princess with very long legs. That's how come she could run so fast and not trip on her bow and arrows. Look, I'm going out for a coupla hours. You be okay?"

"Sure. Bring back ice cream. Chocolate."

"Say goodnight, Gracie."

But sometimes I couldn't summon up even half a heart for the game, and ice cream, even chocolate, would've curdled inside me. On those occasions I would mumble my "sure" and wish him out the door before my impotent tears began to flow.

I can tell you what my first retrievable memory is:

I am sitting in a corner of an unfamiliar room, one eye shut, the other pressed against the peephole of a kaleidoscope, fixed on the stained-glass patterns inside that change at the slightest move of my hand, loving the look of them, frustrated that I can't save the ones I like best, keep them forever, because if I could, I would be safe—safe from what I don't really know; I have no recollection of feeling scared . . . exactly. At a table in the center of the room, men are smoking and dealing out cards, slap, slap, slap. They give and take red, white and blue discs from each other; that makes a louder sound. They don't talk much, except to repeat words like "raise" and "call." From time to time some of them look really mad at each other or like their stomachs hurt bad. One of them is George. My age would be five—that's my best guess.

When I recall that little girl I begin to pity her, want to fold her in my arms. And then I bring myself up short and stop it. George was a singleton in his heart, a gambler in his blood and bone, a man unsuited in his nature to be a parent, yet his daughter never went cold or hungry or threadbare, nor was she abandoned or afraid she might be—never hit, never threatened, never made to feel boring or burdensome.

Quite the contrary, my father tended to me (for if not, who did change those diapers, fill those bottles with milk?) until I was old enough to begin some tending of him. And how heady is that: to be necessary when you're too young to have earned anyone's confidence, too young to deserve such importance! I chose to think of myself as cherished, if not in the orthodox way a parent cherishes a child, then in another way. Back then, George depended on me, and I depended on that. You could say ours was a house of cards in more ways than one, a house where laughs and music punctuated the states of emergency—or the other way around. Nevertheless, it was ours . . .

A tap at my shoulder: Sheilah's forefinger, insistent in its touch. As I turned, I saw the gleam of gold and copper, a ring I'd made her fifteen years ago. "Earth to Gracie. This is too much stuff for you, right? I'm overloading you with information. Here's the thing, though: You'll live in that little apartment for now and you'll work for me, but in what—a few months?—you'll be designing again, and then—"

"No, I won't," I cut in. She had touched a nerve and the pain was sharp.

"You won't? But that's crazy. You design jewelry, that's what you *do*, who you *are*. How you make your living. Since we were kids it's always been—"

"Look, I said 'won't'; I mean can't. My hands are not steady, okay? *Satisfied now?*" It came out like the sudden snarl of an animal stroked the wrong way. "Christ, I'm sorry," I said. I looked at her hurt face and remembered that she'd gone through her own hell and bounced back. The animal I felt like was a swine. "Sorry, really," I said. "Give me half a minute to catch my breath, Sheil."

"Don't *you* be sorry, Sweets, *I'm* sorry. I was moving in on you—occupational hazard. I'm a headhunter—that's what they pay me for," she added with a small, determined laugh. "But look, your hands will be fine once you . . . settle back in, and even if . . . well, you wouldn't have to actually *make* the pieces any more, just design them. Oops, there I go again." She shook her head, the glossy deep red of her hair a match for the darkest of the autumn leaves. Like all her gestures, it was big enough to draw attention to itself.

"I had an offer a few months ago to just design," I said. "Gun motifs with my name attached to them. Some outfit wanted to sell them on cable TV. 'Outlaw chic' was what they called it in their letter."

"I'm not even going to ask if you're kidding, I'm sure you're not. But you know that kind of sleaze isn't what I'm talking about. My GraceL pieces are the ones I always reach for—just like everybody who owns them. You've got a gift. Of *course* you need to keep using it."

"I'm not a sketch artist, okay? I'm a jeweler. Was. I *was* a jeweler who made things and then had some of them reproduced and marketed very profitably. However, a jeweler who can't hold a welding torch steady or set a stone right is no jeweler. So, that's it."

"But—" The sharp twang of rebuttal made my teeth grind. She might apologize but she never, ever gave up.

"Sheilah. *No.*"

She held up one hand, palm out. "Peace. You know me, the single-minded striver, universal caretaker." She gave a little "heh heh" of a laugh. "Prototypical only child of an alcoholic."

I pictured a pale, willowy blond—two drops of Mayflower blood in her veins and lots of attitude about it; drinking vodka, pretending it was ice water. She called herself, grandly for the run-down Washington Heights tenement where we all lived, Mrs. Carpenter-Donlan: the Carpenter to mark the blue blood she claimed, the Donlan to prove someone had married her once.

"Remember how she used to keep at me?" Sheilah asked with the rueful tone that mention of her mother usually triggered. "My pan face, pug nose—and God how she hated my freckles."

"All of those are long gone, Gorgeous. Actually, I always thought your freckles were kind of cute. So, has Mrs. C-D softened with age in the last seven years?"

"Oh right! She keeps the booze in better check, at least around me because she's just a little scared I might cut her off otherwise, but she's still the killer she always was and . . ." Her eyes flicked away from the road ahead to give me a stricken glance.

"What're you gonna do, censor every word you say in front of me? You know, up there we'd use the word about ourselves, some of us would. Maybe saying it is just easier than not saying it." I didn't add that others of us would not talk that talk ever, and anyone who dared it in their presence could end up with a cracked rib or burned arm as a penalty for bad judgment.

The set of Sheilah's face still telegraphed discomfort. And why shouldn't she be uneasy? Why would any civilian be at ease with one of us?

"Come on, finish what you started to say about your mother."

"Oh, same old same old: I don't tell her to go to hell. She lives like a rich lady, sips her Smirnoff in a fancy glass a block away from me in Murray Hill. I pick up the tab and buy her extras tied up with ribbons, and I still can't catch a break with her."

But she kept on with the minuet anyway, courting, wanting, hoping. Hell, she'd named her firm Carpenter-Donlan Associates, brooking no argument from shrink or friend.

In a fast turnabout, which took me by surprise, she said, "Paul was such a bastard, such a beautiful bastard—that voice, like a TV evangelist. He could sell you salvation, or the Holland Tunnel ten minutes after you found out he didn't own the Brooklyn Bridge you just bought."

This was not new territory for us. She wanted to talk about Paul, about the rest of it, trawling maybe for some way to see into my head, to truly understand. "The voice was a lot better than any TV evangelist," I said evenly, "but please, I don't want to go there."

"You're going to *have* to go there sometime." I went often, not with any company though. She knew as much as she knew; lawyers and shrinks knew what I'd told them. Sheilah continued like a stream running where it always ran. "Grace, you could have pleaded *innocent:* self-defense, temporary insanity. Better lawyers would've done it, I *told* you that. You'd applied for the restraining order—"

"It was not self-defense," I said for not the first or the twentieth time, "not the way the law means that. And if you think I was nuts you've got ample reason, but again, not legal reason." From a standing start, my heart began to pound like something needing to get out.

"The man *stole* from you, wrecked your business. I swear if anyone did that to me, I'd—"

"You don't know what you'd do," I said through gritted teeth. "Could . . . could we just not talk for a while?"

We drove on, quiet except for the white sound of good tires on good pavement, until Sheilah turned on the radio to the lulling beat of some easy-listening station. After some Joni and Beatles and Bonnie, I was the one who broke the silence. "Seeing any new men, lately?" It was an olive branch—better for us both than a lame explanation or another apology.

"Uh-huh." She always was. "Briefly." That too. "Well, not *that* briefly, about five months. I didn't mention him when I came up because . . . I don't know, maybe I thought he'd be something and I didn't want to jinx it. Anyway, he was a sports agent: tall, cute, nice sense of humor—very high powered. But he'd have these headaches at the end of an evening, so after a while I began to figure there might be someone else on his screen. And of course there was. Not some cute little actress or model, though. Guess what, my competition was the second-string goalie for the New York Rangers. Can you *imagine?*"

Her lips stretched into something halfway between smile and grimace. She was trying to entertain me and I could've kissed her for the effort. Then she grinned for real and the taut, ivory face relaxed. For a moment she resembled Sheilah Donlan of twenty-five years ago, before her features had been chiseled, laminated, peeled and implanted up to her standards, or her mother's—Sheilah Donlan, from a time when we were sure we'd grow up invincible because we were tough willed and loaded with desire.

"Love you," I said.

"You even love my big mouth?"

"Even that," I said. "Hey, who else would've schlepped up there almost every week for seven years to spend half an hour with a cranky felon in baggy green pants?"

"Can I say something? Promise you won't get mad."

I took a very deep breath. "Shoot," I said.

"A couple of your friends called me—Danton Redondo, Jan Simone. They want to see you, Gracie, but they don't want to . . . you know. Your new number's unlisted. I said . . . well, you'd call them."

There are two kinds of prisoners, the kind who live for visits and the kind who barely live through them. The first are mostly people with families, the prospect of overnights in a prison trailer with husband or kids their searchlight in the fog. I'd been the second kind: no family, only the fog. And thirty minutes of stilted small talk with someone who can go home only made the fog thicker. One by one, I'd turned them away or turned them off. Except for Sheilah who had just kept coming and, don't ask me why, but she would stride into that visitors' room, her hair a flaming rebuttal to the soiled sterility, and I'd be glad to see her. Most of the time I would be.

"I just couldn't handle it when people would come up there," I said. "I was awful. I'm surprised Danton or Jan or anyone wants to bother with me. I'll call them—but maybe not right away. I need some time to kind of learn . . . how to be."

"Of course." Half a beat. "Just one more thing?"

"I may be thinged out, Sheil."

"The hair. It makes you look like Joan Baez playing Pocahontas's mother. I mean, a long, white braid? You're forty years old!"

My laugh was pure relief. "Pocohontas's mother was probably dead by the time she was forty. But I get your point."

"Good, because I've booked you with William at Garren tomorrow at two-thirty. Garren, the hair place at Bendel's? He's a genius; he'll have you looking like you again. Even better now that you've lost—how many pounds?"

"I don't know how many pounds, but you have to know I'm *not* me again—and a haircut won't change that. I'll tell you what, I'll let the genius lop the braid off because I don't want to embarrass you in your office, but the gray hairs stay gray. I've earned them and I own them."

CHAPTER TWO

We hit the apartment just after noon. After a quick tour of my new home, its drawers and closets and the contents Sheilah had put in them, she announced we were going out to lunch in "this great new place on Columbus." Then a funny thing happened: My motor stalled out.

"I . . . can't," I said, my voice small inside me. "I don't think I can go." The foggy dread that had begun to drift in on the ride down had settled thick and deep. I knew if I ventured outside this still unfamiliar nest now I'd be unable to put one foot in front of the other reliably. Sheilah gave a quick understanding nod and dashed out for remarkable corned beef sandwiches, which we devoured faces down, not talking much. As soon as we were done eating, she jumped up from her chair, gave me a hug and a reminder about tomorrow's hair appointment and left mercifully fast—signaling that I was not the only one ready for a break.

As the door closed behind her I wondered how I'd feel if our roles were reversed. Bet I'd be rethinking the ex-con's stability, asking myself how she would work out day to day in my office, whether I'd bitten off more than I really cared to chew.

"Harder to hit a moving target, no matter what way it's moving," George used to say. The advice had served me well in circumstances beyond any he or I could have foreseen. I took it once more now and walked. On the move it was easier to stay in the moment, think harmless thoughts. My harmless thought now was to learn this space, to claim it.

Two chunky rectangles almost identical in size, a short slim one connecting them—the whole thing originally a wing of the apartment next door. The front room was a living room with an open kitchen tucked into a far corner, the back one the bedroom. The narrow connecting hall contained the tall entrance door, and opposite it a small bathroom was installed in what had been in fancier times a large closet. The ceilings were ten feet high, the floors a nice honey color, a little wavy with age, the walls a butter yellow, newly painted, I thought, by an amateur in an upbeat mood. The furniture was minimal and offhand—items handed down or picked up here and there.

When I stuck my head out my new bedroom's window, the wind that hit my cheek smelled of Paul, a trace of pine and ginger peculiar to his skin. He played these tricks on me, or I did on myself. He'd turn up at the damnedest times in the damnedest ways: in dreams of course, but also on the jog back to my cube for a lockdown count, or while I munched a handful of popcorn in front of the rec room TV, too powerful, too palpable to be a ghost. Sometimes he'd talk into my ear as though through a tiny radio speaker, wooing, scorning, surprising—all the things he did. On occasion I could sense him coming and block him, other times, no such luck, he'd zoom in under my radar.

The window faced north overlooking what might have been intended to be a city garden, but received too little sun to motivate any gardeners. A single scrubby tree survived, fighting for its life and good luck to it. Despite the rotten view the fall air was crisp, clear and weightless—the kind of weather that polishes up everything in sight and puts a gold halo around unseen possibilities just beyond the horizon. Not Paul's kind of weather . . .

October, the Taconic Parkway lavishly flanked by a split sea of flaming trees: I feel drunk on color, over the top vocalizing about it.

"Optimist season," Paul says, taking his eyes off the road to throw me a glance that makes clear he has my number and it doesn't rank high in this respect. "Fall grabs people who enjoy being fooled, the ones who can pretend they don't know what they know. That spectacle out there is death in fancy dress. The leaves you're so enthralled with have no life left in them. In a week, maybe two, those branches will be bare as jackal-picked bones. How does that strike you?"

"As bullshit and high drama. It's not death out there; it's life," I shoot back, exasperated that what stirs me should repel him, surprised that my brilliant brand-new husband doesn't grasp what seems so simple. "A few months later spring comes, and it all happens again."

"Exactly." His voice drops half an octave as he clinches his point. "That's what qualifies you: you still don't see."

I didn't then. Later, I learned about Paul and autumn—and that "Death in Fancy Dress" was in fact the name of one of the dark poems he wrote in dark moods. But maybe Paul didn't see as clearly as he thought either—not about autumn or about me. Maybe Paul, who covered all his bases all the time, failed to appreciate the danger in ripping the scales from an optimist's eyes, as though the act were no more than peeling a Band-Aid off a skinned knee: a fast, stinging yank and you're forced to look at what's underneath: to know what you know—what you'd *have* to know if you allowed yourself to really see.

I shot Paul dead in a single incredible, logical, lucky, unlucky, mortal, immortal second. It happened in an October. Of course it did.

"Grace Leshansky." I said my name aloud to hear the sound; in my prison cot I'd whisper it under my breath sometimes, a kind of mantra to keep me from getting lost entirely. The name would be on my new checks. It was already on my driver's license and my passport, both of which needed renewal. I would have no use for a passport until after parole was over, which didn't seem a high priority problem just yet.

"Grace Leshan . . . sky," I called out the open window at the tough, stunted tree, my voice shimmying out of control like a car on ice. At Bedford Hills I'd been Boudreau, strapped face-to-face with Paul's name, each time I heard and responded to it—eight, ten, twelve times a day—an extra lash of punishment.

I filled my lungs with autumn, held onto it for a few seconds, then let it go and slammed the window shut, my unreliable hands stuttering a bit as I did it. For more than an hour I had been pacing the place like a zoo critter scoping out a new cage. I walked it once again, this time in slow, measured steps, finding small features to notice: the pleasing egg shape of a dented brass closet doorknob, the big-bellied shadow a toilet cast on the bathroom tile.

Much of my time in Bedford Hills had been spent hitching short rides on these thought trains to nowhere. They tended to begin with, say, speculation on the shape of a fellow inmate's thumb—broken perhaps, the bones imperfectly reknit—or a count of the number of steps across the hypotenuse of my cell, wondering who its previous inhabitant might have been; why she'd lived there; what had become of her: useless meanderings, except for their potential to distract the mind; so, useful after all.

"When the past's up in flames and you can't see a future through the smoke, you climb into the Now, Gracie. Zip it up around you like a spacesuit and keep your tuchis in motion." Childhood counsel, dispensed in a rasp of a voice permanently singed around its edges from too much fire and smoke. George's hand would be unsteady sometimes when he said this kind of thing and his fingertips ice cold as they played at the side of my neck the way you'd fiddle with worry beads. His words were meant to be jaunty, a try at making a joke of having to once more scoop up our stuff for a quick flight a step ahead of the landlord or the sheriff or an enforcer way more impressive than either of those. But he'd be too transparently scared to pull it off, and I'd know that he needed me to be not scared a bit. Funny, most times I wasn't.

George was gone now—gone maybe in the way he'd always feared he'd go; then again, maybe not. Deep in my 3 A.M. heart I believed he was alive and shreds of evidence kept that small, square window of hope propped open. But in forty years of life I have been wrong more often than right.

Nevertheless, George was gone. A slammed door of a word: gone. It isn't an absolute though—not the way dead is.

It had been almost nine years now since I'd shared a joke, heard an aria, kicked back, blown off steam with my hapless, quirky, endangered father. Most of those years I had spent in prison. Now only hours out I was freshly lonely for him with an elemental, childlike longing that jerked the string between my heart and mind and sent me tumbling back through the decades.

The early times were here and now, all the good times, all the terrible ones, all the places we'd lived, decamping from one to another often in a hell of a necessary hurry—the basement flat in Bensonhurst with its smeary half windows; the pink bungalow in Miami Beach where water bugs big and brown as Hershey bars would zip across cracked, turquoise Formica; the two rooms over someone's garage in Chicago; the motel room in Vegas with the broken blinds that made the Desert Inn's flashing neons an all-night light show beside my bed. Clearest of all, I remembered the Washington Heights apartment we'd lived in most of the time, the place we called home—home meant that we taped opera and museum posters to the walls, that I cared enough to paint one of those walls orange to make the place seem brighter, that Sheilah Donlan lived two floors upstairs.

Maybe the one conventional thing my father ever did was to get his CPA credential, which was how he more or less supported us—not with a steady job that would keep him from taking off for Vegas or Hialeah or Saratoga, but freelance gigs here and there, heavy around tax time. "Taming the numbers," he called it. He was a wizard with numbers. He could make them sit up, lie down, roll over and play dead. Routine stuff, he called it, but he wasn't looking for professional challenges. He already had his numerical challenge: gaming numbers that remained forever wild while he chased them like a butterfly hunter, catching one from time to time in his net.

I saw George teaching me the old Burns and Allen routines, relics of his early childhood, a time he'd developed a crush on and decided to preserve in himself—everything from the chalk-striped suits and wide ties he favored, the pocket watches that kept getting sold and replaced, to a taste for old slang and games of chance and the company of gangsters.

Once I'd learned the patter and songs and time steps, the two of us would bat them back and forth, eyes streaming with laugh tears, performers and audience both.

George: *"Name me three kinds of nuts."*

Gracie: *"Walnuts, chestnuts, forget-me-nuts."*

George: *"Say goodnight, Gracie."*

Gracie: *"Goodnight, Gracie."*

And then there was our song: George: *"I love you, love you, love you, dear, I cross my heart it's true. Do you believe me?"* Gracie: *"I do."* Burns had written the lines, unaware how precisely they would sum up a future George and Gracie.

George Leshansky would bet his life on anything. And his Gracie would believe anything.

CHAPTER THREE

By late afternoon there was no cranny of the apartment left to explore, no diverting small thought left to think, no housekeeping chore. I had taken down the dancer's posters and hung some of the paintings Sheilah had brought from my old loft on their hooks. The others I placed on the floor propped against walls so as to avoid banging new holes in a place that was not really mine. I put my sculptures where I thought I'd enjoy looking at them, changing my mind a few times.

Finally, I sat down heavily on a rattan chair with tropical-fantasy cushions, let my head loll back, shut my eyes and let my mind off its leash. It ran to dig up an old picture, a picture of the girl who wasn't scared facing down a large stranger at her door. His name: Josh Pyatt.

I had just turned nine and was the tallest girl in my class, by a lot. We were living in Washington Heights—our first of three times in that apartment. It was about five o'clock in the evening. I could see that George was worried by the way he kept pacing the living room, eyes darting toward the front door.

"Would you sit down or something," I said irritably, wondering whether he was thinking about us moving again, hoping not. School had just started and the girl who lived upstairs was in my class and on the way to becoming a friend.

He played a little tune on my neck with vampire fingers. I pulled away. "Sorry, kiddo. It's just . . . hey, Gracie, do a pal a big favor?"

I shrugged. *He's going to ask me to do something I will hate, like dropping an envelope of money off at the luncheonette, having to wait there while the guy in back with eyes like sunny-side up eggs, only the yolks are blue, counts it bill by bill and tells me I can leave.*

"That buzzer downstairs is gonna ring. You go to the intercom, and you tell the man I'm out for the night, that you're here with your friend Sheilah doing homework and later you'll be sleeping over at her apartment."

But when the ring sounded, it wasn't the downstairs buzzer, it was the doorbell, four feet away from us—and anyone on the other side of it could hear *La Bohème* swooping to its highs and lows on the record player, which didn't sound so much like a third-grader's homework. We both froze for a second. George went a greenish white. He started fast toward the bedroom door, then kind of skittered back to me and tickled my ear with a hot whisper. My heart gave a whacking thump and suddenly I needed to go to the bathroom seriously. I nodded to him and he disappeared into the bedroom. Only for a second did my feet beg to follow after him. I called out to the door, "Wait a second."

After I was sure he'd had time to get into the closet, way back behind the winter coats, I made myself go to the door and flip open the peephole. The man had a face like a bear, a big, black face with small shiny eyes. "Who is it?"

"I'm Mr. Pyatt, a friend of your daddy's." The voice was like dark honey with sand in it.

"My . . . daddy isn't home, my friend's here. We're doing homework." I turned away for a second and said, "No, Sheilah, it's not your mother yet. It's my father's friend." Then I made myself eyeball him again through the small hole.

Pause. Beat, beat, beat. I wondered if he could hear my heart. "Grace, that your name?"

"Yeah."

"I want you to open the door, so's I can see you better."

"I'm not allowed to open the door when my daddy isn't home," I said like little Susie Cream Cheese, and all I was thinking was, What if he breaks it down? Can I bite his hand? Hit him with the desk lamp?

"I told you. I'm his friend." My eye, staring through the peephole, was dry and itchy, but it felt like the only way to fight him was eyeball to eyeball. "Open it, honey."

"*No.* You have to come back another time."

And he laughed. "I got a kid myself. He's a real pisser, just like you. You are a good girl, Miz Grace. You tell your daddy I said that. And you tell him he been a baaad boy, so I'm gonna be seein' him."

As I opened my eyes and reestablished contact with the yellow walls of my new home, it came through to me how much of life I'd seen through a peephole of one kind or another, the view limited, vivid, all-absorbing, but often manipulated by forces beyond my sight lines—which brought me right back to the question I'd ducked and avoided all afternoon.

Within reach of where I sat was the small suitcase that held my few belongings from Bedford Hills. I nudged it over with my foot, bent to unzip it and felt around among many sets of official papers for the unofficial ones I wanted. My fingers knew them very well: seven number ten envelopes, each containing a single sheet of paper folded into precise thirds. I laid the envelopes out on the table beside me like a poker hand. I didn't need to remove the sheets to know what they said; they all said precisely the same thing:

"*I love you, love you, love you, dear, I cross my heart it's true. Do you believe me?*" Just the pair of lines from the old Burns and Allen song, typewriter typed or computer printed, I couldn't tell which. That was all, no return address, each time a different postmark. Once a year every year I was in prison they had arrived—in July just in time for my birthday, the last one three months ago.

Do you believe me? After George's disappearance, all of Paul's persuasive power had pushed me to believe my father was dead, that he had been killed.

Paul: "He died fast, Grace. He died on the run like a deer. No months of terror, wondering if and when and who would take him out."

Grace: "But he couldn't have just . . . left. He wouldn't. Not without telling me. And they're thinking Michael killed him? Not Josh but Michael? I can't believe—"

Paul: "Believe. Believe George is dead. Believe it because it's the truth."

And so I had begun to believe. Real bone-deep, no-hope belief had taken months to seep in and pull me under. The feeling of it was something like drowning slowly in cold water—skin, blood, heart freezing over degree by degree. Later, too late, Paul had said other things, hinting that the truth was that George had escaped, and then going back on that—skating in verbal zigzags, like an Olympic champ on ice thinner and thinner and thinner.

But in prison, once the first of these letters before me on the table arrived, I began to nurse the shard of what Paul had said that I'd hoped was true: that George was alive but too scared to contact me in any fuller way. As the letters kept coming, the feeling grew stronger: a flower not quite choked by the weeds of doubt around it: what if the letters were a trick of some kind? A trick of whose though?

While I was restrained behind bars and barbed wire, it had been fairly easy to lie in my cot in the dark, early mornings and plan strategies for finding George—for making my own similarly coded contact with him. But now that I was free, and half-dreamed plans could move into action, the playing field was changed. A blind chase after seven anonymous pieces of paper could in fact lead nowhere—or worse, could put George in jeopardy. The slam dunk of that might just finish me off.

The letters did exist though; they weren't from nowhere; someone, somewhere had meticulously sent them to me. Someone. *So what do you say, brave girl? Any guts left?*

It wasn't a matter of guts alone. To follow those letters wherever they led would require inner changes—changes perhaps impossible for me to make. A devout believer with a peephole view would fuck this up royally. I would need to know what I knew, to have peripheral vision, if not eyes in the back of my head. *I haven't got it in me. I don't think so.*

From a standing start, my heart raced ahead of me the way it had in Sheilah's car, and my hands began to tremble. I gripped the chair's arm and felt leather under my fingers—my bomber jacket, tossed there when I'd first come in. It was black and soft and twenty years old, born in Italy. Sheilah had brought it along this morning, knowing it was a favorite of mine. I had bought the jacket with most of my first check for jewelry sold to a Soho shop: an optimist's purchase if ever there was one. I stroked it and concentrated on trying to make the strokes smooth, even: the strokes of a woman whose hands were firm and sure.

It took a while to calm down. Once I did, I felt my father's urge to be on the move. At the same time, I was queasy about leaving this newly familiar burrow to walk the streets of what used to be my city. I was a damned refugee here now, hardly knew the language. I hailed from Bedford Hills Women's Correctional Facility. I knew the drill there: how to go along, get along; how to duck anger coming your way and stuff your own; how to make the small, well-timed joke; how to give and take the bits of warmth without which you feel like you might die—and most of all, how to pass through the stifling boredom that can make you wish you could.

And as I gave the leather one more absent stroke, I saw that if I stayed put in this chair tonight I might as well be locked in back where I'd just come from. I hauled myself vertical, slipped the jacket on and zipped it up to the neck.

On the round, blond dining table Sheilah had left a new wallet thick with cash and a ring of keys with a tag that read "I Want It All." It made me smile. I stuffed wallet and keys into my jacket pocket. "I am going out," I said to the room. Hearing my voice felt reassuring, as it had when I'd called my name out to the crippled tree in the courtyard. "I'll be back for last count."

CHAPTER FOUR

walked west to Broadway and then downtown toward Lincoln Center about a mile away. In the five-thirty swarm of people getting home and going home, an oddly familiar glint caught my eye. I turned to see a bracelet I'd made nine years ago sticking up in the air like a signpost. It was on a woman's wrist and she was hailing a cab. Sheilah owned that piece too, and I'd liked it well enough to have kept one for myself: a two-and-a-half-inch cuff of brushed steel with three triangles inlaid in twenty-four-carat gold; set into the middle triangle was a softly buffed piece of sea green bottle glass.

The woman wearing it was small, chic and ageless, with the taut air of someone waiting expectantly to be given what she wants simply because she wants it with a powerful urgency—different from Sheilah and me who also wanted, but expected to give to ourselves. Though this woman was dark, rather than pearl blond, she reminded me more than a little of Marina Beck: Paul's Marina—though Marina would hardly be wearing anything made by my hand.

I could see her, hair and sequins flashing, the cords on her neck standing out, as the well-known husky voice introduced "Boudreau's latest and,

I'm going to promise you, finest work." She sponsored those readings several times a year, insisting that the world would soon recognize what she already had: Paul's literary greatness. I willed myself to stop the Marina train of thought before it plunged into a darkened tunnel and got stuck there.

Rush hour now, but I had no doubt that within a minute or two a cab would pull up to the curb at the bracelet woman's feet to discharge a passenger, who would then hold the door open while she got in. I didn't stick around to check on it—probably I didn't want to be proved wrong about her—or maybe I didn't want to be proved right. I walked quickly ahead, able after a moment or two to smile at my own foolishness. Walking here in the slate blue twilight gave me the feel of being inside a very good painting, every element arranged for effect and yet in some way more real than life.

A piece of life intruded, the way it does: in the middle of the next block my new shoes began to pinch at the toes. I suspected that if I backtracked to the apartment to change into the sneakers I was accustomed to, I might have trouble leaving again. And wouldn't you know that a mere three steps ahead the painter had placed a store window displaying every sneaker ever produced in the first, second and third worlds? I sashayed into the place, and ten minutes later out again on a cushion of air, about ninety-three dollars poorer and in an unaccountably good mood. I threw my head back and looked up at the darkening, perfectly clear sky. *Tonight is a gift. I may not deserve it but I accept with thanks. I will not waste it.*

In a small restaurant crowded with early diners I ate hot Hunan pork and dry sautéed green beans and tree-ear mushrooms in brown sauce, then headed down to Lincoln Center and walked the complex, electric with crowds anticipating pleasure in the hours ahead. This was a place filled with memories for me—good ones only. George and I had come here often. When he was flush, we bought opera tickets; when he was flat, we watched the crowds go in and then rushed home to play our record of whatever it was they were hearing at the Met. Either way, we'd have a good time.

Later, once my jewelry began selling, a Met subscription for us had been my first gift to him, the look on his face one of those rewards life coughs up occasionally. Fourteen years we'd had that subscription. I think the last time I cried actual tears was when I wrote from Bedford Hills that I would be unable to renew for the coming season.

The Met was doing *Traviata* tonight. Seats were sold out but a woman stood near the box office anxiously waving a single ticket she needed to unload. Yes, in keeping with the evening, it was center orchestra and, no, I didn't hesitate for a second before handing over a hundred sixty dollars—I'd have paid double for it this night. There was plenty of time to start worrying about money tomorrow, and I would have to: I'd left the apartment with five of those big bills, now I had two and change. It goes fast.

The hours, on the other hand, were proceeding with a lovely slowness, luminescent as a string of pearls hanging free of any relation to real time or real trouble. Cinderella's night at the ball must have been this way and there's a good chance everything that came after, including marrying the prince, was a letdown.

"Wait for the second act," said the slight young man with a wispy beard beside me, "the new Russian baritone singing the father is to *die.*" I nodded and studied my program—not only the Russian baritone, but every name in it was new to me. After "Sempre Libera" I applauded the soprano till my palms stung, and then I clapped them some more. "I've heard her in better voice," my neighbor whispered in an eye-rolling tone. "I haven't," I whispered back.

During intermission I strolled the grand mezzanine, glassed-in view of the plaza to one side, tall Chagall panels to the other, and bought a glass of champagne. Twelve hours out of prison, at the Met, sipping bubbly with what George liked to call the swells. As I raised my glass in a toast to the moment, echoes of "Libiamo" filled my head, floating me upward to join the other flyers escaping into the magic of Chagall's sky.

"*Cin cin.* You know Raymond's working on a *genius* thing—*Traviata* with the sexes upside down. No, no, *think* about it. I'm putting my money right where my mouth is and if your brain isn't up your ass, you'll . . ."

The speaker was somewhere right behind me. I did not need to see her to identify her. That certain hoarse drawl was unmistakable. Only Marina Beck sounded like that. A small, electric chill ran through me. Superstition, pure superstition: I had *not* conjured up Marina by thinking about her on Columbus Avenue. As coincidences went, this was no big deal. The woman was a producer of plays, a sponsor probably of Lincoln Center. It was hardly remarkable that she'd be at the opera—some night, this night. Still, I found my hand gripping the champagne flute hard enough to risk breaking it.

I put it down on the bar unfinished and moved for a quick getaway downstairs to my standee's stall. But as I hurried around behind her, she swiveled unexpectedly and threw her head back to stare me straight in the face. Some mix of dislike and guilt, maybe a stubborn bit of vestigial self-respect mixed in, wouldn't let me cut and run. I stopped and returned the stare.

"He was a *true* genius," she said more quietly than I'd ever heard her say anything. I had nothing to say in response, yet I couldn't seem to break the eye lock. I stood studying her extraordinary face, the crimped pale hair, blue eyes framed in heavy mascara, red cupid's bow, white powdered skin: in my old habit of likening people to paintings, she'd always been a Schiele—essence of the decadent, menacing glamour of the German twenties. But her appearance was markedly changed in a way that reminded me of the highly colored dead trees that appeared so often in Paul's poems. I knew she was not quite sixty but she looked a decade and a half older and frail inside the bright drape of her clothes. "You killed my life," she said. There was nothing frail about the pure hatred in her pouched eyes. That was vigorous enough to make my breath catch in my throat. I turned away and escaped fast.

The final act of *Traviata* was gorgeous. I'd always loved the ironic ache of that opera, but my high in watching it was gone.

"Is that baritone fantastic or what?" my neighbor with the wispy beard asked.

"Or what," I agreed sourly, though the baritone had been fantastic indeed.

"And she came right up to speed in the last act, didn't she? Heartbreaking, the "Addio del passato"–I mean, she's no Callas, but . . ."

I think I ran most of the way back to the apartment. Cinderella, a stroke after midnight, the trappings and illusions of the magic evening expired.

CHAPTER FIVE

I never saw Josh Pyatt lay a hand on George, though I came to know very well he sometimes did, leaving colorful bruises that needed warm compresses or ice packs for pain. It didn't happen often, just often enough to make the prospect terrifying when luck began to turn bad. George never seemed angry at Josh or at himself, just very frightened beforehand, knowing it was coming, then chastened afterward, the way a kid might be with a just but brutal father. It was like a deal they had: when George misbehaved, Josh punished him, within bounds, more in sorrow than in anger. Then George would swear to be good, forage harder, more imaginatively, after some cash to pay up, and it would blow over—until the next time, which could be months, sometimes even a year or so away when things were going well. But there would be a next time. There always was.

The day Josh had made his surprise appearance at our apartment door, George had not yet met him, only heard about him—heard enough to be extra scared of the new guy on the job, bigger and blacker and more aggressive than the old-timer he was replacing as a collector for those uptown loan sharks we were perennially in hock to.

The Big Vig, George took to calling him, a pun that made Josh laugh if he was in the right mood. In the wrong mood nothing made him laugh and you got out of the way if you could. "Vig," cute nickname for vigorish: the ten, in desperate times twenty, percent a week interest that is shark heaven and gambler hell.

An effective collector earning a cut of what he recovers makes out very well, as Josh was bound to. And he did, gradually expanding from a freelancer employing his own two hands into an entrepreneur employing a crew of other hands—except for the times he just felt like using his own. As his business grew, his relationship with George altered; there was a crucial change in its balance. On the one hand, I noticed that George seldom got smacked around even when he was deep in the hole, and on the other—astonishing—he would have Josh over for long evenings of beer and Chinese food ordered in.

Those Josh evenings were weird, off-kilter for me. I could have made myself scarce, gone upstairs and visited Sheilah instead of sticking around. But I didn't. Why I didn't was something else beyond my understanding.

As with so much that happened, I watched the action—not only watched but participated—and yet remained oblivious of the whys behind it, or what was truly at stake. I understood only that while I anticipated those evenings with dread, there was a kind of hectic excitement to them. Described in terms of color, the feeling would veer between a sick yellow green and a hot orange red. Kaleidoscope colors fascinated me as they had when I was a little kid. Lately, I had begun to string colored glass beads on strands of wire, weaving them into intricate designs that would not disappear at the turn of a hand.

Though Josh was a big thumb overhead, casting a shadow always, able to come down on us whenever he wanted, there was also a fascinating aspect to his power and the way he used it. My first take on him as a big, black bear proved pretty accurate. Like a bear he was slow, then suddenly quick—warm, almost cuddly when his dark honey voice would tell tales of an Alabama childhood, handed off from relative to relative. But unpredictable: the bear could turn vicious in a second for his own reasons. The

"I asked you a question, Georgie, I want an answer" or *"Tomorrow, not Thursday"* or *"Why'a my not laughin'?"* never came out as a roar, yet the low growl was as heavily threatening as a raised paw coming right at you.

We formed an odd threesome over the egg rolls and spareribs. Like vaudeville performers each of us seemed, if not a caricature, then a distilled essence of a real self. George, the court jester, did astonishing tricks with numbers, tap dancing for the king's applause, not scared but nervous, at the edge of being scared, like someone on a boat ready to become seasick at the next dip. Josh was a king ready to be amazed and entertained but a king nonetheless, wanting his orders fulfilled and prepared to turn mean on a dime because he was also a bear. Then there was me, the chorus, not really part of the main action. One minute I was on the sidelines weaving my bright beads, the next dropping in a smart-ass kid crack with the occasional deliberate "fuck" or "shit" thrown in to show I was brave and sassy—the way George depended on me to be, the way I liked being. And if the prospect of the bear's paw overhead ready to swat me for rude language sometimes rattled my unreliable gut—well, I liked being brave enough to risk that. And in fact no swat landed. Not on me.

I remember asking George once after such an evening whether this whole remarkable thing he did with Josh was about his pride, "Like you need him to see you being smart, this clever expert, not just—"

"Not just a pathetic loser, shaking in his pants? Nah, Gracie, not pride. I'm a little *shtunk* with too many bad habits to have any pride at all, not a drop. But I've got half a wit and I feel pushed enough to figure I better use it for what it's worth. So let's say it's about leverage, about storing up nuts for the winter in case it's a really cold one." As he said this he looked sad and uncharacteristically wise, like a fortune-teller looking into his crystal ball at a future he didn't like but knew was coming.

Josh: "Now how could that apply, Georgie, what you just said?" His trunk of a neck extended as far as it could go in George's direction, reaching out for more than he was going to get. "*Walk me through. If we call it a livery business, where do we get the kind of records you're talking about to look kosher?*"

George: "*Well, Big Vig, theoretically, just theoretically, if you allocated X amount of income to capital improvement of the garages and then depreciated . . .*"

And so it would go, George in control for just these moments when he turned the spigot on oh so briefly, and back off again to munch a sparerib and tell a joke. Josh Pyatt, ambitious small businessman increasingly needed a smart accountant's counsel. The thing that got through to me only later was that Josh, suspicious of the people he worked for and the ones who worked for him, trusted George—trusted him because he owned him and would continue to. For his part, George dispensed advice with what even I could see was an eyedropper—just enough of it to keep the beast mostly at bay. That was the game.

Then during the summer when I would turn seventeen, the game, which had been played in measured volleys for almost six years, went bad. Maybe George was getting too tired, maybe Josh was getting too impatient, maybe both—I really couldn't say. Since my own life had lately expanded to include boys and hanging out downtown and selling my jewelry on weekends at an improvised stand on the edge of Washington Square Park, my mind was not much on George and I tended to skip the Chinese dinners.

It was a beating that set things in motion: not the bruised lip that occasionally appeared during these years when George got far enough behind that his dollops of advice didn't cover the vig—or perhaps when Josh thought he needed a reminder of who was in charge—but a real beating.

The day it happened I came home with a good jewelry haul in my pocket—sixty-two dollars—swinging the door open, ready to brag a little. I found him doubled up on the floor, crying. His trousers were undone and pulled down to his knees and the loud striped boxer shorts he wore were sadly out of synch with the welts and beginning bruises on his thighs. I had never seen him this way, and I had never, even in his worst panic, seen him cry.

The floor seemed to go soft under my feet. I knelt at his side, seasick with fast boiling rage and fear. "God, oh, my God, I'll kill him," I mumbled. "I'll go find him and kill him. I have to kill him." I repeated it over and over like a mantra as I stroked his forehead, wiped his tears and mine with the tail of my shirt.

"No," he groaned. "No, don't talk like that, Gracie. I don't like to hear you talk like that. And it wasn't him, wasn't Josh who did this—some new hot dog of his making his bones on my skinny white ass. Bastard pulled me into the alley." He tried to laugh but I could see it pained him.

"I'm gonna get you to the hospital. You've probably got stuff broken." Broken. George. My father. Broken like a . . . thing, like a toy. I turned away not wanting him to see my face.

"No, no hospital," he said, the raspy voice a bit stronger. "I managed to get myself upstairs and there's not squat a doctor can do for cracked ribs except let 'em hurt, which they do."

He could . . . he could've been killed. For the first time in my life I felt truly like a kid—no one to be depended on. "Well how do you know you're not bleeding inside?" I asked weakly.

"Because a kick to the balls doesn't make your gut bleed."

"You say he didn't do it. But he *did* do it. If he ordered it, he did it. How could he . . . ?" Stupid to even finish the question. Josh could do anything to George because that's who they were; after years of settling into a sense of safety—delicately balanced maybe, but safety—I was sharply aware of real danger. "Why, George? Are you that far behind?" He didn't answer. I looked at his pale, set face and thought I could see the underpainting of fear still there from the moment the goon grabbed him. "I wish he was dead." I had never spoken truer.

He shook his head no. "I'm not that far behind," he said after a moment.

"Then *what?* Did you give him bad advice about numbers? You can't. *I* can't. One of these days he'll . . . Ah shit, George, you're gonna have to *stop* all this." The kid was blathering: if he could stop, he would have—it hadn't taken me seventeen years to know that. "This is dangerous stuff, don't you see?" I added quietly, willing my heart to slow down.

"Unfortunately, I do see. I'm gonna ask you to run a bath for me but not yet, in a while. Look, we're going to Miami for a while."

"No! No, I . . . shit!"

He held up his hand. "Okay. You're not crazy about it. Why should you be? You got plans and—hey, you could stay with Sheilah and her mom instead. I bet I could fix it. How would that be?"

"Rotten," I hollered, furious suddenly at him for his haplessness, and then just as quickly at myself for being selfish pig enough to make his time harder than it was. "I'm going where you go," I said and tried a smile. "You may not be perfect but you're the only family I've got."

He made a move to get up and a spasm of pain crossed his face. He lay back down. After a moment he said, "You got a grandfather over on Sutton Place, believe it or not. Pretty fancy, even his name—talk about assimilated."

Never a photo, never an anecdote: this was a step onto totally unfamiliar ground. "How come you're telling me this now?" I asked, my voice tiptoeing.

"Dunno. Maybe what they call intimations of mortality." He saw my look and said, "No, no, I'm not checking out anytime soon. I guess the way I felt today when this ape began to pound on me reminded me of old times."

"What do you mean?"

He gave a little laugh. "Daddy-o always thought if he whaled me hard enough I'd sprout up tall and ambitious, turn into the son he wanted— kind of a rougher version of the girl kissing a frog to get a prince, and just about as effective."

The seconds dragged while I waited, afraid that if I pushed he'd close right up.

"Doctor Junius Lester was a bad guy," he said, "he terrified an undersized kid. And you know what? He may've made me suffer but I made him suffer too, just by being the unclassy little twerp I was. That's given me some satisfaction through the years, let me tell you." I felt the love swell up in me, crowding out any remaining scraps of bad stuff. I would protect him with my life.

I was down on the floor beside him now, propped up on one arm, my own tears streaming freely. I leaned over and kissed his cheek. "See? You're a prince now. Hey, where'd you get a father called Junius Lester? And *doctor?*"

"At the name-change office and Columbia University: surgeon, wouldn't you know? He was born Julius Leshansky. The Junius was a touch and a half, right? Pretentious asshole—rode horses in Central Park, in an outfit yet. I left the day I was eighteen and reclaimed the family name on my first win at Aqueduct." He rolled to his side, wincing, hoping to find a more comfortable position. It didn't look more comfortable but it was a first move toward getting up.

"Why don't you just lie still for a little?"

"I'm okay. I'm good."

"So what is it, no apples in our family tree only bananas?" It was a knee jerk with us, making the other one laugh. He did and the effort of it pained him. "I'm sorry. Take it easy. You don't have to talk any more." I said that, but God, I wanted him to continue.

And he did. "There are apples. I called her Ma. Good lady, but scared to death of him, scared to open her mouth to him. She gave me three hundred bucks to help me get away, saved it up. She used to play cards for money on the sly."

"Are you . . . are you in touch with her?" It was like discovering a secret door in what had always been a solid wall. To give it an opening push was as daunting as it was alluring.

"No. Better that way. He'd've taken it out of her hide. Anyway, she made her getaway too, died a couple of years ago. I saw the obit in the paper. I was not mentioned." He took a long breath, which seemed to hurt. The lines in his pale face were like cracks in plaster.

"You look awful. I think the emergency room would be a good idea."

"Nah. Go get me a shot of scotch or whatever we've got and run a bath now, warm not hot."

I was back quickly with the scotch—just some Dewar's neat. Alcohol didn't interest George; he was a quick-belt-at-disaster-time kind of drinker.

He downed it at a gulp. "Ah, Gracie," he said a second or two later, "I'm not worth spit to you. And no, you don't have a mother who'd be any good either. I saw your face. That's really what you want to know, right?"

"Yeah," I said, making almost no sound at all, afraid to stop his flow.

"She had to go back to her people." He held his hand out to me. "Help a fella up, okay?"

Grasping my hand he hoisted himself to a standing position. I held his arm and we walked to the bathroom.

"The Indian princess?" I asked, nervousness putting a flutter into my throat. I coughed hard a couple of times to make it stop. "She went back to her tribe?"

"Something like that," he said quietly. "Gracie, she's on the other side of the world and might as well be on the other side of the moon—if she's alive at all." Then in the thready voice he started to sing, . . . *do you believe me?* And through a throat raw with emotion and silenced questions, I sang my answering *I do.*

He freed his arm from mine and held onto the sink. "Turn off the taps, kiddo, and leave me alone. The old man doesn't need you to give him a bath yet. I got some things I need to think over."

"Like what?" The sound of his voice rang an alarm bell.

"Like . . . scoot now. I'm gonna be in here for a while. Start our packing for Florida, but not too much stuff, okay?"

CHAPTER SIX

I awoke in the touring dancer's bed, a futon on a low wooden frame, with a sensation of being on a small boat, a gentle rocking so lifelike that until my eyes opened I was sure I could reach out a hand and dip it into the fragrant water of a large lily pond. But of course there was no water, no pond. The time was five-thirty according to the clock on the small side table. Despite the fact that I'd gotten to sleep past one, this was the time I was used to the flashlight of morning count clear in my face—you were allowed to go back to sleep but I usually didn't.

It seemed as though that part of the inner clock was working according to habit, but since yesterday, nothing else concerning time was. Live action scenes streaked and swirled through my brain at will, cutting through zone after zone and leaving me with the jet lag of an untrained space traveler, fuzzy about where I truly was at a given moment, the *now* turning without warning into the *then*.

Last night's adventure seemed weeks, years ago—or maybe it had never happened. Maybe I'd been here all evening in this strange apartment sitting in a rattan easy chair covered in tropical print conjuring up George and Josh—and Marina Beck. Maybe I'd been lying in this bed dreaming of hearing *Traviata* and had never actually gotten out the door. Then I saw an unfamiliar pair of sneakers on the floor and a Met *Playbill* beside the clock on the table.

"Get a fucking grip," I said aloud, in this way I seemed to have quickly acquired of talking to myself. People who live alone probably do tend to talk to themselves. Maybe a few spoken words clear the head of its endless smoke rings. But that was speculation: until now I never had lived alone—always with George, then with George and Paul, then with several thousand women, all of us miscreant wards of the state.

I pulled my naked body out from between the sheets. It had been more than six years since I'd slept bare, with nothing but the brush of cool smooth sheets and air against the skin. It felt like freedom. It used to feel erotic. Paul, who was capable of giving the world's best massage, had always said I'd be a full-time voluptuary if I weren't so damned practical. Practical. *Was it practical to kill you, Paul? I don't think so. Practical would've been to run as fast and far as I could, taking care not to look back over my shoulder and turn into a pillar of salt.* I wondered whether a pillar of salt was equivalent to a sea of tears with its water boiled off.

This morning the notion that Paul was dead seemed bizarre. Some mornings at Bedford Hills had been that way. I would open my eyes, hazy, confused about where I was, then the reality of what I had done would hit me fresh and hard and I would feel grateful for being where I should be, in a penitentiary. Other mornings, I would have shot him again, this time right between the eyes.

I turned on the shower and let the water soak my long hair, plastering it to my body like so much seaweed. A long, hot shower: it had been a while since I'd taken one of those. Like casual nakedness this was a sensual pleasure long on hold. And like the nakedness, after the first few minutes it didn't seem strange to me at all—which, come to think of it, was strange in itself.

Feeling for a moment almost like a civilian, I dried off and dressed to meet the person who would be my field parole officer, the system's long arm on my shoulder for the next six years. You have a parole officer inside too, the person in charge of evaluating and prepping you for the parole board hearing and, to quote the manual, "helping those incarcerated to develop positive attitudes and behavior." Mine, Ned O'Shaughnessy, had a comfortable McPaunch and seventies sideburns—a nice, laid-back man, who had worked the male side of the system more than fifteen years and found female felons a lot less wearing.

"Look, Boudreau," he'd said in our final session, "it's a crapshoot what officer you'll draw on the outside, but no matter who, the relationship can go hard or easy and a lot of that's up to you. First impressions are important, know what I mean? You want to come on serious and responsible and nonthreatening. Now you've never showed temper inside—well, except the one time and you were a rookie—but you're a presence, a big gal. Also, you killed your husband, and *not* because he was beatin' on you. Hey, this isn't a rehash here, but it can affect how some people might look at you. So watch it is what I'm sayin', be extra careful. Oh, and a little humble wouldn't be bad, okay?"

With this in mind I put on the clothes I'd worn yesterday, the gray pants and black sweater Sheilah had brought—classic and careful. The alternative was jeans or a choice of those items from my prior life she had judged fit to survive, most of them kind of flamboyant for the occasion. I braided my damp hair fairly tight, wound it up into a large bun and used some blush and lip-gloss. The woman in the mirror looked civilized, serious and definitely nonthreatening.

As I walked into the living room, I saw the George-Gracie letters spread out on the table just where I'd left them. Suppose I *did* decide to go looking. Where would I start? The first postmark was . . . I told myself to quit it. Today was today: a day to register at the parole office and have a haircut.

There was a fresh carton of orange juice in the fridge. I poured myself a large glass and downed it without coming up for air, then another. I gathered up the letters, put them back into my suitcase and stowed it in the bedroom closet as far back as it would go, which wasn't very far: every time I opened that door I would think about the letters. I'd think about them anyway, it didn't really matter where they were stored. And when the letters were on my mind, I could never avoid replaying what might have been if I'd kept my eye on George, as I should've, at what anyone—a dropped-in Martian—would have realized was a time of danger.

The Manhattan parole office was way west on Fortieth Street. With plenty of time to get there before nine, I bounced down Amsterdam on the soles of my new sneakers—the black pumps waited in my shoulder bag for a last-minute switch. It was one of those sunless mornings that people sometimes say turns everything prison gray. As I'd grown familiar with a prison landscape at close range, I'd seen that its color palette runs less to grays than to dusty browns, dead greens and dirty whites.

"Cool," a trash handler said, looking me over as he dumped the contents of a barrel into a sanitation department grinder truck. I gave him a thank-you smile and walked past. What was cool was a Japanese kimono-cut coat made of jigsaw puzzle pieces of diverse black fabrics, the design of a friend from the old days, a souvenir from a world where dramatic personal decoration was intrinsic to the way we were, and creating it was the way some of us made our livings. It had been a joyous life for me. This morning the coat served as a kind of talisman, which is, I suppose, why I was wearing it when the Burberry trench in the closet would have been more suitable. Besides changing out of sneakers, I would take Keiko's coat off and fold it over my arm before entering the parole office: a six-foot woman in a garment of striking shape might be considered threatening—and probably not humble.

The office was green, the benches for waiting already filling up quickly by the time I arrived. Females of all shapes, sizes, ages and shades: it was women's day; the sexes are kept separate as they are on the inside. I presented my release papers, checked in and took a seat beside a Hispanic girl of nineteen or so, who looked strung out on something, maybe just on her own existence. A girl: she was a girl. Many of the girls in the room were girls not women, never mind that some of them were noticeably pregnant. What hits you is that same thing that does in prison, how young most of them are.

A majority of the women and girls at Bedford Hills were drug offenders of the small potatoes kind—not dealers themselves, just mules for their dealers, husbands, boyfriends, pimps. But many of them had drawn terms longer than mine because of old New York State drug enforcement laws: the Rockefeller laws, called for the misguided governor who'd signed them—laws that nobody I'd ever met in the prison system or out considered fair or useful, yet were still there on the books kicking ass.

After a few minutes a stocky black woman who looked and sounded like an Army sergeant called out loud, "Boudreau," and told me when I marched over to her desk prepared for what might be tough duty, that she was not my officer, that Ms. Carlson, who was, had been detained, and did I want to wait or make an appointment to come back.

"How long do you think the wait would be?" I asked.

She shrugged. "Couldn't say. Now, I can handle your prelim interview, but you'll need to come back tomorrow and meet with her—or you can have a seat and take your chances waiting. What's your pleasure?"

"I'll wait." There was one common thread that ran through the criminal justice system: you waited—everything took lots of time, if not always for the reasons you expected. "Maybe I'll get lucky."

"Maybe you will," she said with a smile that touched one corner of her mouth.

I went to the farthest back of the benches and shut my eyes. This was one of the times that Paul appeared with no warning at all.

The suddenness of it produced an unlikely laugh that turned heads in my direction. Paul in one of his Gallic moods would call my laugh *le rire de la liberté,* though this laugh had nothing to do with liberty, but with the rusted irony of being fettered forever. Sometimes at a peak of exuberance or exasperation he'd turn to French, that half smile of his implying how English couldn't *quite* precisely convey what was in his head or heart. In the retelling this sounds repulsively affected, but if you were there with him, inside his force field, it was just the opposite. If you were there with him . . .

The week after we'd met, Paul Boudreau took me to France. It sounds like a cute anachronism, "took me," but that is what happened. He had made all the arrangements before calling me at the office—fait accompli.

"Come on, it's just for a long weekend—give yourself Friday off, we'll be back Monday night. We'll go to Mont-Saint-Michel. The *son et lumière* will be on, and I'll get to introduce you to my *grandmère*. She lives in Normandy not so far from there. If I had an upbringing, she was it." Pause while my mind stalled. "What I mean is," he said, "it's my special part of the world and I want to give it to you for your birthday."

"How . . . ?" Never mind that this was almost a month early for it, I had never had a birthday surprise before. Not to say that July twenty-third had gone uncelebrated, just that my own hand had always been involved. I didn't think Paul and I had even mentioned our birth dates, I had no idea when his was.

"How did I know? I asked your father." George, who had met Paul briefly twice, had reacted in a way I had not seen him react to other friends of mine—even painters, actors, writers and such, with a bit of fame to their names. He'd seemed awed. "That guy," he'd said, "that guy could be Jesus Christ or Satan, take your pick."

"How about the Pied Piper?" I'd answered, trying to make him smile.

I'd gotten no smile, just a speculative look. "Maybe," he'd said after a moment. "You want to watch it."

"Can't take my eyes off it," I'd said with an exaggeratedly wolfish grin. We dealt with questions of sex, George and I, the way we dealt with everything: honesty without revelation, laughter the lubricant for rough spots. He let me know that he "saw" women "when the tide rises," but I'd never met one, or pushed to. He had given me a short, clear course on avoiding pregnancy several years before I had any use for the information, and told me to trust my gut and never be a jerk. I had been a jerk—a first-class jerk—but only once.

"This one may be serious, George," I said. "You need to know that and," I smiled the way you can at old miseries after enough good years have intervened, "I hope I'm not being a jerk again." His return smile said he hoped so too.

I had been to France more than a few times by then, but never to the northwest coast. The Breton-Norman terrain was wild, more primitive, more Celtic looking than French—or what I'd thought of as French—and I loved it instantly. On the second day Paul took me to Mont-Saint-Michel, the enormous twelfth-century monastery on its own island just at the point where Brittany becomes Normandy. In summer the place was open to visitors at night, its ancient stone walls and parapets dramatically lit, echoes of Gregorian chants bouncing off them, while hooded monks moved around in utter silence lighting tall tapers.

We walked up the stone steps, higher and higher above sea level, not talking, just absorbing the form, the textures, the grandeur of the setting with all senses. The crowds were not heavy that night and it was late enough that most of the inevitable souvenir and food shops on the lower levels were shut. When we reached the top the light and sound show staged for summer visitors hit with marvelous effect. I threw my arms around him. "Thank you, *thank you*, thank you for this." He murmured something in my ear; I felt the hot breath but didn't hear the words.

Much later we went back to the small inn he'd chosen and made love for a very long time—and for the first time. Despite the voltage between us, despite the fact that I'd crossed the Atlantic with him on a week's acquaintance, we had done no more than kiss and touch through layers of clothing. Paul had been the one to hold off. "Hang in with me," he'd say softly each night, as he pried us apart, "this is going to be extraordinary; it needs to season."

Delay was an unfamiliar seasoning, one that proved erotic in its own way, an exquisite sensation somewhere at the cross-section of pleasure and pain. Another exotic spice heightened the effect: I was entirely unused to being under someone's control. How could he have known I'd cotton to that? A more disturbing question is *why* had I cottoned to it?

What happened in the high, pillowy bed was indeed extraordinary. Paul undressed me very slowly, each square of bared skin new territory: a master explorer, mapping my body, charting each point of ignition and assessing whether the touch of fingers, tongue, teeth or simply expelled breath would drive it craziest. His penis was a slim, elegant instrument. It stayed hard after I had come and come and come, hollering out each time like some manic cowboy in love with the ride. He came too, finally, hard and in silence.

Afterward, we lay together slick and salted, my ear resting on his chest, while our breathing made its way down to normal. His heart marched like a strong, steady soldier. "Oh, my God," I whispered.

" 'If you fear death now is the time to fly.' "

I raised myself up on an elbow. "What?"

"Dante," he said, laughing, "the lovesick poet in *La Vita Nuova,* wondering whether to risk gazing on the lady. I've risked gazing at you."

I laughed in pure joy.

He rolled on top of me again and I could feel him harden against my belly. "I could drown in you," he said, like someone seriously considering that possibility. "It's like fucking the whole damned ocean."

The following day, we drove to his grandmother's house near Honfleur, a couple of hours north—a thatched cottage out of the pages of a *National Geographic* or a high school history book, charming and bigger than it looked at first. Paul explained that the house had been in her family for generations. "She's a LaClade, Norman for centuries. The Boudreaus were Parisians— some Austrian and Hungarian on that side too—writers, scientists, café rats some of them. Flashy, but they didn't have the LaClade staying power."

As I listened to Paul talk about Boudreaus and LaClades I was acutely conscious of George and me, two vestigial Leshanskys alone together in a pocket empty of history.

The LaClade I was about to meet was Paul's mother's mother, who after his parents had died in a motorcycle crash when he was twelve, had taken over. She had used their insurance money and added to it out of her own pocket to pay his way in good boarding schools in America and Europe and brought him to live with her during vacations. "She speaks no English," he warned me. "She's also a little deaf and kind of frail generally. Her heart . . ." His hand swiveled back and forth on its wrist, indicating a touch and go status.

Grandmère opened the door to us and we entered a world that could have been a century old or twice that—wide board floors, dark furniture, not grand but noble with multiple lifetimes of service, rugs with their colors faded to a lovely blur, all of this lit softly through mullioned windows. The old woman wore a dark, ankle-length dress with a cream lace collar and cameo brooch, a costume almost. Her face was fine boned, beautiful even at eighty or whatever age she was, and her body moved like that of a much younger woman. She was small but had the kind of bearing that could hold a stage. I remember thinking it must run in the family. She embraced Paul wordlessly, then reached out and grasped both my hands. *"Chère Grace, bienvenue."*

"Merci," I said, which pretty much exhausted my French.

She and Paul chattered quickly and with some animation, looking at me and then at each other as though the two of them shared a secret. She reached over and patted his cheek and whispered something. Then he turned to me and said, "She thinks your eyes are beautiful windows into a beautiful soul. I told her I think so too, that she's a good judge of character. She has a special lunch prepared—my favorite. I hope you like rabbit in red wine."

Later, Paul and I went for a walk while his grandmother cleaned up the dishes, my offers of help vigorously and smilingly refused. Her palms had scooped air like a farm wife shooing chickens as she'd moved us toward the door almost singing, *"Non, non, non, non, non."*

Swinging our clasped hands back and forth like children, we walked down the hill from the cottage to a stream where Paul had fished during boyhood summers here. The late afternoon had a freshness rare in late July; the landscape's cool greens were varied, each shade distinct from the others—I counted eight of them. It was no wonder that Boudin and his impressionist buddies had gravitated to this area.

Paul told me bits and pieces about his reckless parents. "A crash waiting to happen," he said. "A motorcycle, as it did happen, but it could as easily have been a car, motorboat: whatever they did they did it too fast, without looking. They were like Fitzgerald people, sparkling and doomed. And completely selfish—neither of them gave a thought to a little boy who just happened to be theirs." In his tone there was a wounded bitterness that told me the pain would not ever go away.

I took his hand, raised it to my lips and kissed it, overcome with a sympathy that deepened and strengthened my love for him. "Lucky you to have had all this beauty to come home to," I said. "I guess sometimes a treasure turns up in the bottom of the trash basket."

He laughed. Right then, he looked like a figure in a French eighteenth century pastoral painting, the color high in his cheeks, the fair hair riffling a little in the breeze. The pale gray transparent eyes fastened on mine as he said, "You're another treasure. You said last night that you loved me. I love you too. You know?"

A wave of something that felt like fear took me by surprise. After a beat or two it passed. "Is that a statement or a question?" I asked.

"Both. The question part is just as important as the statement. I need you to *know* that I love you because it's true, and don't ever forget that."

"Are you going to give me reason to?"

"Maybe," he said quietly, less assured than I'd heard him, and shifted his eyes away. Then he looked back at me, broke into a grin and said exuberantly, "What I mean, *ma femme*—and I hope you will be that, my wife—what I mean is . . . ah, who knows what I mean, except that I love you in my way, which is the only way I know how. I want us to be together."

My eyes flooded, and I was swept along in a current of pure feeling. I didn't try to stop its flow, and then wound up laughing instead. He kissed my open mouth so the laugh went into his. Later, we sat on the bank of the fishing stream and I said, "I come with some baggage, Paul. Your parents died. They were risky people, you said. Well, so's my father. George is a gambler, a serious one, which causes him to have to work for a man who's pretty risky too: a bad guy. Part of the reason we live together, though he'd never admit it, is so I can kind of keep an eye on him. That's not the whole reason," I added quickly in some mixture of loyalty to George and plain truth. "I also—this probably sounds crazy to you—I like his company. Look, the arrangement is not ideal, I know, from your point of view, but it's . . . how I need it to be."

"And if you felt any different I might not want you," Paul said slowly. He had a voice of many colors—no regional accent, no theatricality to it but, like the best actors, what he said sounded significant and realer than real.

As we were leaving the next morning, *Grandmère* looked at me hard, the frown lines deepening between her eyes, her delicate face taking on for the first time since our arrival a cast that seemed worried. *"Paul,"* she said, *"est un homme extraordinaire. Comprenez?"*

That I got. *"Oui. Extraordinaire.* Don't worry, I'll be good for him. I will. *Bon. Je suis bon,"* I said, damning my inability to communicate. She nodded gravely. I thought she understood me but she did not look relieved.

———

"Boudreau. *Boudreau.*" The official blast from the front desk cracked my reverie in half.

"Here," I said jumping up. "Right here."

My parole officer turned out to be a thin blond with thin hair and a thin tense mouth. She was likely in her thirties but seemed at once older and younger. She wore a navy blue business suit and white blouse, which looked like a uniform and wasn't. I noticed that the pinky finger on her left hand was gauzed and bandaged. "Patty Ann Carlson," she said, not extending the other hand to shake. The perky Patty Ann was about as suitable a name for her as Theda Bara would've been for me. "Sorry to have kept you waiting," she said, raking fingers through her hair to rid her forehead of it. She motioned me over to a corridor of cubicles and into hers. "Have a seat."

My first quarters at Bedford Hills had been a cell with a sink and toilet and a curtain you could pull across the bars for quick privacy while you used them. I'd been amazed for starters by the spirit and ingenuity the prisoners showed in cheering up their cells—printed fabric draped to cover the toilet, photos and drawings taped to the walls, personal knickknacks, magazines, paperback books, here and there on the small side table beside the cot.

Patty Ann Carlson's work space looked bleaker than many of those cells, including mine—no photos, prints, mementos at all, not even a coffee mug, just folders and papers stacked precisely on the metal desk. Maybe it was policy: don't let the lowlifes see photos of the family—but that hadn't been true of O'Shaughnessy; he'd displayed the four kids and the missus proudly on his desk at Bedford Hills. I glanced down at Carlson's left hand. Next to the damaged pinky, on the ring finger, was a thin gold band.

She looked up from my papers and saw me taking stock. "I gather you've got a job lined up, an apartment and some money in trust for you over at Smith Barney as well as the bank."

"Yes," I said carefully, "I suppose you'd say I'm in pretty good shape."

"I'd say." Shit, she thought I was bragging. Twenty-eight thousand dollars in reserve was a Rorschach blot; Patty Ann Carlson saw one picture in it, Sheilah another—I, another yet. My own relationship to money had always been ambivalent. Bottom line, it was not all that different from my father's: money means everything and nothing. For all the anxiety and grief the lack of it caused us, he never gave a rat's ass about the money itself. Getting rich was not why gambling had him hooked. Beating the system was. Winning. Of course, the system beat him most of the time, but once the hook was in place . . .

"Any problems you want to discuss?" Carlson asked, sounding as though it were the end of a day, not a beginning. I noticed that her pretty hazel eyes were bloodshot, like she was coming off a bad night.

"I don't think so," I said, wanting badly to be out of there.

"You'll report here once a week for the first month, then we'll modify it, depending." She gave me the it's-up-to-you look a first grade teacher gives a pupil with trouble in her record.

"What time? Can I do lunch hour or before work?"

"Before work, eight-thirty next Monday. And you understand I'll be making home and work visits."

Unscheduled: she had the right. I knew that and bet myself she'd do it. "I understand."

She stood. "Well, good luck, Boudreau."

"Thanks," I said, quickly on my feet. "You too."

"Beg your pardon?" Her tone was sharp with suspicion. Did she think I meant her damaged finger? Jesus, maybe I did.

"Sorry," I said, "I figure everyone can use a little good luck." She gave me a look and I left knowing it could have gone better.

CHAPTER SEVEN

I walked the few blocks east to Times Square and then up and down the side streets—the theater blocks, where the gloom of the morning felt just right. The sun had always seemed like an unwelcome visitor here anyway—this was nighttime territory: these streets burned bright after dark, worked late and needed to nod off a little during the day.

On Forty-second Street the old porn houses were now renovated into theaters, sterile in their newness and with decidedly nontheatrical names such as Ford and American Airlines. I didn't care for the changes, beneficial though they must be for the city and its tourist trade. The look of the square had changed alarmingly while I was gone: twice, three times as many gaudy, lighted billboards looming overhead, surrounding you any which way you looked. The effect was less of Times Square, New York, than of a Vegas hotel designed to replicate it.

The meeting with Patty Ann Carlson and the prospect of repeating it weekly, of wondering when she'd surprise me at the apartment or at Sheilah's office, had left me rough edged, feeling trapped in a way I hadn't in prison. I tried to think humble, penitent thoughts: *What did you expect, red carpets? You killed somebody—not just somebody, you killed Paul. You pulled a trigger knowing exactly what you were doing and ended him. Period. Don't give me crap about a paid-off debt to society. You still owe, and Patty Ann fucking Carslon is part of the vig you have to pay. Damn you to hell, Paul.* So the thoughts ended up not precisely humble and less penitent than they might have been.

I wandered up Forty-fourth Street, past Shubert Alley and stopped cold, unable to believe that what I saw could be anything but a sick joke on me. Topping the Helen Hayes Theater marquee was a huge silhouetted photo of George Burns. Beneath him, large letters spelled out *Say Goodnight, Gracie.* I approached the theater slowly, my brain on hold but my heart pounding hard. When I came closer I saw that Frank Gorshin (God, the Riddler from *Batman!*) was performing a one-man show as George. It was a show I would keep my distance from—starting immediately.

Ten minutes later I sat in a Greek coffee shop eating soft scrambled eggs and sausages and trying to divert my thoughts with news and comment from the *Times.* There seemed little in the way of good news and the comments were the rehashed rehash that results when nobody knows anything and states it seventeen different ways to add heft to air.

I folded the paper in quarters, stuffed it into my shoulder bag and paid the check, the spicy-rich taste of smoked meat and eggs filling my mouth still.

As I left the coffee shop I began a mental list of things to do. Join a gym was the first. It wasn't vanity driving me. I'd never done the gym routine or done any formal exercise at all as a civilian, but the act of building physical strength had helped me feel safe in prison. Maybe more important, taking my body through the manageable punishment of stretching and bending and lifting—pushing it daily a bit farther than it wanted to go—had let me control something. With Patty Ann sitting on my shoulder and a past that would never let up, I'd need a piece of self-managed personal property now, maybe as much as I had in Bedford Hills. Speaking of management, I was to meet Sheilah at Bendel's for the haircut.

I checked my watch: I had a little over an hour. I'd spend the time at the Museum of Modern Art—a kind of breath mint for my soul.

Starting when I was twelve or so, the Modern (we never called it MOMA) was where I went almost every week, sometimes with Sheilah, but often alone, to stroll among the Monets, the Picassos, the Cézannes, the Matisses—to sit in the sculpture garden gazing up at the thighs of Maillol's indomitable *Earth Mother*.

Of course I visited the other museums, the Metropolitan, Guggenheim, Whitney—and the grand mansions, the Frick and the Morgan—but in those places I was a tourist always, an admiring guest. The Modern was part of where I lived, *my* place. I missed it like hell when George and I had to scamper and hang out in Vegas or Miami or Chicago.

After he disappeared I came twice, just to . . . be here, I suppose. The second time, I found myself sitting on the ground beside the *Earth Mother*, my arms around her powerful leg, unable to stop crying. I hadn't come again until now.

I walked up Broadway and turned east on Fifty-fourth. What I found stunned me. My museum was gone: a vast square block of fenced-off construction site. The first thing that flashed through my mind was that I must have gone nuts—that another bombing had happened here and I somehow—

"Moved," said a deep voice at my shoulder. "Moved to Queens, while we build the new place." The wide-shouldered guy in construction boots and vest gave me a New Yorker's smile. "So, you from out of town, you didn't know?"

"Right," I said, "from out of town." I let him give me subway directions to Queens and moved on east toward the river, my mood darkened another shade or two. Maybe a look at the water . . .

I arrived at Bendel's on the dead run, out of breath and ten minutes late. Sheilah was waiting at the Garren Salon entrance, checking her watch for probably the tenth time. Her face as she looked up and saw me was tense. "I'm sorry, Sheil, really stupid, I lost track. I dropped in at the Modern and found that they'd taken it away."

That broke through her irritation and made her smile. "All those Saturdays." She reached out to embrace me the way women friends do, but her motion was quick and somehow I didn't expect it, so instead of moving toward her I pulled away. In prison your body becomes wary, careful not to send an inaccurate signal to a fellow inmate.

"Hey, sorry," I said, my arms open now to give her the stalled hug, "that was a jailhouse reflex. I've . . . been locked up a long time, Sheilah."

She looked at me in a way she hadn't yesterday. Perhaps it was getting through to her that I wouldn't be back to my old self any time soon, or ever. Then she retrieved her smile and motioned me inside the salon. "Come on, William's waiting. He's booked solid and you don't want to make him tight on the other end. William, *William*, she's here."

William was as slim and sharp as a pencil. He was dressed in black, against which his face had the sallow look of someone who didn't see much daylight. His own hair was slicked back and clipped with what looked like a large gold ring into the smoothest of ponytails. Other than that hairclip, he wore no jewelry, not even a watch. He had the authority and dash of a young priest, a man imbued with his God-given mission. He looked me up and down, taking in the patchwork kimono coat and sneakers, as well as the coiled, white braid. "Not bad," he said in an Australian accented voice. "You got the height, you got the carriage, even in sneakers."

I smiled and patted my shoulder bag. "I do have proper shoes with me—forgot to change back into them."

"No need. Great coat. Japanese?"

"Yeah, it is. Look, sorry to keep you waiting." He waved a hand that said not to worry. "Sheilah says you're a genius."

"Except for the color I've worked out for her, which I admit is bloody good, you don't need much genius with Ms. Sheilah. She's got the world's best hair."

"She sure does," I agreed. Sheilah beamed as she always did over a compliment about her looks. "But, William, for me you're gonna have to be a genius *without* color. I'll give you some latitude with the scissors, but—"

"I know, I know," he said quickly. "Madame briefed me: 'no color and Grace is stubborn.' So go get changed and shampooed and we'll comb it all out and see what we've got. Deal?"

"Deal."

Some minutes later I was smocked up and in his chair, my wet head being appraised in earnest. "Okay, Rapunzel," he said, "what shall we do here?"

"Whatever you say. You're the genius, I'm just a head." But I found my heart beating with a nice excitement: a woman waiting to be transformed. An illusion, I knew it was nothing more, but what a surprise to feel that thrill.

"You've got a good face for lots of possibilities, Ms. Bones. I could take a razor to that head and you'd look fabulous."

"I know I shouldn't butt in," Sheilah said, "but you know me. Chin length, center part, shorter in the back, longer on the sides"—the way I'd worn it for a lot of years before Bedford Hills. Putting it back on my head now might be the opposite of normalizing—a daily ironic reminder of how much everything had changed.

"Can I amend that?" William said quickly with the mildness of one not too likely to be overruled. "Bottom of the earlobes, one length all round, part low on the left side. I'm going to feather the black streak a bit so it swoops like a bird wing, and stays out of your eyes: a little spiritual but really hot. What do you say?"

"Yes," I said softly. "Oh yes!" I watched fascinated as he made the first cut and a foot of dense hair dropped to the floor. Beside me in the big mirror was Sheila biting her lip in a visible effort not to interfere.

Swoops like a bird's wing . . . that's what I'd had in mind for the first big piece of jewelry I'd ever attempted, a neckpiece, the stone a wing-shaped cut of red faceted glass taken from a junker car's taillight. I'd framed it in blackened steel and hung it from plumber's chain. "Wing" had gotten me my first fashion press coverage, elicited orders beyond anything I'd imagined. The original—a bit imperfect at one edge—lay in the jewelry drawer in my sublet apartment. It was one of the pieces I had wanted to keep, though I didn't believe I could ever again bear to wear it.

". . . and *voilà*." William gave a final flick to the top of my sheared head and stepped back, his face expressionless, waiting.

I came back from my side trip and studied the mirror. I looked . . . I wasn't sure what the word might be. The black streak swept across my forehead seemed to broaden my cheekbones, enlarge my eyes, while the blunt cut silver sides curved like commas onto my cheeks. I thought of the word: optimistic. If a haircut could look like hope, this was the one. I grinned. "William, you *are* a genius."

"Good-bye Pocahontas's mom." Sheilah began to applaud and then threw her arms around him and whispered something in his ear that made him giggle. "Go get changed, Grace," she said. "We've got things to do."

A few minutes later I was dressed and back. "Come on, Sheilah," I said. "I can't accept it. You're enough of a fairy godmother already." I had tried to pay at the desk and been waved away.

Her red lips showcased the costly perfect teeth in a smile. "My plan, my treat."

"Thanks then," I said, my voice too bright and tight. I walked over and put a folded twenty into William's pocket. He was already immersed in playing with the blond Niagara of his next client's hair, but turned to blow me a quick kiss that ended in a thumbs-up sign.

"I *did* tip him," Sheilah said.

"I know. I just wanted—" Taking it further by even one more word would hurt her feelings. "Okay, lady, you said we have things to do?"

She held up a long index finger. "Shopping: you're going to need a couple of basic pantsuits and things to wear under them. I'd love to have you start tomorrow so that Monday you'll be able to hit it running."

"I'm paying," I said a tad too aggressively.

"Of *course* you are, but I'll have to use my charge cards today and get a check back from you. We'll get the banking transferred into your name tomorrow, too late to do it today. And you'll need a cell phone. Oh, by the way, you *must* turn on the answering machine at the apartment and record a message. Grace, it's important. I tried to call you this morning, pretty early. No answer."

"I was out meeting my parole officer," I said, hoping the ping of hostility I felt had not made it into my tone.

"Sorry," she said quietly. "But please don't get defensive, the phone's going to be central to your work life, you know what I'm saying?"

"I do," I said, my eyes meeting hers. And I did.

Like filling a supermarket cart with basic housekeeping supplies I acquired a generic wardrobe: one black pantsuit, one gray; gray, black, wine and white tops; bras, pantyhose, a couple of belts, a black ankle-long jersey skirt, fairly skinny, and a pair of black ankle-high boots, very comfortable—all from the Bendel's post–Columbus Day sale, which was how come the whole lot cost about twelve hundred, instead of twice that. Two days free, two thousand dollars gone. Patty Ann Carlson flashed into my head. To her I was undeservedly rich, spoiled. Maybe she was right.

"Grace. Gracie! Come *here*. What do you think of this?" We were out of Bendel's, my shopping done, and into Bergdorf's, where I paced aimlessly up and down the aisle of designer boutiques, steering my body like someone driving an unfamiliar new car, while Sheilah tried on clothes. Now I followed her voice into Chanel where she stood before a mirror modeling a purple tweed suit. "Is it great or just . . . you know? Because it's a hell of a lot of money even on sale." This last to the saleswoman as though she might be partly responsible.

"I hate to tell you," I said in the tones of a doctor delivering fatal news, "it is great, so I'm afraid you're stuck with it." I spoke truth: it flattered her slim body, the jacket and skirt adding just the right curves; the color was perfect with her dark red hair and blue eyes—also, every time she put it on she would know it was a Chanel and she would love that.

"Do you know what this *costs?*" she asked, playing devil's advocate against the decision already made. Wisely, the saleswoman, an attractive, Slavic-looking blond about our age, kept quiet. It was part of the game and she knew her moves.

I knew mine too. "I have no idea," I said blandly, "but you work your buns off and you deserve it." Sheilah would buy the suit, but the actual doing of it would take some time.

A couple of hours later, after a quick sushi dinner with Sheilah, I got off the 3 Train at Broadway and Ninety-sixth, practically home and glad to be. I was just rounding the corner of my block, a stuffed shopping bag over each arm, thinking fondly of the New York subway system, when a blinding light exploded in the dark, maybe a foot from my face. I flung the shopping bags in its general direction and screamed—I think I screamed. The light exploded again.

"Hey, *sshh*, it's only a flash." A man's voice. "It's okay, folks," he said to the few people on the street who had stopped, "I was just taking the lady's picture."

The circles before my eyes went from yellow to red to black. Then I saw him. Short, a little plump, curly goldish hair thin on top and massing in ringlets at the sides: an aging *putto* off some third-rate fresco, tricked out in little round horn-rimmed glasses and a tan raincoat. No one I knew. "Who the hell are you?" I asked. We were both crouched on the sidewalk stuffing my new clothes back into their bags.

"Name's Gabriel McCail, Grace. Don't you remember? I covered your case for the *Times*. I tried to arrange a visit up there. I tried a bunch of times but—"

"Oh shit." I tasted pickled ginger, tuna and wasabi as the sushi dinner rose at the back of my throat. I got to my feet and took the shopping bag he handed me. "What do you want?"

"So you *do* remember me?" he asked more anxiously than the question seemed to require.

"Actually, I don't." Not entirely true—the name did have a ring, not from the *Times* but from his unanswered letters asking to visit me at Bedford Hills to discuss what he'd called a project. "What's happened to the *Times*," I asked, "they using *paparazzi* now?"

"I'm not with the *Times* now." The street lamp lit him quite well; he was probably somewhere in his thirties, an angel who'd been fired for nonperformance. For just an instant he looked ashamed of himself. "I'm with the *Post*."

"Sorry for your loss." My legs tingled with an urge to kick him front and center, very hard. "If you were planning on an interview about how I like the Upper West Side as opposed to Westchester, forget it."

"Look, Grace, it's not a spot interview I'm after and you know it. I'm working on a book here, and—"

"*You* look, Gabriel. There's nothing in it for me, talking to you, especially not about a book. I won't even ask how you happen to know where I live, I'm sure you have your sources. But I did my time—uneventfully. And now it's over. Why don't you imitate a person and give me a break."

He gave a cocky little smile. "So you've got a job with Sheilah, huh? I love the haircut, looks good. That kimono coat you have on—you were wearing it the night you knocked Paul down at that gallery opening. Remember?"

This time, my hand shot out and stopped just short of grabbing the front of his raincoat. I looked down into his startled face and dropped the hand to my side. It felt outsized and heavy as stone. "You got an *A* in the Grace Leshansky trivia test. Congratulations." My face burned and the pounding in my ears seemed louder than my voice. "There is nothing you can do to me, *Gabriel.* Nothing. You can embarrass Sheilah, maybe enough that she'll have to fire me. Then I'll go work at Bloomingdale's or McDonald's. It'll be less money and worse work, but I will manage. Do you understand that? Do you get it? I've been locked up for seven years. *I don't have much to lose.*"

I felt sick to my stomach. Once in my second week at Bedford Hills, before my skin was sufficiently toughened, I'd gotten into a stupid brawl in the cafeteria and was written up—just the once. Tonight had been too close a call, and for what? To give a pushy reporter just what he'd hoped to get. He stepped back and grinned, pleased with himself.

"You don't have to say any more. I've got my story—at least for right now." That was for sure. I wondered how my thin-lipped parole officer might react to the shot of my screaming mouth and his account of who said what. McCail was nodding, not at me it seemed, but at whatever was going on in his own head. I looked at the camera hanging from his shoulder and wondered whether I had a shot at capturing and disabling it. I probably did but I knew I'd better skip it. I'd done myself enough damage.

He said, "You asked for a break? I'll give you one—to the degree I can. I'm a good reporter, Grace—was then, am now. I work for *me* no matter who signs the checks." He said this with a note of craftsman's pride that rang a familiar note to another craftsman. Right, I thought, kindred spirits, Angel Gabriel and Killer Grace.

It was either my face registering this or yet more reserves of ego that encouraged him to continue, "Once something grabs me, I'm a fact hound. I dig 'em up and I put 'em together real well. You'd be surprised at some of the things I know—about you and, maybe more important, about . . . well, that's for our next conversation." He patted the camera on his hip and said as a kind of calculated throwaway, "You've heard Josh Pyatt's up in Otisville, right? Couple of months now."

"Yes," I said coolly, "I've heard." Reckless endangerment, racketeering, conspiracy, tax evasion: he'd likely spend the rest of his days there. Finally, one of his long-time people had done what my father never quite did: turned FBI informer. I'd learned the news in a short TV report, not so short that I missed the minor satisfaction of watching the Big Vig hustled off in handcuffs.

The reporter sensed an advantage and pressed it. He was looking for more than a tabloid story now. He was sniffing the trail of his damned book. "But Michael's still free as a bird. All that half-assed smoke and mirrors innuendo, then poof! Think he did it? Think Michael Pyatt killed your father?"

Why didn't my feet just move past him, walk away? "Michael's a doc-tor now," he said. "Did you know that?"

"I don't give a fuck." He'd surprised me with that last piece, as I was sure he could tell.

"Come on, how does it make you feel?" he prodded.

Feel? The question, if I addressed it in any real way, would spark a slow burn that stood an excellent chance of incinerating me from the inside out. "It's past being of any interest to me," I said.

"Ironic isn't it? When they had your dad on the hook the Feebies took a snooze, so confident they snored away their chance. With this guy they took nothing for granted—under surveillance from the git-go. The case against Josh and the bigger fish went off without a hitch."

He was so obviously trying to get a rise out of me that it wasn't hard to deny him satisfaction. I turned and began to walk away.

"My book's not about Josh though, or about you," he called this out to my back, stopping me in my tracks. "Paulie Donofrio," he said just loud enough for me to hear.

I broke into a run then. He did not follow me.

CHAPTER EIGHT

The apartment was as tidy as I'd left it, a quiet refrigerator hum the only sound. But had the place been tossed, trashed, decimated by bomb, screeching with alarms bells I would not have been surprised. The encounter with Gabriel McCail had blown away any lingering wisps of pleasure I'd taken in a haircut, a subway ride—blown them away as though they were cotton candy, which of course they were. The real substances of my life were the ones underfoot: the icy slopes ahead and the scorched earth behind.

He was writing a book about Paul. So many stories, so many layers. How many could he peel off if he kept at it?

Paulie Donofrio. Hearing the name from McCail had chilled my bones. I had heard it before, more than seven years ago from Paul's own lips. It had been news to me then. Hearing it fresh from a self-admiring reporter bent on exhuming Paul at any cost changed nothing about what I knew or didn't know—or what I'd done—but it changed a hell of a lot else. I felt the powerless desperation of a quarry: a fox easily lured this way and that by its hunters, destined to be trapped in the end however long it took to get there. Absurd how a woman is flattered to be called a fox, as a man is to be called a bull when both fox and bull are doomed in the games they're forced to play.

I took off my coat and hung it away along with the purchases of the day. I did these things deliberately, concentrating on each move, letting the routine little actions fill my mind, calm my body. It occurred to me to call Sheilah, warn her to expect to see her name and her company's in the *Post*. That would have been the decent thing to do, but I couldn't bring myself to do it. The bad news could wait until morning; it was already past nine o'clock, they'd hardly stop the presses for this story. To salve my conscience a little, I heeded her instruction to turn on the answer machine and record a greeting. My hand had not trembled when it reached out in the aborted grab at McCail. Now it bobbled the buttons on the machine so that I had to repeat the simple mechanics three times to get it right.

I undressed with the acute self-consciousness of a woman stalked and aware of it, first making sure that the window blinds were pulled shut, then covering myself in a long red hooded tee shirt from the stash of preprison clothes. The nakedness that had so appealed to me this morning was now mere exposure and, as such, dangerous.

I settled into the rattan armchair, my arms hugging each other as though to keep myself together. I needed to think in ways I was not used to. George's embargo on our history had early clipped the wings of my personal curiosity. I'd grown accustomed to his evasions and my own ignorance. And because, presented with lemons, my instinct had leaned always toward lemonade, I developed a certain carefree comfort in the simplicity of being rootless and of not knowing.

In prison my thinking had been without consequence, there was little I could do *but* think. Now, unless I was a lot smarter than I knew how to be I could cause another disaster—not by pulling a trigger myself this time, but by inadvertently putting my father into someone's firing range. Much as I'd have liked to, I could not shrug off Gabriel McCail, self-proclaimed fact hound, as simply a mouthy egoist. He'd entered my gut like an armed intruder, striding around in there as though he owned the place, tossing the names George and Paul and Michael at me like so much underwear out of a rifled drawer, but what was important was that I believed his boast of knowing things about my life that I did not.

Half-assed smoke and mirrors, he'd called the evidence against Michael in George's disappearance. Did that mean he knew George was alive? Or killed by someone else entirely? McCail knew things I needed to know, but I knew things I needed him to *not* know. An arm wrestle between us it would be for sure. My jail-yard muscles wouldn't help me here.

Michael's a doctor now. How does that make you feel? How did anything about Michael Pyatt make me feel? Mostly, I tried not to think of him at all, specifically to avoid the feelings that came with the thoughts—betrayal worst of all. But shutting the door on thought was a luxury I could not afford in the new McCail era. So Michael entered my mind—Michael the boy, as he was when we met.

The summer George and I had spent exiled in Miami after the bad beating was the most silent period I'd ever known. Late mornings George would drive me to the beach where I would swim and walk and read and munch a sandwich and weave some beads on wire. I kept to myself, except for an occasional bit of girl-boy banter with some lifeguard or surfer. Late afternoons George would pick me up. Sometimes we'd go to a movie. What he did during the day I'm not sure, though I got the impression it wasn't much—even his gambling seemed to be on hold. He was barricaded inside his own head, like someone who'd gotten disastrous news from a doctor and was trying to find a new way to exist.

It was a Tuesday night when he made the crying-uncle call to New York. I heard only his end of things. *"Break it, you've bought it,"* he'd said. *"You want me, Big Vig? You got me. Tell me where to report. Sir."* That Saturday, we flew back to New York.

The following day, George and I sat opposite each other, bumping along in an Amtrak train headed north for Rhinecliff, two hours from the city. George had been summoned up there for a several-day work session at Josh's country house, me along because Josh had said, "Hey, don't forget to bring my friend Grace. Got a swimmin' hole here and the city's a boilin' shit pit in August."

Despite his snappy, double-breasted seersucker suit, new white shirt and red tie, George looked shrunken and glum. I was determined to feel the opposite. I had just turned seventeen and was clutching tight to an optimistic view of the future, which had been given a big boost by our move back home. No matter how George saw the deal he'd made, the way I saw it was that he was safe from a potential blackened eye, cracked rib or broken arm lurking around the next corner, and safe from the clammy fear that went with waiting for it. I was ashamed to admit to myself that somewhere under my skin lodged a twisted kind of pride that the Big Vig valued my father's talent enough that he'd gone to desperate lengths to claim it.

"You look like a condemned man waiting for his last meal," I said—a less than literal translation of what I really meant: *Please be happy, so I can be happy. Tell me it's okay.* When he didn't respond, I cranked up my own manic cheerleading effort. "You should be *celebrating,* damn it. You're out of danger, right? No more hiding out in soggy Miami, which we both hate. We're back where we want to be—we can get our Callas records and stuff out of storage, even go to Lincoln Center and hear some live opera. He's letting you work off your debt—*paying* you, for Christ's sake, and if you're lucky this'll be an arrangement that lasts."

"Don't bet the farm on my luck," he said, the left corner of his mouth turning down the way it did when he was being ironic.

"You're home free, George. Don't you *get* it?"

He gave me a smile that looked seasick. "My darling daughter," he said softly. I searched his face for the beginnings of a joke and didn't find one. For all his love of twenties shtick and Italian opera, George was not sentimental in matters personal: words like "darling," even "daughter," were not much on his tongue. "I get it," he said, the smile gone.

Josh picked us up in a large station wagon. Beside him in the front seat was a boy about my own age, who looked as unlike his father as I did like mine. Even seated, I could see he was at least as tall as Josh was but half as wide. That was not the only difference. My jewelry work had made me superaware of shapes and textures. I noticed, for example, that the son's face was a perfect oval, sharp featured, earth brown and matte, whereas his father's was broad, blunt and licorice black with a sheen to it.

"My son, Michael," Josh said with the pride of an owner. He didn't move from the driver's seat to help us load our overnight satchels into the car. That wasn't the relationship; it would have felt weird if he had. What already felt weird was that we were going to spend a few nights up there. Josh had full days planned for George—two, at least. Lawyers and others would be joining them some of the time.

Michael gave me an inquiring look, mumbled hi or hey or some such, and then turned to face the windshield. The late summer day was pretty hot, but good hot—not the damp, rotting hot of Miami summer. The rolling mountains here were an inviting lush green broken by gold and purple patches of wildflowers. That landscape and the back of Michael Pyatt's head occupied my eyes, but I was jittery at George's silence— George, who usually talked more not less when he was nervous. "Are these the Catskills?" I asked no one in particular.

"They are, Grace," Josh said. "Pretty, huh? Folks used to call the part west of here the Jewish Alps. In the old days, city Jews came up here to breathe some country air and," he laughed, "find their soul mates. Your folks meet at Grossinger's, Georgie?" he asked.

"Yeah," George muttered. I gave him a fast glance, but he was looking at his lap. The "yeah" wasn't likely true from the little I'd learned of his parents.

"My place is just outside Woodstock," Josh said. "Summer of Love: you ever hear about that?"

"Sure," I said. "They smoked a lot of dope and listened to great music and fucked their brains out."

After a long beat, the laugh roared up out of him. You could never tell how he'd react to "language" from me; sometimes it made him mad. It was a game I played, but that day I was showing off for Michael, not his father. When I saw Michael's head shake, side to side, very slowly, I figured he must think I was a total moron.

"Beats all, don't it?" Josh asked. "Nigger out of Alabama with a plantation in the Summer of Love." He liked saying "nigger out of Alabama," judging by how often he said it.

The house was no plantation, just a nice, big house up a long winding path into the woods. But the grounds, and there were a lot of them, were enclosed by tallish stone walls topped with ironwork spikier than the design required. A pair of large Dobermans ran out to meet the car. Josh leapt out, patted the dogs' heads and disappeared into the house like someone in a rush to get to the bathroom.

George, who was scared of dogs, cowered in the back seat trying to summon up the inner push he needed to get himself out of the car. "Come *on*, George," I whispered. "They're not going to hurt you."

Michael stood a few feet away, watching. He noticed us making no move to get out of the back seat. "They won't bother you unless they think you're an intruder." The first real words he'd said. "Why don't you go inside, I'll put them in the kennel. As I stepped out of the car, he turned back toward us. Though I couldn't have sworn it was a fact, I enjoyed the idea that he was approving of the red, gauzy Indian print dress and of the body inside it.

It had never occurred to me to wonder what a place Josh Pyatt lived in would look like—or, for that matter, what anybody's place might look like. Our own apartment in Washington Heights had no identity at all, except for the art and opera posters that covered the walls like stamps on an envelope hoping to be mailed somewhere far away. The inside of this house of Josh's looked like a set on loan from *Leave It to Beaver.* It was at least a mild surprise.

We sat in the Cleaver dining room where everybody wolfed down ham and turkey sandwiches and deli trimmings. Josh stood up still chewing his last bite and said, "Georgie and me gonna roll up our sleeves. We got work to do." After a moment George stood too. Michael and I stayed where we were and exchanged glances. If his was coded, I couldn't read it.

"You kids go out have a walk round now, take a swim." Josh's decree was thick and flat as a plank. "Hope you brought a swimsuit, Grace. Must still be a couple of Naomi's upstairs somewhere, but you'd never get into one of those—top *or* bottom."

I saw Michael wish for lightning to strike his father dead and figured Naomi must be his mother. I'm not sure why I laughed then: partly, I thought, to let George know I was okay and partly to let Josh know he couldn't embarrass me with cracks about his wife's body or mine or anyone's. Maybe mainly I laughed because I was wound too tight. It was stupid—dumber than my comment in the car.

"G'wan now, Michael, you take her up to her room." Michael knew an order when he heard one. As he got up from the table he looked ready to take a swing at Josh, but of course he didn't. And George stared down at his empty plate on the table as though the meal really had been his last.

"Do you ever talk?" I asked Michael after we'd been strolling around for ten, fifteen minutes.

"Yeah, I talk. When I feel like it I do." God, he was great-looking!

"Look, I'm sorry I laughed, you know, when Josh said that thing. Naomi's your mom?"

"Yeah."

We passed brilliantly colored, cultivated gardens, then stretches of woods, then more gardens in a landscape that held a visual surprise over each roll of ridge. I stopped in front of one large square where bushes of yellow roses were surrounded with masses of something I'd never seen that was orange and fragrant. I took a long sniff and turned toward him.

"Freesia, it's called. My mom loved doing all this planting. She called it her therapy."

"Is she dead?"

"No. They're divorced. He gets me every August." He speeded up his loping kind of walk to a jog. I followed.

"He was an asshole to say that in front of you about her," I said after a silent while. "I wish you *had* hit him. You wanted to."

"You serious or trying to be charming?" He was wearing a baseball hat and the angle of the peak shaded his eyes so I couldn't see them.

"I don't know," I said. "What do you think?"

"I think you're scared shitless of my daddy."

"So are you. And I'm not sure you're right about me. I wouldn't say I'm scared of him . . . exactly." Of course he was right. I felt the urge to point out that you couldn't be brave if you weren't afraid, but I didn't.

"Well, you should be scared. He's scary."

"If you say so," I said, wanting to get Josh Pyatt's big thumb off the moment. My hair was pinned up in a coil and I felt the full sun at my bare neck and the sweat on my forehead beginning to spill down into my eyes. "So where do we go for the swim?"

"The pond's over the next ridge. Follow me." Sure enough, beyond the small hill it appeared. He tossed the towels and his hat on the grass, kicked off his sneakers and took a long dive in. Since I had learned to swim in city pools where the borders and depths are a crystal clear blue, I was cautious about this very large circle of black jelly that might be bottomless. I walked in gingerly, as though I expected ground glass underneath my next step. The water was cold enough to make my breath catch, and smelled slightly of sulfur and mud, a country smell that I found I liked a lot better than chlorine. I paddled around for a little to get the feel before beginning to swim across in real slicing strokes.

After a few minutes I glanced around and saw no sign of Michael. Just as I was registering that, I felt a sudden tug on my leg, pulling me down. I kicked my other leg hard and reached into the water with one hand far enough to find his head and give it a strong push. He ducked away, surfaced and showed me a large wet grin. I dove under and went for him then and for the next while we played like seals and got acquainted more directly than with clumsy, unreliable words.

Later we lay on the soft grass a few feet from the pond, wrapped in the big towels he'd brought. I could hear his breathing and my own alternating in a kind of syncopated rhythm. I pushed my soaking Medusa hair out of my eyes and looked over at him. His arms were stretched out wide, his legs together: a long, slender cross. His eyes were shut and his lips at rest. The lower one had a slight cleft in its center, which made it voluptuous. I had the notion of licking that lip, but didn't.

"You're really beautiful, you know?" I had never said that to a boy before, or to anyone. At that moment it was simple to say just because it was true. But then, I'd never felt quite like this: all grown up and at the same time brand-new.

"I'm supposed to be the one saying that," he said without opening his eyes.

"But I'm not beautiful. Sexy maybe, but not beautiful." Now he squinted his eyes open, shading them with his hand to look at me.

"You are a faahn looking woman," he said, putting on a black accent to go with the line. His own accent placed him as a private school boy—a certain laid-back ease they had, the ones I'd met: a touch of "I go to Collegiate or Dalton or such, and you don't." Josh talked black and enjoyed exaggerating it, daring you to take exception, wanting you to know you were getting it stuck to you by a black man—a nigger out of Alabama.

"So where do you go to school?" I asked.

"Boston Latin. Boston's where I live."

"With your mother?"

"Right. Except for August. What about you, where do you go to school?"

"Wherever we happen to be living at the moment." I shrugged, playing the adventurer a bit, even though I was speaking fact. Michael and I were both propped up on our arms now, facing each other, big towels draped around our heads and shoulders like a pair of Bedouins. "School starts in a couple of weeks. If I can get back into High School of Music and Art for senior year, that would be good. But we left for Florida in a hell of a hurry, and all kinds of forms were waiting when we got back. It may be too late to enroll now. Maybe not, though."

I saw his jaw clench, but he couldn't hold back. "What *is* it with you? You're like that old joke about the kid who gets a pile of horseshit for Christmas and dances around smiling 'cause she's so sure there's a pony waiting for her. You gotta *know* my daddy's a hungry tiger and your daddy's a scared rabbit who looks like dinner to him. Don't you *get* how bad this whole fucking scene is?"

I bounded up, scalded by shame and anger at hearing a truth I knew better than I wanted to from a boy I shouldn't know at all. "*Me?* Oh, I get it all right. I was just trying to be tactful, not mentioning why we had to run away to Florida. You're the one who doesn't get it. Your father had my father beat up so bad he couldn't walk. And you know why? To force him into taking this job because Josh *needs* him—and he just takes what he needs. Let me tell you he's no tiger, he's just a bear, crafty, mean and kind of dumb. See, the dumb bear needs this supersmart little rabbit to cheat the government out of taxes on money he made breaking bones of gamblers—right, breaking their bones, making them bleed, scaring them to *death*." I had screamed myself hoarse but I was no way ready to shut up. "George didn't want to be part of this. He fought it the best way he could and . . . You think *I* don't get how bad this fucking scene is? It's *you* people who make it like that."

Michael stood too, scooping up the towel I'd dropped and holding it out to me. " *'You people'*? I'm not part of you people. I'm not him," he said quietly.

"You belong to him." I took the towel and slapped it down on the ground hard. It was damp and made a whipping thwack. I dropped it, ran back to the pond and took a running jump in.

I swam back and forth, cutting the circle into quarters and doing it again—and again until I was exhausted. He didn't come after me but when I walked out finally, there he was sitting cross-legged on the bank looking up at me. "I hate what my father is, and I've got nothing against yours. I wanted to tell you." The words came out of him one by one, equal value, no inflection, as though he was typing them on a piece of clean paper. They seemed all the more powerful for that.

I took a step or two toward him and then stopped. "All that yelling I just did's been sitting there in the bottom of my heart since it happened to him, the beating, but I couldn't let it out, not around George. He took weeks in Florida to decide to give in to Josh and I was praying hard that he'd do just what he did, so he'd be safe. I mean, screw the government and their taxes, I just want him safe."

"Amazing Grace," he said slowly. A cool breeze blew across my back and I felt the skin on my arms and legs pucker up to gooseflesh. My nipples hardened into pebbles. I could feel them do it and knew that he could see them through the thin tank suit I wore. "You know, I had a hard time figuring out if you were dumb or nuts or . . . or just brave."

That made me smile. "And which one do you think?"

"Maybe all the above. And sexy. And beautiful."

He stood up. As he did I saw the bulge in his boxer trunks. We faced each other, eye to eye, a matched set—he topped me by no more than two inches. I had been to bed with three different boys during the past year, which put me past the nervous virgin stage, but not as far past as I would have liked. And also, this felt so different it was almost scary—like my legs, no bones in them, were trying to support a full pot of very warm honey. "Is there some place we could be?" I asked, the words flooding with too much breath. "I mean you've got natural camouflage on the ground, but my big white butt would catch the light like a moon and—" I exploded into an unexpected laugh. "Where'd you put those damned dogs?"

"Locked in the kennel. But you're no intruder. You're with me." He took hold of my hand and we ran barefoot into the woods.

Over the next two days, we had sex, made love, fucked, sucked, screwed, scratched that itch as often as we could get away with, which was often. Our fathers were locked away somewhere in another part of the house with other men who came and went, all of them in deep concentration on how to best wash and dry and press and store away Josh's growing fortune.

The few times I saw George surface, I noticed he looked more like himself, energized the way he got when he was figuring horses or handicapping ball games. The seersucker suit hadn't given way to country clothes, which he didn't own so hadn't brought, but the tie was missing and the shirt collar open.

"Looks like it's going okay," I said as I passed him on the stairs one late afternoon, my body tingling, face still sun warm.

He nodded. "Long as they keep those fucking German hounds away from me. I'm in the numbers, Gracie. Once I can focus on the puzzle, I'm good. You're having a nice time?" he asked. It was an apology, I could tell that. That was one thing about being close and separate in the way we were: you read some signals too well and others not at all.

"I'm having a great time. Really."

"Yeah." He did not sound reassured. "Be careful." Something he never had said to me in my life.

"What do you mean?"

"You know what I mean." I did know. What he meant was not a warning against sex with Michael, per se, but a reminder of who we were and who they were—and, that understood, who was more likely to get burned. "But it's probably useless advice, considering the source."

"Don't worry, I can take care of myself," I said, the full faith and credit of my love-happy self-confidence behind it, and leaned in to kiss his cheek.

Late in the afternoon on our last day, Michael and I were lying together in the woods, the same spot where we'd first gone and continued to go. He'd brought some very nice grass down from a stash in his room, and was smoking a joint as we held each other after making love for a long time.

"What's it like to be you?" he asked lazily into my neck while his free hand moved in little circles on my belly, as though his baby were in there.

"I've never been anyone else." I put my hand on his lightly enough so he wouldn't stop the stroking. "Right this minute it's wonderful to be me," I said.

"Yeah, me too," he said after a beat.

"I sometimes think my mother was something brown, or at least tan."

"Really?" He passed me the joint. I toked and gave it back.

"Dunno, never met her, she took off early. How I see her in my head is this big, tall Cherokee maybe, with a long braid down her back. My birth certificate says her name is Sara Leshansky. George says that's not real—that they weren't married. That's all he'll say and it's useless to push him. That pisses me off, but not as much as it did when I was younger. You get used to stuff."

He took in a lungful of smoke and let it out slowly. "Sometimes, I wish I was black like . . . I mean my daddy is hardly what anyone would call a role model, but he *is* black: the man is a black man." He inhaled some more and took a long time to get it out. "My mother's white, and Jewish." he said. "Surprises you, huh?"

"It does. Naomi, your Jewish mother." I laughed. "Think she'd like me?"

"Sure," he said after a pause just long enough for me to notice. "Thing I was trying to say is, we live in a white neighborhood—always did, even when they were together. I go to white schools. I'm some kind of brown white kid." His dislike of that was clear. Then, I guess to switch the subject off him, he asked: "What's it like to have your father?"

"Doesn't have much to do with the word 'father.' It's more like having a terrific brother who gets into trouble. I mean you love him to pieces but you have to watch out for him all the time—like he might go off and get himself hurt or kidnapped while you're not looking. It would be awful to have your father. Does he hit you?"

He took some time to say, "Once. He did it ice cold; beat my butt with a belt. I was nine. I'd called him an ape so maybe I had it coming—but he hit me too hard. After that, all he ever had to do was give me a look. He probably still thinks it was the right thing, you know—give the kid a good scare one time and then he stays in line."

"He's in the scare business, your father. That's what he does."

"I told you I hate what he is. I hate what he does. I *almost* hate him. Any part of me that doesn't must be hooked into the word 'father,' because if the man wasn't my father I could see wanting to kill him." He took another drag and held the joint out to me.

"No thanks. I don't smoke much dope."

"I do. I need to stay mellow." His eyes looked at me and were teary suddenly. He took a final toke, so deep he came close to singeing his long fingers.

———

I got off the train in New York able to float inches above the pavement, smiling a smile that began in the brain and moved straight down to between the legs, not missing a single vital organ on the way: I was in love; my father was out of danger. Two other omens: first day back I learned that the High School of Music and Art had said yes, they *would* take me back and Sheilah had sold five of my bead and wire neck collars to an artsy fashion shop on Columbus Avenue for fourteen dollars apiece.

My seventeen-year-old life had swooped upward like a launching gull, soared beyond what I could have reasonably wished for. It was not like that for long. Quickly I lost altitude and the pavement came up to meet my chin. Michael Pyatt did not call. After three days I called Josh's Woodstock house (the unlisted number pried out of George—the only piece of information in my life I remember getting from him that he didn't want to give). I tried many times, at many hours, no one answered. That was the first wave. The second was worse.

A week later, Sunday afternoon of the Labor Day weekend, Josh came to our apartment. George answered the door and stood there holding it half open, not inviting entry. My heart dropped like a stone down a well, wondering whether his safety would be the next thing to vaporize. But George himself did not seem scared in that way as he asked quickly, "What's up, Josh?" and then reluctantly stepped back giving Josh room to get his bulky body through without having to knock over an obstacle in its path.

"Not here to see you, Georgie," he said. "Wanna talk to Grace." There was something raggedly intimate in the way Josh said my name. Hard to say how it was different from the way he'd said it dozens of times over the years but it was. I was wearing shorts that day and a tee shirt on the tight side. For once in my life I'd rather have been wearing a canvas tent.

"What . . . ?" George began and seemed to lose his nerve. I saw his mouth give a little twitch, which was the only real sign he ever gave when he was frustrated.

"Alone," Josh said, not loud, but that was that for George, whose eyes apologized for leaving me on my own before he began his walk to the bedroom. Until that moment I had never in my life felt abandoned by my father.

"That's fine," I said a little too loud just before he closed the door behind him. Josh was here about Michael's disappearance from the face of my earth. However bad the last week had been, this was going to be worse. My chilled gut knew that if it knew nothing else.

I turned to Josh and asked flat out, "What?"

"Want to sit down, Grace?" he asked the way you might speak to a hospital patient you were visiting. *Was he going to tell me Michael was dead? Car accident? Burst appendix?*

"No, I'm fine." *If he insists I sit, what will I do?*

"Suit y'self," his shoulders shrugged; it was like the movement of troops. "Michael won't be calling you," he said like someone delivering news of a death. "And you shouldn't try to call him." I did not understand a thing, not a thing—except that Josh, who had been all for Michael and me, who had *pushed* us together, was now pulling us apart, squashing us under his huge thumb.

"You're a good-lookin' girl," he said. "Big, strong, the way a woman should be." He laughed in a low phlegmy way, the way he did sometimes when he wasn't amused. "If I . . . if you came 'cross my path when I was Michael's age . . ." I felt my face go hot. I gritted my teeth, forced myself not to lower my eyes and said nothing. "It ain't my call, Grace." Which meant it was Michael's call.

I felt myself gasp and tried to turn it into a laugh. It didn't work. "Don't you worry about that," I said through a clog of fury and shame. "It would've been a waste of time for him to bother calling anyway. To tell you the truth I thought he was nice but we have nothing in comm–" My voice broke on the lump in my throat. I turned fast and walked a few steps farther away. In case I did cry, at least he wouldn't see. It seemed very important that he didn't.

Then his hand was on my shoulder. I pulled away violently. " 'S'okay," he mumbled. "Okay. You're a good girl, Grace. Knew it from the first time you didn't open that door to me." He walked around to where he was facing me. "Here," he said, holding out his hand, which held a fistful of money. I stared down at it, my mind not tracking. He reached for my hand and tried to put the cash in it.

I reared back and shook the bills from my palm as if they were on fire. "If I were fucking *starving* I wouldn't take your–What am I, some *hooker*? Is that it? You and your slimy son, you people are *disgusting*." I ran down the hall to the bathroom and locked myself in. I stayed there for a long time crying hard as I wanted, which was pretty hard. If Josh Pyatt had broken down the door and killed me I wouldn't have cared a damn.

When I came out Josh was gone and George was sitting in the armchair listening to *Tosca* on WQXR. His head was thrown back, eyes shut. I thought he was sleeping.

"Hungry?" he asked, sensing my presence. "It's seven-thirty." I was hungry–not for food but to hear him say, "Look, Gracie, this isn't *Traviata* we're playing here. You're no Violetta and the Big Vig's no . . ." or even, "I told you up in Woodstock to be careful," or, "I'm sorry, kiddo, I feel like hell for you." No, I didn't really even half-expect that last one. All those things may have been in his head, even somewhere near his tongue, but they were not words George Leshansky could say. They would have made what had just happened realer than he could stand. What he said was, "Pizza or Chinese?"

"Pizza's okay," I said, stupid with the pain. "Keep him away from me. You just keep him away." He nodded okay.

The money was nowhere in sight. Had the wad of cash gone back into Josh's pocket or into my father's? I didn't ask. George and I never talked about the incident at all. Probably there was nothing to say that would have helped. Still, I would occasionally ache to ask him how he could have known it would end badly—*did* he know or had he just been guessing when he'd warned me to be careful? To say, yes, it *was Traviata,* some horrible modern version with no good tunes or costumes. And we could laugh maybe and melt the tension, some of it. But I didn't say word one, because I would have had a hard time then stopping myself from going on to ask how he could have walked out of that room and left me there.

———

The phone rang, not an especially blaring ring, just a usual one, but it brought me back to where I was—in a stranger's armchair, printed with flamingo on the wing. I listened to the second ring and the third, imagining hello in George's voice, in Josh's, in Michael's. When the machine picked up, it was Sheilah I heard, saying how much fun the day had been for her, hoping I was ready to "hit the ground running" tomorrow morning.

I got myself out of the chair and stretched my arms high as they would reach, then went into half an hour of bends and stretches, leg lifts and crunches, bent on whomping up endorphins to help combat old sadness and new tension. In eight hours I would be starting a job in a field I knew only through bits and pieces I'd heard from Sheilah. Seven years locked up had given me lots of training, but none of it relevant, I thought. I'd never worked in an office, not a real one. What if I let Sheilah down?—Sheilah, who was paying me not out of some corporate pocket but out of *her* pocket.

CHAPTER NINE

"Hey, Cynthia," I said to the woman behind the desk. You could call her an office manager, bookkeeper, executive secretary and be right on all counts. She had been Sheilah's right hand for almost ten years: a record. It was twenty to nine. I was reporting for my first day of work in new clothes, old Burberry, and over it all a mantle of determined good attitude. I glanced around the reception area—all smart, light earth tones, wood and slate—and remembered with a zinger of irony that it was in this office that I'd first laid eyes on Paul Boudreau.

"Hey, Grace. You look *good,*" Cynthia said. She had the face of a highly intelligent chipmunk, a resemblance heightened by her glasses, spiffy hexagonals, the frames dark blue to match her eyes—a change from the plastic horn-rims I remembered. She stood and held out her hand.

"And you. Look at you! Love the glasses."

"Not to mention the fifteen pounds my middle can't seem to get rid of. Sheilah took me shopping for the glasses: Christmas present. Your hair has that William look to it."

"Right. Yesterday. Bedford to Bendel's faster than the eye can follow. How are the kids?"

"Great. Katie's eleven now, all honors classes, and Sean, he'll be eight in January–hits a ball, *fuggedaboudit!* I don't know–was he born yet when–"

"About to be. You must have your plate full–the kids, all this."

She laughed. "My secret weapon is Tommy. If you're going to work for Sheilah Donlan and even think of having kids, it helps to be married to a good guy." Suddenly, she looked at me the way Sheilah had yesterday when she'd used the word "killer": the way you might look if you'd mentioned the three-minute mile to a man with one leg or next New Year's Eve to someone with a bad diagnosis.

"It's okay, Cynthia. Really. Some husbands are good guys, some not. Just like wives." It was surreal, standing in a Madison Avenue office in a new suit reassuring a nice woman who felt bad because she thought she'd made me uneasy about killing my husband. "So look," I said quickly, "tell me about my job."

"Come on, let's sit. Want some coffee?"

I nodded.

"Here's the thing," she said, after we were settled, mugs in hand, behind her big slate slab of a desk. "We've got two relatively new hires ourselves: Craig Tarbell, this brilliant researcher, he's been here almost six months. I mean he hardly ever leaves his desk but what that man can turn up on his phone and his screen, you wouldn't believe. And then there's Teresa Woo, Sheilah hired her four months ago. Good recruiter, finance and accounting specialist, hope she lasts. Seven searches in-house right now, two of them for GreenTree Bank, biggies: a Chief Technology Officer and an EVP, Marketing. Sheilah is handling those herself. The other five are for First America, the credit card company: two Marketing, three Finance, they're Teresa's–with input from Sheilah, of course." An eye flicker passed between us to acknowledge mutual understanding. "Teresa's on the road now meeting candidates, back Monday, and Sheilah's off to Dallas and San Fran Wednesday."

"And I'm going to be setting up those road trips for them?" *Okay. This is going to be okay. I can do this.*

"Yup. Like putting together a jigsaw puzzle–flights, meeting rooms, hotels. You want to pack in as many meetings as possible on a swing without making it too crazy. That's one part of it, the other is candidate/client meetings. Teresa should have one of her final slates in order by the time she gets back, she's already seen two candidates she likes, and we've reserved dates for them to go out and interview at First America. She needs one or two more solid candidates to round out the slate—and expects she'll have them by the time she gets back. Then, over to you."

"Okay."

"It's tough sometimes. Each candidate meets with say four or five people at the client company, also some clients put the candidates through a battery of psychological tests—you know, critical thinking, leadership, plays well with others. You'll have a contact at the client company who'll put the agenda together on their end, and you'll clear it with the candidate and arrange the travel and hotel and all."

"So I deal with the candidate and the company and try to keep things on track."

"Not always easy. Candidates sometimes want to cancel or reschedule after the whole thing's in place, and you could just—" She pantomimed a wring of neck. "What you have to do is twist their arm without pissing them off."

"How about between trips? What's the rest of my job?"

She laughed. "Believe me, in this office there's enough work for . . ."

Just then, Sheilah emerged from the conference room at the end of the hall, followed by a young man with a Midwestern face, carrying a briefcase. "Thanks for coming in, Jeremy. I'll check out the dates you gave me and see what we can set up in Wilmington. I think you're going to have a blast meeting them—and vice versa." He told her he was really looking forward to it. She gave him the smile, full wattage. "Hey, you sure I can't wrap up that croissant for you?" she coaxed like a mama. "Better than anything they'll give you on the plane." He declined with thanks. Twice. "Need the men's room before you go?" He declined that too. She fetched his coat and suitcase out of the closet, shook his hand and out the door he went.

Then she made for me like a targeted missle. "What *is* this, Grace? How could you not call and *warn* me?" She'd learned about McCail, but how?

I'd bought the *Post* at a newsstand on my way here and the story and photo were not in it. I felt like a kid caught with contraband at school—or a con nailed for an infraction by a guard.

"I was going to tell you first thing this morning," I said, careful to look her in the eye the way I would the guard. "I was too bummed out about it last night. It wasn't in the paper. How did you know so soon?"

"It's all over the Web," she said coldly. "News travels faster these days. It doesn't give my company's name, but it does give mine: 'A Madison Avenue executive search firm owned by her childhood friend, Sheilah Donlan'—something like that. You should have called me, Grace."

"I know. You're right. Does he . . . give my address?"

"No, just Upper West Side." So he'd given me one break. "He did mention that you were wearing the coat you wore when you decked Paul at the gallery that time—maybe you'd better leave it in the closet for a while. I printed the thing out, I'll show you." Her voice was sour. "God, that picture with your mouth wide open! You looked . . ." I didn't know whether crazy or violent was the word that didn't leave her tongue tip.

"He took me by surprise, the flash half blinded me. Look, we may as well say it: all this baggage of mine may be more than you bargained for."

"No, *you* look. Stop it about the baggage, okay? So the flash took you by surprise. This takes *me* by surprise, that's all. I'm *allowed* to be upset."

"God, of course you are. I wish I had warned you, Sheil. I'm sorry." A hug would have been the thing. I even felt like hugging her, but somehow I couldn't. Knowing it was too formal for who we were to each other, I stuck out my hand to shake, hoping she'd understand. She met me halfway, the grip on both sides strong enough to say we were trying to be okay.

After we'd released hands, she asked Cynthia, "Did you get to mention the name thing yet?" At the negative headshake, she turned back to me. "Cynthia and I have been batting it around. We're going to give you a stage name, kind of. I think you'll find it easier too, particularly with the kind of thing that happened last night." She was certainly right, I just . . . I'd gotten attached to being Grace Leshansky again. I felt reflexively disappointed—and petty and foolish for feeling that way.

"Is there a name you have in mind?" I asked.

"Well, we thought—just Cynthia and me, I haven't discussed anything about it with the others, Craig and Teresa just know we're getting a new staff member—we thought let's leave your first name alone and call you Grace Lester. How does that strike you?"

With a small shock—I'd never told Sheilah about Dr. Junius Lester. So much I'd never told her, which she suspected and which hurt her. She deserved a better friend than me, I thought. *I* deserved a better friend than me. I'd trusted both too much and not enough. I knew that; I just didn't know why it was. "How about Leslie," I said. "Grace Leslie, I like the sound of that better."

"Fine," she said. Her palms clapped in a that's-attended-to gesture. "Grace Leslie. Now let me show you where you'll be working, Ms. Leslie. We've put you over in Craig Tarbell's territory, through there." She pointed to a door at right angles to the office entrance. "I was lucky enough to get hold of a small office right next door, where I could break through. Come on, I'll show you." I gave her a glance, wondering whether she was placing me in the new space because memories of Paul might spook me less there—and decided I was overthinking things.

I followed her through the connecting door into a clean, white, no-frills reception area. Against one wall stood a smart steel desk equipped with two phones, a computer, three stacks of file folders and some yellow pads and pens. A long table with a fax machine on top of it and filing cabinet underneath occupied the adjacent wall. Mine: Grace Leslie's. I itched to start—to touch the stuff.

"This is you," Sheilah said, "and right behind that closed door is Craig. Now this office has its own entrance from the common hall, and what it says on the door and in the lobby directory is Leland Consulting, even though Craig's a Carpenter-Donlan employee. He picked Leland, said it had good, old-line authority, the kind of name people tend to think they've heard before and—you know—trust."

"Sounds like the CIA."

"You got that right. Recruiting research, *real* research—I'm not talking networking to find people's out-of-work golf buddies—the good stuff is an undercover operation. I mean we're looking to ferret out executive information companies don't want us to have because we're going to use it to entice their best people away. And all of that goes double and triple with the background checks we need to do now. It takes a lot of ingenuity, poise and very creative lying to get the hard facts and inside buzz. Craig is . . . incredible."

"So I hear from Cynthia."

"He's got a whole rep company of characters he pulls out; he's like a one-man show. And he plays that computer like a Steinway. You wouldn't believe what he can track down on-line." She chuckled. "I don't know how he does it . . . he tells me it's better I don't."

I decided to ask the question. "So how come I'm here in his war room instead of–" My thumb pointed back toward the connecting door.

"Only place I've got desk room for you. Hell, Teresa's workspace is a remodeled supply closet; she uses the conference room when she needs to spread out. Fortunately, we don't need to keep any word processing bodies on site. We all do our own computer work, except for, say, a long, formal report with graphs and charts, which we farm out to an office services firm downstairs. I tell you I *love* technology. It has trans*formed* our business!" Now fully immersed in her element, her mood was upbeat, laced with an enthusiasm for her game as authentic and infectious as any basketball star's or tennis pro's. "Want to meet Craig?"

"Absolutely," I said.

"Now I have to warn you. He's . . . different, a real original–eccentric– and not exactly thrilled about having a roommate." She knocked softly at the closed door and opened it a crack to peek her head in. After a beat, she opened it wide enough for us to get through; then she turned back to me with her finger to her lips and motioned me inside.

". . . No, no, I'm up here in the New York office. Yeah, that's right, Leland Consulting. We're doing some comp and benefits reengineering for Corporate. Ha ha, it sure is about time! And line managers like you are a priority. Yeah, tax impact's the thing, what it's all about, right? Hey, you know, I think I may be looking at an old org chart here. Hexter is still the CTO in your division, right? Okay, who're his direct reports now?" The young man had his chair positioned to lounge, feet up on the desk. He wore a headset leaving his hands free to work the keyboard of the laptop that rested on his stomach. "Uh-huh. *Uh-huh.*" He signaled Sheilah a vigorous thumbs-up. "Ah, so you have a new boss too. And how long's she been with the bank? Ah, from Citibank, no? Oh, Wells Fargo, my mistake. She is? No, no, no, don't worry about that—confidentiality's not my middle name it's my *first* name. Hey, this is way useful here, many thanks . . ."

He kept on in that vein for another ten minutes or so, lifting bits of information like a skilled pickpocket. He was maybe thirty with the pale face and classic features of a Greek statue in a face a bit too butter-cheeked to suit them, and a head that was shaved totally bald. His eyebrows, dark brown and bushy, also looked as though they belonged elsewhere, on a cowboy maybe. He wore a black tee shirt and above its collar a Ping-Pong ball of an Adam's apple bobbed up and down his long neck as he talked.

On the phone he'd sounded slightly southern fried but no way cornball. Warm and casual, confident in a way that inspired confidence in return: you'd tell this voice whatever it asked you, of course you would—and it knew how to frame its questions so as not to raise hackles or flags. He had a gift for the grift, this boy. It was a talent I was overprimed to recognize.

"Curtain call," Sheilah said with a big smile. He rose and took a bow. Once he was standing, I saw that he was shorter than I'd expected. The slightly bowed legs in black jeans had a working cowboy look that seemed a match for the bushy eyebrows. "Meet Grace Leslie, our new scheduler, your new neighbor."

"Hello," he said neutrally. "Welcome," he added because he had good manners. As far as I could tell from the two words, the southern accent had vanished.

"Thanks. I hope I won't be too much of an intrusion on you," I said.

"I'm sure it'll be fine." His face and tone let me know the opposite was true. Just what he needed: a stranger camped outside his door while he worked his magic—I couldn't blame him.

"Hey, I have to run," Sheilah said. "I've got this meeting in ten minutes and I need to prep. Those folders on the desk are for you to look over,

Grace—give you some background on the current searches and the candidates. See you at twelve-fifteen at Cynthia's desk, okay? Any questions before that give her a shout, extension three-four-five. After work, I'll show you how I want your on-line files organized. Meantime, get acquainted with the computer. Craig, have you got a few minutes to show her how to get on-line? I would myself but I've got a meeting." His "yes" was anticipated—not waited for, and not actually voiced.

Once she'd gone, I noticed him looking at me speculatively, his eyes as bright and opaque as green olives. Sheilah had made a point of saying that only she and Cynthia knew my real name, but that didn't mean that this man who played the computer like a Steinway had not seen McCail's photo and story on the Internet "Yes?" I asked, "do you have a few minutes for me?" *Oh yeah, he'd seen it.*

"Sure, just after this call I've got to make. Sorry for staring. You reminded me of . . . something." *And you remind me of something too.* As though he'd seen my thoughts flash across my forehead, he smiled and said, "Surprises come in thirty-one flavors."

I forced a smile back and went to sit at my new desk. Craig Tarbell closed his door. Once it had clicked shut, and I was alone, the memory that had followed me into Sheilah's office this morning sat beside me.

A party, big and noisy, maybe two hundred people gathered to celebrate Sheilah's great new space on Madison Avenue. After four years in business with her income ratcheting up at a steep angle, she'd taken the plunge and moved from a couple of rooms in a group office suite to this smart spread of pale leather, grained wood, granite, steel and large pieces of abstract art.

I stood beside Sheilah in the small kitchen while she finished giving the caterer chapter and verse on how to properly arrange hors d'oeuvres on a platter and the bartender hell for running out of Perrier. She turned to me and grinned. "Offices for a grown-up, right?"

"A pretty militant grown-up. Ever considered changing the company name to Attila the Headhunter?"

"I don't think that's funny, Grace," said Mrs. C-D, who was swanning around the place like the Queen Mum.

In an exchanged glance Sheilah and I recapped years of shared history and exploded into hilarious laughter, hers a soprano trill, mine an overture for the bassoon.

As I was wiping the tears from my cheeks, a man came jogging into the room, an extraordinary man: he seemed to reflect light, give off his own rays. His hair was blond, almost platinum, long enough to flop a bit as he ran. His eyes were the faceted pale gray you see in very old, expensive crystal chandeliers. They caught the light in a startling way, an effect heightened by lashes that were dark, thick and perfectly straight. His brows, dark too, and a rather strict mouth gave him a gravity that suggested a saint in a medieval painting.

His compact body moved with the assurance of a home-run hitter rounding third base. I seemed to be the home plate he was headed for. He did not say a word before he took my hand, the one that wasn't holding a drink, drew it to his lips and tongued it right at the sweet spot for an astounding ten seconds. That would have likely earned any other stranger a swift kick in the balls. Deserved. But I did not kick the man, nor did I pull away my hand.

"I've always intended to marry a laughing Valkyrie," he said.

"Do a little more of that and I'd say you've got a good shot." The sexual buzz I was enjoying was strong enough that I heard its rush in my ears and felt my knees go spongy. I had not felt this level of amperage since my seventeenth summer—since Michael Pyatt.

"This maniac is Paul Boudreau," Sheilah said. "I told you about him the other day, he's my new money manager—on his way to making me rich enough to afford all this. *And* I hear he writes poetry: the Renaissance man. Paul, I want you to meet my best friend, Grace Leshansky." She held her arm in front of his face. "Ring; bracelet: GraceL, both of them. Ever see better design?"

He didn't answer her question or give any sign he'd heard her. "I wasn't kidding," he said, studying my face as though he were taking a course in it. The couple of inches I had on him required a slight tilting back of his head.

"Well, maybe I'm not kidding either." It slid off my tongue like a perfect fried egg off a flat skillet. It was nothing I would ever say, not in flirting, not in any circumstance. Marriage was not what I had in mind for myself. I was about to turn thirty, making what seemed to me unbelievable money for doing what I would be doing for no money—enough to have just bought a West Village duplex loft with room enough for George and me to be together and separate. I was enjoying the hell out of the downtown social scene, complete with men for all occasions—straight, gay and undecided. In short, my life was straight up. Still, it seemed to me I was not kidding.

Craig sauntered out of his office. "All yours. So the Internet's new to you?" he asked innocently but with a twinkle.

"Okay," I said, sure now that I'd been right. "I know that you know— and now *you* know that I know that you know." I put my hands out palms up. "So, the photo's not my best angle."

He grinned like a boy. I had caught him a tad off guard—well, maybe I had. "I thought it was *very* Susan Hayward," he said. "Now I know you were probably trying for Bette." He shook his head. "But Susie's who you got."

"Not Marie Windsor?" The name of George's favorite B-movie bad girl sprang unexpectedly to my lips and made me smile. Craig was no sun god, just an almost handsome guy with a profitable talent for manipulation, but I'd better keep some distance. There's not much similarity between a black cat and a panther either, unless a certain curl of lip or flash of predatory eye sets off a shock of recognition in a sensitized observer.

He pulled an extra chair over to my desk. "I'll be your cyberspace coach . . ."

Craig was a good teacher. Then again, the rudiments of e-mail were not hard to pick up. Carpenter-Donlan had its own e-mail entity, so my address was simply, gleslie@carpenterdonlan.com. "And if I want to open another account, a private one?"

"Do it on AOL, Earthlink, whatever. I'd probably say AOL for you, at least to start. You'll find it easy; it's the provider most people use—other than techies. We can punch it up now if you want. You'll register, give them a credit card number, pick a screen name and—"

I cut in fast. "It's okay. I'll work it out later." I wouldn't have a credit card until after I'd sorted my banking out with Sheilah at lunchtime—and I didn't want an audience while I picked out a screen name George might recognize as authentically me—if he was alive and had a computer and wasn't too scared to risk searching. "Sheilah says you do amazing things with this magic box. How . . . how might an amateur go about finding someone? I mean, I've been away seven years and there are people I might want to—"

"I get it. There are a number of ways." He proceeded to show me a few: ICQ; sites like Classmates; search engines. As he did a few quick demonstrations I saw how skilled he was. "There are also on-line phone directories, if you happen to have a notion of current name and locale," he said. "That's an easy way to go, and it's surprising how often it works. Doping out the e-mail handles people hide behind can get to be like cracking a safe—you know, listening for the little clicks."

"I'm not terribly good at little clicks," I said, suddenly uncomfortable with the closeness of someone whose profession was psyching people out. "Well, look, I've taken up more than a few minutes of your time—and besides I haven't even cracked this pile of folders, so thanks and . . ."

He gave a little comic bow. "Glad to be of service, ma'am," and off he went back to being the wizard of whatever Oz he was running at the moment.

Before I opened the first folder, I let myself wonder for a second what I *would* call myself on AOL. Gracie something. But there'd likely be a few other Gracies.

CHAPTER TEN

Three and a half weeks went by pretty easily, except for my visits to the parole office–weekly reminders that I was on a leash that could be jerked, and my nose rubbed in any mess I made. Gabriel McCail's recounting of "six-foot Grace reaching for this reporter as he snapped her picture" had triggered a starchy warning from my PO to keep my hands at my sides in such situations: "In your pockets, if you have to." I'd said "Yes." Yes was most of what I said to Patty Ann. It seemed the best way to go.

Otherwise, the McCail story had not been much of a hassle in the end. It was gone from the Internet before the day was out and appeared in a single edition of the *Post* on an inside page. Fact was that the current life of an ex-jewelry designer who more than seven years ago had shot her husband in a domestic dispute was hardly compelling, even to Web chat junkies or readers of the *Post* or the supermarket tabloids, who had plenty of tastier stuff to snack on.

Gabriel McCail did not appear again.

As Sheilah had promised, there was plenty of work for me at Carpenter-Donlan, and I was good at it. As I clicked "Send" or negotiated with Platinum Travel which flight plans would work best, I was often conscious of feeling pleased to have my days filled with a set of challenges that were immediate, limited and absorbing—absorbing enough to keep my mind quiet and pointed straight ahead most of the time. Meetings got scheduled and rescheduled. Sometimes candidates or secretaries got short or sharp or bitchy with me. I did not get short or sharp or bitchy back: I had been in training for this job for seven years.

I'd spent hours using the search engines and techniques Craig had shown me for finding people on the Internet. I'd looked under Burns (many, but not so many Georges); I'd looked under Lester (lots of those, a few Georges); I'd even tried Leshansky (none). The AOL screen name I'd chosen was gracieido. No one but George would spark to it; if he were looking for a Gracie, he'd recognize that one as uniquely me. I opened my account the minute I had a Visa card. That had been more than two weeks ago. I'd sent out a bland "I'm here and I do. Please write" to all the George Burnses and a couple of Jlesters, even to a single JuniusL (his father's name had been Junius, after all. I'd thought, just maybe . . .) The yield had been several courtesy "You've got the wrong guy" messages and a lot of spam— nothing else. I continued to check a few times a day, even though I'd tried disciplining myself down to one.

Speaking of discipline, a funny thing happened on the way to the gym. I looked in the window, saw all those people pumping all those machines and I couldn't bring myself to open the door. They looked so locked in there. Instead, I bought some good running shoes, a sweat suit and a pair of twenty-pound weights. I'd get my endorphin fix inside my own walls or out in the open air.

The Sunday of my first free week, I ran/jogged/walked all the way downtown on the west side and stopped for a long time up on that platform near Stuyvesant High School overlooking the scooped, walled void where the World Trade Center had stood. Firemen, cops and haul-away trucks were long gone, no filthy air, no smell. My mind's eye filled them in—filled in the exploding buildings, the flying specks of people. If life had gone a different way I'd have been at my studio on Broome Street that morning, four blocks away from Tower One. If . . . I headed back uptown with no detour to the studio or to the loft on Hudson, where life had gone the way it had—by my hand.

During these weeks, time ran like a stream that had cut itself a shallow bed to flow in, a safe course that might stay intact until the next storm blew it to hell. I took long reacquainting walks around the city, seldom going inside even a museum. To wander outdoors looking at this shop window, that building façade, those people, with the freedom of a bee in a field of flowers was all I craved at the moment. I went to a couple of movies, shows—once the ballet. Except for a few dinners with Sheilah, who had been out of town a lot, I'd kept my own company.

Halloween night, I had moseyed down to the Village to watch the annual gay parade, a treat of lights, camera, action and defiant joy I'd always loved. This time I deliberately stopped first on Hudson Street, in front of the loft building where I'd lived—where *we'd* lived. Maybe I intended to try and strip the place of the mythic power it exerted in my mind by looking it in the face. The mellow old brick and plaster façade was calm, impeccable; it had not imploded. I gazed up at the fifth floor as long as I could stand to. No tears; I guessed they really were gone. I made a quick left turn, hurried down to Christopher Street and joined the manic crowd, weaving my way in and out of groups of exuberant strangers.

Just as I'd found myself a good vantage point, a brief gap between floats framed a familiar face: a snapshot glimpse of Craig's bald-headed profile. He was standing diagonally across Christopher from me, one arm around the leather-jacketed shoulder of someone whose face was turned the other way, pointing at a particularly outrageous float about half a block away. For a moment I wanted to wave, call out, make contact—be there with a friend, I suppose—but the moment passed. The next morning at the office I didn't mention having seen him.

Craig and I had managed with each other in a kind of delicate balance.

From time to time he made sure I remembered that another human being crowding his space was not his heart's desire—a roll of eye at the blizzard of paper on my desk or the slam of office door if my phone dealings were loud enough to annoy him that day. At other times the technique he used so well on the phone would beam itself at me—a thumbs-up on an over-heard fragment of my candidate handling, a random smart comment, an offbeat joke he somehow knew would tickle me.

He had the skewer tongue and nicely depraved sense of humor some gay men have, and the give and take with him brought back my best times—times immersed in art and fashion, when work was more fun than fun. On the other hand, the repertoire of accents and personas that served Craig so well in his work, the shifting moods, the targeted charm, contin-ued to ring too many alarm bells. We had not exchanged a serious personal word. That was the way to keep it, I knew—and yet I kept feeling we might.

Now, at six-thirty on a Monday evening, I sat at what had come to feel like my desk e-mailing meeting schedules to GreenTree Bank candidates as though I had been doing it all my life. I heard a key turn in the lock and looked up to see Craig, who'd been gone most of the afternoon. "Hey," I said, "what're you doing back so—" Just then a new e-mail flashed onto my screen: a candidate needing to cancel with Sheilah, who was on the road expecting to have dinner with him tomorrow. "God *damn* it!"

"Yeah, I'll second that," he said sourly.

His office door shut—not with a bang this time—and I focused on try-ing to resurrect Sheilah's dinner date, and when that didn't work, putting together alternative travel possibilities that wouldn't leave her twiddling her thumbs in San Francisco unless she felt like it.

"Could you come in here, Grace?" He stood in the doorway like a Boy Scout at attention and spoke in the no-accent accent—Midwestern?—that seemed to be authentically his.

"Give me a minute. I just want to finish a sentence and send."

"You've taken to all this like a duck to Grand Marnier," he said. "I sup-pose I shouldn't be surprised."

"Just don't strike a match close by." I was not entirely joking. The "all this" could go up in flames any minute of any day; there were so many possible ways to torch it.

A few minutes later I walked into his office to find him sitting behind his desk, apparently doing nothing but waiting for me. "At your service," I said, sitting myself in the leather chair facing him. He looked at me and nodded. "Well, *what?*" It came out sounding like an impatient mother whose kid won't say what's gone wrong in school when something clearly has.

His face was flushed around the edges, like a kid's with a fever. "Look," he said, "I know you didn't raise your hand, but I'm going to call on you anyway because I'm a drowning guy and you look to me like a life preserver."

"Life preserver? *That's* how I look to you? You've got a good sick sense of humor, Craig, and I like that in a man, but even so you'd have to see that I am treading water as fast as I can here. A sparrow sitting on my shoulder would pull me under. Why me?" It was the question I'd never asked Paul. "We hardly know each other, Craig. You have friends. I've seen them in and out of here."

"Sure, plenty of friends. I'm so good at friends that I'm locked in. Know what I mean?"

"No, I don't."

"I've done such a Goddamned brilliant job of packaging and selling myself like a brand that help, help, I'm a prisoner in a Coke can—no, wrong image, not a Coke can, a robot: I'm a prisoner inside a highly evolved robot. Just press the right buttons and he'll be whatever you want. But it's *me* who's trapped in there. I can't get out!"

"And are you packaging and selling yourself to me now as this . . . prisoner?" I asked this curdling inside because I understood what he was saying better than I'd have liked to. "One prisoner to another, is that it?" I wanted to get up and leave—go for a run, run home. I wanted the safe, easy pleasure of being alone.

"Nah, it's not about that at all. It's about . . . Grace, I've watched you and I'm a pretty good watcher. No, I take that back, I'm a *great* watcher. You're like a dowsing rod for truth, I can tell that about you."

"Oh right," I said, thinking again of all the truth that had been posted like a billboard two inches from my nose, and gone ignored.

"Well maybe this just has to do with your sense of *me*. I can tell that you *know* me—and you don't buy me. You don't buy my act—acts. Not one of them, you don't." He made his points as persuasively as any of his cast of phone characters: the consultant, the book researcher, the conference planner, the think tank guru. The urgency was ramped up by his eyes, which seemed all the greener as they willed me to see through him. Was he leveling? Paul wouldn't have been. With Paul this would just be another layer, the layer that seemed so solid you thought it *had* to be bedrock.

I needed badly to lighten this up. "You are a drama queen, Craig Tarbell, you know that?" And he laughed like no laugh I'd heard out of him before: a loud, wild trill that included snorts like reverse sneezes. "Okay, nobody would dream up a giggle like that," I said, "so let's call that spontaneous and say there is hope for you. Look, why do you want so much for me to buy or not buy your acts? What the hell do you care what I think?"

He scrubbed at his laugh tears with his fists and then shook his head. "Ah, I don't know. Maybe I'm just a fag in search of the right hag."

"And you figured me for a hag in waiting?" Until then, I had been sitting stiffly in the chair, completely still, as though keeping my body behind some imaginary line where Craig and whatever he was selling, could not touch me. Now I leaned forward, my forearms resting on the desk. "Or is it that since you know I was married to a con man and blew him away, you're hoping if I get to know you better I'll do the same for you?"

"Maybe," he said blank of expression. And then, "No. What I hope is that you'll help me open up my works and see what I want to do about what I find in there."

"Kaleidoscope," I said almost to myself.

"What?"

"Nothing. I want to make something clear. Whatever I feel . . . think about you has nothing to do with any moral judgment about your work. Hey, companies don't own their employees; I think headhunting's a legitimate business and that you're a great performer who deserves to make whatever you make and probably more. What you're spotting in my reactions has to do . . . not with you. I. Don't. Know. You," I added one word at a time, giving street directions to someone who didn't understand the language.

"Now that's not true," he said flatly—correctly. "Even that first day you looked at me like I was someone you recognized." Again I wanted out of there, but stayed in the chair and heard my stomach rumble in a complaint that felt more angry than hungry.

"What's your problem, Craig? Tired of getting it up every day for the performance? And then keeping it going till it gets to be sleep time, if you *can* sleep. Or is it the other way around? Is it all so easy it's stopped being any fun?"

"All of those things, of course," he said, the color gone from his voice, which, like Paul's, could strum the rainbow like a harp. "There's another thing here. I've met someone, hardly know him, just a few weeks and he's not even my usual type but . . . it's almost like if I talk about him it'll dissolve, what I think I'm feeling. It's been a while for me since I've felt anything without artificial flavor or other additives. Grace, I want to be real for him, even if he can't tell the difference—*especially* if he can't tell the difference. But *I* have to be able to tell the difference, and that's getting harder."

"Did it occur to you that what you might need is a good vacation or a few shrink sessions?" It was a straight question, but not a serious one—not in the sense that I'd have believed a yes answer.

"No, I'm beyond sending myself into the shop for a quick fix. Think I haven't tried all that? I have. Okay listen: I'm from Salt Lake City, haven't been back there in fifteen years. I've got a mother, a father, two brothers and three sisters. There. I never tell that to anyone."

I thought of Paul's confidences—revealed, he'd claimed each time, only to me:

"I was three credits away from my doctorate in philosophy at the Sorbonne—I'd even done most of my dis, 'Machiavelli vs. Sartre in Time of War'—and I quit."

"But why?"

"Bored, I suppose. I'd done all the thinking I wanted to do about it. Fini."

Three months later: "It wasn't true about the Sorbonne. My only formal graduate work was at Wharton—MBA. What is true is that I didn't finish. I do get
bored."

I shrugged. "And maybe it's true or maybe it's a con within a con
within a con. I don't give a damn if you come from Utah or Mars but believing isn't something I do easily these days, Craig. Also, I have no magic
for you."

He popped out of his seat with the spring of a jack in the box. "Good.
I've got more magic than I can deal with already. I need what people like
you call integrity. I need a conscience. I need . . . dinner's what I need.
Would you have it with me?"

CHAPTER ELEVEN

My cell phone rang from inside the bag at my feet just as I was sampling the scotch a waiter had placed in front of me. Other than the bit of champagne on the Cinderella evening at the Met, this was the first alcohol to pass my lips since the night before I shot Paul—a night every part of my body remembers as well as the day that followed. It had been scotch I'd drunk that night. The taste intensified the illusion that Paul sat at this table now with Craig and me. And in a way, of course he did.

The phone in my bag rang a second or maybe a third time and I reached down for it.

"Grace." Sheilah. I knew it would be Sheilah—and yet every time I picked up a phone there was a sharp particle, like a grain of grit in my gears, that half-expected George's voice. "I got him!" she said, her triumph pealing into my ear.

"Great. How?" She was telling me she'd nailed the canceling candidate, glued the broken dinner meeting back together.

"I hunted him down like a *dog*, that's how." I found my face stretching into a wide smile as I listened, almost as proud of her as she was of herself. She went on with a play-by-play as vivid as live commentary on a close Wimbledon final. "The secretary kept blocking me, see: he was in wall-to-wall meetings off-site, unreachable except by voice mail on his cell, which of course he didn't answer. So I phoned around, found out where the meetings were and when they were likely to break. Then I left him another voice mail telling him I was right there at the conference, in the lobby. I guilted him about how I'd come three thousand miles to meet him, to have this dinner. This time he called me back, a little sharp, a little annoyed. So I made nice, then I carrot and sticked him: tempted him with more options, bigger sign-on bonus. Bottom line: I'm meeting him at seven. Heh heh."

"You're amazing, Champ." I took another sip of scotch, privately toasting her.

"I should only be so persuasive in my private life. Hey, what's that background noise, sounds like music?"

"Restaurant. A group just started to play."

"What restaurant?" Craig raised his eyebrows at me across the table. "Sheilah," I mouthed. He nodded and then shook his head no.

"Don't know the name," I said. "It's in Chelsea, way west."

"You alone?"

"No." I waited a beat longer than I would have liked before saying, "With Craig," knowing she wouldn't be pleased to hear it. "We were working late. Talk to you when you get back tomorrow. Good luck with your dinner."

"You too," she said, painting a lot of nuance into two short words.

"You shouldn't have told her," Craig said after I'd put the phone away.

"Why not?"

"You're going to make me spell it out? Okay. She doesn't want us to have a relationship that she's not part of. She's proprietary about you and she thinks I'm weird—which I am, but she thinks it for the wrong reasons. I've kept double arms distance because that's my best shot at making this very lucrative job last. Otherwise, she moves in and breathes your air. So to Sheilah I'm a statue on a pedestal with a chain around it and a little sign that says, 'Do not touch.' "

Every word he said hit its mark but I wasn't going to trash Sheilah with him. "I'm not looking for intrigue, Craig. I'm very picky about which lies I tell these days." I drank a little more scotch.

We'd walked the few miles south and west from the office to get here. Craig liked to walk as much as I did—or said that he did, despite the fact that his legs, being short, had to speed up while mine had to slow down if we were going to keep pace. By the time we arrived I knew his favorite bad movie *(Valley of the Dolls),* good one *(Raging Bull);* music (anything that doesn't use a synthesizer); country (Italy); foods (rare hamburger and pistachio ice cream). I knew that he lived in a loft on Nineteenth Street a few blocks away from where we were now sitting and that he came to this place often enough that the hostess and waiter greeted him by name. He learned similar data about me: we saw eye to eye on *Raging Bull* (I kind of preferred *Mildred Pierce* to *Valley*) and on Italy, which might have won my heart over France for its sheer spontaneity, even apart from the fact that for me France and Paul would remain too tangled for comfort. We had not, by mutual agreement, talked about much else yet.

"How do you like this place?" he asked.

"A lot so far," I said. It was pleasantly dark and big enough to accommodate live music. The lighting was orangey like firelight. "The music's nice, that bluesy wahwah sound. You've heard this band before, right? I saw the guy wave to you."

"Yes. I play a little myself. Sometimes. So, what're you in the mood to eat?" He seemed withdrawn suddenly, awkward like someone on a blind date looking for conversation. I ordered a Cobb salad and he a cheeseburger. I stayed with my scotch and he had another beer. "I'm not from Salt Lake," he said suddenly with a slight drawl. "I'm from Atlanta. My mother teaches chemistry at Georgia Tech and my father's a doctor—was; he died two years ago. I have a sister in Dallas and I talk to my mother and sister every week." And then he laughed.

"I don't give a rat's ass where you're from. What are you trying to do here?"

The laugh died. "I don't know. I honestly don't. This afternoon I went out for a walk—just a little break—and I found myself over by the Plaza not able to breathe right. I mean it was a perfectly nice October day and I couldn't take a real breath. I stood there propped up against the side of the hotel looking like a drunk and afraid I was going to fall down. It passed but this isn't the first time it's happened."

"Been to a doctor?"

"Oh yeah. Anxiety. After all the tests that's what he said. Probably he's right." He took a serious bite out of the cheeseburger and chewed it waiting for me to say something.

He had not come right out and asked about Paul, not ever, but his desire to know crackled in the air. And for the first time I seemed to want to tell someone—no, not *someone:* Craig. It wasn't because I trusted him. God, no! It was because he'd understand.

"Paul used to cry sometimes—I mean really cry. He'd go to bed, pull the covers up under his nose and cry and stop and cry and stop. It could last hours or a day. It didn't happen often, only three, four, five times in the two years, but it was alarming, like this remarkable creature, so strong, so surefooted, was being massacred from inside. I almost expected that the tears would turn red like blood."

"And it came at you from nowhere, just when things were at their best?"

"Yes. Yes, usually that's exactly the way it was. Is that . . . has that happened to you?" My heart quickened with eagerness to hear his answer.

"Sort of. Of course I'm no magnificent creature."

"Tell me about the 'when things were at their best' part."

"Well . . ." He picked up the hamburger, ready for another chomp.

"Put that thing down, okay? Talk first, then you can eat every last bit of it."

"Sorry." He put it down and glanced at it longingly. For someone who had attached to me like a limpet in his need he was having trouble taking a next step. "When I've pulled off something really cool—you know, some construct that opens the tap all the way, so I get every damned piece of information I'm looking for from one single source instead of six—sometimes, just sometimes, after the firecrackers stop popping I find I don't want to see or talk to anyone, including myself. Even a movie doesn't help; even sex; even playing piano. In fact, that makes me feel worse. So I just curl up in bed and jerk off for a while. And then I do start to cry." He had said these things to the hamburger. Now he looked up and across at me as though waiting for a specialist to announce the diagnosis.

"I don't have any answers, Craig. Sorry. I have a question though. What if you changed jobs? What if you did something completely else all day—something that didn't use that part of you?"

He laughed, not the manic giggle, a sad chuckle. "So I wouldn't be conning twenty-four seven? Let me tell you something. My first job out of college was selling stocks. I was great, so great I almost got myself arrested. What I do now gives the same buzz, pays damn well and is a lot safer—though one company, which shall be nameless, tracked me and showed up at my then office with the FBI threatening some misrepresentation or suspected industrial espionage charge. Anyway, I had to sign a paper about keeping off their turf, and you know what? I fall asleep at night figuring bulletproof strategies to worm my way back in there. What I'm saying is different church, same pew—I always find that pew."

"With people too? Lovers? Friends?"

"I've already told you the answer to that," he said. "But there's this certain new lover I mentioned, and," his hand half reached out to me, "a certain new friend . . ." He shook his head slowly; his eyes looked moist. He picked up what was left of his burger. "Eat your salad, it's getting cold or warm."

"No, not yet. I want you to hear this. Paul and I first met at a party in Sheilah's office. It was the most spontaneous, amazing thing for the two of us, or so I thought. Within a week I went off to France with him to meet his grandmother who lived in Brittany. We got married pretty soon after that. On our first anniversary he took me back to France, the south this time." As I started to tell him, I grew barely aware of talking. I felt as though we were there, Paul and I, in an Avignon café, sipping *citron pressé* under the shade of a square umbrella on a very hot afternoon.

"Ever think about fate?" Paul asked me.

"Sure," I said lightly. Everything about this day had been light—light as a pale yellow balloon floating on warm blue air. "I kiss the ground daily that you happened to be at Sheilah's party and that I happened to laugh loud enough for you to hear."

It was true—mostly true. Life with Paul was exhilarating: his sudden notions of where we must go, what we must eat, which new move we must try in bed; of which book, music, painting I needed to experience right now; of why *this* theory was utterly wrong, while *that* one was irrefutably right—all of it shone so bright that the rest of the world, the Paul-deprived part, seemed only half-lit in comparison.

There was another aspect, one more seductive than I admitted: the experience of being looked after—cooked for and cosseted; finances managed by an expert with my interests front and center; my father enfolded and enjoyed, concern for him shared for the first time.

I had a partner. So if we hit a bump here and there—the flash of my temper, his occasional murky mood or abrupt silence—those were quickly passed over, mere reminders of how good we had it most of the time. Even the more puzzling aspects, such as the changing scenarios of his past, shifts in time and place that didn't jibe, I put it down to a kind of poetic license, a need for drama to match his broad imagination. After all, who was I—I who had no history at all—to deny him the pleasure of playing with Boudreaus and LaClades as though they were toy soldiers to group and regroup as the spirit moved him?

"But do you *believe* in fate?" he asked.

"If you're my fate," I said, "I'm glad to believe in fate. If we just happened randomly, I'm glad to believe in chance."

He traced his forefinger around the outlines of my mouth, something he liked to do. "What if I told you that it didn't just happen?" It was his storyteller voice, inviting the listener to settle in for the good stuff.

"Meaning?" I felt the tingle of something part excitement, part dread.

"Meaning that fate plays out far better when it's shaped by a good hand for a good reason."

A kind of chill quivered under my skin, despite the heat of the summer sun. "And that hand would be yours?" I asked.

Then he told me the story, presenting it like a beautifully wrapped gift revealed in stages, one layer of tissue removed at a time. What had seemed so crazily romantic, so much of the moment, had been planned, every move scripted like a movie, down to where you could see the camera angles catching certain highlights. Paul had known exactly who I was, had checked me out in the flesh at a gallery opening months earlier and given himself a short, comprehensive course: everything from the company I'd started and how it was doing, to my taste for John Garfield movies, Italian opera and Hunan pork, to the reprobate of a father who lived with me and how close we were.

By the time I first laid eyes on him he had already chosen me to be his mate and gone about designing a first encounter that would be . . . everything it in fact had been.

As he detailed his Grace research—the people he'd talked to, what information he'd looked for and where he'd found it—there was no mistaking his self-pride. And once all the wrappings were gone, I saw the gift for what it was: a chance to examine the works inside the kaleidoscope, to see just how the bits of colored glass and shards of mirror were put together to craft the illusion. What cracked my heart was not so much the learning how I'd been fooled but having to look at the magic deconstructed piece by piece when all I wanted was for it to last.

"Why?" It was less a question than a kind of half-numbed reflex of sound making.

"Why?" he echoed. His crystal eyes scanned my face and perhaps found what they were looking for, I couldn't tell. His hand had covered mine sometime while he was talking. I jerked my hand free and the sudden motion seemed to reconnect some loosened wire inside me.

"Yes, why? *Why?* Why all that lying, fiddling, manipulating? Stalking— you were *stalking* me! Goddamned *hello* would have done it. I'd have been your *femme* in three seconds if you'd just been . . . you knew that, right? You must have. Right? *Right?*"

"Right," he agreed, maybe because until he did I might just keep hollering the stupid word. He didn't reach for my hand again, made no obvious move toward me, yet it seemed to me he was nearer than he had been a moment ago. "I made something unique happen for us." I could feel the warmth of his skin but that was crazy, he wasn't close enough; it was just his smell of pine and ginger in the warm air. "I loved every second of it," he said slowly, no trace of a smile playing on his lips, "and so did you, Grace. Didn't you? Be honest."

"I am *always* fucking honest." We locked eyes, squaring off. After long thick seconds I admitted the obvious, "Yes, I loved every second, but that's not—"

"No buts. It was what it was. I *gave* that to the two of us and I continue to love every second of the memory."

"It's like that Erasmus thing you gave me to read, isn't it?"

"*In Praise of Folly?*" A teacher encouraging a student who'd done the homework.

"Yes. Where everything makes marvelous sense, only then you see that it's Folly talking, so the whole thing is a cheat."

"No, no. See, the irony is that it *is* sense, no matter who speaks it, or how many twists it takes. What's true is that I love you—every flesh and blood millimeter of your body, every cell in your brain and instinct in your soul. We are perfect together, you and I."

My gut lurched, flailed like a caught fish, desperately but briefly. The pleasures and comforts and excitements Paul brought were a hook deep in my innards. I felt the pain of it now, but had no will to fight free. So somehow I quieted down and tried to find a place to fit this gift he'd given, a way to accept what Folly described as love.

I made myself touch his hand, which almost immediately felt familiar to my fingers again: my husband's hand. "Why did you tell me?"

"To bring us closer. I feel very close to you right now. And that's not Folly speaking." He leaned over and kissed my neck lightly, just in the spot where certain nerves come together.

I saw that Craig's eyes were fixed on me, narrowed in concentration or pain. "Jesus," he said, "it hurts."

"Oh yeah," I murmured. "It does. Did then, does now."

"What a selfish prick I am, I wasn't even feeling it for you—only for me. Listening to that story was like hearing my fortune told, having my palm read, and finding out that the future is as bleak as I thought. I'll be thirty day after Christmas."

"Paul was thirty-two when he . . ." One sleepless night in my cell, I'd vowed never to let myself off the hook by referring to Paul as simply having died. ". . . when I killed him." I looked into my glass, thought about denying myself another sip and then took one anyway. "So you've got a little time to straighten out, Tarbell—if you can."

"He did it all the time, the bait and switch?"

"Do you?"

He nodded. "I have. Want to hear?"

"No."

"You said he cried after he'd pulled off a coup. Did he that time?"

"If he cried, I didn't see. But I managed to get away from him for some long, solitary walks around Avignon. I said I was searching for design themes for new pieces. It turned out to be true—I did find some. No, the first time I saw Paul cry was a month or so later. We were back home sitting in the kitchen having some coffee and I asked whether he'd heard from his *grandmère*. She'd write him letters fairly often, always sent me her love. He put down his mug and gave me the kind of smile a chess player might give just before saying, 'checkmate.' Or maybe I just imagine it that way now. Remember, by then I knew a side of him I wished I didn't.

"He said, 'Grace, she died.' I looked back at him. Telling it now, I almost wonder if I suspected what was coming. But no, I don't think I did or the shock would have been muted, at least a little. 'And she wasn't my grandmother. She was a friend, an actress—a very good one. I wanted—'

"I pitched the mug with all I had. It grazed the side of his head before it hit the fridge and broke on the tile floor. He ran down the hall toward our bedroom. I sat still for a long time. See, I was deciding that no matter what, I needed to get out of the marriage. I would give up what I had to give up. I had managed without foot massages and gourmet dinners on the stove for thirty-one years. I had handled my own money, if not brilliantly, at least well enough to have some. I had looked after my father. And I had had sex, maybe not quite as bravura but . . .

"As I got close to the bedroom to tell him he had to pack up and go, I heard the sobs. They were deep and gulping, like . . . like a child down a well with no hope of escape. I went inside. I did hesitate at the door for a while but I went inside and I held him. I didn't tell him to leave. You know, back at the office, I asked you why you chose me and you said I looked to you like a life preserver. Ironic, no? I never asked Paul why *he* chose me. Maybe I knew."

"Maybe you did," Craig said seriously. "I'm sorry."

"For what?"

"For you. Right this second, it's you I'm caring about." There across the table he seemed like someone I'd known a long time.

"Hey, Tarbell!" The voice came from the small bandstand. "You ready for your dessert?" The speaker was a big-bellied guitarist with lots of facial hair, and clearly the leader of the group. Craig put his hands out and wiggled the long, slender fingers that seemed, as so much of his body did, to belong to another person altogether. Then he got up and walked slowly to the front of the room where the pianist clapped him on the back, made an it's-all-yours gesture at the instrument and walked away toward the bar.

For the next say forty-five minutes they played, Craig fitting in with the others as though he did this every night. Maybe he did. He worked intricate harmonies around bass and guitar solos and then they turned the tables and supported him while he played Gershwin and New Orleans blues and some modern jazz new to me. The set finished with a trumpet and piano duet: a pared down yet utterly nongimmicked version of the Pachelbel *Canon*. It was thrilling; the applause said that everyone in the room, waiters included, agreed.

"So that's the other side of it for you, huh? Sheilah told me going in that you play the computer like a Steinway. You play a Steinway the way a

Steinway wants to be played." We were on the street in front of the place now. Its name I saw was Mac's. "Do you crash and weep after you pull off a performance like tonight's?"

"No. Strange maybe, but I don't." He yawned so wide his jaws might come unhinged. "Playing piano is a different kind of good feeling for me."

"I know what you mean," I said quietly. Oh, didn't I just! For the first time in quite a while a memory filled my senses: the joy of working a piece of metal into a shape I'd imagined—the instruments steady in my hand, the silver growing warm . . .

We walked quietly together. A lot had been said. Too much? "Cab for you?" he asked. "I'm just around the corner here."

"Nah. I'll walk to Eighth and catch the bus."

"See you tomorrow then," he said and quickly leaned over, neck stretched up, to brush a kiss on my cheek. I did not flinch; neither did I make a move to kiss him back. But I didn't mind the kiss.

CHAPTER TWELVE

The phone was ringing as I turned the key in the lock. I got it one ring before the machine would have. "Gabriel McCail, Grace." I'd known he would turn up again, I just hadn't known when. In fact, I'd been surprised he'd stayed away from me this long.

"A little late, isn't it, Gabriel?" I glanced at my watch: quarter to one.

"I called earlier tonight, couple of times. You weren't home, so I figured I wouldn't be waking you." How he happened to have my unlisted number was too boring and pointless a question to bother with. If he right now mentioned the half-moon birthmark on my left buttock that wouldn't surprise me either.

"You didn't wake me. What do you want?"

"How about thank you for a start?"

"You're welcome."

"I meant *you* thanking *me*. I did you more than one favor in that story."

"Thank you." This need McCail had for a round of applause should have been obnoxious but somehow it was faintly endearing. I asked the perfunctory question: "Is there something else?"

"I'm writing my book, Grace, with your help or without it. I'd rather it was with."

"Oh, I'm sure you'd rather. But what's in it for me? I'm asking you seriously. I'd almost be tempted for money—enough money." I'm not sure why I said this. I am sure it wasn't true.

"Bull*shit*. Money wouldn't do it. That's not your button."

"Okay, I don't want to. Even you can understand that."

"I understand. My job is to make you want to." Otherwise known as twisting my arm. I wondered how hard he'd twist, what holds he'd try to use. The undertone in his boyish voice said he had some moves in mind. I realized the arm wrestle had begun. I tried to think of a way to make him be the one to cry uncle, and couldn't.

"You covered the case, you've done your digging into Paul's past. Marina Beck can bend your ear for hours on his genius and trash me in pretty colorful language—she's probably already your new best friend. But if you think there's any way I'm going to whisper intimate revelations into your ear, you're dreaming. It'll never happen."

"Never say never." This time I didn't respond to the bait. I wanted to hang up but I lingered the way I had when he ambushed me in the street, held by what he might say next.

He said, "Michael's a resident at Columbia Presbyterian Hospital." I pictured his Cupid mouth close enough to the receiver to kiss it. "Pediatrics. Up there in Washington Heights, you know the neighborhood." He paused; I waited. "All that old circumstantial evidence, all that buzz, all that zilch about him killing your father: you're old friends. Why don't you just plain ask him?"

"And why don't you just plain go straight to hell?"

Now I did hang up. My heart bounced around as though it had suddenly shrunk too small for the accustomed snug fit. Hard to tell with someone like McCail what was bluff and tap dancing; what was substance. Clearly he knew things, but *which* things? Did he know whether George was alive? He'd thrown in that Michael and I were old friends. I needed no reminder of that as my mind flashed back more than a decade.

It was 1991. Since Paul and I had been married a mere month at the time I was still blessedly oblivious of his sleights of hand. I had not yet seen the man who lied and cried and lied some more. No, that October I was a ripe melon, fat and juicy and sweet, basking in sunlight.

I can see Paul and me on a certain Saturday afternoon marveling at the Matisse cutouts on exhibit at the Modern, holding hands as we moved from one to the next, the exuberance of the art a match for the mood of the moment.

"Oh, to have a talent like that!" I said.

"Simple and perfect," Paul agreed.

I threw both arms around Paul's neck and said into his ear, "I could fuck your brains out right here."

He dipped and, hand quicker than eye, slipped his finger under my long skirt and inside my underpants to touch the magic button. I shivered head to toe. "Hail to the homecoming queen," he whispered back and made me come again. That we were on a secret island unnoticed by the sea of people around us turned up the volume of each thrilling second.

I wasn't aware that Paul's attention had shifted until I heard him say, "No one is such a liar as the indignant man."

I turned my head and saw he was saying this to a tall man about twenty feet away. Almost fifteen years, but my brain took him in with no search time, as though he'd been there behind my eyes unseen, yet somehow tracked year by year. Despite the addition of a trimmed beard capping his chin like protective cotton wool and a few added pounds—very few—on his shoulders and chest, the boy who had been my first tutorial in love and loss seemed not all that changed.

Michael Pyatt, grown older but not grown up. He moved closer to us. I saw his jaw muscles tighten. He seemed ready to speak, then didn't.

"My phone number's changed," I said, "I guess you had a hard time finding it when you got around to trying." I said this with a nasty smile on my face, and felt almost cheated to find the long aged pain inside me as inert as dried gravy at the bottom of an unwashed pot—there, but no juice in it to stir up.

"No excuse," Michael said quietly, "no good one," and shifted his eyes to Paul. "Maybe you picked the right quote to throw at me, asshole," he said, "but if you think I'm gonna stay and play Nietzsche cards with you, forget it. I am out of here. It's been nine years, Paul. Let's make it another nine. Shit like this reminds me loud and clear why we're not friends any more." He turned away and stood, head forward, ready to move but not moving; his thin frame in that posture might have been a model for Giacometti's walking man.

The quake had been so sudden and severe that it took this long for its impact to register: by some freak coincidence Paul and Michael were friends—old friends, ex-friends. In the second rumble, I realized that this meeting was *not* a coincidence.

"I guess the joke's on me," I said, "a pretty grim one. Am I the only one who sees it that way?"

"Hardly," Paul said. "Just look at Michael's face."

"I can't see it, I can only see his back. He's leaving in case you hadn't noticed. But I see *your* face, Paul. So it's your private joke, is that it?"

"Not a joke, nothing like a joke. This is serious—a strategy."

"Well, I don't know what's in your head and maybe I don't want to know. You call it serious, I say sadistic. I could just *kill* you right now, I really could." An expression: only an expression that time. It launched me into a volley of how-could-yous and why-would-yous, which sputtered out fast into wordless outrage that had nowhere it could or really wanted to go.

"It was not sadism, I promise you that," Paul said to me with a quiet urgency, soul mate to soul mate—and then, to Michael, who had turned toward us and retraced a few steps, "I wanted my best friend back and, given the circumstances, I couldn't see how to make that happen except by surprise. I was scared about how you'd react, both of you—or rather I *knew* the reaction I'd get: a pair of No's. Grace, I should have told you the first time you mentioned the name Josh Pyatt to me that I'd known the man for years—that Michael and I went to college together. And I think I would've said it, except then you mentioned Michael, what happened between you two . . . you can see the spot I was in."

I lost custody of my eyes. They darted to Michael's face, which was tight, skinned back in rage. I remembered him looking just that way when he'd wanted to hit his father for making a lewd joke about me not fitting into his mother's bathing suit. I felt my own face go hot.

"The last thing I wanted to do was cause you pain. *Je t'aime plus que tout.*" Paul whispered the endearment to my eyes the way he often did, in the middle of a thought. "But once I'd let that moment go by, Grace, there was no right time to tell you the truth." His hands went out, palms up, asking what else could he have done in the circumstances but contrive this abominable scene.

"You wouldn't know truth if it bit your balls off," Michael said flatly. "You are a fucking liar."

"That oversimplification is a lie in itself. What I am is a creative worshipper of truth. Lots of things are *true,* but some truths are staggeringly important and others are insignificant. You've been jackassing all over the world for the last nine years, Michael. Have you found what you're after?" His cheeks were pink as a working athlete's on a hot day. "Didn't think so. I'm sorry, friend. That's the best I can say: I'm sorry."

"You ever thought about starting a puppet theater?" Michael snapped. "That creative enough for you?"

He had half a foot on Paul and slim as he was, he looked fit. I wondered what it was that stopped him decking Paul right there with Matisse looking down from the gallery walls. Or maybe that's just what I felt like doing. The stuff about manipulating unimportant truth in the interests of *über* truth smacked of the bits of Nietzsche he quoted from time to time.

"Step away, Paul," Michael said. "I mean take yourself a little walk. I want to have a couple of words with Grace. Alone."

Paul hesitated only seconds before nodding and moving to the other end of the gallery. Michael drew closer to me but not too close, about three feet away. "Are you good with this?" he asked.

"Dunno. I'm still reeling–kind of. But . . . it was a long time ago with us. We were kids. I can't summon up those feelings now, not the love not the hate not the . . . maybe it's because I'm so damned happy these days."

"True? Is that true? Are you happy with Paul?" He focused on my face analyzing it micron by micron.

"With Paul, with my work—the whole package. Yeah, I am happy. Very. Were you and Paul best friends?"

"Yes." He seemed ready to say more and didn't. I didn't ask for more. Whatever had split was almost a decade old.

"Seems a shame to hang onto an old grudge." He nodded as though something were paining his neck.

Paul returned, walking slowly. He said with a kind of shyness I'd never heard in his voice before, "I wanted to make it happen, *comprends?* I thought that here," he held a hand up pointing at a cutout in full leap, "with these leaps of faith all over the walls, and the three of us together . . . fresh start? I love you, both of you. We're going to be such good friends."

Paul had made his sale; he always did. We did become friends, such good friends. And friends can prove at least as treacherous as lovers— maybe more treacherous because the betrayal is unexpected. I mean lovers are steeped in sex where friends are steeped in trust.

———

That day had been awful at the time; the memory felt worse reconsidered in the light of all that had happened since. I stripped off my clothes and sank into my bed, suddenly and deeply exhausted—emotions played out. My mouth tasted of old pennies. Within moments I'd fallen asleep, but not before wondering whether I would actually go up to Washington Heights and confront Michael—to "just plain ask him," as McCail had coyly suggested, or to wring his Goddamned neck no matter what he had to say?

CHAPTER THIRTEEN

Tuesday, eight-thirty had emerged as the regular time for my weekly check-in at the parole office. Out of the last four visits, Patty Ann Carlson had been late for two. This morning was unprecedented: she was both at her desk and in a good mood. Little flush of color in the cheeks, lips turned up slightly at the corners, not smiling but inclined to smile—even the thin, blond hair had a bit of bounce. The hand bandage I'd seen at our first meeting was a couple of weeks gone now, the sprained finger, or whatever, healed. Today her previously unvarnished fingernails were freshly polished a shell pink.

I, on the other hand, had woken up this morning feeling like an under-cooked scrambled egg. In the hour it had taken to shower, dress and get here, nothing had improved. McCail's strategy was working on me, as he knew it would. Faked-out fox: maybe that's what I was in the end. But it wasn't the end, not fucking yet, it wasn't. I told myself that without much heart behind it.

"Good morning, Grace."

"Good morning."

"You can call me Patty Ann. I've had the feeling you're not sure what to call me."

I was reluctant to use the little girl name straight to her face, fearing maybe an inadvertent smirk on my own. "Patty Ann," I said carefully. "Thanks."

"How're things going for you?"

"Well. Very well." I stopped myself before asking the question in return, remembering the first time we met when I'd wished her good luck and she'd seemed to interpret it as snotty.

"Any problem on the job?"

"No, just the opposite."

"And what about your jewelry?"

I froze. More accurately, my blood went cold—that's how much I didn't want to talk about that. "Nothing about it," I said evenly.

"I used to see your pins and necklaces and things in the fashion magazines." She read *fashion* magazines? "We've met what, four times now?" *Five, if you include the first one.* "I haven't seen you wear any jewelry at all." Was this on purpose? Was she trying to stick it to me?

"I guess if I want to again I will."

The smile that had waited on her mouth since I'd arrived blossomed. It didn't look malicious. "Very good looking, what you design. Too much for my wallet to swing but very nice."

Go fuck yourself. It's not hard to turn into a paranoid bitch, or a skinless crybaby either. "Thank you," I said.

The session was over shortly after that, Patty Ann reminding me that she'd be making an office or home visit sometime soon. In my current frame of mind the mention was like a sharp flick on thin skin and made me speculate on her possible sadistic leanings.

When I was outside the parole office door I switched to the sneakers in my bag and headed east toward the office at a brisk walk. I was sorry the distance wasn't more than the scant mile it was. The wind against my face was cool but not strong. It felt soothing as after sunburn salve.

Once when I was maybe twelve or so, George gave up gambling, suddenly and for no specific reason I knew of. "That's *it,*" he'd said one night as he walked in the door of an apartment where we lived briefly over the mechanic's garage in Chicago. It was sometime after midnight. I was asleep on the couch. I opened an eye and grunted. Sure, I remember thinking sourly. *Right.* My silent doubts were countered with a strangely hearty, "No, no more. Chips cashed in."

Within a few days he was set with a nine to five at some bank, where he cashed in his personality along with the chips. He came home, spoke little; went out not at all. He stayed with it a couple of months. Maybe the period was briefer even than that and seemed longer because of its dryness. It was as though the unruly landscape of our lives, admittedly choked in some parts with weeds but nevertheless green and dotted here and there with flowers, had turned to sandy brown. Then one Saturday morning I awoke to a faint breeze directly under my nose: George, waving a pair of American Airlines tickets to New York. My father was back to normal, and selfishly, no matter what, I was glad to see him.

Curious that I'd retrieved this particular memory while walking from a parole office to a safely dull job that paid me a living wage. The subject, I realized, was desire: quickened blood, lift to the heart. George got it from gambling, figuring how to win. I had gotten that high from making a new piece of jewelry that pleased my eye and hand. If he really was still alive, did he gamble still? Did he get that kick, however briefly, from time to time? If so, maybe he was one up on his daughter.

"Late for you," Craig called out from behind his desk. "You okay?"

"Fine. Ten's as good a start to the day as nine, don't you think?" The walk had stretched longer than it needed to—I'd gone twelve or so blocks out of my way just to stay outside, moving. It had helped smooth me out. As I looked through the open door at Craig, I thought of friendship and betrayal—of Michael and of Paul. I put my brown-bagged tuna sandwich on the desk and kicked off my shoes. "Why don't I shut your door," I said, "and spare you the sound of me playing Ping-Pong with Platinum Travel." I did that, picked up mail, E and voice. I did my morning check on gracieido@aol and found the mailbox empty of anything but bargain airline offers. When I dove into the day's work the distraction it provided was as welcome as a pool on a hot day.

Quickly it got to be two forty-five. Craig's door opened. A crescent of winner's grin dominated his face. "Looks like you've had some good hours," I said.

"Depends on how you're looking. Got blown off by a couple of tough cases—wouldn't give me diddly squat." His laugh cackled: the tang of challenge had piqued his appetite. He would sharpen his claws and teeth finding a way in and would relish every second of it. "Want to come over to my place tonight?"

"I don't think so, Craig." His eyes went blank for a second and then refocused on me brightened, recharged for the task of changing my mind. "No," I said. "Don't do it; don't try to sell me." His responding smile was rueful and too appealing. "You know, Tarbell, you might just be a hopeless case."

He held up his hand, palm out. "Did I scare you last night? Say too much? Hear too much? Maybe it was just a crazy impulse, put it down to that."

"Don't you dare trivialize it," I said sharply, surprised that it really mattered to me. "Impulse maybe—and if that's true, be glad you're still susceptible to a flat-out impulse now and then. I don't regret telling you what I did last night. You understood about Paul in a way that not many people could. And I want to know that the things you said about yourself resembled pieces of Paul—just *pieces*. You're not his twin or his clone. For one thing, you're a way better musician than he was a writer. But here's the thing, I have more shit to deal with than you know about. You reached for the wrong life preserver."

"Then how about we just see if we can be friends? You already know the worst and you don't need to trust me for anything, so maybe we can kick back and make each other laugh—maybe only that for now. I like you."

I looked at the odd mismatch of features that was Craig and couldn't help but like him back. He was a liar like Paul was a liar, like George was a gambler—people whose life force lay in taking risky routes. Yet last night Craig had yearned to give up his game, to cleanse himself of it for his new love—*or said he did*. I held my hand out. "Friends for now," I said. We shook hands, formal as a pair of minor dignitaries who had just signed a deal.

"You sure you don't want to come over?" he asked. "Giant hero sandwiches from Manganaro's. My TV has a flat screen. Cigars? Cigarettes?" He gave his hips a little swivel, which produced the laugh he was looking for.

"How about the new boyfriend? He coming over for giant heroes?"

"Hope so." The olive eyes turned quickly serious. "I wouldn't mind you meeting him. He's . . . argh, I don't know what he is. Maybe that's part of his charm. Hard to pin him down."

"Not tonight, Craig, I'm feeling a little . . . I dunno. But I'll come another time. I'll meet him. Promise."

Hard to pin him down. I thought of Michael, remembered ringing the front doorbell at his apartment building a couple of days after George had disappeared and the rumors of Pyatt involvement were flying—remembered leaving there unanswered, as I'd hung up my phone unanswered by Michael or even by his message machine. And I knew I would not be able to resist trying to pin him down now.

After a moment Craig said, "Can't get him out of your head, huh?"

"Your boyfriend?" He'd startled me good and he knew it.

"Nooo, a different him." I stared at his now bland face, my heart full of something more and less than anger. "I could see someone was on your mind and took a shot it was a male. I make my living manipulating people into telling me things," he said dryly. "Sorry."

"Don't say you're sorry when you don't mean it. You are like a fucking performing seal. What are you looking for, a raw fish?"

"I *do* mean sorry. And you're right, it *is* like a trick—seal's trick, card trick. Slap my silly face next time. You've got full permission."

I turned away and picked up the phone. "Cynthia, I'm cutting out a little early. GreenTree interviews are set for the whole CFO slate for next week and Teresa's Chicago trip's scheduled Thursday, Friday. I'll copy you on the e-mails before I go. No, no, no, I'm fine, just a bad headache."

CHAPTER FOURTEEN

I rode Duke Ellington's A Train. I've always liked the elegance of that piece of music, which George used to render in his smoky George voice when we'd stand on the platform together waiting for the train to chug in. This was the train of my childhood, the train that connected Washington Heights to anywhere I wanted to go.

I could have cried—would've if I could've. As it was, my eyes were dry. Behind them, as the train made its uneven progress toward 168th Street, the stop for Columbia Presbyterian Medical Center, flashed views of Michael Pyatt—bright, translucent fragments grouping themselves into designs of a friendship that developed over almost two years: a friendship blown apart in a mess of truths and lies. The larger pattern I still did not comprehend, yet I knew there must be one.

After Paul's jury-rigged reunion amid the Matisse cutouts (a touch of irony, of cruelty, of poetry in his chosen setting? All of those probably) Michael, who lived and worked in the Village a ten-minute walk from the loft, hung out with us a lot. Sometimes it was just the three of us, sometimes—seldom—George would join us. Oh, and sometimes there'd be Michael's girl of the moment, an Yvette or an Astrid or a Mai . . . my memory's run out of their names. But mostly it was the three of us. Many glasses of wine, many more cups of coffee, much, much talk. Except about his father: talk of Josh was tacitly off limits, at least when I was present. Michael did see Josh, I kind of knew that—knew also, since he was always short of money, that he was not living off him. At the time it was all I wanted to know on that subject. At the time . . .

I saw Paul standing, spoon in hand, at the stove stirring something garlic fragrant in a big pot—a *paella* or a *zuppe de pesce*. He had the air of a ship's captain keeping his vessel on course just so. Michael and I sat side by side on tall chairs on the other side of the counter that separated the open kitchen from the loft's main living area.

We lounged with glasses of white wine, keeping the cook company. Michael wore, as he always did then, black jeans and a black turtleneck or tee shirt, which underscored his wiry thinness. The small beard was like part of the uniform: a black chin yarmulke. He worked a clerk's job at the Strand Book Store on Broadway and Twelfth Street—a thirty-year-old college graduate who'd wafted around Europe and Africa for nine years before returning to New York empty.

"Have to admit it, man," he said to Paul, "you weren't all wrong that day in the museum. I lit out but I never did find what I was looking for."

"Maybe you did find it," I said, "and didn't recognize it."

"Maybe." He nodded. "But isn't that worse? Hey, maybe I'm doomed to roam the earth in a permanent state of transition—making my way to some 'there' with no map."

"The Wandering Jew?" Paul asked with a knowing chuckle. "Transition's our home state, *mon cher*—you, me, her, we're all *en route* to destiny. 'Our destiny exercises its influence over us even when, as yet, we have not learned its nature.' Remember? But here's the difference between us, Michael: I've learned about my destiny and you haven't a clue about yours."

"You want to play Nietzsche? Here's one coming at *you*. 'Look into the abyss long enough and you become the abyss.' "

By then Paul had fed me bits of Nietzsche to read and I understood the quotes well enough, but the vocal subtext and the traded looks between them stamped the communication as coded and private. "Let's be practical here," I said, overcheerful in some effort to cut through my own unease, "just fasten onto something you might be good at and might like to do—and maybe that'll turn out to be your destiny."

———————

Another evening, months later.

"Hey, George."

"Hey, Michael," George mimicked straight-faced.

Michael had arrived at the loft just as George was about to leave, a poker game likely; though those were questions I still did not ask because the answers never told me anything. If George was surprised some months earlier by Michael's sudden, coincidental return to our scene he had given no indication of it. But then, George had a way of appearing unsurprised at anything—a bite-sized piece of personal pride, I'd always thought.

I had to admit to myself that George and Michael did not like each other, hadn't from first meeting. I knew part of the distaste had to do with mutual blame over treatment of me. But whether they realized it or not, there was more: though the bonds were quite different, each knew that the other was tethered to Josh, and the knowledge, rather than creating empathy, embarrassed them both. I always imagined that when, accidentally, their eyes did meet it was like looking into a mirror and seeing a face you wished weren't yours.

"Have a good time," George said, opening the door to leave. "Improve your minds." In an hour or so Michael and I would be going to hear Paul read some of his poems. Marina Beck, as usual, was sponsoring the event at the Soho Playhouse where a show she'd coproduced had opened and quickly closed.

"Guess I couldn't persuade you to come hear your son-in-law?" I asked—useless wallpaper question.

"Not if it was Edgar Allan Poe reading his stuff. Poetry ain't my line, unless it's Gilbert and Sullivan or Rodgers and Hart." He raised his hand high to signal good-bye and left.

Paul's poems, which had neither rhyme nor rhythm, were dark and as hopeless as a walk through quicksand. They were not my line either, though I'd been to four of these readings and never said so. And the Marina-led discussion of symbolism and language that would follow the reading—I cut the thought off cold. The fact that Marina, the patron and flame keeper, and Grace, the Philistine bride, did not cotton to each other was hardly surprising, but I did feel guilty for disliking the poetry that Paul considered his "real work."

I offered Michael a drink and we settled on a couch with a bottle of Beck's apiece. We'd spent little time alone together and both of us felt jumpy; it was there in the air. His face had a resolute set, which made me feel he was going to bring up something red-lined important that I did not want to hear.

He took a swig as though it were a drag on a joint, put the bottle down on the coffee table and said, "How much do you know about Paul?"

Shit. "Enough to know that I love being married to him." Michael didn't say anything, just waited. I felt the blood rush to my face. "I know his parents were killed in a motorcycle accident."

"No they weren't," he said quietly. "That's not how they died."

Don't you know I can't hear this? There are embellishments—okay, lies. Don't you know I know that? But once the spool begins to unwind . . . don't you know how much I can't bear to give up what I have now? "I don't need to know how they died," I said.

And finally, a bright spring Saturday afternoon, the sky a hard, baked pottery blue.

Michael and I strode down Mercer Street, side by side—big strides, keeping pace the way a pair of long-legged people can. I'd taken him down here to Soho to shop a great linen sale. The girlfriend of the moment had claimed at dinner the preceding night that his studio apartment was stocked with two hand towels and no pillowcases that didn't have holes in them.

"You're too short to be a basketball player," I said, "so that's out." It was a riff we did sometimes. Apropos of nothing, he'd point out how he'd never get a liquor license because his father was a crook, so forget opening a restaurant. I'd just nod, but on another day, equally out of context, might mention that law was out for the same reason, also because he didn't talk enough bullshit to be a lawyer.

"Something I want to tell you," he said now.

"Ground rules," I said quickly because he had a certain serious sound. He knew what I meant: nothing about Paul.

"Okay. Ground rules will be observed."

"So?"

"Day after you left Woodstock my mom showed up to drop off some books for me and my daddy started teasing her with how Michael had a big, beautiful white girlfriend. It was the way they had with each other. I told you my mother was white, but it wasn't so much race that divided the two of them as it was class and everything in that package: he was trash, a hunky crook with lots of money and she was a college girl with a sense of adventure—and no money after her parents cut her off for marrying him. In the beginning, when I was a little kid they had sex going for them. By the time they split all they had was . . . what you'd expect: bitterness, hate. When she found out that your father was a gambler and on the payroll, she went through the roof, insisted on taking me back to Boston with her right away. He didn't stop her—I'd've only been staying another week anyway.

"On the way back she let me have it. She was a good debater; she'd been a college activist, right out there about race and war and any other issue she got her mind around. Anyway, her winning line to me was that I'd be putting you and your father in danger if I didn't walk away. 'What if you and this girl go sour? What if she decides to break up with you, hurts your feelings? You know Josh Pyatt's temper, Michael, almost as well as I do.' She knew what buttons to push."

"Oh." I didn't know whether he heard me; it didn't matter.

"I could've called you. I could've written. I could've tried to explain. I knew how you'd feel and I didn't do jack shit for you, didn't—"

"Stop it. You don't have to do this. Really."

"I *do*. I—"

"You know, fifteen years ago I'd've given a kidney to know why you dropped me cold, just so I could find someplace to put the fact of that— someplace where it wouldn't stab my gut every time I moved." I kept walking, looking straight ahead. It was four, five steps before I realized he had stopped. I turned and went back to him. "It stopped hurting a long time ago. I was punishing you just now, turning the knife."

"I deserve it and more, but thanks for saying that anyway. My mom died of breast cancer that following summer. I wanted so much to see you, talk to you, but somehow I couldn't. Whether it was what she'd said in the car that day or just that by then I was too sad and embarrassed—I dunno, probably never will." The little chin yarmulke looked soft, vulnerable. I had the impulse to touch it but didn't.

"Oh, Michael . . . the way things turn out."

"Yeah." He smiled just a little. "You were my first girl."

"Well, you weren't my first boy—just my best. That counts."

"Counts for a lot." He put his arm around my shoulder and squeezed hard.

"I mean my best up until—"

"Just shut up, I know what you mean," he said, no anger in it. "How about we stop for a cup of coffee?"

We did. We settled into a tiny booth in a Bleecker Street coffee house, where we dipped chocolate-edged biscotti into espresso and talked about nothing special for an hour or so. At some point, for no reason I can remember, I felt a renewed urge to touch his soft, black beard. I gave in to it this time—reached across the table and cupped it in my palm for perhaps a moment longer than I'd intended. We left the espresso bar and went our separate ways.

That was eight years ago—only weeks before George disappeared, months before I killed Paul. Bizarre ways to mark a calendar.

The A Train kvetched its way into the 168th Street station. I felt an unsettling familiarity, as though I'd been here yesterday and every yesterday for years. The station was huge. The grim light bouncing off the areas that were white tiled gave the effect of a mammoth men's room; the rest was a gray cavern, the kind of station where footsteps behind you were good reason to get to the stairs and up them fast. I'd done that often enough in my years here that it had become just another fact of life: nothing to be alarmed about as long as you were alert to it—and brave.

The station was crowded now; it was almost five. I walked the stairs up to the street more slowly than my normal pace, realizing I was going toward this meeting out of the unaccustomed urgent need to know whatever was the truth—even to know that George was dead, after all, and the letters a trick—a final trick by Paul, or by someone else who knew somehow about our George-Gracie routines? But no one did, no one alive.

The back of my neck was damp with sweat and the hands I jammed into my pockets were unsteady. I felt anything but brave. What's more, I felt suddenly free of any need to *act* brave. It occurred to me that an admitted coward is sometimes more able than a hero to take risks just *because* the coward feels free to hide or scream or run like hell if things go bad. Was I learning late a lesson my father had not intended to teach?

I looked around at the unlovely neighborhood, a mere three blocks from my childhood home base, and breathed deeply its damp, faintly cinder-smelling air. The hospital center was enormous, its own city. It looked unchanged from the place where I'd gone as a child for this or that shot and to have an arm I'd broken at the skating rink set.

In the oddly direct way things sometimes happen, when the elevator door opened on the pediatric floor, the first thing I saw was the back of a tall, black man on his way down a hall. It was a broad back, heavy as an old tree trunk, straining the shoulders of his blue hospital coat, yet he moved with the bouncing lope of a lithe animal.

I stood for seconds watching him walk away before I started quickly after. "Michael?" I asked, not sure I'd said it loud enough.

He turned. From the front the difference eight years had made was even more marked. His chin was bare and square, no longer protected by the little beard of uncertainty. I studied the hard-planed face and tried to locate someone I remembered. Maybe in the mouth with its bisected lower lip? The shape was there but less vulnerably ripe. There was a new narrowness to the eyes, which made them look darker, opaque. He'd said once that he could look into the mirror and see his mother's face in his face. I wondered whether he still could.

While I had been studying him he had been studying me. My changes were as marked as his. "Grace," he said: an announcement of the inevitable. My arrival was a blow but it was no surprise.

The inside of my chest had begun to burn as though a thousand bees had gotten trapped there and were doing their best to break out. "You bastard." It came out quiet, muffled by pain.

He shut his eyes, as if he had the idea that when he opened them there was a chance I might be gone. When he did and I wasn't he said, "C'mon," and motioned me to follow him. We turned several corners and ended up inside a small linen storage room. He shut the door and leaned his body up against it to prevent anyone joining us. So, finally . . . Finally what?

His face was tense, lips tight, governed against saying more than he wanted to. "I didn't kill your father," he said, five flat words. "That's what you came to find out."

"You could have told me that years ago. How about when I tried to call you right after it happened? How about when I rang your apartment bell and rang it and rang it? You were gone. *Friend*. Not good enough now—not good enough to just say what you didn't do." It was hard to talk. Physically, it was hard.

"Jesus, of course it's not good enough. It's true enough but it can't be *good* enough: too much piled on top; too much rotting away underneath. Don't you see?"

That damned question was like a hosing of cold water, dousing out everything except the need to know. "Don't I *see*? No, I don't see."

"I didn't kill your father. I can't make you believe me but it's true."

"I've been told a lot of 'truth'—by you, by Paul, by George. But always pieces—a fractured truth, then another one. What I call those now are lies. No, *worse* because they're more subtle, more deceiving. So tell me, God-damn you, tell me about *Enforcer's Son Seen Near Leshansky Loft Night of Disappearance*. Tell me about *Michael Pyatt May Have Driven Kidnap Car*. And, oh yes, *Michael Pyatt FBI Material Witness?*"

"How about *Pyatt Arrested*—want to know about that part?" he asked bitterly. "What about *Pyatt Released?*"

Behind me was a stepstool for reaching the upper shelves. I sat myself on it because my legs didn't seem able to keep doing their job. "You either killed him or helped him get away, or you covered for someone who did one of those two things—because you weren't in those headlines for no reason; and you didn't go missing from my life for no reason. You say you didn't kill him—now, standing here in this linen closet, you say that. So tell me, which of the other three things happened?"

"I didn't kill him," he repeated giving me opaque eyes. "And my father didn't either. I can't swear to that, but I would stake my life on it."

"And why in hell should I believe you?" The question was more than justified, yet I did believe him—mostly because in my heart I believed George was alive.

"From your point of view, you've got no reason to trust me at all, about anything. But I just told you the truth. Not the whole truth, but the piece I told you is pure. And it'll have to do. It's all you're gonna get."

I rose from the ladder and moved closer to him, as though I could exert more pressure with less distance between us. About a foot away I stopped; it was as close as I trusted myself to get before I lashed out or crumbled. I locked eyes with him. "Tell me this then, is George alive?" I asked and swallowed hard. "At least you owe me that much."

He shook his head slowly as though it were very heavy. "Yes. Rather, I hope so but I don't know."

"What do you mean you don't know? You *do* know!"

"I don't. How old would he be now?"

"Seventy . . . five? Six?" How bizarre to not know your father's precise age. He'd once said a vague something that made me think he was over thirty-five when I was born.

"People can die around then, if their genes say so." The thought of George just dying had not occurred to me and was in its way as big a shock as the sight of the changed Michael. "I repeat, I don't know."

"Stop saying that. There's *a lot* you know, like *where is he?*"

"You're wrong. I don't know where he is." He took a long beat before he said, "How much do *you* know, or think you know? What did Paul say to you?"

"On which day?" The words even tasted bad.

"Go home. Get out of here." His voice was rough edged, harsh.

"Who're you talking to, a fucking dog?"

"Sorry. Look, nothing I can tell you will change a thing. Nothing."

"You brought up Paul. Did Paul know or was he just blowing Paul-type smoke at me? He said . . . so many different things, about George, about himself—about what might have happened, should have happened. He'd tell me George was dead, and better off that way. Then he'd tell me that George was alive . . . somewhere. He'd say you must have killed him for Josh's sake. And he'd say . . . he'd say Michael couldn't kill a bug."

His hands hung fisted at his sides: huge, brown knots, tensed to strike out. His eyes were moist now, tormented. "Grace, *listen* to me, you've got a life left. So do I. Neither of us has a shot unless we're rid of this."

"It's my father you're talking about, not an *it*—not a sack of garbage to be *rid* of."

He let out a long breath and unclenched his fists. "Sorry. But you need to consider this. Say your father's alive. If he wanted to find you he could. He doesn't." The statement needed no embellishment. "Let it be over, Grace," he said quietly. "It *wants* to be over. You're throwing yourself away coming here."

I'd already done that. I had thrown myself away years ago. The thought must have been obvious on my face. I knew by his that he'd read it. Suddenly the little room was very warm: I could smell the fresh hospital linen and Michael's face had broken into a sweat. "I treated you like shit as a lover and I treated you like shit as a friend. Do you expect better from me now?"

"No, but—"

"I am an asshole bastard who gave you a lot of grief and stood by while . . ." He reached for my arm and pulled me toward him. The grip of his hand even through my coat was some kind of shock. I didn't try to fight him off; maybe that was the reason. For a moment his face was close enough that I felt the warm breath on my cheek. I had the crazy idea he was going to kiss me. Then he swung open the door with his free hand and hustled us out into the corridor, where he turned me loose. "Go. Just . . . go!" Not until he'd turned the corner at something close to a run did I register that on those final words he'd begun to cry.

Unlike Paul, he did not want me around to see his tears.

CHAPTER FIFTEEN

I
t was rush hour on the subway going back downtown, the car filled with people trying not to bash against each other. For most of them, the ride was likely a twice a day habit. Habit . . .

Fear; desire; habit. Maybe habit is in the end the most powerful of the life forces: the easiest to acquire, hardest to give up. Or course habit is an alloy of the other two. Anyone who's worked metals knows an alloy is stronger than its individual components. The habit of a selective blind eye had been a necessary condition of being my father's daughter and my husband's wife. I'd thought I was watching out for George; I'd thought I saw Paul's need for drama, for stories. I'd thought that if I stayed vigilant we'd all be okay. It is hard to be vigilant with a blind eye.

It was sheer coincidence that I had come home from the studio early that particular day. Bad shrimps in a Chinese restaurant or twenty-four-hour flu, whichever it was had given me a marauding upset stomach. By two in the afternoon I'd completed my fourth dash in an hour from worktable to bathroom and been told firmly by my assistant to get the hell home—that toughing out the day (also habit) would be hard, at least as hard on my co-workers as on me. Coincidence: in fiction it's all-important, the magic moment, lucky or unlucky, that changes everything; in fact, except for being on the wrong plane or in the path of a stray bullet, a moment of coincidence changes nothing—it only seems to.

The loft's entrance was off at one end of the hall, the living area at the other. As soon as I'd opened the door I heard unfamiliar male voices. At first I didn't make out the words but something in the men's tones set off childhood alarm bells and made me slip off my shoes and move quietly to where I could watch and listen unnoticed.

George, Paul and three men I did not know were locked in tense conversation. George, looking like an old small boy, was seated dead center on the couch, flanked by Paul and one of the men. The other two sat on chairs drawn in close on the other side of the coffee table.

"He's not gonna answer that and you know it," the large, heavy-jowled man seated beside George said in a singsong voice, identifying himself to any six-year-old with access to a TV set as a defense lawyer.

"Oh, he'll answer," said one of the pair of dark-suited men in the chairs, his eyes fixed on George, not the lawyer, as he spoke. "One way or another he will," the other one added. Fancier looking than cops they were, with a more self-important sound to them: FBI was my guess; right, it turned out.

"What are you offering?" Paul asked, cold steel in his voice. "You're in a position to cause my father-in-law grief, nobody's disputing that. But he can cause *you* grief too, just by holding his teeth together. And you know I know what I'm talking about. So tell me, what are you going to do for him besides rev your engines and make noise?"

This was a Paul I had not met, and I'd met more than a few by then. The one sitting beside my terrified father, hand clamped on his forearm, was a war-toughened soldier in one army or another. *And you know I know what I'm talking about:* Crook? Cop? Spy? He could have been any of those, my husband of almost two years—any of them. Reality had me cornered, no way to rationalize, shrug off: I had *no idea* who he was.

"Couldn't've put it better myself," the lawyer said, plainly wishing he could but needing to mouth a line for the record anyway.

The older of the FBI agents ignored him and said to Paul, "As you say, you do know the turf, Paulie." He let out a dry cough of a chuckle. "You and that mother of yours—you're some pair." *So, no fatal motorcycle accident either.* Paul stayed silent. After a beat, the agent said, "Look, I'll give you and your father-in-law two concepts to mull over: federal prison and witness protection. Either-or, but he's better off in our hands, no matter what. You can fill in the blanks for him if you haven't already."

My gut lurched, threatening to give up anything left inside it. But there was nothing left to give. My hand at my mouth did not quite muffle the sound of a deep dry heave.

Everyone shut up and turned in my direction. I walked into the room as though negotiating a tightrope. I did not trust myself to speak without retching again. Paul stood up and George, whose arm he still held, stood up with him. As I stared at them, they both looked alien, their features disconnected from any form I recognized in the way a printed word you focus on too long becomes a meaningless grouping of letters.

Paul said, "Grace, I don't know what you heard but—"

George interrupted. "Gracie, I wanted to keep you out of . . ." It was the first sound out of him, the whine of a guilty child.

"Congratulations." The poisonous mix of bile and tears that filled me soaked the word in something like hate. "Looks like you succeeded."

"Ms. Leshansky," the younger of the agents said, his voice professionally gentle, "your dad's in big trouble here. You'd be doing him a service if you—"

"Stuff it, Kramer," Paul growled like an animal ready to bite. Then his face smoothed out, as though an invisible iron had been run across it. "We know your terms; we understand the offer," he said, the quiet businessman now, ending a meeting. "We'll get back to you. End of day tomorrow, you have my word. Our family needs some time alone."

I almost gagged again—maybe it was Paul giving his word, maybe the reference to our family. I swallowed hard instead. The agents exchanged quick glances, came to silent agreement and picked up their briefcases. The lawyer stayed where he was. "You go too, Jake," Paul said holding up his right hand as though to take an oath. "No deals without your input, promise. Call you after we've had some time with Grace."

They left quickly. I think I wanted to go to George, put my arms around him, shield him from the nightmare threats that were just beginning to take definable shape in my head, but I felt rooted to the spot where I stood. Maybe some part of me was scared that if I got within arm's reach I'd slap him instead.

"Ah, Gracie," he said, sounding more like himself now that it was just the three of us, "I knew from the beginning how this movie was gonna end—knew it like you know you'll die one day, but you ignore that fact because you don't know when. Seems like when has come around. I knew better than to go on the Pyatt payroll. I should've taken a beating here and there and just sucked it up, huh?"

What you should've done is stopped gambling. Wouldn't that have been simpler? It was a useless moment for a useless reflection. Also useless was painful hindsight: I would have *had* to know for years, if I'd let myself know it, where the path I had counted on to keep George safe must sooner or later lead. Josh Pyatt's career and income and reputation had grown steadily and predictably to the point where the Feds found him worth their bother: an important fish even in a good-sized pond. And where would that be likely to put Josh Pyatt's accountant?

Paul moved to give the embrace I seemed incapable of delivering. He wrapped George in both his arms for a long time. "Don't lose heart, George. We'll work this out. I swear we will."

"I am on the edge of throwing up as it is," I said, each word grating past the rock in my throat. "Hearing *you* swear anything, *Paulie,* just about pushes me over. I am pretty dumb, we can all agree on that, but I do get the fact George's signature is on lots of papers that lie and break laws, and the choice is either to rat out Josh Pyatt or get locked up. Am I missing anything here?"

George glanced over at Paul, as though asking permission to speak. Then he turned back to me and shook his head very slowly. "No, Gracie, you're not missing a thing." Had his neck shrunk? I could've put a finger between it and the shirt collar. He was so skinny. Could I have really not noticed that much lost weight? He had been quiet recently, come to think of it, unusually quiet. What fucking planet was I living on? How much else had I avoided seeing to protect my Paul habit, my little bubble of back-rubs and smart investments and literary tutoring and great meals and lays—and yes, less worry about George because I had such a capable, interested partner?

I walked over to George and put my hand on his cheek and let it stay there. After a moment, I turned to Paul and said, "You go somewhere, I don't care where. Whatever you tell those guys you are not part of 'our family'—and I need to spend some time with my father."

The pale, crystal eyes looked at me coldly the way they had at the FBI man who'd called him "Paulie"—but only for seconds. Then I saw the gaze, still fixed on me, soften. "I love you both. If you ever believed anything, believe that."

I remembered a hotel room in Normandy:

"I need you to know that I love you because it's true, and don't ever forget that."

"Are you going to give me reason to?"

"Maybe."

I was fresh out of belief. I said nothing, just waited for him to turn and go. I heard the front door close and actually went through the exercise of checking that he was in fact gone.

"Come on, let's sit," I said and George obediently settled on the couch, right in the middle, just where he'd been when the men were here. I started to go sit beside him and then changed my mind and sat across so I could see his full face better. "George, this is *Gracie* here. How—" I stopped myself asking, "How could you not have told me?" and changed the question. "How long has this been going on?"

"Week, week and a half, something like that."

"Well what happened exactly?" I was trying to stay calm, to filter panic or anything else that might spook him from my voice. "Did they just show up here? Telephone?"

"They contacted Paul."

"Paul. You mean *Paulie?* What in hell is all this? Is he FBI? Is he a mob guy? Is he—"

"No, no, no," he said fast. "No. Your husband had the bad luck to have a father not so different from yours. His dad was a low level . . . something, I'm not sure . . ." His eyes looked furtive but I didn't press him. "Anyway, he—the father, Donofrio was his name—became a government witness, went into witness protection. So-called."

"And?" But I already knew what was coming next.

"He's dead." George's face was blank. It reminded me of too many colors running together to make no color.

"I'll be right back. My stomach . . ." I bolted out of the chair and dashed for the nearest bathroom, which was behind the kitchen. "Don't move," I shouted as I ran.

"Don't worry," he shouted back.

My gut writhed for a while, insisting it still had something to rid itself of. It was wrong. All that was left was a hopeless terror, which doesn't exit through the upper or lower roadway. It just sits inside you, mangled and immobile like a wrecked car. I washed my face, rinsed my mouth and returned. He was still there. I went and sat beside him.

"What're you going to do?" I asked softly looking at my lap. My eyes studying him now would shame him.

He didn't answer right away. "I'm gonna take the fall and keep my mouth shut is what I'm gonna do."

"Prison. Is that what Paul told you to do?"

"Didn't need anyone to tell me, Gracie. I'm me; remember? It's all I *can* do. Rat out Josh Pyatt? I am too plain fucking scared."

"How long? How long could you get?" Was this real: George and me sitting together on the couch here speculating on how long he might spend in a federal prison? The rest of his life, or pretty damn close.

He put his hands on his thighs and rose the way he often did from a couch or deep chair, popping up like a small jack-in-the-box. "Look, we've got time to talk about all this. Days, weeks, we've got. Maybe it'll all look different in the morning."

"I don't see how." He reached for my hand. His was icy, the way it used to be when I was a kid and the luck was running bad and the man might come to the door. I stood up too.

"Tell you what," he said, and I was half still in the past, expecting him to tell me to pack up our stuff, just enough to tide us over in Miami for a while, "you've got a bad gut and my head's killing me. You go swig some Pepto-Bismol and I'll pop a couple of aspirin and I'll take you to the movies over on Nineteenth Street."

"Movies?" I echoed. "What's playing?"

"Who cares?"

We came home hours later after multiplex hopping to two of the twelve films on offer. I think one was a comedy. Small sips of Coke seemed to have quelled my stomach and George's headache was gone, or so he claimed. Paul was not at the loft.

"I know it's only ten," George said, "but I'm wrecked. Haven't had much sleep recently. I'm going to bed."

"Sure you won't sneak out?" I asked, trying a smile that must have looked as pathetic as it felt.

"What're you talking about?" he asked fast with an unfamiliar edge to his usual rasp.

"Joke, bad one. I meant to a poker game. Sorry."

He patted my arm. "We've had some fun, right? Plenty of shitsky, but a few good times."

He was preparing for what lay ahead: preparing us both. Instant tears flooded me and I struggled to keep them contained. "Lots. Not a few, *lots*. Listen, I have the father I want. We'll . . . think of something. We'll . . . you're right, let's get some sleep."

"You know, my father had those yellow eyes, just like yours," he said. I almost told him then that I knew he did. But if I did, I'd have had to tell him about my stalking of Dr. Junius Lester. He gave a smile that looked real, if wan, and said, "Sometimes it's the only way I know for sure we've got the same blood in us. You're a champ, kiddo, always have been." He shuffled his toes in a little soft shoe and began the Burns routine, "I love you, love you, love–" Then his voice cracked. "See you in the morning," he mumbled and started up the stairs to his room.

The morning came but I didn't see him. He was gone.

CHAPTER SIXTEEN

I touched the door of my apartment, unsteady fingers gratefully stroking its shiny red paint, applied by the dancer no doubt over the original dingy gray for upbeat effect. It didn't matter that the paint was beginning to peel in spots, or that the door was dented around the keyhole where a new lock had been sloppily installed and at the bottom where someone, sometime had kicked at it: touching this door was like knocking wood for luck right now.

I was out of breath, having run from the subway in wrong shoes for running, out of heart after seeing Michael and reliving the hours before George disappeared. I'd gone up to Washington Heights to get the definitive word on whether George was dead or alive. I'd left convinced that, barring a heart attack or some such, he was alive. Somewhere. I had also been forced to face the fact that he either did not dare, or did not want, to see me. The prison letters in my closet were his way of letting me know he was okay—and loved me, whatever that meant to him.

But I would have to let go now. It seemed unlikely that George was in any actual danger from an imprisoned Josh Pyatt, though I could hardly be sure of that. But there was Gabriel McCail, who had more than hinted at how ready and able he was to hunt down anyone intrinsic to his precious book.

So it was over. My father was not dead and gone, but alive and gone. I'd never known Michael the way I thought I had—two separate times: Michael the boy, Michael the young man. The almost stranger I'd seen today, I did not know at all. Yet I believed the partial truth he'd told—maybe because he hadn't passed it off as the whole truth. Maybe . . . I turned the key in the lock and opened the door to my apartment. My apartment.

As I walked inside, I had a try at accepting that the bond between George and me had never been what I'd supposed or he could not have simply left without telling me, no matter—and in the instant another piece of truth hit me with its sharp edge: George's fear trumped any other card he held. He would have done whatever he thought necessary to escape. So if he was not kidnapped that last night we spent together, then he knew he was leaving. Taking me to the movies one last time had been his way of saying good-bye.

A woman with long, white flowing hair parted straight down the center, iridescent peacock feathers sticking out at crazy angles all over her head. How do they stay in, I wonder. Are they glued in place? Drilled right through her skull? I am looking at her up close, face to face but she doesn't seem to see me. She is tall—my height—but her shoulders are broader, arms rippling with muscle. I make sounds—not words, but indefinable sounds—to try and get her attention. "Pocahontas," I say. "Pocahontas's mother." Finally she looks straight at me. "Who the hell are you?" she asks. We are almost nose-to-nose now and suddenly I'm numb with surprise. I say, "I'm you. Don't you see I'm you?" The words catch in my throat. As I realize I've been staring into a mirror. She shakes her head no, and turns away. And in that second, the mirror shatters as though someone has fired a bullet at it.

I awoke to find myself curled into something like fetal position, my behind hanging off the narrow black plastic couch, and sobbing so deeply that nothing in the world existed but me and pain. Finally I sat up, looked around through stinging slit eyes and waited for the hiccupping sobs to

slow. At first I looked for landmarks of our Washington Heights apartment, the opera posters: Albanese, Callas, Tucker—taped to gray white
walls. Gracie, I was Gracie.

I ached as though everything inside me had been rubbed raw. It took a
while for the dream to echo back. For seven years I had been that woman.
She wasn't much and nobody would want to be her, but at least she was
real. She'd done a crime and she was doing time: she was a prisoner. Who
the hell . . . *what* the hell was I now?

A flat blat of sound pierced through. It took a second, more insistent,
ring of the downstairs buzzer to get me off the couch and into the kitchen
where the intercom was. I heard Sheilah's voice. ". . . in a cab back from La-
Guardia, just an impulse," little heh heh heh of a "you know me" laugh. "I
thought in case you were home we could send out for food and catch up."

The world stopped its crazy spin. After the first stab of outrage at being
invaded, I felt glad she was here. It came through to me that her emphatic
smile would be the kind of tonic it had been when she'd appear at Bedford Hills. I pressed the enter button and headed for the bathroom, where
I doused my swollen face over and over in cool water and then drank
some out of cupped hands. I felt clearer in the head but looked like an Es-
kimo with a bad cold. The doorbell rang.

Sheilah had been on the road interviewing candidates since last
Wednesday. She'd flown home today via Chicago, catching back-to-back
meetings at O'Hare. Her face was clean of its usual perfect makeup and
her hair had grown a couple of weeks beyond its need for the master cut.
It had been a tough week for her.

I reached out arms open to hug with no flinch or hesitation. "You look
wiped," I said.

She hugged back hard, the way she did. "You too. Cynthia said you left
with a headache."

"Yeah, well . . ."

"You've been crying. Ah, Gracie . . ."

I wished she hadn't called me Gracie just then. It gave my heart a
twang that threatened to make more tears come. "I was bound to cry. I
just . . . hadn't gotten around to it till today."

She nodded. "It's good, a good thing to cry. Saved my bacon a thousand times, still does. You remember what a crier I was when we were kids. She'd say something to me about my crooked teeth or my freckles or whatever—Christ, could she pull my chain. I always wondered how come you *didn't* cry."

Because big, brave frauds can't risk tears, they might dissolve like an aspirin. "You latch onto some way of getting through and that's what you get used to doing, I guess."

"How's your headache?"

"Gone now. I'm fine. But you, I'm surprised you didn't just want to go home and crash."

"I suppose that would've been the smart thing but . . ." She grinned a good grin. "I met someone on the plane back."

"Tell, tell. Come on, give me your coat."

She handed it over. I hung it in the closet and while I was doing it I glanced down and saw the satchel where George's letters were. If I meant what I'd been telling myself in the hours since I left Michael, the thing would be to throw them away—let the past be over. I shut the closet door firmly. "Pull over the flamingo chair for yourself, it's way more comfortable. I'll take the couch—it's a bitch."

"Got a Coke? Not diet, I need the sugar as well as the caffeine. And I'm starved."

I made a face. "Not sushi, okay? I'm not in the mood for raw fish. How would you feel about pizza?" Before she had a chance to answer, I added, kind of ashamed of myself, "I don't have any Coke, diet or not, but I'll make you a pot of coffee and you put in all the sugar you want."

"Sure. Is there a great pizza place? Could we have sausages and peppers and . . ."

". . . and pepperoni and extra cheese." We saw eye to eye on embellished pizza and always had. There was a stack of take-out menus in the kitchen drawer; they appeared regularly under the door. I hadn't yet used one of them. "I don't know about great, but this says real coal oven so maybe it's good. Coffee'll be ready in a minute." I corkscrewed open a bottle of red wine, one of several liquor store items sitting on the counter, bought on impulse one day, not broached until now, poured myself a glass and noticed my hand was trembling.

"That's a lot of wine there," Sheilah said. Like most AA's she was unfazed by others drinking in her presence, unless she considered them drunks or at risk of becoming.

I gave her a look and kept my mouth shut. There was in fact a lot of wine in my glass. I sipped some off the top and went to the phone to order the pie.

"They say about half an hour for the pizza," I said and I drank some more wine.

Sheilah, who had fetched her coffee and was sipping it, made a mental check mark. "Got anything to munch on meantime? Crackers? Potato chips? Do you . . . you know, keep food in the house?"

"Do I keep food in the house? You sound like some sitcom mother visiting a daughter who's just left home." The truth was I kept only morning food—coffee, orange juice, English muffins and butter. This was a place I slept in and left from. "Want an English muffin?"

"No, I'll wait for the pizza." Good thing: I remembered belatedly throwing out an empty carton of them yesterday. "But that's what I'm meaning, Grace. You live here. Booze and coffee, not even a *cracker?*"

"Whatever lurid picture you have of it, I don't live on booze and coffee. I just haven't gotten around to— Look, stop this, would you? I'm dying to hear about *him*, the guy from the plane."

She leaned forward in her chair, girlfriend-style. "He was sitting next to me, we were in business class so it was only two across, with some space. We started to talk—well, I guess *I* started because he was really kind of attractive in a craggy, Lincoln-faced way and no wedding band and a good shirt, and a *great* briefcase."

"You were drawn to his briefcase?"

"Part of the package. After all, I am in the people assessing business, though you might not believe that when you look at some of the guys I . . . anyway, I'd finished those pretzels that they serve with the drinks and his were just sitting there, so I asked if he'd donate them to the fund for hungry women executives. He laughed and said it was his favorite cause. I tell you, Grace, we didn't stop talking the whole flight back—except he did doze off for an hour or so." She held up her index finger, "He's a lawyer," her middle finger, "He's divorced—twelve years, no kids—lives on Central Park South," ring finger, "not involved with anyone right now"—pinky, "*and* he likes Sondheim and Porter and Bobby Short." The hand made a fist and punched the air. "Yes!"

I seconded that with my own "Yes!" hoping Mr. Lincoln was as good as his briefcase.

The phone rang. "Hey." Craig, sounding a bit subdued.

"What's up?"

"Not me. My angel came over, but he stayed a hot fifteen minutes. No, scratch that, it was a *cool* fifteen minutes. His mind seemed to be somewhere else. I wonder if—"

"Look, I'm going to cut you off. Can we talk about this tomorrow? I've got company."

"Aha, sorry. Is it your 'him'?"

"No, and don't be nosy. I'm not one of your research projects, okay?"

Sheilah was gazing at me speculatively. "Research projects? Was that your pal Craig?"

"Yes," I said, the *s* hissing more than I'd meant. Sheilah hated to be excluded from anything. If two friends of hers were being mugged together, part of her would crave to be mugged too rather than be left out. My version: her version would speak to loyalty and rejection—many times it had. This issue went back to grade school with us. It stayed in its box most of the time.

"Sheilah, I have had to account for every move I've made in the last seven years, including trips to the bathroom. I love you but I won't have a hall monitor on my tail."

"I'm not intending to be a *hall monitor.* What am I supposed to think? Last night you're out clubbing. You leave the office early with a headache and now you're downing a tankard of wine."

"I left early," I said, stiff with anger at needing to say it, "lots of times I've stayed late."

"That's not what I—"

"Maybe not, but you felt you had the right to say it." And maybe she did. If I needed a reminder that our relationship was changed because of that, I had one.

"Forget I said it. I'm thrilled with the job you're doing at the office; this isn't about that and you know it. Remember when I got out of rehab? You picked me up from Four Winds and stayed with me that night."

"Yeah, I do."

"And my mother called just as we were walking in the door and you wouldn't let me talk to her?"

"You didn't want to talk to her."

"No, but I thought I had to, so I held out my hand for the phone."

"But you *didn't* have to, not right then."

"That's just what I mean. You knew that and I didn't. What I'm saying is that you don't always know what's in your interest when you're fragile."

"Fragile?" I hated the word applied to me. Our eyes met. I couldn't read her mind, but the disquieting thought in mine was that less than a year after she'd left rehab, she had moved her mother from Washington Heights to Murray Hill into an apartment a block away from her own.

"I was like an ice sculpture back then," she said, "*that* fragile. It felt like any strong emotion might be meltdown. The only place I felt safe was an AA meeting. I went to two a day for the first, oh, six months or so."

"You did good," I said and meant.

"Whether you admit it or not you're fragile now. What I'm trying to say is you've been through hell; don't you think I realize that? But you have to give it up. I see that look you get sometimes and I know you're missing George or . . . maybe thinking about Paul. You know, no matter how crafty and smart and charming, he was just *nuts*. That awful poetry! After I got to know him a little better I took my investment money and gave it to the stodgiest firm on Wall Street to manage."

"Very wise of you," I said tightly.

"Damn it, I'm *sorry*. I don't mean to make you feel worse. Oh, Gracie, just wear a great pin on your jacket. It'll be like reclaiming a piece of your-self. Yes?"

I managed "Yes." Even when I wanted to embrace her, I ended up wanting to push her away. She hadn't said one word off target but target shooting was badly timed tonight no matter how worthy the motive.

Before she could fire off another insight, the downstairs buzzer rang. The pizza had made it here early—and before we opened the box I would switch the conversation back to lawyer Lincoln with the good briefcase, or die trying.

"What's his name," I asked.

"Todd. Todd Berenstain."

CHAPTER SEVENTEEN

I slept fitfully, plagued by a weird dream that had to do with artificial legs. I was in a shoe store, but instead of trying on shoes like everyone else there, I was trying on one after another mismatched pair of shiny plastic limbs—some full-length, others knee down—strapping them on, trying my best to walk. None of them was a good fit and I stumbled, never reaching the little floor mirror down at the end of a long corridor. Now awake, I was almost embarrassed by the too obvious dream language. Christ, had I lost even my imagination?

Damaged I was: why fight a losing battle against what was true? I got out of bed and told myself to feel thankful I was not looking at the barred door to a cell, even a cell in an honor dorm; thankful that I had a decent job in a city I loved and the freedom to do what I wanted nights and weekends; thankful for Sheilah who cared about whether I lived or died. I found myself adding a little thanks for Craig Tarbell, despicable tendencies and all, because he was fun.

I laid out my mat in the corner of the bedroom I used as a gym substitute, and worked out for a sweaty half an hour with the ten-pound bells, including plenty of knee bends and sit-ups—to prove to myself I still could, I suppose. The twenty-pound weights sat in the corner seeming to dare me to take them on. I didn't. Other than running, I had exercised hardly at all these weeks and my legs felt it now. As I made myself do another thirty of everything, I pictured Michael the way he'd looked and sounded yesterday: a man intent on getting on with his life, pushing me to do the same— a push not all that different from Sheilah's in the same direction. By the time I'd done the morning's final sit-up and made my way into the shower, I was still telling myself how right they both were. Then, as I turned on the tap, I was blindsided by a memory: the night George left.

Paul had come home to find me on the couch, where, after George had gone upstairs to his room, I'd fallen into one of those states that feels like you're water skiing the surface of sleep. He woke me massaging my shoulder.

"Come to bed, darling, it's cold in here." He sounded so exactly like himself, so *normal,* that the previous seven or eight hours might have been no more than a toxic fantasy.

I sat upright fast; the only light in the room was coming in off Hudson Street. I had not been dreaming. "Don't touch me, okay? You are Paulie Donofrio, no person I know. What I *do* know is that you are up to your ears in this . . . this mousetrap they've set for George. For weeks— months?—you've sat with me, eaten with me, looked at me, fucked me and never, never said a word about it. So . . . I conclude you are a monster and I don't want to be anywhere with you, especially a bedroom."

Even in the dimness those pale gray eyes caught the light—they always did; whatever light there was went there and then beamed at whoever he fixed on. "Paulie Donofrio was a kid who learned about mousetraps very young," he said. "He watched a trap spring on someone close to him and there wasn't a damn thing he could do to stop it." He said this with a dry sadness in his voice that sounded beyond tears. "I haven't been Paulie Donofrio for a long time, Grace. If you believe nothing else you've ever heard or will hear from me, believe this: I love your father and I would die before I'd do him harm."

"I think the Believe Paul account is a long way into overdraw," I said. But it wasn't entirely true. Despite all the senseless lies he'd told me, despite what I'd seen and heard today, I did believe him here, in this moment. I believed he cared for my father.

He sensed that, of course. "I know you don't want to share a bed with me right now, so how's this? Go have a good long bath and then go catch some sleep in our bed. I'll sleep out here. We'll talk about all this in the morning."

"Isn't it morning now?"

Paul looked at his watch. "Technically. Two-twenty."

"Where have you been?"

"With Marina," he said. "I had dinner with her to go over her portfolio, remember? I told you in the morning before you left for work." *The morning? Told me? Yes, so he had.* "Evenings tend to go late with her and I didn't rush home; you didn't want me back here."

"No, I didn't." I stood and stretched my cramped arms. "I don't want 'our' bedroom. You take it, I'll get myself a blanket and stay here on the couch." Which I did and, surprisingly, fell into a deep, solid sleep.

———

What if I hadn't? I wondered now as the warm shower sluiced over me. What if I'd spent the next six hours sleepless like some normal, worry-sick daughter? What if I had sat there awake? What if I had gone up the curving staircase to the second level of the duplex and knocked on George's door—again like some normal, worry-sick daughter? Would I have heard him leave under his own steam? Would I have heard him being taken away?

"What if," used as a pair, should be deleted from my vocabulary. "What if" was a phrase pregnant with regret and hope and terror, and once it got its foot inside your door, it gave birth to all three. The way things had worked out, hope was the weak triplet, too puny to make it. I should get rid of the letters. I should call AOL and cancel the gracieido e-mail account.

I poured what was left of the coffee I'd made for Sheilah and stuck it into the microwave to heat. It would taste like tar, but coffee was one thing I didn't have to start from scratch this morning if I didn't feel like it—a small thing, but still . . . I took it into the bedroom and opened the drawer where my jewelry lay. I looked down at the selection of pins, bracelets, rings and neckpieces (no earrings: I'd never liked feeling them clipped tight on my lobes, nor the notion of having holes pierced through parts of me). It would be a good thing to do, I thought, to wear one of them today—let Sheilah know I'd heard her: let *myself* know.

The iron and gold pin, a square inside a square inside a square, an opal at its center: that would look great on the left shoulder of my gray jacket, not too high. I touched the pin, admired it as though the artist who'd made it were an old friend. But I could not make myself wear it. Not yet.

It was Friday morning. Two days had gone by smoothly, so smoothly since I'd seen Michael. During that interim, I had stocked the apartment with other than breakfast food in case someone wanted to eat there. That someone could very well be me—soon. And last night while I was watching the late news I went to the jewelry drawer and put on a gold and acrylic neck-piece, which rested against my breastbone with just enough heft to feel good. As I slumped in the flamingo chair the lamplight flash made the clear acrylic inset gleam like fire.

Just after nine, I paused in Sheilah's office doorway with some print-outs I'd brought her. She was on the phone but motioned me to come in. "I can come back later," I mouthed, but she shook her head and pointed to the leather chair opposite her desk. It's awkward to sit directly facing someone who's on the phone—you have to look up, down or sideways to avoid becoming a staring distraction, plus you become a captive audience to a performance that could have a long running time and a boring plot. Whoever it was on the other end had kicked off the conversation by annoying her, judging by the expressions marching across her face. I looked at the papers in my lap, pen poised to make notes on them.

"Yes, Stan, we do have to get this straight. But *don't* tell me I went behind your back. I did *not* go behind your back. I have my own relationship with Greg and it's a long and deep one on both sides. We talk all the time."

Stan was the head of Human Resources at GreenTree Bank and Greg was the bank's CEO and Sheilah's cornerstone client for a decade now.

"Yeah, I think I do know what your job description is. I wrote it, after all. Heh heh." But the heh heh was forced. She didn't like Stan Lockert. "Arrogant little prick," had been her assessment on a visiting day up in Bedford Hills when she was hot on his trail, recruiting him. I'd liked hearing about her business: she told the anecdotes well and with full passion—also, it had given us something to talk about besides me. "Why go after him then," I'd asked. "Why? Because he's the best and Greg needs the best."

She had been Greg Frost's right-hand headhunter, the one he had trusted to find an A-team to transform an almost defunct savings and loan that he'd picked up for small change into the twelfth biggest bank in the country, bucking hard to make the top ten. GreenTree had been the making of Sheilah's business. Not that the bank was her only client now, but the rosewood and steel desk she worked on, the glove leather chair she swiveled back and forth as she talked, this suite of offices had all been paid for with GreenTree fees.

But the money was in some sense secondary: Greg's "Go get 'em, Tiger"; the long one-on-one strategy sessions; the phone calls that studded her days and nights like stars; the live, vibrating connection was everything to Sheilah—more urgent, more satisfying than any boyfriend or crush she'd had, more important even than the cash to an ambitious girl who'd grown up poor.

"Look, Stan, you run GreenTree's HR. I report to you. That's worked fine, right?" Long pause. I heard her sigh heavily during his response, and so, likely, did he. "I just think that bringing in another search firm to do a search as crucial as Marketing EVP makes no sense." Beat. "No, no, no, I never complained that we were overloaded, I just said that I thought the marketing job could wait until we closed the finance search . . . yes, right. I *did* think it was something Greg should know about." The pause on her end was long enough to make me glance up. She was not giving him pointed sighs; she was very quiet. I saw that her face was stricken as an unexpectedly slapped child's and quickly returned my eyes to my lap. "I see," she said quietly. "If that's what he said then we will." Her voice was quavering just a little. "But not right now. I have a candidate waiting to see me and . . . okay, yes I'll e-mail you."

I didn't hear the click of the phone in its cradle. After a second or two I raised my eyes and saw that she had hung it up, but not in any angry burst. She was in tears. I went to her and put my arms around her. Her head burrowed against my stomach and beat like a heart there as she sobbed. "Oh, Sheilah, oh, honey, it'll be okay. That little bastard—"

"It's not him," she moaned, "it's Greg. Greg didn't even call me back, he called *Stan*—and he said, 'You people . . . you people need to stop squabbling.' Gracie, I was just part of *you people* to him." So Great God Greg had sold her out, left her to the mercy of an underling—an underling she had hired.

"I know," I said. And I did. Betrayal is betrayal is betrayal. It tastes like iron filings and it smells like shit.

The phone on the desk rang. "Pick it up, okay? Say I'll call back in a few."

It was Cynthia. "Hey, Grace, it's you I'm looking for. You've got . . . a visitor. A Ms. Carlson?"

Sheilah gave me an inquiring look. "My parole officer," I said. "This is what is called in the manual an Unscheduled Visit. She's allowed to make them at work or at home. Feel better. It really will be okay." I didn't quite know what I meant by that except in the general sense that most things become tolerable once you get used to them. The power of habit.

Patty Ann Carlson looked both younger and more vulnerable away from her grim cubicle. She stood in the reception area sizing up the smart, expensive surroundings a little like Alice saying to herself, "So this is Wonderland." If she'd lose the dowdy blue coat and tilt the beret at a good angle, I found myself thinking, she'd actually— Then she looked my way and I quit my fashion makeover fancies cold. There were two reasons: One, I saw that flicker of resentment in her eyes—if I had any idea I'd imagined her dislike, I knew now it was real; and two, I noticed a decided puffiness on her right cheekbone, noticed also a faint bluish tinge there that makeup base couldn't quite hide.

There was the splinted bandaged finger she'd had at our first meeting, now this. If the blow had landed an inch or so higher she'd have had a spectacular black eye. This time I had no doubt. *Why don't you just leave him?* The question had barely formed in my mind before I realized that it was about as useful as asking George why he didn't just stop gambling.

"Hello, Patty Ann," I said, "can I take your coat?"

"No, no thanks. I won't be staying long. How are things going, Grace?"

"Fine, just as fine as they were Tuesday." *Stop it. Do not be a smart ass.* I didn't recall that instruction in the manual but it should be there, just in case someone who has taken a life gets the notion that free on parole means free of annoyance. "I mean . . . fine," I said lamely.

"I know what you mean. Nice office. Lovely surroundings to spend your time in."

"My actual surroundings are a bit plainer. Come on, I'll show you." I took her through the connecting door into the Leland Consulting space and pointed out my desk. I was glad to see that Craig's door was shut. My phone rang. I bent over and picked it up. It was a techie candidate calling to give me two possible interview dates, each with a set of time restrictions that was likely to pose problems for Teresa Woo, whose trip I was scheduling. I told him I'd get back to him by the end of the day.

"I don't want to keep you from your work," Patty Ann said. "Would it be possible for me to have a quick word with your boss, Ms. Donlan?"

"I really don't know Sheilah's schedule. Cynthia Lafferty, the woman you met at the front desk could tell you."

"No, that's all right," she said, reaching into her bulging briefcase and coming up with a large plain brown envelope. "I'll leave this for her at the desk. She just needs to fill it out and get it back to me as soon as she— What are you *staring* at?"

At her bruised face, of course—like the idiot I was. "I wasn't aware I was staring," I mumbled quickly as I lowered my eyes, unsure exactly where to look. "Sorry. So, if that's it I'll see you out."

"I can see myself out," she said.

I gave her a few minutes to do that and then went back in myself to check on Sheilah. Her door was shut but I could hear through it that she was on the phone in animated recruiting-style conversation. Good for her.

As I turned to leave I almost collided with Teresa Woo the technology headhunter who was heading for Sheilah's office.

"She's on the phone," I said. "I have your Texas trip about set, except for two pesky guys."

"Yeah, well . . ." She gave an impatient glance to her watch and then to Sheilah's door. Teresa was on the road a great deal. Almost entirely our contact had been by phone and e-mail: if I'd seen her five times in the past weeks it was a lot. She was a young woman—maybe thirty—who presented sleek as an officer on the *Starship Enterprise*. The message was, "I'm smarter and cooler than you, and you'll be sorry if you don't listen to what I say." She gave the closed door one more glance and did a neat military about-face. "Thanks, Grace," she said over her shoulder, "I'll look for your e-mail."

Craig was not in his office but had left a note propped against my screen: "Brunch Sunday? Noon. My place. You, me, HIM. RSVP." At the bottom was his address and phone number. I had been supposed to meet HIM last night, but he had canceled at the last minute so Craig and I, just the two of us, had gone and had burgers at the place where he played piano. "This guy's real, right?" I'd asked Craig, half serious. "With your little quirks you might've invented him."

"Oh, he's real, all right, maybe too real," Craig had responded. "There's a downside to being in love. If he doesn't call I feel ready to hop on top of the piano, cross my legs and sing Helen Morgan torch songs."

I called the number and said to the machine, "I'll be there. Does HIM have a name?" Then I put in a solid two hours of work, had the good luck to click into place the last pieces of Teresa's trip and finish scheduling a day of interviews and testing for both GreenTree treasurer candidates who'd made the final cut.

I checked for gracieido e-mail and found nothing except the usual crap. One day I *would* cancel the account—maybe the same day I began to wear jewelry.

The connecting door opened and Sheilah's face appeared. It wore a smile only slightly wan. "I filled in that form your parole officer left and sent it off. Thanks, for . . . you know . . . earlier."

"You okay?" I asked.

"Pretty much." The smile broadened. "I'm running now. Todd called. I'm meeting him at the Carlyle for a drink. Then, who knows? Maybe his place?" She held up crossed fingers.

After the door had closed I stood up and stretched out the kinks. A run would feel good but a glass of red wine might feel better. I took myself home and poured one—not too generous—while I heated up a can of Progresso chicken soup out of my new larder. I had the feeling of holding myself in a delicate balance, keyword: moderation. I sat in the flamingo chair sipping and browsing through that morning's *Times*.

I'd turned the soup off and was down to a slick of red at the bottom of the glass when I reached the arts section. My eye was drawn to her name— a wondrous instrument, the eye: in a broadsheet gray with small type its radar zooms in on a combination of letters with personal meaning. A new play in verse about Lucrezia Borgia had opened downtown at the Cherry Lane. I can't say whether the critic liked it or not; I didn't read that part. What drew and held my eye was the producer's name: Marina Beck.

She'd been a bitter old woman the night we'd seen each other at Lincoln Center, but as I looked at her name now, I saw her the way she was when I'd first met her, lounging like a twenties vamp on a low French leather sofa in the library of her house. She'd say things like, "By the time I was fourteen I was the most accomplished whore in Wheeling, West Virginia. Light me a cig, Boudreau, would you?" Holding up the birdbath martini glass she carried with her to parties because she hated "dinky glasses," she'd say, "There are four ways to get real money: work, steal, inherit or marry. Of course if you marry, you have to pick smart and divorce smart." Colorful, the slick magazines called her. Well, she was that, I suppose.

When Paul and I met he told me he was between apartments, told me he'd sold his at a profit too good to resist and was staying at a friend's house while deciding what to buy. We'd returned from the Normandy trip full of marriage plans, including logistics of his move into the loft—wall of bookcases to be built here, another closet there, new bed? One early Sunday morning in the midst of such a discussion, he said, "You've met *Grandmère*. Now you need to meet Marina." A smile half mischievous, half guilty—a boy's smile: "The friend I've been staying with, I want you to meet her."

"Her?" I smiled back at him. Nothing to send up red flags, we were playing the Getting to Know You Game. After all, in real time we'd been together only a few weeks and had lots to learn about each other—rather I had lots to learn about Paul.

"Her," he said. "Her name's Marina Beck. You may have heard of her—or not."

It took a few seconds. "I think I've *met* her actually, small blonde with big checkbook? She put some cash in a show friends of mine did." He nodded, the smile still playing at the corners of his mouth, waiting for me to be surprised. I recalled an imperious, chin-forward bearing, something like Gloria Swanson in *Sunset Boulevard*, a slinky purple dress, a thin-lipped, berry red mouth opening and closing fishlike on the cigarette that moved in and out of it. Oh yes, surprised I was but no way jealous. "Paul Boudreau, you are a man of . . . should I say many parts?"

He applauded, a slow few claps. "And you are *une femme superbe*. Marina is important to me in ways upon ways upon ways, as I am to her. We are close. Not as close as she may think." He smiled at what was clearly a private joke.

"How does she like your suddenly up and marrying someone else?"

"Not much," he said, "but she's prepared to live with it."

Something in his voice or face caused the crackle of distant static in my head. "I'm not really good with ambiguity, Paul. I mean, tell me a thing—even a bad one—and I try to find a way to deal with it." That sounded so heavy. "Or don't tell me at all," I said with a grin, "and I won't know."

"I understand that about you." *Didn't he just? Oh, didn't he just.* "The question here is, were we lovers? The answer is, never. Have we shared a bed? That's a different question. The answer's yes."

"Fair enough," I said.

"Always ask, Grace. I mean that. Always ask me."

"He's gone, Paul. George is gone. Did you . . . was this your doing?"

"He cut and ran, Grace. The right thing: he's a gambler; he gave himself a chance."

"But this is no game. How will we keep Josh from catching him and—"

"And what? Whacking him? We can't. At least it would be quick and clean."

"Don't give me 'whack'; the word is 'kill.' Quick and clean? He'll be terrified."

"And what do you think he'd be in witness protection? Scared every minute of every day for weeks, months, years—until the day the Pyatts nailed him, which they would."

"Pyatts? You mean . . . not just Josh?"

My hands fluttered a little as I folded the *Times* back to the front page, folded it again and put it carefully on the floor beside me. Then I took my empty wineglass to the kitchen counter and refilled it close to the top. I looked at the chicken soup, already forming a skin on top as it cooled. I wouldn't be eating for a while.

Damn you to hell, Paul. Damn your shape-shifting answers. If you were alive I would wish you dead. But would I kill you? I paced and drank. Now there was a question.

CHAPTER EIGHTEEN

I awoke to sunlight and to a terrific headache. It took most of Saturday morning to shake off the feeling of having spent the previous evening in a whirlpool, pulled down and further down. Recollections of Marina and Paul had predictably given way to recollections of George and Paul, as well as some of Michael. The red wine bottle had been emptied, the chicken soup never reheated or eaten. This was no good, I thought, not any good at all. A plea in a hospital linen closet: *"You need to get rid of this. Let it be over. It wants to be over."* As though the It had a life of its own. But the hitch was that its life was braided into mine—and while the surgery to remove it might be lifesaving, the operation was as delicate and dangerous as separating Siamese twins joined at the heart.

On that inspiring thought I pulled myself out of bed and into the bathroom, where I swallowed some aspirins with handfuls of water and had a hot shower. Then I marched myself to the kitchen. The saucepan of uneaten chicken soup waited like a long-suffering Jewish mother. I shut it up in the fridge and made myself bacon and eggs instead.

The day played out pleasantly in small, easy events. For one thing, I had a haircut; in four weeks' time the shape of it had begun to erode. No

Bendel's; no William. Hair was not where my three hundred bucks needed to go. I mooched around Broadway, Columbus and Amsterdam until I found a small shop that looked hip but not fancy. The Chinese woman with the scissors reminded me a bit of Teresa Woo at the office in her cool self-confidence.

"Can you kind of keep the line?"

"Sure." She ran her fingers through it. "You come back two hours. I do." I did and she did. Fifty dollars, sixty with tip; it was fine.

Back on the street, I found myself saying softly, "Okay. You're okay." I'd already done groceries a day or two ago. Now I visited the Pottery Barn and a shop called Surprise! and another few stores whose names I forget, gathering things to turn the touring dancer's apartment into home. While I shopped I tried and almost succeeded in holding off the sense memory of cheering up a cell.

I bought a comfortable green canvas lounge with blond wood arms and a nice shape, then a silver metal standing lamp for behind it and a low wicker cube for beside it; after that, an Indian bedspread to throw over the ugly black plastic couch and several pillows, various shapes in primary colors, to anchor the spread in place; finally a big midnight blue woolen shawl which I saw blanketing my shoulders or legs as I read or watched TV on a winter night. My last purchase of the day was a six-pack of wineglasses and another couple of bottles of red wine to go with them. The wine was going to help me through, and a nice glass to pour it into would make the drink feel festive rather than remedial.

By the time I'd made my second trip back to the apartment I felt filled with virtue, ready to go for a short run in Riverside Park and then pick up a bag of mesclun to go with the pasta and marinara I'd cook and a movie from Blockbuster.

I was in sweat suit and running shoes, ready to go out the door when the phone began to ring. "There is no one you want to speak to just now, no one you're expecting to call," said a small internal voice, "do not go back." I didn't obey. I turned the key in the lock, ran to the phone and caught it just before the machine clicked in. Instantly, I was sorry.

"Hi, Grace." I'd known McCail wasn't done with me. Of course I'd known that, but someone with as long a history as I in not knowing what she knows reverts to type easily.

"Gabriel, you are not what I need right now," I said crisply.

"I *am* what you need, you just don't know it." I let that one go by and waited. But I didn't hang up, did I? "We got off to a bad start, Grace. My fault. It was just that I wanted to get your attention."

"Plus you wanted what the *Post* paid you."

He laughed. "Okay."

"Well, you got it, my attention. But you're not going to keep it very long, so tell me what you want that I haven't already said no to."

"It wasn't *only* to get your attention that I *paparazzied* you. I was pissed at the way you blew me off–no answer, no chance to make my case." That ego of his again: You could punch him in the mouth and he wouldn't complain; he'd wipe the blood away and start talking again but the man couldn't stand being ignored. "Grace? You're still there, aren't you?"

"Yes, but the answer's still no. I can't think of one reason, not one, for me to want to help you write that book."

"Here's one and it's a biggie: I told you I was a good reporter and I am. Also, I've put in a chunk of research–a good few years." He paused. "I know things you want to know."

A wavering alcoholic must feel this way, able to imagine the rich, mouth-filling burn of scotch. George must have felt this way after the brief, barren time when he gave up gambling. My addiction was not the knowing of "things," just the knowing of *one* thing: *So tell me if you can, you angel-faced little creep, where is my father?* But if he could, he was a man with a live bomb in his hand. I had a quick flash of George hiding in a closet crouched behind a curtain of long garments, the door swinging open by the triumphant hand of Gabriel McCail.

"That's where you're wrong," I said. "There is nothing I want to know." I put the phone back in its cradle.

The next morning the time dragged gloomily until noon when I could show up at Craig's brunch and hide out from the thoughts and impulses, which kept threatening to snap their bonds and gallop off into bad places. I made myself put on clothes from the old days: a big purple sweater and jeans and green cowboy boots and Keiko's kimono coat. They were clothes, I told myself: I owned them; I liked them; I couldn't afford to replace them. And good memories permeated the fibers the way beach smell does a swimsuit or perfume a ball gown. *Keep the good ones; toss the rest.*

I was working at bluffing an upbeat mood to bring to Craig and his boyfriend. Bluffing, you learn in prison, can be useful—what they call in all those step programs, "Fake it till you make it." Again I opened the jewelry drawer and slipped a bracelet that looked like charred chain mail edged in gold on my wrist. Tomorrow, I said to myself. Tomorrow I will wear this bracelet and I will call an old friend: I'll call Danton, go down to the show at his gallery and have lunch.

I stopped at Zabar's, the Upper West Side's gift to people who love food—any kind of food, but especially smoked fish and meat and pickles and spicy salads and crusty breads—and bought some black olives with rosemary and some fresh bright green ones that tasted only of olive, not of salt. Then I walked the three miles down on Broadway, taking a turn west to Ninth Avenue after Lincoln Center, where I lingered. *I know you're officially dead, George, but tell me, is there opera where you are? Do you ever go?*

Craig's building was on Tenth Avenue near Twenty-sixth Street, part of the farther reaches of Chelsea that had become chic while I was gone. He buzzed me in and stood looking down, waving me up as I mounted four flights of corrugated metal stairs. He was excited—happy excited—an unaccustomed glint in his olive eyes. A gorgeous red silk shirt replaced his usual black turtleneck.

"You look like a kid at Christmas," I said, his good mood an emotional vitamin shot. "Though everything I know about kids and Christmas I learned at the movies."

"Poor Grace," he said, craning to kiss my cheek. "We had Christmas and a half in Shaker Heights."

"Shaker Heights?"

He held up his hand. "Swear. And I'm not scamming you so don't haul off and smack me. Only truth from now on, me to you. Vice versa? I've got one sister still in Ohio and a living mother. My dad died last year. He was an uptight shit."

"My father," the words felt dry in my mouth but I made myself say them, "thought Christmas was a crock. It had less to do with him being a Jew than with being a skeptic." I thought of Sheilah, Christmas deprived too. Under mostly silent protest, she spent that day with her mother, the two of them dressed in the new outfits Mrs. C-D called "our presents," sitting in a fancy church pretending to be part of the congregation of strangers and afterward going out to a "nice" restaurant. The annual Christmas tree in her own apartment rivaled the one in Rockefeller Center.

"That is one swell bracelet," Craig said, taking my hand and lifting it up for a better look. "Yours?"

I nodded. "A kind of debut. I want to wear my stuff again. I thought I didn't, couldn't stand to—didn't deserve to. But I was wrong. It feels good to see my bracelet on my wrist, even if my damned shaky hands won't let me make another one. I put this on today because I was going to be with you."

He gave the mesh of the bracelet a light kiss. "Thank you."

"Speaking of swell," I said, "this is some swell place to live."

"It is, isn't it? Wait till you see the loft." He motioned me inside to a single large space, maybe fifteen hundred feet with what looked like sixteen-foot ceilings. A half-wall near the back partitioned off what must have been his bedroom. The walls were rough whitewashed cement, and the light through long, narrow windows cast sculptural shadows, which would change with the hour and the weather. The floors were stained black and all the furniture—stark modern shapes—was black too. The only slash of color was a very large painting of a bright red eagle with an expression that was not threatening, but not unthreatening either.

"Great," I said.

He grinned. "Truth now, could you live here?"

"No, but I do love it." I slipped off my coat and draped it over a square black ottoman, where it almost disappeared. "Here, I brought you olives. The green ones match your eyes."

He took them and set about opening the containers. "How'd you know I like olives?"

"Didn't, just figured."

"Not Angel's taste though."

"Olives."

"No, the loft," he said strategically placing twin white bowls of olives on a black rectangle of table already stocked with bagels, cheeses, lox and salads. "Want a drink, Bloody Mary, wine, something?"

"Rather have some coffee and if you don't mind, I'll sneak a nibble even if the big He isn't here yet. I'm starved. Angel? Is that his name?"

"Angelo, really. I call him Angel because I like it—also it sits better on my heartland tongue. Angelo Sweeney, don't you love it? Father Irish, mother Italian. He'll be here any time now. Help yourself to food and drink and take a seat."

"And you'll give me the quick briefing?"

"You bet."

Half an hour went by: a cup and a half of coffee, cream cheese and lox on a bagel went down easy. Craig toyed with a beer, too excited to eat, too excited to do anything but talk. He told me, for starters, how he'd looked up from the piano keyboard at Mac's late one night and spotted Angel sitting at the bar, how they'd made eye contact that seemed at once different from any eye contact in his thirty-three years, "even with my mother when I was two; even with my gym teacher when I was twelve; even with . . . well, you get the idea. He's got these blue eyes, so damned blue, and he made me feel like he knew me down through all the layers."

"That's what you said about me, wasn't it? That I looked at you like I knew who you were?"

"Right, and that's important because of what I have with him. See, you get me and a lot of what you get you really can't stand—you want to kick its ass black and blue. But with Angel that first time it was like I was the single, unique thing those blue eyes had ever looked at. You know what I mean?"

The sun god jogged into Sheilah's office kitchen, drawn by the sound of my laugh. "Yeah, I do know what you mean. Craig, that was how long ago?"

"Six weeks, almost seven."

"How well have you gotten to know him? I mean a soul-touching look is galvanizing but then what?"

For a second he looked pained, then he took a bird sip of his beer and made the face of a kid swallowing brown medicine. "Well, after I'd fin-ished the set that night I joined him at the bar. As I was walking over he started to clap, you know applaud, but making no sound, just pantomim-ing it. When I got there, I was about to run some smart opening line, but then I didn't—it seemed too . . . and he said, 'Would you believe how many years I've been looking for a beautiful bald piano player?' Okay, I see it on your face. Barf if you have to."

"No, it's not that," I said quickly. "Hey, mating talk sounds inspired to the mates and dumb to anyone else. But your Angel's opener set off an alarm because it reminded me of—what the hell, if we're friends we're friends—it reminded me of Paul."

"Paul? I thought *I* reminded you of Paul?"

"You did—do in some ways, but only some ways or I wouldn't be here eating your bagels. Maybe I'm just Paul-spooked today. The reporter from hell's been on my tail, poking and probing about him and . . . never mind. So, go on, we've got six, seven weeks to fill in and," I glanced at my watch, "the Angel will be here any minute, no?"

"Right. I'm surprised he isn't here yet. But he's a poet and time doesn't work the same way for them." He held up his hand as if his palm could move to erase the reaction he expected to see. "Okay, I know Paul wrote poems too, but this *isn't* Paul we're talking about." The hand went down and the voice softened. "I don't even know why I said that, I should have known it would ring your bells." He sprang up from his chair and began to prowl the big room. "Shit, it's hard to be spontaneous for a gamer like me. What Angel makes his living at is research—not my kind of research,

research for encyclopedias, reference books. Keeps him traveling, gives him a window into amazing stuff."

"Fine, we'll get Sheilah to find him a job. Stop writing his résumé. What about him and you?"

He walked back toward his chair. "Amazing. In bed, wooo! And out, there's an attention we seem to pay to each other, a kind of heightened awareness, like when one of us lifts an arm the other one can feel the air move six feet away, you know?"

"I used to think so." I looked away, not wanting to leave my dark footprint on his romance. "Have you and he spent a lot of time together?"

"Well, here's the thing, and it bothers me a little. At the beginning I was . . . I didn't know what hit me. We saw each other boom boom boom first few weeks. Then one night in bed he was telling me about having witnessed an execution in Texas and I said that my uncle was on death row there, which was a total lie—and I realized I'd told him two others that week. That freaked me: I did *not* want to game with him—not with him. So after that night I made myself take a time out; when he called I'd be busy or have a headache or whatever. I was so scared I'd fuck it up. Then, once I'd kind of enlisted you as my Jiminy Cricket, I thought I might have a shot at making it. And it's been good, Grace, really good, only—"

The phone rang. He sat still, hands on his knees, premonition darkening his eyes. Then he rose and hurried to answer. His back was to me and for what seemed a long time he was silent, just listening. He could have been a life-size sculpture called dejection. Then he said, "*Shit*, Angel . . . yes, I know, I know but Grace is here and you *know* I . . . we talked about it. You wanted to meet . . . of course, of *course* I understand but . . . okay, sure."

He walked slowly back to me and said, "That's it—second time running he's done that recently, bugged out at the last minute. Always a good reason but . . . you asked me if he was real." I heard a shimmy in his voice. "Maybe . . . shit, I feel like a teenager ready to weep."

I got up and went to him arms open wide. "Come on, let mama give you a hug." He walked into the hug as though it *was* his mama's, and I patted his back the way she might do.

CHAPTER NINETEEN

"You know, maybe Mr. Angelo Sweeney is just as scared as you are about how it's going to play out for the two of you. Tell you what—Mama says, let's get out of here and take a long walk, blow out some cobwebs." I wasn't any more certain than Craig was that his angel wasn't just dumping him. But I had a powerful desire to make my friend feel better, and damn, that felt good to me!

We walked clear down to the southern tip of Manhattan and caught a ferry for Ellis Island, where neither of us had ever been. Since Craig's people, both sides, predated Ellis Island, as such, we made our mission tracing the immigration of Leshanskys. And the computer yielded up Fyodor in 1905 and Rubin and Sarah in 1908. None of the names rang a bell.

"I think I'll adopt Rubin and Sarah," I said. "I like the sound of them and that'd give me a grandma."

"You want to tell me about George? I think maybe it's your turn to talk—I've been going on and on for hours about my . . . do I call it broken heart or dented pride?"

"Probably some of each, but if he dents you much more in the heart or elsewhere, figure it's not an accident, it's a habit and . . . look who's giving advice! I was about to tell you to cut him loose."

We were outside now, at the slip where millions of the washed and unwashed, including three Leshanskys, had first put a foot on American soil. I felt proud and moved as a corn-fed tourist. Paul would've laughed at me, the way he did about autumn, reminding me what squalid tragic lives a great many of those hopeful huddled masses had in fact lived out.

Fuck you, Paul. A lot of them had good lives, wonderful lives—well, at least better lives than where they came from. I took a deep breath. "I have to think finally that I was more dependent on my father than he was on me, though that was the exact opposite of how I saw it. He was kind of a throwback—this gambler in snappy clothes. And he loved the old-time entertainers, sang all the songs. That's why my name is Grace—Gracie: he was crazy about Burns and Allen. I . . . you're gonna have me in tears here."

"Do you think he's dead?" Craig asked. "I'm sorry, I did get a lot of the old coverage off the Net."

I shrugged because I needed the practice. " 'S all right: public information is public. I don't know if he's dead or alive, and may never. I hope he's okay . . . somewhere, but I need the not knowing to not matter."

He took my hand; his was very cold. "Did you love him? I mean really love him?"

"Oh yes, so much—and not just because he was my father but also—"

"No, no. I meant did you really love *Paul?*"

I took my hand out of his. "Don't ask me that, Craig. Any answer I'd give you would be a lie once it was out of my mouth." The wind came up and caught hold of the cowboy hat he wore, sailing it up, over and out. It landed on the water. "Shit," I said, "that was one great hat."

He reached for my hand again. "C'mon, let's go catch some coffee. I'm freezing my balls off here—and Angel may still have some use for them."

I gave him a light hit on the side of his shaved skull. "*You* may still have some use for them, asshole."

"I love it when you talk dirty."

———

I stopped by Sheilah's office the next morning before hitting my own. She was sitting at her desk wearing the Chanel suit I'd supported her buying a month ago, my second day out of prison. A month can be the snap of fingers, the blink of an eye. This month had lasted half a lifetime.

"You look spectacular," I said. Her cheeks glowed, smile flashed bright.

"It was a gooood weekend. Friday night was just fabulous—well you know how I adore Bobby Short. And then Saturday he took me to lunch at Aquavit. He is just—oh, Grace, he's so *appropriate.*"

It cracked me up. "That may be the most romantic thing I've ever heard anyone say."

She laughed with me while she held up crossed fingers. "You know what I'm going to do? I'm going to give a party—nothing fancy, kind of impromptu—I was thinking say next Tuesday. It would be a great way to sort of . . . introduce him—and look, this just occurred to me: my party would also be a good occasion for you to break the ice with your old friends. Just tell me who to invite."

My heart took a little skid. Just because it made me nervous didn't mean it was a bad idea. "Okay, good," I said. "Danton Redondo, for sure." As I said his name I pictured the little Oscar Wilde of Soho and felt a twinge of appetite to see him again. "I was going to call him myself today." I held up a hand. "Swear I was." As my sleeve fell back I saw her eyes register the chain mail bracelet on my wrist. "And you could ask Jan. I wonder if she's still buying jewelry for Barney's. I think two's about enough on my end for now. Oh, you could call Keiko, except she's probably in France for the shows about now. I wear her coat every time I want to feel good."

"You're feeling good today. I've always liked that bracelet. I'm glad to see it on you." She tilted her head and studied me some more. "Haircut works." Her phone rang. She said her name with the usual welcoming glissando. But that was the end of that. "Yes, I did tell her to have you call me . . . correct. I have no intention of paying it . . . sir. Ex*cuse* me sir, that was *not* the price you quoted for the letterhead and I . . . not *true.* No! I made no alterations that could possibly cause the price to almost *double* and . . ." Sheilah's wars with vendors, tradespeople of all kinds, were legendary. What most people didn't understand was that it had nothing to do with her being mean or stingy—she was quite the opposite—it was just that she craved a win way more than they did. I raised my hand good-bye and made a quick exit.

As I approached the reception area I heard Teresa Woo's voice, a fast rat-tat-tat with a hiss to it, the kind of loud whisper that carries better than usual conversational pitch.

"I can't. I can*not*, Cynthia. I don't think this is going to work. For God's sake, I ran my own business. I came here with that credential: I know technology; I recruit senior technologists. My track record is excellent—and I won't live with her looking over my shoulder and second-guessing *every* . . ." She broke off as I came into view. "Oh, Grace, I got your e-mail," she said tonelessly. Her delicate features looked disarranged: a cherry blossom slightly crushed. "Thanks. I'll let you know if I make any changes." She obviously wanted me not to linger. We had a common goal there.

"Fine," I said. "Morning, Cynthia. Craig in yet?"

"No, and he won't be. He just called in sick—flu maybe. My guess, he'll be out a couple of days, he sounded awful on the phone."

"Too bad," I said, halfway through the connecting door. Funny, he'd been fine, if a little smashed, when I'd left him at about one. I punched in his home number and got the machine.

"Must've been the river wind," I said. "Seriously, if you're sick and not playing hooky, I could bring up some chicken soup after work. Now that I've acquired a Grandma Sarah such things come naturally. Give me a call when you feel like."

He didn't. After work, I stopped at Papaya King for two hot dogs with sauerkraut and mustard and a large squeezed grapefruit juice and went home. When the phone rang at about nine I was certain it would be Craig.

"Paul Donofrio, nine years old, saw his father die of a gunshot to the back of the head, the classic mob execution of a betrayer. Young Paulie watched through the cracked door of the garage where he was hiding. He watched it happen, but couldn't do a thing."

Did my gut lurch? Sure it did but not in a big way. The edge of shock value grows blunt with repetition and the smack of McCail's truncheon was no longer a surprise.

"What are you looking for, Gabriel, applause? You're not going to get any here."

"*It's the worst thing in the world,*" I mumbled, *my face numb from too much crying. George had been gone two days.* "*Running like a rabbit, knowing you'll get caught.*"

"*You don't know the worst thing in the world.*" *Paul lay flat on his back in our bed, tears beginning suddenly to stream from his eyes and run sideways off his face into his platinum hair, into his ears.* "*The worst thing in the world is hanging in, waiting. The worst thing in the world is being a kid of nine hiding in a garage, watching through a crack in the wood while they frog march your father out of the house and blow the back of his head off. Witness protection? Balls.*"

"I assume that's the opening of your book you just read me," I said. "Very dramatic and all, and I don't know where you got it. But it's not news to me, if in fact the story's true. Since you're making a study of Paul you must know by now that a lot of what he said wasn't."

"See, that's exactly why I need your help. So you knew his father got whacked in witness protection. An intriguing symmetry there, don't you think?"

"I try not to think too much, Gabriel," I said sweetly. "It's a lot easier that way. Have a good evening."

I hung up. A slight queasiness, just that—just enough to remind me that whatever you've lived is called your life: yours. You can try hiding the pieces you want to disown, or hiding *from* them, but in the end you don't forget, not unless your brain short-circuits. I had to wonder how long it would take McCail to get around to tracking George. Not very long, I thought: intriguing symmetry was a chilling phrase. The queasiness got worse and I felt myself beginning to spin out where I couldn't afford to be. I looked down at the phone and wished it would ring, Craig on the other end.

Like a miracle, under my gaze, the phone did ring.

"Hi," Craig said, the usual energy missing from his voice.

"Believe it or not, I conjured you up. I'm a witch. Are you feeling really rotten?"

"Yeah." After a few seconds he added, "It's not the flu though."

"You're . . . not sick?"

"No I'm not sick. And I'm forcing myself to call you and say so."

"Okay."

"I told you I wouldn't lie to you. I woke up this morning with a bad case of the sads. Not a crying jag, just a—God this is hard—a loathing for myself that feels like worms under the skin. I'm going to take a couple of days off, partly because I gave such a bang-up performance for Cynthia that my . . ." that cackling laugh of his, "credibility demands some recovery time." I heard him sigh like the air leaving a punctured tire. "So, I didn't lie but I'm going to skip the chicken soup, and even skip talking to you, much as I love you. Gotta go now."

"Take care of yourself. I'll . . ." But he was no longer with me.

CHAPTER TWENTY

Craig returned to the office Monday morning after a full week's absence, looking as peaked as though he really had just recovered from the flu. We hadn't talked much during the week he was out. The couple of times I'd called to check on him, he was still buried under what he called "the sads" and not up for talking.

"You okay?" I asked when I walked in to find him already at his desk.

"Will be. Thanks for giving a damn."

I wanted to ask him if Angel had shown up or called but something in his face made me feel like the question might wound. "You going to Sheilah's party tomorrow night?" I asked instead.

"Rather have my fingernails pulled out one at a time," he said, not smiling. "She e-mailed me an invitation and I told her I was feeling weak and probably wouldn't be up to socializing by Tuesday. Not a total lie, see? I'm not in the best shape, Grace. Angel—I don't want to talk about it."

"Well, holler if . . . you know . . ."

"I do know," he'd answered with a half smile.

"And you do the same, Grace. I'm a piss-poor friend right now, but that said, if you need me you holler too. I'll hear you."

"Well, you're in luck. I'm not needing to holler just this minute."

Sheilah's party was called for seven-thirty—Tuesday being what she liked to call a school night. She had taken the afternoon off to prepare her apartment for the do and herself for lawyer Berenstain. They'd seen each other a good few more times by now and he'd taken her to places she loved going: "Gramercy Tavern, Gracie, and more Carlyle, and Lespinasse. It's not just the places. He is smart and funny and . . ." That good grin of hers. "You'll see for yourself." Her parting words to me before cutting out at noon were, "Get there on time, okay?"

I left the office at a quarter to seven and strolled down Park toward Murray Hill. My general mood was no way as up as it had been last week when she'd proposed her party. The phone exchange with McCail had gotten under my skin and sat there like a rash, reminding me of his irritating existence. Irritating in another way was the stubborn shred of hope that George would one day come looking for me in cyberspace, which kept me checking e-mail several times a day whether I intended to or not.

As I approached Sheilah's building, my mind had drifted eight years into the past, to the time after George left and I fell apart. Those first few months I drew a kind of chalk circle around myself, stood in the center and burrowed into work. Often I stayed all night at the studio making pieces unlike any I'd made before, pieces with a reckless edge to them: rings and pins and bracelets that featured smashed fragments of the most beautiful, expensive glass I could find and break. I would buy Tiffany, Baccarat, Lalique and take a hammer to them, then select the shards I wanted to frame in roughly twisted gold and silver. They sold, sold well. Something about being able to display a craziness that isn't yours: own it, wear it, put it away in a box at night knowing it can't get out and do you in. Risk-free risk, at least that's how I came to see it later. I kept none of them for myself.

During that period Paul asked no questions about my comings and goings. When I was home he'd pour me a drink and I'd drink it; he'd ladle out hot soup and I'd eat it. He didn't try talking much but I'd catch him looking at me sometimes, the pale eyes concerned but calm like someone attending to a sick child. And then I did get sick. A cold turned to pneumonia, which dropped me suddenly, like a club to the chest.

Eleven days later I was released from the hospital, and in an odd turnabout that I still can't explain I turned docile, dependent on Paul as though I were his pet, looking to him for sustenance and affection. I wanted to see or hear no one else. It was early summer then and he'd take me for walks like a dog; he'd feed me tasty nutritious food, make gentle sweet love to me. I did not have to do a thing. My father's disappearance had itself disappeared, leaving no ripple. Michael had not been charged nor had he ever turned up. I no longer cared: guilty or innocent he was guilty in my heart, if not of murder then of betrayal, but I did not have the energy even to wish him dead. And work seemed an activity from a distant past: Paul assured me that he was on the case—the studio was managing to coast while I recuperated; there were after all plenty of orders to fill.

Then in September I learned that while I'd been off the planet my business had gone bankrupt. The impact jarred me awake; that was one thing it did. And rage, flash frozen with shock, boiled. Paul had done this; he did not even try to deny it. There were losses in investments he'd made for his clients—investments where he was liable. He'd covered them with the skin off my back. He could do that because he was—had become—my business partner, though that was not exactly how I'd understood our deal. But apparently I had signed papers. I could sue of course. I still can see his mouth as he said that: severe, serious, with what I thought was a smile playing at the edges.

The incident at the Huffman Gallery when I pushed him into the canvas was not the first time I raised a hand during that final month.

"I'm here for Sheilah Donlan's party," I said to the doorman. "Grace . . . Leslie."

He consulted a list, gave me a nod and smile. "Seventeen J."

"I know." In the elevator I practiced an inner shrug. It was a party, not all that big a party. I'd see Danton and Jan. I'd meet Sheilah's Todd. It would go how it would go. I'd been to parties before—I just had to get the hang of it again.

I hung my coat on the big guest rack in the hallway and took the proverbial deep breath. The apartment door was partly open and I heard voices—enough of them to go with the coats on the rack. I checked my watch—only ten minutes late. I was kind of relieved that the first face I spotted in the entrance foyer was Cynthia's. She walked over and gave me a kiss, the way you tend to do at parties, even to people you've just seen in another setting.

"Hey Grace, I didn't see you with your jacket on at the office. The pin's great! I don't think I know that one."

It was a matte gold triangle with a steel rivet set like an eye near its top point. "Probably not. I made just the one piece . . . a long time ago."

I heard the cadence of Sheilah's voice coming from the kitchen. I couldn't make out the words but the tune was familiar. She was instructing person or persons to do something her way instead of their way. Cynthia and I exchanged a glance.

"The new man'll be here and of course she's always edgy when her mother's around, she said."

"Her mother? She invited her mother?"

Cynthia gave me a what-can-you-do smile. "Well, she didn't exactly *invite* her."

"Oh."

"Plus she's got some grief with Teresa Woo."

"Yeah, I figured. Is Teresa leaving?"

"Don't know. I hope not. But she's not coming tonight and I know Sheilah invited her. Look, don't get bogged down with this now, Grace. There are a couple of people in there who've been asking for you."

"Right." Instinctively I'd placed myself with my back to the room while we were talking. *Chicken.* "See you later." I turned and marched straight ahead into Sheilah's pretty living room—nineteenth-century England recreated in a late twentieth-century apartment: flowered chintzes against apricot walls topped by white crown moldings; polished walnut parquet and pale oriental rugs.

Maybe a dozen, fifteen, people in groups of two or three stood drinking and chatting. I spotted no familiar face. At the far end of the room I did see a back I recognized: a slender broad-shouldered woman almost as tall as I, her red gold hair a stylish chaos of cascading ringlets. She wore a long red knit dress. I headed for her and gave her shoulder a light tap. When she turned to me her eyes asked, "Is that—"

"Yeah, it's me, Jan," I said with a smile.

"Oh, my God, Grace," she said, "you look . . . I mean you look really good."

"And really changed. It's okay, Jan. I'm used to it but you're not." We embraced, and I remembered how difficult it had been to walk into Sheilah's hug that first day when I arrived at Bendel's. So I had come if not a long way, some part of a way.

Jan Simone was a jewelry buyer for Barney's, the only department store that had carried my stuff; otherwise I'd sold through galleries or boutiques or to private clients directly. But Barney's was into edge, especially in the eighties when it was a downtown store. "You look great as ever," I said. "I admire your taste in jewelry," I added, referring to a rusted iron and silver pendant around her neck.

She laughed. "I didn't wear it just for tonight. I mean I *did,* but I wear it a lot anyway."

I noticed that her face at close range had a strained set to it like someone with a headache she wasn't about to give in to. "Before you ask, I'm not with Barney's anymore: hard times there, mean guys. I'm in Soho now. Rescued by Saint Danton. I'm doing this and that at the gallery."

"Is he here?" I asked. "I don't seem to see him."

"Sure, just over at the bar behind that good-looking gray-haired guy. Hard to see Danton in a crowd at first."

At that moment, Danton, tonight in a purple velvet suit, emerged from behind the gray-haired guy and made his way to us carrying two glasses of what looked like scotch. He handed one off to Jan and said to me, as though we'd seen each other yesterday, "Come on, Mizz Grace. Bend over and let me kiss that cheek."

I turned around and stuck my butt out at him, then turned back and leaned my face down to where he could reach it. We both laughed, not forced: an old mutual joke can work wonders. Danton Redondo hit five two when he stood up very straight, which wasn't most of the time.

"I'm gonna say you haven't changed a bit, Danton. And that just happens to be true."

"Believe it." His small graceful paw of a hand cupped Jan's chin. "I was just slipping Jan here the name of my plastic surgeon."

"Well, don't bother trying to hook me up with the good doctor," I said. "I'm too far gone and besides I can't afford it." This was not so bad; it felt easy, fun.

Danton's brown face was all points: chin, nose, beard, mustache—like a cartoon of a pirate who happened to favor a dandy's clothes. He was from the Mississippi Delta and claimed that four kinds of blood cooked to a syrup in his veins. And underneath all the flash was a pragmatism as solid as any on Wall Street or Main Street or Pennsylvania Avenue: his gallery on Prince Street showed what sold and skipped what wouldn't. His motto was: "I'm a businessman not an art lover."

A hand clapped my shoulder. "*Gracie*, I didn't realize you were here." Sheilah in brown silk palazzo pants and tunic and beside her, the gray-haired man Jan had called good-looking. Sheilah smiled wide. "Grace, this is Todd. Todd, Grace—my best friend since third grade." She held her arm out at him. "Bracelet, GraceL—she made it. Great, huh?" If I had shut my eyes I would remember a different party, almost the same words of introduction from Sheilah. *Grace, this lunatic is Paul Boudreau.*

Todd the lawyer made no move to kiss my hand, of course. We just made the usual pleased to meet you noises. He and Sheilah, side by side, might have been a handsome successful couple out of a glossy magazine, the print beneath their photos describing the fullness of their life together: the small dinners, large parties and evenings for two that Sheilah craved as a companion piece to the work life she'd already attained. Her desire seemed to fill the air around them; it had a texture to it. I wished I had the power to sweep all the preliminaries and obstacles out of the path and speed them from here to there in the instant.

One of the servers held out a tray with red and white wine on it. I took a red. Another offered a tray of hors d'oeuvres. I skipped that. Just then, Mrs. C-D in stormy blue sailed toward us from out of the kitchen clutching a water glass of clear liquid (which might have been water but likely wasn't) as though she were preparing to christen a battleship with it.

"Grace dear," she said, "I hardly recognize you. You're so much . . . thinner."

"All that gruel." All right, I was playing to Danton, beside me. And he did laugh. "Nice to see you, Mrs. C-D," I said, the good girl, partly in penance. "You look . . . splendid."

"Ah, thank you." She took a very healthy pull from her glass. "Well, I hope you're enjoying working for my daughter," she said with what passed for a chuckle. "It must be a bit hard to begin in a new field at forty." She spoke in what Sheilah and I used to call the memsahib voice, the one she might have dispensed to a cleaning woman, if she'd been able to afford one back then.

"Mother," Sheilah warned. Then her eye lit on the foyer where some new people had arrived. "Oh, there's . . ." I didn't catch the names. "Let me go say hello." She did, her mother right behind her.

I took a sip of wine at least as hefty as Mrs. C-D's of gin or vodka. I saw what Sheilah had meant about Todd Berenstain's face being Lincoln-esque. It was, sort of: a Lincoln with an insinuating smile. "So, Todd," I said, "what kind of law do you practice?"

His eyes, dog brown and keen, met mine. "Criminal," he said, lobbing it in almost straight faced. *I know about you.*

"Been there; done that," I said. I felt a pat on my thigh and turned to Danton, whose hand it had been. "Jailhouse blues isn't your final song, big lady," he said quietly and slipped his card into my jacket pocket. "When you're ready . . ." I ruffled his crisp hair; it was easier than saying that I had this shaking hand problem: that I wouldn't–couldn't–be ready. "So, Todd, have you met Danton Redondo and Jan Simone?"

"I have," he said. "I've enjoyed the Redondo Gallery often. About two years ago I came within a hair of buying a sculpture from you, Danton–an open-work iron bull. You wouldn't remember, but we talked quite a while," he said smiling down at Danton.

"Next time make a better decision and I'll never forget. I do remember the piece."

"My decisions have improved by leaps and bounds these last couple of years. Here's the thing: I couldn't afford it then; now I can. Hey, Jan, both our glasses seem to be empty. Shall I get us refills?" Were the dog eyes wolfish as they switched their gaze to Jan or did I imagine it?

"I'll walk you over to the bar," she said.

The front door opened again and a couple I didn't know walked in to a big greeting from Mrs. C-D. From where I stood at the far corner of the living room my view of the foyer was partly blocked. It was not until I heard Sheilah's voice say an emphatic "*No.* I didn't invite you here," that I craned my neck around to get the full picture. It wasn't a couple who'd arrived, it was a threesome: the third person was Marina Beck.

I glanced back at Danton and mouthed, "I'll be right back," and moved quickly toward them, with the vague idea of containing her there in the entrance foyer, which fortunately wasn't all that small.

"I came with the . . ." Marina turned to the man, "what was your name, honey? Ah, the Cunninghams. I came with the Cunninghams. Now how about a drink, Sheilah? It's been a long time." She produced her famous oversized martini glass from a green lizard satchel and held it out for the taking.

"I don't care if you came with God," Sheilah said. "You're leaving."

Marina raised her arm and pointed a red-tipped finger at me. "But I understood that friends of Grace are welcome here. I see Danton Redondo right over there. Why not me? See, I'm even wearing a GraceL pin, badge of the club."

I could have stayed out of it. If it's not your beef stay out of it: if you don't learn that in prison you've learned nothing–and probably acquired some battle scars in the bargain. But it *was* my beef and it threatened to lay a steaming turd in the middle of Sheilah's meticulously planned party. But maybe the most important reason was that it galled me to be scared of Marina. The sight of her at Lincoln Center had shaken me to the core. The sight of her here did too. I felt my face flush with a shame that went beyond any feelings I had for Marina Beck.

"You wanted to see me again that much?" I said, closing in on her, as the couple she'd come in the door with moved quickly into the living room, away from the fuss. I gave Sheilah's shoulder a squeeze. "It's fine with me, Sheil. She'll say what she has to say right here and then she'll go. It's perfectly fine." It wasn't fine. Cushioned as I was with wine and people, the pin that glittered on Marina's lapel gave me a sharp jab. It was from my crazy period: a jagged shard of beautiful old ruby glass buffed smooth at the edges with a gold lightening bolt running through its middle.

She waved her empty glass at a passing waiter. "Put in two ice cubes for a couple of seconds, throw them out. Pour in a good vermouth and pour it back out. Then comes the gin: gin not vodka—Tanqueray if you have it, otherwise Bombay. Not the blue one, though; it's sweet. Fill it to one inch below the top." The waiter, who had "actor" stamped across him, head to toe, recognized who she was: a producer through whom he might get work. He took the glass from her hand, staring at her like a subject undergoing hypnosis.

"Go talk to your guests, Gorgeous," I said softly to Sheilah. "You don't want Todd to get lonesome." He didn't look lonesome at all, in a corner, deep in conversation with Jan. Sheilah spotted them too and took off with no protest.

Marina was dressed in a gray green man's suit, custom-tailored to her hard little body. With her crimson lips and green eye shadow she looked ready to play the emcee in *Cabaret*. Her eyes shone hard and bright from their nests of wrinkles.

I recalled the night I met her—*really* met her, with Paul. She'd scrutinized me something like the way she was doing now and said, "I don't often get surprised but when Boudreau told me he was moving out to

marry *you*–" And she laughed loud, with an open mouth. "Do you understand what you've got here, Grace Leshansky?"

Back then, not wanting to wreck Paul's evening, I'd pussyfooted, forced
my own laugh and said, "I hope I understand," or something equally
inane. Now I said, "Could we cut to the chase, whatever the chase is
tonight, Marina? We are natural enemies and always were. What else
would we be? You hate me with damned good reason, I really do understand that. In your eyes I robbed the world of a great writer–and in anyone's eyes, I robbed you of a–" I cut off, astonished because my voice was
shaking with a welling of tears that had moved in quick as a sneak storm.

Fortunately the waiter arrived with her martini, a lemon curl and an
olive beside it on the tray. "I didn't know which you'd prefer," he said, his
young voice extra resonant.

"Both." She dropped them one by one in her drink, took a taster's sip
and nodded. "You're a peach, and a quick learner. You straight or gay?"

The kid was a kid and he blushed like one. "Straight," he managed.

"Good," she said. "Maybe we'll see each other again," which robbed
him of his stage presence entirely. "I have a play on at the Lortel. Leave
me a message with your name and number. Go on now, other people need
refills."

After he'd scampered, she fixed her eyes on me, no banter in them at
all. "You did rob me. And you owe me."

I'd worked at stuffing my emotional laundry back in its bag during her
little riff with the waiter. But some note in her voice made my hands feel
at risk holding a glass. I put it down carefully on the hall table, but not before swallowing another mouthful of wine. "Owe you?"

"Owe me. I'm a plain speaking woman. I get what I want because I say
what's on my mind."

"Bullshit, Marina. You're anything but a plain speaker. You package
yourself as one and you're very good at marketing." When you get a long-
held two-bit insight off your chest satisfaction ought to come along.
It didn't. She was here for some real reason, not just to play gotcha
games.

A smile stretched her chalky face. "I came from nothing. All I owned was my life. I can package and sell me any damned way I choose. Paul and I had that in common. He did it his way, I do it mine. We were soul mates. That's what you robbed me of: my soul mate. And who were you? Nothing but a big, sexy, dumb bitch with clever hands and a little talent for making something to pin onto my jacket."

"Just shut up. I don't owe you listening to that."

She sipped at her drink. "Where's your wine? Scared you'll get stinko and do something you shouldn't?"

I looked at her, the poisonous red mouth, the ruined white face. After a moment, I turned away and started toward the living room.

"Backing off?" she called.

"Bet your ass," I said over my shoulder. "I killed someone you loved. You want to challenge me to a duel about it now. I won't fight."

"I heard tell he was someone *you* loved. You come back here now. I have something to say to you."

I did. I would take one more verbal punch from her, whatever it was. I'd forced Sheilah into letting her stay. I couldn't just walk away and let her ruin the party for everyone. "Get to it now, Marina, whatever it is, or I'm going to the buffet table."

"Here it is. Boudreau is not going to disappear like a rock thrown in the water. You may have shot him dead but I won't let him die. I'm his literary executor and the world will know him and his work."

"Fine. Go have it published. You've got money to spare; put out a leather-bound edition."

"No. He wouldn't have wanted vanity press. He would've laughed it to hell and back."

"That's all the stuff is worth," I said almost under my breath, knowing I should have bitten my mouth shut.

She moved toward me. For a second I thought she was going to toss the martini in my face, but she didn't. She raised the glass to her own mouth and drank some. "No, Paul Boudreau is worth a best-selling book. And he's going to have one."

"Fine. Good luck. What's this got to do with me? I'm assuming you don't want me to write the forward."

"Does the name Gabriel McCail ring a bell?" She had me flash frozen, just as she'd meant to. "Boudreau's work—some of it—will be part of Mc-Cail's book. He needs some cooperation from you to make that book work. You owe *me* that cooperation, and if you don't see it that way, take another look or you'll be sorrier than you are already."

She downed the last few drops of her drink and put the glass back in her satchel. "That's all I had to say to you." Her skinny hand went to her lapel and stroked the gleaming red glass in the pin. She was savoring the drama of the moment. "Love this. I wear it all the time."

CHAPTER TWENTY-ONE

had no heart to stay there, no heart to be anywhere—except perhaps behind cinderblock and barbed wire where I belonged in more ways than one. I stared at the front door still sick with surprise, not trusting myself yet to review with any logic what the hookup between Marina and McCail could mean to me or to George.

"I don't know why you encouraged that woman to stay so long. *And* I cannot fathom why she didn't contact you at your own apartment instead of ruining Sheilah's party." The indignation fluted into my ear from behind: Sheilah's mother at her most aristocratic.

I walked away without turning around, absurdly more angry with Mrs. C-D than with Marina. I headed for the buffet table, not because I could have swallowed a bite of anything, but just because it was crowded and busy and seemed a good place to be unobtrusive.

"Whatever she had to say, she's just a piece of flashy performance art," said Danton who had materialized by my side. "What can she really do to you?"

"Nothing," I said. *Maybe something.* I supposed he was more right than not. Marina could give McCail money and whatever facts were in her head. She *was* performance art: an opening act softening the audience up for the real thing. How real a thing did McCail have? Suddenly, my head began to reel and it felt hard to catch a full breath. Shit, to pass out right in front of Sheilah's beautiful buffet table . . . "I wonder if you'd do me a favor, Danton. I've got to get out of here. I mean if I could just slip away and you could tell Sheilah—the others too but especially Sheilah—that I . . . you know."

"I do know. You go home and put your feet up. I'll take care of it."

"Thank you." I kissed the top of his head.

"But only if you promise to call me. Some things I want to talk about."

"I will. It . . . may not be for a while but I will call."

I stood on the corner of Thirty-seventh and Park filling my lungs, gulping in cold air as though I'd never get enough of it. I didn't want to go home and put my feet up. As much as I'd wanted out of Sheilah's party, I realized that I didn't want to be alone and spend the night focused on Marina, on McCail, on Paul. I wanted to be with . . . a friend. I reached into my bag for my cell phone and punched in Craig's number. While the call was going through I looked at my watch and found it was almost nine-thirty. I had no sense of how much or little time had passed and was faintly surprised it was still that early.

"It's Grace," I said when he answered. "I couldn't . . . I left Sheilah's party. How would you feel about my coming to you now? I think I need—"

"You get your tush in a cab and come ahead."

Craig opened his door dressed in red silk again, this time Japanese pajamas, bare feet. He looked a little silly but the sight of him warmed me.

"Craig-san, I'm so glad to be here." We embraced, close and quick. I slipped my coat off and threw it on one of the black chairs.

"The party must've been stress and a half—you look grim. Come on, give the jacket here, get comfortable." I handed it over and he hung it on a steel coat tree.

"Ta," I said and tried to smile but couldn't. "I'm not in great shape. I just felt like I needed to be with you, just specifically with *you*, so . . . whatever you are and whatever I am, I guess we really are buds." Something that looked troubled flickered on his face. "What is it?"

"Nothing." He leaned over and kissed my cheek. "We are for sure buds, I don't know that I've ever felt this easy with anyone in my life. It's just that we're not alone tonight. See," he jerked his head back toward the semi-walled off sleeping quarters, "Angel's in there."

"Shit," I said under my breath, unable to help it.

He took both my hands in his. "No, no, please. Don't pull away. Tell you what: he's putting some clothes on. But look, once the hellos and all get said, he'll go home. He's fine with that. And I'm dying for him to meet you after—what's it been—three near missses?"

"Sure," I said awkwardly. I felt suddenly hyperconscious of my size, the air I displaced around me: one huge, hulking problem for Sheilah, for Craig—a boulder in the middle of the road. I might as well—

A man in jeans and tee shirt stepped out from behind the half wall. I was maybe fifty feet away and the lights were turned fairly dim. But as he drew closer, which he did slowly, sauntering, I saw that his figure was short and slightly chubby, and his blond hair curled into ringlets.

For what seemed a long time nothing happened: I felt nothing, said nothing. My eyes did register the image before them but any connector to the brain was lost, blown out by surprise.

"I'm sorry, Grace," the man said, almost shy. I had not heard shy out of him before. "After your call I thought of leaving, but then . . ."

I stood, stupid as a cow. Angel: Craig's object of desire, call to mend his lying ways, prime reason for seeking a friendship with . . . who else? Paul Boudreau's wife.

Angel Gabriel. Coincidence? Don't make me laugh.

"Then I thought maybe this isn't such a bad thing," Gabriel said.

"It's a very bad thing," I said, my lips stiff around the words, as though the language were foreign. I spoke not to Gabriel McCail but to Craig's white face, which looked set in a masklike stillness. Shock? Guilt? My mind flashed the awful picture of Paul springing Michael on me at the Matisse show.

"I don't get this," Craig said. "I don't get what you're saying, either of you."

"You don't?" I felt myself slide as I had with Paul that day into lead-footed sarcasm, weapon of the pathetically impotent. "What's the act I'm hearing now, Craig? The graduate student researching a paper? The management consultant doing a marketing study? The lovesick truth teller? Is he from Cleveland? New Orleans? Which one of your cast of characters set me up here? Who the hell *are* you, you *freak?*"

"Hey lady, just a second," Gabriel cut in with the authority of a holder of good cards. "Think about it. *You* were the one who called tonight. He didn't expect it. This just happened, maybe God meant it to."

"You and God, now there's a pair."

"Just a fucking minute, both of you," Craig said. The look of him had altered from a moment ago, his face hard and wary as a cowboy's walking into a new bar in an old Western. Yet another shape shift? The red Japanese pajamas, big white bare feet: an absurdly wrong costume. "Somebody spell me out in simple English what this *is*."

Gabriel said, "It's got a few moving parts to it, Craig, and–"

"Shut up!" Me: louder than any words spoken so far. I pointed to Gabriel. "What is his name, Craig? Tell me his name."

"Angelo Sweeney–Angel . . . to me."

"No, that's not his name. His name is Gabriel McCail. He's a reporter. He works for the *Post.*"

I saw the cowboy veneer begin to crack like a plaster cast falling off his face. He giggled that crazy high giggle of his. He started and couldn't seem to stop. Then tears began to run down his face and still he didn't stop.

"He didn't know," Gabriel said to me quietly.

Craig's manic laughter was beginning to wind down. None of what was happening seemed quite real, which is one way of looking at something too real to bear.

"Get out of here, Angel." Craig's order was toneless, the endearing nickname ice cold.

"Craig," Gabriel said, stretching out the vowel center in a way that sounded intimate. "I said it had moving parts. One of those parts is the way I feel about you—which I admit isn't the same way I felt when we started."

"We?" Craig gave what sounded like a fresh burst of laughter, but it died fast. "Conned," he said. "My own medicine and didn't I just lap it up. You sitting there at the bar clapping away, little smile, just enough. You're good, really good. Now, you tell me you've got a wife, three kids and a dog in a split level in New Jersey and I'll tell you you're the best I ever met."

"I don't," Gabriel said. "Not even the dog. I am a true blue faggot, my darlin'. And all yours. I'd love to demonstrate that to you right now but I'm a little scared you'd knock me on my ass if I tried it." For a second my eyesight refracted through a different lens and I was able to see Gabriel as Craig must see him: not as a slightly dissipated short man with thinning curls and a little belly, but as a teasingly sexy angel boy, all pink and gold, and now turned naughty.

The two of them faced each other like a pair out of confessional television: the deceiver and the deceived, the air between them thick with the charge of their own drama—you could almost smell the electricity. It was plausible, so plausible. But what if I was simply watching another piece of scam art? What if the only deceived believer in the room was, as usual, me?

Something about the scene put a chill on my own heat. If Craig had been an innocent dupe wouldn't Gabriel's prodding him for information have raised red flags? After all, panning for that kind of gold was how Craig earned his living. On the other hand, probably not: sex in skilled hands is a better blindfold than any silk scarf. And who should know that better than I? I grabbed my coat and slipped it on, pulling it tight around me as though the layer of cloth offered protection from both these men, for that's what they were to me now: conjoined twins.

"I'm out of here," I said, my hand on the doorknob.

Craig whirled like a clumsy dancer, almost falling over. "No! *He's* out of here. He's done. Grace, I didn't sell you out. You have to—"

"It doesn't matter Craig. He's here, I'm here. I can't—"

"You have to believe me."

"You know, I *don't* have to. What I *do* have to do is find a way to live and to feel . . ." The word in my head was "safe" but somehow I couldn't say it. I felt my hand on the knob begin to tremble.

Gabriel cut in almost lazily, "Paulie Donofrio met Michael Pyatt when he was twelve, right after his father got whacked—best friends on and off ever since. Josh Pyatt swears he had nothing to do with the hit but—who knows?" His cherub smile challenged me to leave without biting at that. I opened the door and kept my mouth shut. "And you're dying to know where I got that, aren't you?" *Take a step over that threshold and close the damned door behind you.* I started to do just that. Gabriel said, "Michael has been a really good source for me."

It hit the mark—as he'd known it would: a punch line that punched the wind out of me and made the next breath something to work on. Despite that, I couldn't help glancing back at him before I left. He leaned against the back of a tall black chair, a lounging pose that looked unnatural because he was hardly the lounging type. The last thing I saw before I shut the door behind me was a red blur charging like a Samurai fighter; the last things I heard were the sound of flesh smacking flesh and a sharp yelp of pain.

CHAPTER TWENTY-TWO

An old favorite joke of George's: Two Jews about to be executed. One hollers out, "Fuck you, you Nazi bastards." The other one whispers to him, "Shhh, Yussel, don't make waves."

I would make waves of biblical size and I would surf the tops of them wherever they carried me. I didn't feel like I had anything to lose.

I covered the blocks to Eighth and Twenty-third with no sensation of feet on pavement. Down the steps into the subway: the uptown A Train was pulling into the station just as I swiped my card. Its prompt arrival–at my service–put me for a moment inside the woman I'd seen hailing a cab as I'd strode down to Lincoln Center my first night out of prison. Of *course* you get what you want because your want throws out long orange licks of flame, your want has tiger teeth in it, your want has the might of right. Fear? Memories of that were distant, something imagined a long time ago.

I landed on Michael's pediatric floor at just after midnight and almost collided with a young nurse on the run. "Dr. Pyatt?" I asked.

"Just coming off shift I think, unless he's left." She shrugged and hurried away.

In fact he was in the locker room slipping into his coat. I wasn't any more surprised to find him than I'd been to find the A Train showing up for me, and he didn't look surprised either.

"I'm not going to let it go," I said, feeling a kind of calm settle in—the calm of telling, not asking.

"No, I guess you won't." His face gave nothing—no anger, no shame, no apologies.

"You're a liar, a treacherous liar." My eyes were on that beautiful mouth of his: the good source. "You're worse than McCail. Maybe you're worse than Paul. McCail's obsessed with his book. Paul was obsessed with recreating who he was. What are you obsessed with, Michael? Do you at least have a reason, a conviction behind what you do?"

"There's always a reason, isn't there?" I half expected that he'd bolt. Michael had been a bolter as long as I'd known him. But he didn't look about to cut and run, as he had last week. I remembered how in the two years I'd known him as an adult—thought I'd known him—I could often predict what he might do, when he might be about to break with the latest girlfriend, how he might react to something Paul was in the midst of saying, or I was. I remembered also that in the big things, where Michael was concerned, I'd miscalculated. Always.

"Where are you headed?" I asked. "I mean now?"

"Home."

"I'm coming with you."

"Uh no . . . no, you can't do that."

A recognizable signpost: the liquid glint in the eye meant a woman. "You're living with someone." It was not a question and he didn't answer. I said, "Well, I live alone. You come home with me." I saw the hesitation and found my arms and legs bracing to block him just in case. It would have been useless of course: I was strong but it would have been like tackling a train.

"Okay. You don't have to bring out the cattle prod and cuffs. I'll come quietly. I've got a couple of conditions though: I need some food, and a drink might help."

"No weed? Think you can manage without that?"

"It got to be simpler to learn to skip it. And as you know, I go for simple."

"I have scotch and wine at the apartment—salad and sliced ham and cheese and bread. You can scarf down all of it but I'm not going to sit around in some restaurant or bar and pretend we're old friends having a reunion."

We went downtown by cab: one had pulled up to the hospital entrance as we were leaving. Michael grabbed it. "I'll pay," he said.

We barely spoke during the ride and were relieved of any responsibility to do so: the driver, a passionately articulate middle-aged Haitian, kept up a running commentary on the sad state of the world, what with people all over the place thinking they can just shoot and bomb anyone they please. He had no way of knowing that one of those people was sitting right behind him. Was a second one sitting beside me? Funny, even when Paul had me convinced that George was dead, I had never fully believed in Michael as his killer. Had Michael, wherever the hell he was when he heard the news, instantly believed in me as Paul's killer?

Maybe accusations of treachery between us, spoken and unspoken, were a two-way street. I'd killed his best friend.

Michael ate. He followed me through the door, put his leather jacket on a chair back, opened my fridge and ate what he laid hands on. He ate as hungrily and mechanically as a furnace stoking up its fuel. He ate in silence, standing up at the kitchen counter. While he was doing it, I went into the bedroom and took off my coat. Only when I saw the white of my shirt did I realize that my suit jacket hung on a coat rack in Chelsea.

Craig Tarbell, dupe or conspirator: the thought of his shaved head and stunned face—those silly red pajamas—it hurt my heart either way.

I considered getting out of my shoes and didn't, who knows why? Too informal maybe—or maybe I had the idea Michael would do a sudden Michael, make a run for it, and I'd have to run after him. I'd never catch him, of course. I used the bathroom and gave my face a cool wash.

When I came back he was finishing up his feed. "Sorry, we were one doc short today—never did get lunch beside a candy bar from the machine." He rinsed off the fork and knife he'd used and walked past me to the couch. His size made the apartment look like a kind of playhouse. The disproportion was even more notable with him sitting dead center on the slim, mingy couch, draped with my improvised Indian spread: giant attends sixties tea party. "I'm all yours," he said flatly.

"You forgot to pour your drink. Think you can manage?"

"We'll see. You want to talk; we'll talk. I tried to tell you last week I don't have the answers you're looking for. I don't know where George is, do you get that?"

I nodded. "And I also get that you wouldn't tell me if you did."

"True. So there won't be much satisfaction for you tonight—except you'll have reason to hate me more than you do already; that might give you something. Go ahead. Shoot." I was standing opposite him, other side of the slatted coffee table. His gaze clicked into mine for just the second that it took to acknowledge the inadvertent pun—and the fact that many expressions in the normal vocabulary had shadow meanings for me.

"I have something else to ask you," I blurted. "Did it surprise you that I killed Paul?"

"I . . ." His hand rubbed at his face, hiding his mouth.

"Tell me the truth, Michael." I felt the blood rush to my cheeks. He'd just told me. "Why?" I asked. "Why would you think I could kill someone?"

"Jesus, Grace, I . . . if the right buttons get pushed, anyone—"

"You're lying. I can see it all over your face. Why would you think I could kill someone?"

He took a deep breath, like someone preparing to dive in under a wave. "You put yourself out there in the wind no matter how strong it's blowing. Always did, as long as I've known you—with George, with Paul. It's one of the things I love you for." My lips opened as I took in a quick puff of air but I didn't say anything. "Paul was a fucking hurricane. You snapped."

"He was your best friend," I said, my hand reaching for a chair back because my legs felt shaky.

"He was nobody's friend," Michael fired back, his voice hard. His fist landed with a soft thunk in his palm: punctuation. "Look, I'm here because McCail told you I've been talking to him. Want to know about that? I'll tell you. The man's obsessed with his book. You said it yourself. He is not going away. After the third or fourth time he contacted me, I decided to make a deal with him. Here's what it is: I'll talk about Paul and me, 1975 through 1994. Anything after that is off limits. I don't touch it; he doesn't ask."

"Why talk to him at all? You just said Paul was nobody's friend, why would you want to see him memorialized? It can't be that you're dying to see your name in print. I'd have thought you'd had enough of–" Suddenly, the shock of what McCail had told me less than two hours ago hit me again and I wanted to slap Michael, slap him hard–feel the sting in my palm as it hit his cheek. "Nineteen seventy-five? You and Paul really go back *that* far?"

"We go back that far." He got up from the couch and walked over to me, his face sad. "Twice, I tried to tell you. It was like a fucking ball of twine. If I could've found the place to start it would've . . . you made it tough, Grace. I did try. I should have tried harder. Knocked you down, put my hand over your mouth."

"Oh right. That was just your style, wasn't it? Coward."

"I was that for sure. Still am, maybe not the same ways. Why am I talking to little Gabriel? For the same reasons anyone talks to a biographer: to get my version on the record. I do have another reason. I want to keep that motherfucker occupied as long as I can with things that happened twenty, twenty-five years ago."

"Rather than eight years ago?"

"Rather than eight years ago," he repeated. "You're beautiful, you know?" he whispered, his voice cracking on the last word. Did he remember my saying exactly that to him almost a quarter century ago as we lay together in prickly summer-smelling grass? Sure he did.

"Don't you dare," I said. "Don't even start."

He took my hand, which still clutched the back of the flamingo chair, and led me around to the front of it. "Sit down, Grace, you look more exhausted than I feel. But if you want to hear what I've told McCail, and some things I haven't, it'll take a while." I sat and he returned to the couch. We were face to face on opposite sides of a low table, separated by ten feet and square miles of ambiguous feelings.

He said, "You probably know by now that Paul's father was killed with a bullet to the back of the head—hit, whacked, iced: all those colorful expressions that make mob lore it's own cute little piece of folk art. What you may not know is that Paul saw it happen, or says he did. Well, first time I met him he said that. Another time he told me he and his mother weren't home when the crew came. I tend to believe the first version, but it *is* Paul we're talking about here so who knows? Let me . . . let me go back.

"November of seventy-five is when I met him. I was thirteen, just turned. Life was pretty rocky in our house right then. My parents were getting ready to split, which they did right before that Christmas. Can you imagine their sexual superglue held for fifteen years? When I was a little kid I used to hear these growls from their bedroom and think they were fighting, about to tear each other up alive." He paused for a beat, halfway into a turn down a road neither of us wanted to be on. "Paul," he said firmly, back on course.

"One Friday night my daddy came home from the city—chancy thing those days whether he'd be home or not. Riverdale is where we lived: good white suburb, at least at that time it was; good white schools for the brown kid who had a mouth filled with acid rain and sense enough to keep it shut most of the time. Anyway, one Friday night his car pulled into the driveway and there in the front seat with him was this boy, this white-haired boy about a head shorter than me. I saw them from the window, saw his arm go around the boy's shoulder and, I'll tell you, for about a second and a half I was so damn jealous it hurt—*me* who ducked away any time he wanted to touch me.

"He brought the boy inside, along with a beat-up suitcase, and said, 'This is Paulie Donofrio.' And the kid looked up at him and said, 'Paul Boudreau. My name is Paul Boudreau'—said it in this voice way older than he was, said it like he and my daddy were equals, you know?"

This time I was the one who veered abruptly off course. "What I know is it makes me nuts when you—"

"When I say 'my daddy.' I know that. I used to take all kinds of care not to around you, but it is the way I think of him, at least when I'm talking about back-then times. Your father was George to you; mine was Daddy. For me it was just his name, doesn't mean I liked him. Funny, much as my mom got to hate him she always, *always* referred to him as 'your daddy.' These days I tend to call him Josh more often than not. But I'm gonna say what I say, and you're gonna have to deal with that if you still want to hear all this."

"Point taken. Sorry. I do want to hear all this."

"Well, back to nineteen-seventy-five then. The kid talking up that way tickled my daddy. He gave one of his big laughs and said, 'Yeah, Paul Boudreau. This is Paul Boudreau. Michael, you take him out back and shoot some baskets, he'll be with us for awhile.' By the way, Boudreau wasn't a made-up name. Like most of Paul's stuff there was some grain of fact. It came from generations back in his mother's family." He laughed. "Unless it didn't.

"I can see that first night so clearly. Paul and me standing half-faced away from each other in this phony mock-up of a big all-American backyard we had: wrought-iron benches, basketball hoop, apple trees and all. It was dark and chilly. After a while of nobody talking, he stepped around to where he could make eye contact—always such a thing with him, using those pale eyes. That night they caught the bit of light from the half moon like wolf eyes. He was the one who started to talk, of course.

" 'I've decided to be a writer,' he said, like I'd asked him.

" 'Really? I thought you might be holding out for President.' "

" 'I don't think so,' he said. 'I'd be Machiavelli's prince, if I could, but the President has too many rules. A writer can do and say whatever he wants as long as he can make people believe it. He can write philosophy or poetry or plays or movies. Anything. It's wide open. What about you? What're you going to be?'

"I'd never heard of Machiavelli or his prince and this kid damn well knew that. 'A fireman,' I said straight-faced and nasty, 'maybe a cop. Or maybe I'll decide to go into the family business and fuck people over.'

"He moved up close to me and said real quiet, 'I saw them shoot my father. I was reading in the garage, only no one knew that. I was supposed to be at school—we were in so-called witness protection up in Lake George—but school was boring, bunch of dumb kids memorizing things they didn't understand, so I cut out and sneaked back home to read. Two guys: one of them walked him out of the house and the other one shot him in the back of the head.' He pointed his finger and pantomimed firing. He told it like a story about other people: no emotion, just the plot. I said to him, 'I think you're just telling me something you read in your garage. Or maybe you're trying out some movie you want to write.'

"And he said, 'No, this is real. I'm telling you because you're the first person I can really tell—you know, around my age and who'd understand.' I made sure to keep my face in neutral—you know, not to be uncool, but I'd never felt more like a sheltered middle-class kid than I did at that moment. He assumed that being my father's son and all . . . hell, I'd only seen things like that on TV or in the movies. He told me that it had happened less than a month ago. October."

October. It hurt like hell, the way melodrama does when it happens to be true—a shard of it cuts through your skin and draws blood. I could have cried for the boy Paul. The details Michael was recounting differed somewhat from the ones that had made me weep the first time around (in that version the family's witness protection had been in the Colorado mountains; Paul had been asleep in his room, awakened by his father's terrified pleas.) but the gist was the same and I, like Michael, believed its essence. "October," I said and tried to swallow. It took a couple of tries.

"I'm sorry," he said, standing up. "I'm giving you pain, telling you more than you need to know."

"No, no. Stay put. I'm okay. Sit down and go on. Please. Where was Paul's mother? And how come Paul got taken up by Josh after his father was shot?"

He stretched his arms out and up and then gave his back a two-handed rub. "Mind if I pour myself a little more scotch?" I shrugged. "Want some?"

"No."

"I'm gonna sit down here on the floor," he said when he came back with a squat glass about a third full, no ice. "That's one bad-ass couch." He lowered himself on my side of the slatted table and rested his elbow on the bright new stack of floor cushions. "Paul's mother. As I understood it, she was in Vegas. I think she became a dealer. I've never laid eyes on the woman and Paul hardly ever mentioned her. Josh never did either, except once he did say that a hamster had better mothering than Paul did. I somehow got the idea that she may have dropped the dime on her husband, though I don't *know* that. As to how my daddy was involved, I don't have a real answer to that either. He always said he just took a shine to the boy, felt bad for him, wanted to help out."

"A natural benefactor, Josh. Okay, sorry. I can't seem to resist. Go on."

"Of course you're right, there must have been more. The late Jojo Donofrio ran a very small-time book somewhere in the Bronx; Josh made some collections for him; Donofrio went into witness protection owing him money. Look, I don't think he ordered the hit but I can't swear to that. I can tell you Paul didn't think so because I asked him once. I also asked him how come a wannabe Nietzschian *übermensch*, a Machiavellian prince like him had any use for a lowlife like Josh Pyatt. What he said was that he admired my father's brutal grandeur, which was just another way of saying that he admired power."

"Yeah."

"He told me how his father was scared shitless the whole time they were in witness protection—about a year I think."

"Sixteen months and two weeks the way I heard it."

"He said the man could hardly walk when they took him, that his knees were wobbling under him. He peed his pants."

My eyes shut for a moment and burned under their lids. They still did when I opened them. "It doesn't matter whether he saw it or just imagined it, does it?"

"No, hell either way. The thing was he also blamed his father on some level for being a coward, blamed him for caving to the Feebs in the first place. Easy to get sucked into what's brave, what's brutal—moral, not moral—whose hat's what color."

"Is that really what you think, Michael?"

"I don't know. Maybe. I can tell you that I remember Paul saying how *my* father would never turn, never, and I remember feeling proud of Josh. Now that little glow lasted about three seconds, but I did feel it. And I do know the color of my daddy's hat."

I hadn't been aware of Michael working on his drink until now when the last sip disappeared. He looked oddly at home there on the floor, this large man sitting with his legs folded Indian style, almost at my feet. "I have trouble with hat colors," I said. "Good thing I look better in black than white. So . . . you said Paul stayed with you through Christmas. What after that?"

Michael looked down into his empty glass and then up at me. "He left, went out West where his mother was. Right after Christmas my mom and I left too and went to her folks in Boston. If there'd been e-mail then Paul and I probably would've been on-line a lot. The way it was I'd sometimes get a book in the mail with a note telling me which passages, what pages. Machiavelli, Erasmus, Nietzsche—hooked me through the brain. He always knew the best bait to use on someone; he flattered the hell out of me."

He sprang up from the floor, agile as an athlete. "Can I get you a drink now? I'm going to have another. Yes it *is* a crutch, at least tonight. I'm coming to a couple of parts I didn't tell McCail. You might want a crutch too."

And what was the matter with using a crutch if it eased the pain of walking? "No," I said. "If it's going to hurt I'd rather feel it flat out. I can't even really say why."

"I know why," he almost smiled, the way you might if you were proud of someone very close to you, "because you're still out there in the windstorm." He went and poured himself more scotch and was back quickly, back down to his place on the floor a little farther away from me this time.

"In the split, as you know, Josh got me for summers and part of every summer Paul would fly east and come to Woodstock. That summer I met you, he'd left less than a week before you and George got there. I loved spending time with him, considered him my closest friend, yet the funny thing was we almost never, except for that first time when he told me about his father, talked about anything personal. It was like the big revelation got the blood brothers thing out of the way, cleared the decks for philosophy, ideas—the better stuff, not to mention safer. For all the Frenchiness he started to put on, I was the one who came up with Sartre. I was proud as a dumb peacock about that one: for ten minutes I knew more about existentialism than he did."

As he talked I could see the two boys sitting at the edge of the pond in their swimsuits, young, so young. The image was heart cracking. It must have been for Michael too, no matter what he said now about Paul being no one's friend. He took a long pull at the scotch and I wished I had some.

"Grace." The way he said my name marked an end to poignant pastel souvenirs. "Paul learned about you when he was sixteen. He learned about you from me."

I nodded automatically while I took it in. Creepy as it made me feel, it made sense: boy gets laid; tells good buddy all about it. But Michael was looking at me with eyes full of meaning I didn't quite get. "Spell it out for me, Michael. I'm the kind of person who needs it spelled out."

"After my mother persuaded me to drop you for your own good—" He shook his head. "No, that's not fair. I let myself listen to my own fears and doubts about getting mixed up in a bad situation: your father, my father . . . 'coward' you said tonight. Anyway, I was not in good shape after that and suddenly, big surprise, Paul turns up in Boston. He hadn't mentioned it when I saw him that past August, but here he is in October living in my city as what they call an emancipated minor—he'd made himself a grubstake in the stock market, had his mother making trades for him since he was fourteen; never said a word about it to me."

"If it was true," I muttered.

"There's that. But however he got to Boston I was so glad to see him I almost kissed his white wolf face. I wanted to talk and talk and talk—and not about anything in any book; I wanted to talk about you, and as I got going Paul listened harder; you could almost see his ears perk up."

"Please—"

"No, they didn't perk up at sex talk. In fact he kind of passed that off with that little indulgent smile and said, 'I'll give you some Dante to read, lovesick swain. He had his Grace too, only her name was Beatrice.' What Paul was hot to hear about was George: George reminded him of his father. 'A certain kind of little fish who always gets caught,' was the way he put it. Am I telling you I'm sorry every other sentence, or do I just think I'm saying it? I *am* sorry."

This time I got up—not to get a drink but out of a need to move, to know I could walk away. "I knew he'd picked me out. Toward the end I even kind of knew it had to do with George and his father—but I hate this anyway. I *hate* it." I stumbled over a hassock and felt suddenly that even my own legs weren't under my control. Michael was quickly at my side, his arm around me, hand clasping my upper arm the way a doctor might help a wobbly post-op patient—a doctor with scotch on his warm breath. I jerked myself away from him hard. "*Why?* Why did you stand by and let me marry him? How could you if you—never mind the if. How could you let me walk into that?"

"As usual," he said, "I wasn't there. That's me, the amazing vanishing man. I was hacking around Europe—those damn aimless asshole years. I had no clue about you and Paul. He and I were out of touch. We'd had a big blowup right before I left. Money. This should ring a bell for you, he stole two thousand dollars from me. He said borrowed but he stole it, forged my name on a check. I only caught on when he was putting it back in my account. But that's not the point: I'd've *given* him the damn money—it was my daddy's anyway—but he lied to me and stole it.

"I was back in the States a little over a week when I walked into that setup at the museum. And it was my daddy along with Paul who pulled it off. He was the one who told me Paul was living in New York, big success as a money manager, newly married to a real nice girl—and here's his number, son, give him a call. You know, I never even brought it up to Josh afterward, never asked him why he fucked me that way. Fact is, once I thought about it, I knew. Revenge is part of his DNA. He wanted to teach me a lesson, punish me for cutting him off, which I did—must've called him four times in ten years. I wish he'd decided to just let me have it straight in the face with that big fist instead."

I was leaning against the wall for support as I listened. Every last bit of strength was gone. Briefly, as I'd charged out of Craig's loft for Washington Heights, juiced with outrage, I'd felt righteously powerful. Every ounce of that was gone. Michael had raised the red velvet curtain, given me a glimpse of the pulleys and strings inside the puppet theater where I'd been an unwitting performer. It was worse than a cracked-open kaleidoscope, much worse. "Pour me some of my scotch," I said. "You can't not know what you know, but you can wish you didn't know it."

He took my arm now, just my arm this time. I glanced down at the brown hand, large even for someone his size, and felt the warmth of it through the white silk of my sleeve. George was far from my mind, I realized—Paul was too. Front and center was a pair of seventeen-year-olds who for a few days had taken a manic delight in each other, unaware that they stood not a chance in hell of having a forever after together.

CHAPTER TWENTY-THREE

awoke to a sweet throbbing in my crotch and a wicked throbbing in my
head. My mouth felt as though ashes had been rubbed inside it. The
last impression on my brain had been of Michael walking me into the
bedroom, his hands slipping off my shoes, guiding me onto the bed. I
thought I remembered his voice saying love words very softly in my ear.
Had we? Then I checked under the covers. Except for the shoes, all my
clothes were in place: black pants and white silk shirt, bra and pantyhose
underneath them.

My hand went between my legs and extended what was left of my first
wet dream in a very long time. When I turned my head my cheek brushed
a piece of paper—a note: *You said your weren't going to let this go. I don't want
to let you go. Not this time. Far as alcohol or weed, you're a cheap date. Always
were. I'll call you at Sheilah's office later.*" He'd scribbled his cell number, an
afterthought, across the bottom corner.

Michael's words in my hand made me smile. Then without warning
tears began to flow—no sobs, just the tears, streams of them flowing sideways into my hair and ears as I lay there stuck in a traffic jam of feelings.
The clock beside me said seven-nineteen: time to get up and go to work,

so I did. I drank a lot of orange juice, swallowed a couple of aspirin, took a long shower and felt better than I had any reason to. The good spirits began to cave when I thought of Craig. I knew I could manage facing him, thanks to some useful human relations training in the Bedford Hills boot camp, where you could no way count on avoiding people you didn't care to see.

Good morning, Craig. Good morning, Grace. He would go into his office and shut the door. I would sit at my desk and begin the day's scheduling. Whatever emotion threatened to flood me, I'd swallow it whole and hope it stayed down. Actually, my work was about caught up which, when I thought about it, might not be such a good thing for my longer-term prospects there, especially if Teresa Woo left. Maybe Cynthia needed a hand with some of her bookkeeping or bill paying or—hell, I didn't care, I'd vacuum the damned carpets to earn my paycheck.

Sheilah and I bumped into each other in the lobby at ten of nine. She pulled a wheelie suitcase behind her, prepared to leave that evening for a recruiting trip to London. Her face stiffened at the sight of me. "Sheil, I'm sorry about cutting out like that. You give great party, you really do. Danton did tell you I was leaving, right? I just . . . after the thing with Marina, I couldn't hack it and I didn't want to rain on your parade."

"I understand." That may have been true, but it didn't mean she forgave. Silently we walked to the elevators.

"Are you very pissed with me?" I asked.

"Should I be?"

Shit. "Well maybe you should. Look, I suppose I could've insisted that Marina get her ass out of there. I guess I was just too bullheaded to let her think I was . . ." Something kept me from saying the word scared. ". . . rattled."

"I guess so too. *I* wanted her to leave."

"I'm sorry. I really am." A low-level ache behind my eyes reminded me I'd had too much alcohol and too little sleep. Sheilah was looking at me speculatively. I glanced up at the digital display: both elevators were on a twenty-something floor. I wished some other suits and briefcases would arrive and move in close to us, but we were alone. "What did you think of Todd?" she asked. The question was neutral but the jut of her chin as she asked it was not.

"He's attractive," I said carefully.

"Well, that's pretty lukewarm. Your friend Jan wasn't lukewarm though." *Uh oh.* "Every time I turned around to do hostess things there they were, heads together, nose to nose practically. Even my mother noticed." *I'll just bet she did.* "Grace, I know you can't stand my mother but she's not unperceptive."

Only when Sheilah felt all other roads were dead-ended did she align herself with her mother, but I would have had to be more nuts than I was to put my foot in. I had nothing constructive to say, not even that I liked the man. "Come on, Sheilah, from the little I heard he was talking about his tastes in art." This was tap dancing and maybe Sheilah knew it. Todd had been flirting with Jan and she'd been flirting back. Finally the elevator arrived.

Its doors opened and we got in; it was just the two of us. Something about an elevator's confines either promotes or discourages eye contact. Sheilah and I made it. "Is that what's really bothering you?" I asked. "Todd?"

Her eyes glistened with hurt, anger and blame about to turn liquid. She had been betrayed not once but thrice: by Teresa Woo who was about to bail on her, by Todd Berenstain whose eye had wandered, by me who had put my agenda with Marina ahead of the social welfare of her party. In all three cases she had put out to the max, done it all with care and flair, but the payoffs hadn't come—not the ones she'd had in mind. She'd done her part; we had not done ours.

We were thinking the same thoughts. "I try so . . . it's not worth it!" she snapped, her mouth close enough to my nose for me to smell the coffee on her breath. I wanted to say, "Rest on your oars a little—don't always try so hard," but she would have taken that as a slap at her. The elevator door opened on our floor and she raced down the corridor.

Cynthia, at her desk, looked up at me. "She's, uh, really upset, Grace."

"I know. We came up in the elevator together. I may be part of what she's upset about."

"I think it's really the Teresa thing that's getting her. She was hoping so much it was going to work out."

"And you think that it's definitely over?"

"Who knows? They're both away these next few days. Maybe . . . maybe Teresa will see things another way. She can make a lot of money here. It's a matter of her ego. And Sheilah's Sheilah. That's how it is."

"Yeah. Cynthia, by this afternoon I'll have some . . . free time. Got anything you need a hand with?"

She took a beat before saying, "Let me go over some things. Maybe."

"Good." I moved toward the connecting door and couldn't resist asking, "Craig? Is he coming in today?"

"He's at his desk."

The door to his office was closed; I could see the thin outline of light from inside, hear indistinct phone sounds. My suit jacket was draped on the back of my chair, the square of brushed gold and steel pinned to its shoulder. The sight of it brought back last night's scene in his loft: McCail stepping out from behind the half-wall of the bedroom. I took kind of a long time rolling the jacket just so into the smallest possible cylinder.

Good morning, Craig. Good morning, Grace. The neat roll of jacket disappeared into the bottom of my bag. I checked my phone and screen messages, then I punched up gracieido.com as I did morning, evening and sometimes in between. It had gotten to be a kind of tic. I'd been out of prison for more than a month now. If George was alive, he'd know how to contact me easily. He wouldn't even have to track me down on e-mail; he could call Sheilah for a start, if he didn't for some reason still sense danger, even though Josh was already convicted and locked up—he could if he wanted to. That was what Michael had said: if he wanted to. My mailbox displayed the usual junk. I closed it, spread out my note pads and dialed Amex Platinum Travel.

When I went out for a bite at two, Craig had still not emerged from his office, nor had Michael called. By the time I returned at three-fifteen, the door to Craig's office looked dark around the edges and I heard no sound from behind it. Cynthia had given me a few message slips but none of them was from Michael, nothing on my voice mail either. I was wondering what make-work project to dream up when Sheilah came through the connecting door.

"I've got car service waiting downstairs," she said. "I'll be in touch when I get there."

"And I'll e-mail if anything comes up." We took a beat, both kind of mulling. I took the first step and she met me halfway. We hugged tight. I would have said something loving but my mind stalled about what it could be. Instead I raised my fist in the We Shall Prevail gesture we'd used on and off since we were kids. She raised hers in answer and left quickly.

I went back on-line and answered a couple of new notes confirming candidate appointments and travel arrangements. Then, because I had nothing in the way of work to do, I clicked once more into AOL and looked at the screen name in front of me for a while: gracieido. Sentimental kid thing, that name, I thought absentmindedly. I was too old for . . .

The mindless finger action came close to erasing the single new message from allenbirn@hotmail.com. I stared at the blue-highlighted line, then at my rigid index finger inches above the mouse, fighting a crazy urge to click on "Delete" rather than on "Open." Allenbirn: I'd moused around the Internet trying combinations of Burns and Allen and George and Gracie and so on, but not this one. I remembered now that Burns's real name had been Birnbaum, spelled, I thought, with an i. A laugh seemed to echo in my head. Paul's mocking ghost?

My finger began to tremble and came down hard on "Open." The message read, *"Cross my heart it's true. Do you believe me?"* I replied the automatic, *"I do"* and rode a wave of sudden nausea because it wasn't true: I had no reason to believe him—presuming it *was* him. I believed it was, though my track record for accurate beliefs left much to be desired. Could Paul—even Paul—have worked out this elaborate a posthumous scam? I tried to remember how much George and Gracie shtick we were doing in the Paul years. Not much, I thought, but I couldn't swear he'd never heard us play with the little patter song.

I allowed no time for internal debate before typing an additional reply: *"I'm trying to stay zipped up inside the Now, but I can see the smoke's pretty thick ahead."*

I waited, summoning him up in my head, visualizing his stubby, agile fingers working a keyboard, trying to force an answer by the sheer power of my concentrated desire. It did not happen.

At a little past four the phone rang, delivering Michael.

"You holding up?" he asked.

"As long as I don't look down." But I *was* looking down—at my AOL screen, which as I spoke displayed a new message from allenbirn. My heart raced. *"Remember to just keep the tuchis in motion."* Oh joy, oh rapture! That was George talking our private language. Was this the way a mother felt when her toddler spoke its first real words? Michael heard my gasp.

"Sure you're okay?"

"Oh yeah. I . . . I'm *good.*" I was dying to shout out the reason into the mouthpiece but caution prevailed.

"I get off at five," he said, "which means six if I'm lucky. Any possibility of seeing you?"

"Yes." The word crackled with pent-up emotion, part of it legitimately about him.

"Excellent."

"Look, this time let's not talk about Paul—or about . . . anybody's father. Last night was amazing for me—not so much surprising but amazing. I guess I'm saying . . ." I found my mouth going dry; my hand gripping the phone was damp. "I really haven't got a clue who you are."

"I know who *you* are."

"Who? A white-haired woman who hangs out in the wind like a tattered flag?"

"You're Grace," he said quietly. "Look, how about I pick up some real food, good bottle of wine and come over to your place?"

My hand squeezed the phone hard. "No."

"No?"

"You put me to bed last night—took my shoes off and tucked me in. Tonight, if you came over I'd open the door and we would be in bed before you got to put the food bags down. I'm not ready for that. No, I'll say the truth: I'm *too* ready and I—"

"You don't need to explain. Countersuggestion?"

"Maybe an early dinner somewhere we can just talk."

"Old friends having a reunion?" he asked ironically. "We're that too."

We settled on a place around the corner from me on Amsterdam. The second I hung up I typed an answer: *"I try to keep the tuchis moving and the mind quiet. It doesn't always work. I went to Lincoln Center to hear Traviata my first night out. Do you get to hear opera where you are? Will you tell me where that is? Are you okay?"*

There was much more I wanted to say, but the thoughts were a cement block in my head. At the moment I couldn't hack one from another and didn't want to take the time to try. Eagerness to hold onto the give and take, to keep it going, was way stronger. Just as I pressed "Send" the phone rang.

The caller was Gabriel McCail. I couldn't even call it an unpleasant surprise: it was no surprise at all. In fact, had he not called me I'd have called him, if not today then fairly soon. Michael's strategy of manipulating the reporter with selected tidbits made sense. Now that George and I were in contact it made more sense.

"I'm sorry about what happened," he said, sounding boyish.

"I'm sure you are," I said through a grin. "Black eye? Not a tooth knocked out, I hope."

"Just a fat lip. Occupational hazard, I could say."

"You could say."

"But it wouldn't be the whole story. And I go for the whole story."

"Oh yes, you told me that the first time we met."

"Grace, Craig didn't know." He said it slowly, one word at a time. I didn't respond. "I swear on my—"

"Your what? Journalistic integrity? Reputation?" Perhaps he was speaking true about Craig, but it didn't touch me as much as it should have. The damage was done: Craig's and my friendship was too new, too fragile to survive distrust. You can glue a broken cup back together again if you want to enough. What you can't do is fail to see the cracks—or be confident that the cup will hold water. "Can we get off this and cut to the chase, Gabriel? I think I'd like to talk to you." My clammy palms let me know I was nervous: George was somewhere to be found and I didn't want him found by Gabriel McCail. "Not on the phone. Maybe we can get together later in the week."

I'd taken him by surprise, which was satisfying. It was a moment before he said, "Fine. Tonight?"

"No, I can't tonight. Tomorrow would be good—time and place up to you."

He laughed merrily. "Outstanding! I'd ask you to my place, but it's . . . small. How about Marina's house at seven tomorrow? She's letting me use her library for interviews."

"I'll be there."

No quick answer from George on my screen. And there still wasn't one an hour later when I was ready to leave. I hoped my questions hadn't given him second thoughts—or was that hope merely a bounce-back of my own Paul-spooked doubts? I sent one more message. *"One more thing. Would you tell me what you remember about the kitchen where we were that last time in Miami?"*

When an answer didn't come in ten minutes, I closed down my computer for the night. I was already half out the door when something pulled me back to my desk and made me reboot, download both ends of the George correspondence onto a floppy to file on my laptop at home, and then delete all traces of it. Paranoid fallout? Maybe. Then again—I glanced at the door to Craig's darkened office.

CHAPTER TWENTY-FOUR

sat at the far end of the small, darkish bar playing with a glass of seltzer with lime in it, waiting for Michael. He wasn't late; I was a little early. I'd gotten the idea that I wanted to watch him walk in just to have a fresh first glance at him, a first glance not refracted through regret or anger or need—if such a view was remotely possible.

There he came through the door, wearing what he'd worn yesterday, jeans and a beat-up brown leather bomber jacket with some blue shirt visible at the neck. He was what you'd have to call a hunk—a hunk with a lope. The several other women who turned to look at him silently agreed. His skin was the same matte mahogany it had always been, but in that moment, having nothing to do with shades in a palette, he looked blacker.

"Hey." He clapped both his hands over mine. "Am I late?"

"No, I'm early."

He parked his butt on the adjacent stool. The position strained the seat of his jeans very nicely. He gestured at my glass. "Vodka?"

"Seltzer."

"Should we get a table?" The bar was beginning to crowd up with after-work drinkers, most of them not ready to sit down and eat yet. I wasn't hungry either but somehow I felt tongue-tied, empty of anything to say—absurdly like a shy girl on a first date.

"Let's stay at the bar awhile. It's . . . comfortable." More comfortable than sitting eye-to-eye across a table making small talk because the bigger talk was stuck somewhere down inside you—jagged chunks of it that were painful to say and painful to hear.

He shrugged and asked the bartender if Sam Adams was on tap. It wasn't, so he settled for a bottle. When it arrived he tipped it up and took a pull. It was the way he'd always drunk beer—made you thirsty to have some, even if you didn't care for beer.

I looked away from him, into my glass. "Where were you, Michael, all the years? Where did you go?"

"Away. That's my pattern, right? I left the country the day after the cops turned me loose. I went a lot of places. I was in Ivory Coast when I heard about your shooting Paul."

"The news didn't send you flying back to New York."

"Would you believe me if I told you I'd have been on the first plane back if I could've?"

"To sit with me in the courtroom while I pleaded guilty? To drive me up to Bedford Hills when I surrendered myself? Sure, I'll believe anything, Michael. You know that about me."

His face had a desolate look to it, the kind of caught and hopeless expression he'd had the first time I'd confronted him at the hospital. That time he'd said that neither of us had a chance unless we were rid of *this*. He reached for my hand. "No, don't pull away, I want to say something and I'll be able to say it better if I can hold onto you—at least your hand. Okay?"

"Yes." I felt my hand close on his in return.

"There was nothing in the world I wanted eight years ago as much as I wanted to come and be with you. Doing that would have helped me but it would have hurt you—hurt you bad in ways you don't know about. If you believe nothing else out of my mouth, believe that." His hand grabbed mine tighter. "You must've figured out by now that I was involved in helping George cut and run. I played a bit part and there were strings attached to my doing it—strings that tied me up in ways I hated, and still hate. What I told you last time was true: barring natural causes he should be safe and alive. Somewhere. That's all I know about your father."

His grip on my hand eased up, but mine on his stayed firm. "I said on the phone this afternoon that I wanted tonight to be about us, not about Paul or anyone's father. I don't have a clue in hell, any more than you do, if that's possible. Maybe . . . maybe we should just let things be what they are." My eyes were trained so intently on his face I felt like I could see blood in turmoil underneath the skin. He looked ready to speak but instead just nodded. "We're not just old friends having a reunion," I said, "let's go to my place after all."

Sex is like water; it goes where it wants. Ten minutes later I was turning the key in the lock of my apartment. And then, hardly inside the door, coat still on, I checked out. Someplace in my brain I was dimly aware of a tall woman frozen in place in a traveling dancer's living room, unable to make her legs move her from here to there.

It took Michael a moment to realize that I'd left the scene, was no longer with him. He walked back to where I was standing and cupped my face in both his hands as though it were an object fragile and valuable—a Ming vase. "Grace?" he asked softly.

"I dunno, dunno . . . I never had sex with Paul again after George . . . I mean, at first I was furious. I could've killed him right then because he'd taken my father away—*mine*—and cut me out of the whole thing, and then mind-fucked with one version, then another and . . . I got sick; I mean body sick. That took everything away. I had no will left, no anything—not even my anger. After I got out of the hospital, for a few weeks he fed me soup, spoon by spoon. He cooked it and he put it in my mouth and I let him. He stroked my head, rubbed my feet and I let him do those things. I was like this big dying, beloved dog he was tending. But we never made love any more—we never fucked either."

All of this had rushed out of me in a whoosh of words so thick you could almost see the fused mess of it fall to the floor, too heavy for the air that carried it. All the while Michael's hands stayed where they were, framing my cheeks like a warm poultice.

"Grace, Grace, you don't need to–"

"I do. I *do* need to. I need to let you know how it is, so listen. You know what seven years in prison's like? It's like nothing–I mean *nothing:* a void. It has to be that way or you couldn't stand it. So you do it day by day, thousands of blank days, with a little laugh here, a little anger there, but mostly nothing. And either you touch someone and someone touches you–man, woman; guard, inmate, doesn't matter–or that doesn't happen and you are untouched; not to *be* touched. Hell, I didn't even dare touch myself because I . . . I don't *know* why . . ." I was panting now like someone running too fast and my face was cool with sweat. One of Michael's hands moved from my cheek to my mouth where the palm rested warm and dry against my lips.

"Can I help you take off your coat?" I nodded. He helped me gently, so gently out of one sleeve at a time. "Good." He held my hand now. "If you want me to leave now I will leave." I didn't move; I wasn't aware of breathing. "That's a hard offer to make, and mean," he said. "But I do mean it. Would it be better for you if I went?"

Such warm hands. I looked at him. He was not Michael–well, except for the souvenir of his mouth–but he was no stranger either. The face I saw, its broad hard angles of jaw and chin, its forehead showing hash marks of a stubborn will and some hard miles of its own, made my eyes blur with a kind of pleasure-pain. My hand had been inert in his. Now my fingers squeezed back hard. "Maybe it would be better for you to go, but I'll bar the door with my body if you try."

Time passed, I don't have a clue how much of it. I remember every second of clothing pulled off, dropping to the floor in clumps. I remember the melting look on his face and the wetness I felt on mine–tears or sweat or both, who knows? I remember anticipating the heat of him before I was close enough to feel it. And I remember a hot-wired jolt from his mouth on my bare breast. After that there was nothing distinct to remember. Nothing was separate from anything else, no consciousness of *he did* or *I did;* no technique, no moves. Nerve endings rang, openings were filled, tentacles reached for what they needed—pure sensation: hot, moist color, whirling fast, spinning us into a jelly.

Then we slept, my head resting on Michael's chest: I'd wake up intermittently and feel his sleep-breathing, deep and regular in my ear. We understood each other easily and precisely. What a shame, I thought groggily, to ever have to bother communicating through the mess of talk.

The bedside clock read two-twenty. I heard him groan and propped my head up on my hand. "Hi."

"Hi." He reached up a paw and ran it lightly down my face. "Hungry? We never did eat."

My stomach responded with a small growl. "Should we get up?" I asked reluctantly.

"No, stay. I'll see what there is and bring it back here. Eating in bed at two in the morning, what could beat that?"

"You're kidding? We just *did* beat that by miles." I licked his neck and gave it a light bite where it met his shoulder. "How about I eat that?"

His head ducked under the covers and between my legs. "How about I eat *that?*"

"Oohh, no fair. I could die so happy right this second."

He surfaced and got out of bed. His naked body was a Goddamned treat, the muscles firm but not aggressive, enough beef to make things comfortable. "Me too," he said and I could see the real world creeping back into his mind, which meant it had begun working its way back into mine too, and would arrive momentarily like a slightly late train. Dying happy this second would be a slam dunk. Living with what came next would not be.

He turned toward the door and started for the kitchen. "You are some piece of ass, Doctor," I called after him. The train was chugging into view and I wished I could stop it coming.

My eyes closed. Unexpectedly, what I saw behind them was my old studio—my first one, the one where I worked before the business grew to where I needed a team of assistants and the space to house them. And I felt that singular ping of joy that came with the precise tap of my jewelers hammer on a piece of silver. Tonight that recalled joy swirled like rich cream into the blessed aftershocks of sex.

Michael marched back into the bedroom with a green metal tray he'd found somewhere in the kitchen, on it a jar of peanut butter, one of raspberry jam, a stack of Pepperidge bread, a knife, a quart of milk and a single glass. He carried the tray high, his naked body all the more elegant in its darkness. "Her Nubian slave presents Cleopatra's picnic," he said.

"Cleopatra accepts with great pleasure."

He handed me the tray while he got back under the covers beside me. I placed it carefully across our thighs. We fell on the food like wolves. He poured milk for me into the glass while he drank his straight out of the carton, head thrown back, the same way he downed beer.

"You haven't touched your milk," he said, his mouth glistening with white drips.

"Don't like milk. You always loved it. I remember that. Think it's because you had a mother you adored and I had no mother at all?"

"Nah. I don't go for that kind of Psych one-oh-one. I think you just don't like milk." He lifted the tray off us, put it on the floor and gave my neck a lingering wet kiss that made me growl. "Here's some better milk, happy cat. You are golden, you know? I never noticed it as much as now; maybe it's the light hair, but your skin is pale gold. You used to say your mother was an Indian. And I'd think, yeah, right, and I'd picture George holing up in some Arizona reservation. But in India I saw women who reminded me a little of you."

"India?"

"Yeah, I was in Calcutta five months—and Afghanistan, the Palestinian refugee camps. Docs Without Borders, I did that for two years after med school. The kids, they got to me. A lot of loss, the kind that cracks you right in the heart. But sometimes you win. And those times are worth everything. I lived for them. Still do."

I sat myself up against the headboard, covers drawn high, chaste. I smelled the familiar-unfamiliar salty after-whiff of sex. And I could also smell the separate smell that was Michael: clean sweat, a little like sawn wood but sharper. "Blows me away, that you've done that. Awe might not be too strong a word," I said and meant. "You never said you wanted to be a doctor."

"That's because I never thought about it. I worked at the Strand Book Store. Remember?"

"I remember. And you dated every Scandinavian blonde in lower Manhattan."

"You used to call them the Utes and the Ullas."

"You mentioned the other night that your mother was a doctor's daughter. Maybe that's why you landed in med school"

"Nah. If you're thinking I had fond memories of going to grandpa's office, forget it. After my parents split we moved to Boston because that's near where my mom was from—Milton, specifically. But it never really worked with her family. She couldn't really forgive them for cutting her off and they couldn't forgive her for marrying Josh—and with me in the picture they couldn't even pretend it never happened." He crossed his hands behind his head, making a nest for it, and looked up at the ceiling. "How come I'm a doctor? Chance . . . and a few other things. Remember how we used to joke about a career for me? Well, a black criminal's son who came damned close to being indicted himself doesn't have a lot of options open to him—especially when he's thirty-two and has no sense of rhythm. Seriously, as I said when we were in the bar, after they turned me loose, all I wanted to do was get the hell away—far away."

"I do know what it's like being in custody," I said. "But then again, I did the crime."

"Look, I'm not saying what I went through compares to what you went through. It doesn't, but it was a bad time for me after George left. I thought I knew what I was letting myself in for, but I was such a dumb fuck, such a baby, I didn't know jack shit. See, some way I had the idea I was invulnerable—not *übermensch* garbage like Paul's Nietzsche riffs, more like nobody could really *do* anything to me because I hadn't really *done* anything. And I had an alibi all in place to prove that, a good lawyer. After all, this is *America*. Naïve as it sounds from my daddy's son I did not fear law enforcement.

"But here's the thing, I wasn't who I thought I was. In my deluded head, I was a white guy who happened to be brown—lived in white neighborhoods, attended white schools, had white friends, white lovers; read the same books, laughed at the same jokes, looked down on the same people. Shit, I never even saw Harlem till I was sixteen or so and then only a few times Josh took me there like some tour guide; that was *his* place and one thing my battling parents saw eye to eye on was keeping me clear of it.

"However . . . how*ever*, when the cops and the Fibbies got hold of me, none of it was about my accent or my clothes or my college degree. I was a nigger: a badass nigger son of a badass nigger daddy. 'What do you call a nigger with an alibi?' one of them asked his partner. 'Burned toast,' the other one said. I guess it was a routine they did—scared me shitless. But you know what? They were right, right enough to jump-start my brain: wake-up call."

"They weren't right, Michael. Don't give me that bullshit. They *weren't* right—any more than the Nazis were right when they gave the Jews a wake-up call."

"You're looking through the wrong end of the telescope. We know what we think about racist cops and Nazis, that's an easy one. You want to draw a parallel try this one: the assimilated Jew who imagines he can trade his willingness to blend in for a different set of roots is in for the same kick-ass surprise as an assimilated black who pretends his skin color is the result of some kind of random accident with a paint can."

"No! That kind of bullshit thinking gives them the high ground; it lets them win. You can't just lock people into some artificial—"

"Not artificial—*essential*."

"—category because racists want it that way and, hey, they'll put you into it anyway, so why bother. That is dumb and cowardly and—"

"Sssshhhh." He was up on his elbow now, and leaned over to kiss me lightly on the mouth. "We're not going to end this debate tonight–or probably ever. Probably good to have it though–to keep having it."

I stroked his cheek, which was beginning to get sandpapery with needing a shave. "You put yourself through all that abuse for George. You never even liked George."

His eyes slewed over to meet mine. He didn't answer that; didn't need to. What he'd done–whatever exactly that was–he'd done for me. *Thank you? Do I say thank you for daring a reckless act that may have saved my father's life, while wrecking mine and ending Paul's?* "Tell me," I said. "Tell me what happened after the cops let you go."

"I was out of here like a bat out of whatever bat hell is. I knew what I wanted–oh yeah: I wanted to live on an island, water all around and no white faces in sight. I wanted grass and girls, weed and women; some books, some CDs and no stress. Grenada's where I went."

"Grenada? Isn't that where Reagan did some stuff back in the eighties?"

"The very same. In 1983 Marxist rebels grabbed control and Ronald Reagan sent Marines in to squash it. You could see that as a valiant intervention by the guys in the white hats or, alternatively, as a hippo sitting its ass on a caterpillar in someone else's garden. I was not a political animal in 1983, and I'm not really now, but I knew it was a tiny black island democracy. Good enough for me, especially since I'd heard cannabis was a key crop. It also has a medical school where a good many of the students are Americans who couldn't get in back home. But some of them are islanders, and one of those I kind of owe my life to. She was the one who pushed and prodded me into applying." *Of course a she; it would be a she.* "I'd started hanging with her–by the way, only the second, no third, black woman I'd ever been with. She was sharp and pretty, and she had a certain focused energy that could pull a lot of dead weight, kind of like an expert lifeguard. God knows what she saw in me. I was a sorry mess, high half the time, almost catatonic the rest."

She saw in you what I saw in you at seventeen, see in you now, as much as you've changed: body and soul–and there is that mouth. You are a sexy beast, Michael. "Maybe lifeguards like rescue missions; that's why they're lifeguards," I said half sourly.

"Anyway," he said, "she, Cecily, got the idea that med school would give me what she used to call 'a central organizing principle.' At first, I blew it off. You know, 'Right, weed fiend doc who came this close to being in jail. Want me for your physician?' But she'd come back with, 'Maybe, if I didn't have a better choice.' After a while, it began to get to me. I was on the edge of going nuts doing nothing except thinking and grieving when I wasn't fucking and smoking. So . . . I did apply. I cut way back on all four of my previous pastimes and for four years I was like an object caught in a wind tunnel: just me and the work in there. At the end of it, out came Michael Pyatt, M.D." I heard the pride, and he was well entitled to it. However, I was not entitled to what I was suddenly feeling.

We were sitting upright, side by side in the bed now, none of his skin touching any of mine. "Congratulations," I said, meaning it, but something in my tone drew his questioning glance. "Sorry. It's hard not to be jealous."

"Of Cecily? That's long over. We–"

"No, asshole, not of Cecily, of the *work*. You're doing work you love. I used to do work I loved."

"Jesus, Grace, I'm the one that's sorry for being such a clod. But you'll design again; you'll get back to it. You're not going to be Sheilah's secretary forever. That's just a–"

"I'm not her secretary–unfortunately. If I was, my job would be way more secure than it is." I gave a poor excuse for a laugh. "And you sound just like her, about my designing again. The fact is I won't make jewelry because I can't. You're a doctor. Haven't you noticed how unsteady my hands get?"

"Yes," he said quietly. "Little tremor sometimes, not all the time."

"Enough to put a jeweler out of commission. It started soon after I got to Bedford Hills. I'd drop things. I was doing pretty well keeping my mind in neutral, only to be skunked by my damned hands."

I let out a long breath, pushed the covers aside and moved to get out of bed. He caught hold of my arm. "Grace, no. Don't go. Please don't go.

I know how you felt about your work and I remember how I used to envy you that feeling. Let's just say I didn't think."

"Not your fault, Michael. Ah, look, maybe there's just too much shit between us. Maybe . . . I'm not who I was. I did the irrevocable thing." The words, raw melodrama except for their truth, blasted out of me unexpectedly and scorched the air. I winced as though the smoke were in my face.

"What you did was as much my fault as yours."

"No it wasn't. And it's not something you get to be gallant about because you're feeling gallant toward a woman in bed. I did that thing. *I* did." I was half off the bed, one leg kneeling the other outstretched, toes on the floor. His hand still held my arm. My bare skin felt cold and I wondered what the hell I thought I was doing here.

"You're not 'a woman in bed,' you're Grace. Come on, stay beside me here," he said. "Please. Please?" He let go of my arm and I got back under the covers where I wanted to be.

"You're living with someone, Michael. Right?"

"Right."

"Not Cecily from Grenada?"

"No, I told you that was over. Cecily's back there doing family medicine. We e-mail."

"So, is she black, the one who isn't Cecily?"

A slightly curly smile: "Brown."

"If you think I give a flying fuck whether you're in love with her you're . . . damn, I don't know whether I do or not."

He whispered "no" close enough to my ear that I felt his breath and shuddered with the pleasure of it. I rolled over on top of him and we were off again, speaking a better language.

"I'm not back on shift till noon so just let me . . ." was the last thing I heard him say before he lapsed into heavy, rhythmic breathing, an almost snore: he was dead out, hand resting lightly on my breast.

It is an intimate thing to watch someone asleep. Michael's face, mouth slightly open, looked younger than it did awake. Even so, it was anything but the unfinished face of a boy. I craned my neck around to where my tongue could touch that lower lip. I licked it lightly, very lightly so as not to wake him. It tasted of peanut butter and milk.

A quarter of eight: I hadn't gotten much sleep but I'd woken up with no need of an alarm, not in the least tired. I looked over at Michael, face down now, head turned away from me, and touched the nape of his neck. Happy does not begin to describe how I felt about his being there. On the way into the bathroom I'd caught a glimpse of myself in the mirror and was surprised to see cropped white hair with a crazy black streak rivering through it; surprised to see my own hash marks. I grinned at the face Michael had called golden. *Look who's here: a woman who got laid for the first time in eight years. Hey, Pocahontas's mother, can Pocahontas come out to play? Yes!* My cunt throbbed, skin tingled in memory: it seemed a shame to shower any of that off. I soaped up carefully, one last whiff before it washed down the drain.

The buzzer rang from downstairs just as I got out of the shower. I reached for the towel with a trembling hand and pulled it around my head tentlike, letting it hang free, as though I could hide from the intrusion. It blatted again, the finger pushing at the bell with more insistence: *You'd better be up there.* Before I let the towel drop to the floor, I used it to scrub at my eyes, which were spilling impotent rage. I pulled on my long sweatshirt and ran to grab the intercom phone before the damned thing rang again. I held it to my ear knowing whose voice I'd hear. I wasn't wrong.

"Yes, okay, Patty Ann," I said, "fourth floor."

CHAPTER TWENTY-FIVE

"**N**ice place," she said, glancing around from a vantage point maybe three feet into the apartment. She stood there looking like a visiting nurse in her usual navy blue, holding a furled blue umbrella, which appeared bone dry. "I was out on Tuesday, sorry. I was . . . I had a twenty-four-hour flu." She'd been out several Tuesdays, as we both knew.

"I hope you're feeling better," I said carefully, wishing I'd drawn a PO who seemed better suited to the job—street smart, tough but easy, seen-it-all smile, maybe a little tattoo or . . . what I really wished was to have no PO at all, but that prospect was seven years into the future: in other words, a view so far away as to be invisible to the naked eye. "Look, I'm going to have to hustle or I'll be late for work."

"Well I do, you know, have the *right* to make this home visit. In fact I should've gotten to it before now, but my case load . . ." She walked into the center of the room. Something seemed wrong with her left leg, causing her to favor it, a not so slight limp. She brushed her wispy hair back with her hand. The thin gold wedding band was still in place. *Leave him for Christ's sake, you idiot. You think it'll get better? Hah, come on up to Bedford Hills and talk to a few cons, just girl to girl. You might learn something.*

"No problem," I said, the way we all do—especially when there is one.

Her blue eyes came to rest on the closed door. "Is that the bedroom, through there?"

"Yes it is. There's someone in there sleeping." Beat, beat. "You have the right to look, of course."

"Um-*hmm*." She shifted her attention back to me and again ran her hand through her hair, waiting for me to say something.

"It's a man, Patty Ann." As I used her name, something in her expression said she regretted having invited me to. "He's a doctor and has to go back on duty at noon. If you want to see for yourself, go ahead. Last time I checked the manual it didn't seem I was breaking any rule."

She hesitated for a moment and damn if she didn't limp over to the door, open it a crack and peer in at Michael, longer than needed to confirm that, yes, it was a sleeping man. "Okay," she said, quickly shutting the door and fishing a notebook out of her bag. "What's his name?"

John Smith? "Michael Pyatt," I said, my face and voice competing for which could be blankest.

Hers were the opposite. "Pyatt? Grace, I do *not* understand what you think you're doing. You talk about the manual—did you get to the part about consorting with felons?"

"Michael is not a felon," I said, aware that with her, even if I won I lost. "To my knowledge he has never been charged with a crime."

"Right," she said unpleasantly. "But all things considered, why in the world would he be your choice?" Choice came out of her like a spitting sneeze. I locked my jaws against any one of a dozen replies. The joke on me was how totally on target the question was. "There is something self destructive in you, Grace, I've seen it from the first." A slight tremor of voice let me know that she was angry, not professionally but personally. In her book I was a chronically loose cannon, unappreciative of the cushy second chance I'd been handed. I clenched my jaws tighter. "You'd have been on reduced supervision by now except for a recklessness I sense in you." *Recklessness? I sense it in you too, lady. Sisters under the skin?* "And now *this:* out of the entire population of New York City, why would you even *want* a man who—"

My restraint popped suddenly like a balloon getting one puff more than it could contain. "You know, I'm gonna bet with such a big caseload you have things to do besides ride my tail. The fact is you don't like me. I piss you right off. Maybe because you think I have things too damned easy. Hey. I'm not even *suggesting* you should be on my side, but could we try for neutral?" She stared at me making no attempt to break in and shut me up. Part of me wished she'd do it, yet I couldn't seem to do it myself. "Look at you! You think I don't know who you are? I've been locked up for seven years with women who *were* you. In a way you don't begin to understand, *I* was you. So what did he do this time—push you down? Kick your—?" Now I stopped dead in my mouth-running tracks, my breath like broken glass in a dry throat.

I watched her lip begin to tremble until she trapped it between small white teeth. She stared at me as though I were the one with power over her, instead of the other way around. Then she turned and limp-ran out the door. I watched her, feeling more like a contemptible schoolyard bully than an idiot who had just well and truly fucked herself over.

Before I left for the office, my gut doling out punishment for the outburst at Patty Ann, I leaned over the bed and took my own parting look at Michael. Out of the entire population of New York City why *would* I want a man who . . . He'd rolled over onto his stomach now, head to one side. Carefully, I lifted the covers and peered under at his back—and resisted a tickle of temptation to crawl back in beside him. Instead, I kissed the nape of his neck, very lightly right where the hairline stopped.

"Good morning, Grace." He stood in the doorway of his office, bowed legs slightly apart, knees a little bent like someone ready to defend an assault. His face and eyes looked cool as stone.

"Good morning, Craig," I said, busying myself with hanging my trench coat on a hook and removing my scrambled egg sandwich and container of coffee from the luncheonette bag.

This was how it would be—just the way I'd hoped, and just fine. No wrangles about trust, betrayal, fairness, the meaning and bounds of friendship: like jailhouse cons we'd make it through because neither of us had the ready option to be somewhere else.

Was it possible Craig had been sucker-mugged by Gabriel McCail? Sure. Was it also possible that the scene at Craig's loft had been staged for my benefit? That was possible too—in which case Craig, self-confessed virtuoso scammer, knew damned well that after work today I'd be sitting in Marina Beck's house telling Paul stories to his boyfriend.

"Ironic, no?" he asked raising his brows. It took a split second to get that he must be commenting on his own thoughts not mine.

"I'm sure it is, whatever you're referring to. Most things are." I popped the lid off my coffee and took a swallow. I was still standing. Maybe if I sat down and booted up he'd close his door and disappear. I went ahead and did that; he was still there.

"And who would know that better than thee and me?" I bit into my egg sandwich and didn't answer. I noted the play of a smile on his lips and didn't smile back. I picked up my phone to collect voice mail.

As soon as I heard his office door close I went onto AOL and, sure enough, a message. *The kitchen counter was pink. You called it Pepto-Bismol. The crack was shaped like a giraffe. I get to the occasional opera but it ain't Lincoln Center. I have some records though. CDs but I still call them records. Did you hang onto any of our old ones?*

Yes. Yes, yes, *yes!* Pepto-Bismol. Giraffe. Never mind that he hadn't said where he was now. I hadn't expected an answer to that and the fact that he'd simply ignored the question was so utterly George. His mention of our records flooded me with nostalgia for years that I knew very well had been deeply blemished, but seemed a paradise compared to recent times. I typed back a short one. No questions this time, just: *Yes, but I haven't been able to play them yet. I will now.*

The phone rang. Sheilah. I was glad for the sound of her, and equally glad just now for the distance of an ocean between us. George, Michael, Craig, McCail, Patty Ann: the wall of undiscussables between Sheilah and me was growing higher by the minute.

"Hey, I got your e-mail," I said. "All attended to. I'll send you a revised schedule as soon as I hear back from the Barclay's guy—maybe an hour or two." I did not add that the piece of work I'd just mentioned was all I had on my plate today. If Teresa Woo did leave, how in hell would I earn my keep scheduling for one instead of two? Scary, but I would have to raise it when she got back. "So how's it going?"

"Good." She laughed. "Great, actually. Two winner meetings—well also one loser—and guess what?"

"What?"

"Flowers from Todd. They were waiting at the hotel. Two dozen yellow roses." Delight bubbled up in her voice and my brain instantly recalculated his credit rating. He came up smelling like one of those roses. "And we're having dinner Tuesday night when I get back—just something quiet; he knows I'll be wiped."

"Outstanding," I said.

"Things okay with you?"

"CNN owns my nighttime soul," I lied.

"I'll bet. The Brits think we've got John Wayne running our country. I stay noncommittal. You should too, by the way. I'm serious: do not get into politics with your contacts. Ever."

"Right."

"Got enough to keep you busy at the office, Grace?" Naïve to think I would need to raise the issue. Sheilah, much as she loved me, knew my cost/benefit ratio to her business as accurately as she did that of a piece of software, a phone system, a new chair for the conference room.

"Not really," I said, half relieved to have it out of its box. The other half was causing my hands to sweat.

"I know. Not to worry—we'll talk about it when I get back. I've got some ideas. Oh, and I've asked Cynthia to give you some of her overflow, okay?" It was more than okay.

I typed some letters, reorganized a paid-bill file and, hey—I found myself taking little breaks, doodling. Sketching a pair of stylized wings. A pendant? A pin? Split them up and they could be earrings. Bring them around full circle: a bracelet. There should be one large stone where they joined . . .

I got around to having a salad sent in for lunch just after two. At about the time it arrived, Craig emerged from his office and hurried past me without a glance. His cheeks were flushed, as though dabbed with rouge, but his face looked grim. That would happen, I knew, when he'd pulled off some scheme that pleased him. The high would be followed by an emotional nosedive. Like Paul. We'd talked of these things that first evening when he'd corralled me, saying he wanted my help in purging his old ways, the better to be worthy of Angel. It had been weeks ago—it seemed like years.

Craig and Paul: in my own small way I was as skilled at sleight of hand as they were, having spent the better part of forty years practicing moves that made inopportune facts disappear before the eye. The hitch was that the only eye it worked on was mine. I saw myself earlier this morning, striding east through the park on my way here, skin tingling, motor purring, Michael-filled—joyous for the first time in more than eight years. So what inconvenient material about the source of that joy was I choosing to vanish up my sleeve? A late-blooming racial consciousness, perhaps? A live-in girlfriend of the right color? A stubborn primal loyalty to a monster he called daddy?

The choice to walk away from joy was not one I'd ever made, or let anyone make for me. This morning I'd chosen instead to fly off the handle in a tirade against the killjoy who happened to be my PO. Given it to do again I supposed I'd do it again.

CHAPTER TWENTY-SIX

Marina Beck's house was on Beekman Place, a bow-fronted beauty with large windows that looked out on the East River. I'd been there more than a few times in the Paul years, listened to her stage whispers to other guests: *Boudreau! My financial secret weapon, darlin'—he's almost as brilliant an investor as he is a writer. Almost.* Yet each visit to that place was a reminder that underneath the public performance, the flamboyant arty enthusiasms, there breathed a woman shrewd enough to have held onto her hard-won money, to have invested it quite wisely before she ever heard of Paul Boudreau. She'd bought the house for cash in a distress sale and done it up with superb English antiques—cost, as she was fond of saying, "ten cents on the dollar." All this in the seventies when Paul was still giving his mother orders about silver futures. And *he* was *her* financial secret weapon? I hadn't asked that precise question before but I did now. The answer that sprang to mind was, I don't *think* so.

As I rounded the corner of Forty-ninth onto Beekman I thought of Paul and money: not Marina's, but mine . . .

I half-lay, half-sat against plump pillows, my legs wrapped in an afghan like Elizabeth Barrett Browning on her couch. I had been home from the hospital almost two weeks. My lungs were clear of pneumonia but I was still weak and exhausted. It had been three months since George's disappearance. With the help of my own head games, layered on top of the ones Paul ran, I'd found ways to exist with the idea of his being gone. Sometimes I would imagine him simply away in Miami or Las Vegas—somewhere he'd return from one day without notice, the way the two of us used to come and go when I was a kid. Other times he would become my late father who'd died of an unspecified disease. But in certain unguarded moments I would see the running target, sweating and crying for his life. Brought down or escaped? The question would prod my heart like an icicle.

Paul knelt at my side, talking about money, about his mother, about—what he was saying was making no sense to me—it was like overhearing fragments of conversation in a busy airport; the phrases could have been in a foreign language for all the sense they made. ". . . not a complicated woman, my mother—cared only about what she wanted at the moment. As long as she got her hands on *that* house, *that* car, *that* diamond bauble . . ." ". . . began moving money around when I was fourteen." ". . . too young by law to act for myself, so she opened accounts, executed my trades, did what I told her—and I handed over a piece of the profits." "My partner . . ."

Partner? Was he meaning his mother? Me? To my reeling mind it seemed insane for him to be chatting about these things right now, as I lay there in a state of shock. Moments earlier he had told me in words all too clear that GraceL Studios was on a quick route down the tubes. Its imminent death had to do with "moving money around," he'd said.

"Grace, we'll restructure, get new financing—maybe after the bankruptcy filing's history . . ." *Bankruptcy?* ". . . put together a consortium of investors and go public. That would be bigger than anything you've dreamed of and . . ." His face was close to mine, close enough to slap, to rake with my nails, but my hands stayed quietly clasped together. Those eyes of his shimmered like pools of gray rain. Tears flowing, I realized.

"But orders—we have . . . had. We produced . . . how can you go out of business when you have so much business?" I asked, stupid in my amazement. True, Paul had been investing GraceL cash and mine for the past year and a half; true, he'd been running things since George disappeared and I'd been sick; true, I'd signed whatever— "What have you *done?*"

"My fault; all mine—moving the cash around and then the music suddenly stopped. I needed to cover fast—too fast. Blame me, *ma chère,* blame me."

I think it was the "*ma chère*" that did it. "I do," I said, the breath behind it hot and bitter in my mouth. I threw off the afghan and leapt from the couch, furry black circles of dizziness almost blotting him from view. "Just get out of my reach, you freak bastard, because I swear I'll kill you."

Those words, more than eight years old now, screamed with fresh fury inside my skull as my finger made Marina's doorbell chime like an old music box. The door opened quickly enough to make me feel like Gabriel had been poised there behind it like a jack-in-the-box waiting. He looked like something out of fresco scribbled with graffiti. He wore faded jeans that almost matched his eyes and a yellow shirt a shade and a half paler than his ringlets. His face was purpled and puffed on the right side. So Craig's punch had connected, that much at least was true. He gave me a lopsided smile, which heightened his resemblance to a spoiled angel.

"Right on time, Grace."

"It's my way." I walked in past him and felt my hand stutter as it went to untie my trench coat belt. I knew perfectly well why I was here: to tell some careful lies candy-coated in truth. I'd come to outsmart a smart-ass. *Allenbirn* had made the enterprise more important and more risky. I was growing less sure by the second that my game was going to be good enough, and I felt shaken, undermined by the too vivid recollection I'd just had standing on Marina's doorstep. Also, something was nibbling at the back corners of my brain, demanding my attention, but I couldn't make out its shape or message.

"Want to sit in the library?" he asked. "Marina's going out, but she'll put her head in and say hello before she leaves."

"Hospitable of her." I should quit being snotty tonight—there was nothing in it for me.

I settled myself in a tall straight-backed chair. Gabriel sat opposite me, maybe ten feet away, on a small easy chair, a closed spiral notebook in his lap, pen clipped to the cover. I had turned down a drink; he'd popped open a can of Coke out of the fridge that was part of the room's wet bar. "Grace, look, we got off to a bad start but I give you my word I'm not out to do you harm." I didn't roll my eyes; I'm sure I didn't. "Look, let me rephrase, I won't do you harm."

I give you my word. I promise you. Trust me. Do you believe me? Right: How do you say fuck you in Swahili? "Okay, you won't do me harm." I said. "You've been wanting this meeting since before I got out of Bedford Hills. I'm here. So . . . what?"

"Well, how about I lead off? I'll tell *you* some things that might be of interest." I shrugged. He was going to tell me some back story about Paul—that he'd tortured small animals when he was seven, perhaps, or had been abused by his mother. He'd flash facts like cards pulled from a deck, facts that once might have frightened or fascinated or revolted me, and didn't matter a damn now. No, that wasn't right, they did matter in a terrible way: hearing them would breathe life into the man I'd killed, put flesh back on his bones, and that would be hell. He asked, "Did you know that Paulie Donofrio lived the first eleven years of his life on Staten Island, that he was an altar boy at Saint Cecilia's there?"

"And?"

"And that Jesus reached out a hand to him."

I shrugged again. "Figures."

He laughed. "Hey, I was a Catholic school boy, first grade through half a year of college; no statue gave me a tumble. But you can ask Paul's parish priest, who happens to still be alive. He believes to this day that that statue moved for that boy. He was a kind of magic kid, even then. The other kids thought so too. Paulie was chosen, earmarked. There was some talk at the time in the parish about him being a young saint. Stigmata on his palms and all."

"If you're saying that Paul was a born con man, that's not exactly hot news."

"Any possibility in your mind that he may have believed it himself?"

Something in his face as he asked the question kept me from dismissing it with an automatic "please!" I saw Paul, wonder coloring his face at first sight of the laughing Valkyrie he wanted to marry; love for *Grandmère* gleaming in his eyes as he ushered me into her cottage; passionate conviction roughening his voice when he said George was likely dead—better off to have been killed fast, perhaps by Michael. "Maybe," I said. "Maybe at the time they're selling the con they do believe, the really gifted ones, but . . . never mind."

"No, what? What were you going to say?"

"Oh, just that the Paul I knew packaged himself as a cynical intellectual. One of his favorite books was a skinny little thing called *In Praise of Folly* by—"

He uncapped his pen and flipped open the notebook. "Don't stop. I just want to make a few notes, okay?"

"Fine." It was after all why I was there, to divert him with this kind of thing. "It's by Erasmus, the book—kind of a long essay, where the speaker makes really good arguments about all sorts of things, and just as you're about to buy the logic, Erasmus stops and reminds you that Folly is the character who's leading you along, so of course everything has to be held up to a mirror and looked at the other way."

"Hmmm. Michael told me that Nietzsche was Paul's main man."

"True, and Machiavelli and Schopenhauer, but in some way the Erasmus thing was closer to the bone, his bone, even though it was kind of a trifle rather than 'Great Thought.'"

I saw him warm to the interchange. He tapped his pen against his teeth for a moment and said, "I've read Paul's work—well, the poems and stories that Marina has, which may not be the total body. What do you think of them?"

"Not much. I'm no literary critic, certainly no high-flying intellectual, but I find his stuff the kind of sludge that seems to have no point except darkness. If Paul created a masterpiece, the piece of art was himself not his writing. For what it's worth, that's what I think."

He scribbled down my words and looked up waiting to see if I'd volunteer more. When I didn't, he said, "Jojo Donofrio, the father, was a dapper little guy—you know, a salesman type with a smile and a story for every occasion. But he just wasn't a very successful salesman type. A fuckup, really, from what I heard." *In other words, Paul's George. You've made your point.* He nodded, knowing he had. "Jojo ran a book in upper Manhattan, which was how come he knew Pyatt. The word was Donofrio went into witness protection owing Pyatt a chunk of change." He cupped his damaged cheek gently, almost caressing it. "Now here's a thing I find puzzling. There was a thread of suspicion at the time that Pyatt could've dimed Donofrio out, maybe even had his own crew do the job—or actually done it himself. There were a lot of people pissed at Jojo about his testimony, of course. A few of the guys he gave up landed in Otisville or wherever, and any one of them would have cheerfully put out the hit. Now, Jojo didn't finger Josh, but Josh—Josh Pyatt never really cared for being stiffed—bad precedent in his business; rotten PR." He cocked his head to one side, the better to see what might be going on in my head.

It was this: Paul had seen the men take his father; he'd told Michael that, and me too, which didn't mean it was true. But if it *was* true, and Josh himself had been one of the men . . . "What exactly is it that you find puzzling?" I asked, trying for nonchalance, not quite achieving it.

"The same thing that puzzles you, Grace: the crisscrossed relationships. If Josh really was involved in whacking Jojo, and Paul *knew* it, could Paul—even our Paul—split himself into enough parts to mourn his father, admire the father's killer and become the killer's son's best friend?"

" 'Paul was nobody's friend.' " I repeated Michael's words, hearing shadows of new meaning behind them. I wanted out of there: I was going to screw this up. "You've talked to Michael," I said carefully, "I'm sure you asked him the same question."

"I didn't get an answer though. He said he had no idea."

"And that stopped you pushing? *You,* Gabriel the unstoppable?"

He grinned, liking being teased: it made us pals. "Well, he's bigger than I am."

"Everyone's bigger than you are."

"True. You know your Michael's a strange bird."

"*My* Michael?" My tone was arch, but the paired words did appeal to me.

"All right, Michael's own Michael. Laid back, ten most eligible bachelor type and yet you sense that with the right stimulus he'd—"

"He'd what?"

"Do anything he wanted. Let me ask you a question. If you thought Michael killed your father you'd be steering clear of him."

"How do you know I'm not?"

"Because I sent you after him and you went; I've got my sources at the hospital. But here's the question: if Michael didn't kill George, who did? Maybe your father's not dead at all."

It was both a jolt and a relief to have him get to it so soon. I gave the response I'd planned, and found it hard to keep my voice from catching. My ears felt hot; I imagined them turning a liar's crimson. "It took a long time for me to believe he was, but see, if my father were alive he would have been in touch with me, some way, somehow by now. He and I were very close. I have never heard from him." I saw Gabriel nod and then jot, but his face gave nothing away.

"Anyway," he said, "here we've got this altar boy, saint in training, who by the way seems to have been fond of his hapless dad." He was tapping the pen against his teeth again. "You and Paul had that in common: the dads and the way you felt about them."

"Yes. So what happened to the saint in training?"

"He disappeared along with his parents. And he did a damned good job of it. In Lake George, which is where they went, nobody really remembers the kid. He kind of became invisible. It's not just that they dyed his hair dark, which they did, and put little round glasses on him, it's that the whole personality changed. He went from being a top student to one just below the middle of the class, didn't talk much, no friends."

He was trawling me, trying to emotionally hook me with the boy. Knowing it helped a little, only a little. "That was, I guess, the plan," I said primly, "to make the family unobtrusive."

"Rough on the boy though. Big personality like Paulie, having to hide all that charisma, brilliance–"

I sprang from the chair and walked quickly to the far end of the room. "I don't want to hear any more of this stuff from you. What am I supposed to do with it? *What?* Dissolve into tears? Keep it up and I'm out of here. You want some anecdotes? I'll give you some anecdotes–that's why I came–to give you material you can use, and to get you off my case."

"Okay. Sorry. Come on sit down. Sure you don't want a drink?"

"I've never been surer." I returned to the chair.

He sat waiting for me to talk, and I did. I told him the benchmark stories, the ones that lived all too close to the top of my mind. I told him about our boy-meets-girl. I told him about *Grandmère*. I told him about the marvelous home-cooked dinners and the spur of the moment dream vacations. I told him how I'd handed over control of GraceL to Paul, signature by signature at the ends of long documents with small print, too simpleminded about business technicalities to realize what I was doing until it was too late.

He took his notes, looking up from time to time, giving his teeth a tap now and again with the pen. His relish over the new trove glowed in his face, though I could see him trying not to look rapacious.

"It was never about money for Paul," he said. "I've known that for a while now. The money was a side benefit. All that investing he did when he was a kid was a triumph for him, just another high-wire feat, right up there with convincing the parish about the beckoning statue. He was winning, in charge, making money into more money because he *could*."

"You got it. Winning, controlling: those were what turned him on. And he loved pulling off the big surprise. He'd take you on a magic-carpet ride, then while you were soaring, he'd yank the carpet out from under you and let you land hard on your ass. And then he'd produce a new flying rug.

Maybe his best fun came from getting you to take a second flight; that's where the challenge was."

He put his pen down. "Nietzsche's God man," he said in the tone of a student with a crush on a star professor.

"I guess that was Paul's idea. It depends whose eyes you're looking through, doesn't it? For some of us the word 'evil' does come to mind, melodramatic as it may sound."

"I never looked at Nietzsche before, didn't even know how to spell the name—I was, as they say, never a student, not the bookish kind. But getting into Paul's head was something else. I actually read Nietzsche—well, some of him. You know, in *Ecce Homo* he says he believes only in French culture—regards everything else in Europe that *calls* itself culture as a misunderstanding. Think that's where Paul got his French passion? I do. And what about 'Life always gets harder toward the summit—the cold increases, responsibility increases.' That's from *The Antichrist*—amazing stuff."

"Yes. Did you get to, 'Look too long into the abyss and you become the abyss'? I'm not sure I have the words exactly right, but I've got perfect pitch on the tune." I sure did: I could hear the cadence of Michael's voice throwing the quote at Paul.

" 'Man is a rope stretched between the animal and the Superman—a rope over an abyss.' " He preened like a kid who'd gotten the top grade on the test. "That's where your quote about looking into the abyss comes from too: *Thus Spake Zarathustra*." His face went suddenly serious, though the beam of pride lit it still. "You know, I just realized something. I pulled that scam on Craig because—believe me I may be the least spiritual person you ever met—but it was like I was channeling Paul Boudreau. I set up Craig just to see if *I* could."

"You set up Craig? Are you sure?"

"What do you mean am I sure? I went to that bar where he hangs out and plays piano, set my cute little ass on a stool, clapped my hands—and then held them out and let him fall into them. More to it than that, of course, but . . . you have to admit it was something like the way Paul caught you."

"Maybe," I said, "maybe not. I was easy. Craig's a lot shrewder."

"You think so?" He laughed, the corner of his bruised mouth turning down in a way that made his face look melted. "That means I really do have some Paul in me to tap. Craig fell in love with me because I intrigued him. He was a lonely guy with a fantasy life. He was looking for an angel; I let him find one. Call me a bastard, but I did begin to have feelings for him, I really did. I hurt him, he messed my face up: it makes us even—sort of even. Look, Grace, I can't say I could have planned that you'd show up at his place the other night, but I do have to say that if that hadn't happened, no way you'd be here now. Am I right?"

"You're right." I felt no twinge admitting that because I'd just realized something crucial: Gabriel McCail was far from omniscient. Unless he was the world's premier actor he had no clue that Craig was anything but a susceptible guy whom he'd been able to manipulate into falling in love with him—and providing useful access to me. "Do you know much about Craig?" I asked. "Just curious," I added, light and quick.

"No, not much. He had a rough childhood—dad who beat up on him, humiliated him. Mostly, he wanted to hear about me. You and he patched it up yet? I think he was as upset over losing you as he was over learning that his angel was no angel."

"Cold little reptile, aren't you?"

"Okay, so you're bitter. I can understand that."

"Can you? Your *paparazzo* thing may've helped get me off to a bad start with my PO."

"Speaking of your PO, she's another story, our Patty Ann."

"Yeah, well I think I've figured that one out. She'll leave him one day or she won't, probably the latter."

"He's a cop. She's been gone and back three different times. The woman's unstable, really not suited to being a parole officer. Jesus, she sticks out like a convent girl. She ought to be a kindergarten teacher, which is what she started out to be—was until she got fired for all the absence and—"

"Does anyone get to have a life without your face stuck into it?"

He shrugged, pleased with himself at the backhanded compliment to his skill. "Well, she kind of came up in my research."

"Let's skip her for now, okay?"

He picked up his pen and massaged his teeth with it. "Why do you think he *did* bankrupt your business? Paul."

"Yes, I got that we were back to Paul. He said it was to cover some bad decisions he'd made. He needed fast cash." He'd said that, but he'd also said something else—something I was hardly going to repeat here. The prickle at the back of my neck warned of heavy roadwork ahead. I clasped my hands in my lap to preempt any trembling.

"You don't think he siphoned off the cash to disappear your father?"

You're a poker player's daughter. Play poker. So I said what I'd planned to say. "He wouldn't have had to, I'd have given every cent I had to keep my father safe. But understand this, I was never rich, not say the way Marina is rich. While I had a damned good business, it never made me millions. My distribution was select, boutiques, by corporate standards very small stuff. I made a wonderful living by my lights, bought a nice loft to live in and paid a hefty mortgage every month. Besides, Paul did most of his siphoning after George disappeared, not before. He did it while I was out of commission with pneumonia."

This part was not exactly true: my embarrassed accountant tried to explain that the stealing had begun at least three months earlier—a month before the FBI closed in on George—but that the GraceL books had been so well cooked it had been impossible to detect in time to salvage anything.

"Hmmm," Gabriel muttered, and made some notes. He looked up and asked, "Did Paul really think Michael did your dad?"

"I can't tell you what Paul really thought about anything. He *said* he thought Michael was set up."

He laughed merrily. "Set up maybe, but protected in the end with an alibi that held. If you'd trust me a little, Grace, I'd like to show you I can keep secrets as well as tell them."

"I do trust you a little, Gabriel," I said sweetly, checking my watch. A little over an hour since I'd rung the bell. I rose from the chair. "I hope you've gotten something out of this, because I don't want to see you or hear from you again."

He rose too. "I've gotten a lot. Thanks."

"You're welcome." With this last snippet of mannerly form, I walked to the library door and took hold of the round brass knob. I was done here.

"Grace, why did you shoot him? I mean I know the list of complaints against him, I know you filed for the protection order, I know you've said it was his gun and that he put it there on the table—but still . . . what was in your head when you picked up that gun and fired at his heart?"

I turned and looked him in his eyes. "I have no recollection of what was in my head. He came to the loft. When I tried to force him to leave he took out the gun. He said he had things to say to me. That's when he put the gun on the coffee table between us. He told me I could pick it up and blow him away if I didn't like what he said. I remember nothing else until after the shot." I had said this so many times in much the same words that it felt almost like speaking truth.

We stayed lock-eyed for a few silent seconds. "Now, do I believe that?" he asked. *Do you believe me? I do.* I was hyperaware of the floppy disk in the bag on my shoulder and wondered whether a reply from George sat waiting for me to come home and switch on the laptop. *No, don't even think of George. He'll see it coming out your eyes.*

The brass knob, still in my hand, turned—but not by me. The door opened and I stepped quickly aside as Marina, tricked out in a Marlene Dietrich tuxedo, sailed in. A much younger man, similarly dressed, stood a respectful few feet behind her. He looked slightly familiar but I couldn't quite place him.

"Hello, Grace," she said. My name tasted bad to her. She turned to Gabriel. "She staying for dinner, McCail?" *McCail. Boudreau.* The affectation was silly—as silly as the big martini glass, which no doubt sat inside the velvet bag on her arm.

"No," I said, "she's not staying to dinner, but since you were kind enough to look in on us, Marina, I have a question for you." That I actually asked it was almost as much a surprise to me as it was to her. "Did Paul ever really invest for you or was it kind of the other way around?"

She took another few steps into the room. The young man followed keeping the same few steps distance between them. He did ring a bell; I just didn't know which bell it was. "How do you mean the other way around?" she asked.

"Well, you're pretty smart about wealth; you say it about yourself all the time: poor hooker from the backwaters of West Virginia, rich widow, self-invented . . ." Self-invented: that murmured something back to me, but I was too full of what I wanted to say to slow down and listen. "So when we get down to it, I just don't see you turning over the management of your hard-earned cash to someone as—shall we say artistic or shall we say erratic—as Paul."

"Boudreau was a brilliant investor." She turned her head slightly. The light hit her face in a way that suggested a collapsed wedding cake.

"Right, just like he was a brilliant writer. I know the party line. What I'm questioning is *your* investment in *him*. I'm not saying you didn't give him some money to play with on your behalf. But the big stuff? I don't think so. With the makeup and costume off, you are far too practical. I wasn't but you are. You back this project or that project in a measured, careful way." I pointed at Gabriel whose rosebud of a mouth was slightly open. "He's your current project and Paul's *his* current project. So, bottom line, you're still funding Paul." I glanced at the almost recognized young man, who was fascinated enough that he'd forgotten to be embarrassed. "Is this one here another project?"

"No, he's a good young fuck." Now the embarrassment flooded his face and I did place him: the drinks waiter at Sheilah's party.

"Sorry," I said to him, "this isn't about you." I looked back at Marina's face, tense and worn under the heavy makeup, as though all the warm blood were gone from beneath the skin. "What I'm thinking now is that you were Paul's private bank," I said. "When an investment he did for someone else went bad you covered until he could recoup. Isn't that the way it went?"

From behind me, Gabriel weighed in, "So how come you didn't help him out when he bankrupted Grace's business?" The reporter was apparently unable to resist a key question, even at risk of offending his patron.

"Because I don't like Grace," she said with a deeply dirty look at Gabriel. "I never did."

"And you wouldn't do it, even for Paul?" Gabriel had to push; he couldn't help it.

"No," she almost whispered. Something in her face, in her voice, was off. He'd touched a nerve. Was it the cumulative thrust of our questions, or was it the taunting note in his voice when he said Paul's name? . . . *even for Paul?* It occurred to me as Marina's eyes met mine that she looked different from any way I'd seen her look before—she looked nakedly like a grieving mother.

You and that mother of yours—you're some pair. The FBI agent had sat in my living room eight years ago. I heard his voice as though he were in this room now. And I knew—clear and simple, I knew.

It snapped into focus, complete with the ironic twist that was Paul's emblem. I could almost hear little clicks inside my head as shards of memory found each other and bonded with the glue of logic. I remembered Paul teasing me lightly about having shared a bed with Marina, assuring me it meant nothing really. Had he crawled into bed with Mommy as a little boy? Maybe something a bit racier as a bigger boy? What I was sure of was that he'd stayed on the dole from Mom, enjoying the private joke that witness protection had made it all possible—witness protection, which had not done well by his father. Reparations. And Mrs. Donofrio wanted her boy to be a star. Even now, posthumously, in a tell-all book. *Damn.*

I'd been staring at the floor because it was too hard to look at her while these thoughts whirred in my head. But I met her eyes now, and everything else receded for me—everything except the fact that I had killed her son. "Marina," I said. "Jesus, Marina. I didn't know, not until this second. Paul never told me you were . . . I am so sorry."

"I hope you burn in hell—and very slowly." Her eyes threw out a flame that could have started the fire. Could this be a woman who picked up a phone to call her husband's killer? You bet—but who was I to talk? Without another word, she turned and left, the good young fuck following in her wake.

"Wow," said Gabriel, his voice muted by surprise. "Not bad."

"It *was* bad, very. Not in any way you'd get."

He threw his head back and laughed louder and freer than I'd heard out of him. It must have pained his face but he didn't seem to care. "What the hell's so funny, Gabriel? I wasn't doing a parlor trick, for Christ's sake."

"Life. Coincidence. You. It's amazing how you walk around clueless, not even any apparent *interest* in the clues and then, bam, you nose out something really subtle. So now we share a secret. Tell you what, wanna be my partner? I'll give you a job."

"I have one, thanks. Anyway, you're in no position to be offering jobs, *McCail.* Marina didn't like you butting in, moving things along—and she will get you for it. You may be out on your dimpled ass."

"I don't think so," he drawled out, plenty of air space between the words. "She wants the project almost as much as I do. She's ready to un-veil herself—she just wasn't ready tonight."

My perspective on so much had already started bending, straining to look from new angles. I felt faintly dizzy and suddenly the need to leave her house was more urgent than it had been. "Look, I'm going now." I grabbed my coat and hurried out into the hall.

He followed close behind me. "One thing," he said, mild as one of those dumb like a fox TV detectives, "if Paul bled your business out and didn't ask her for help, wouldn't that suggest he needed money for some-thing he couldn't talk about, even to her?"

I stopped but did not turn back. It was a skinny line to walk, especially for someone thrown off balance. "My guess is that wrecking my business was his point: Paul playing Nietzsche's Superman. If he'd lived, maybe he would have resuscitated it with some dazzling sleight of hand, the best trick of his career. I've given you more than you could have hoped for. Use it. Write your book. Get famous, make millions. But let me alone now, for good."

"Well, I've given you something too, in a manner of speaking. I'll tell you what, I'll stay out of your hair in exchange for an answer to one more question: that art opening at the Huffman Gallery, the night you went at Paul and knocked the painting off the wall. Next day you filed for the order of protection. How come?"

"Because I was frightened, Gabriel," I said. "If you don't understand that Paul was dangerous, you'd better write a different book."

I opened the door, closed it hard behind me and got myself away from there fast.

CHAPTER TWENTY-SEVEN

When I walked out Marina's door it was raining medium hard—a welcome cooling on my scalp, which burned with the red-hot stuff inside it. I hurried west on Forty-ninth, eager to reach home base, grateful to blend into the wet dark around me as I thought. I'd been frightened the night Gabriel had just mentioned. I'd had reason to be.

The show at the Huffman Gallery opened on an unseasonably warm evening in mid-September, the nineteenth it was. I had moved into the GraceL studio the day Paul told me my business was in effect dead. Though my assistants and secretary were interviewing for new jobs, they came to work; we did what we did: pieces got designed and a few of them got produced, though in small numbers. We didn't talk much but a spontaneous embrace would happen, a flash flood of tears, a burst of manic laughter.

During that time I'd thought often of Paul's pitiless take on an autumn tree: death in fancy dress. More than once I had wondered whether he'd knowingly been commenting as much on me as on a season. *Up yours, Paul, I am not dead. And if I have to lose my leaves and weather a winter before new ones come out, I'll fucking do that.* Despite everything, I did hope. And when you hope you are still alive.

Early that evening I went to the loft to rummage my closet for something gutsy to wear. I'd called first and gotten no answer but my own voice on the machine, but when I arrived fifteen minutes later Paul was there looking sparkle-eyed, handsome in gray pinstripes and a yellow tie on a deep blue shirt. He made the beginning of a move toward me, or I thought he did. "Don't start," I said. "I've come to shower and change for the opening."

He opened his arms wide and dropped them quickly to his sides, a gesture peculiarly his. It meant: I have the whole picture inside my head but I can't make you see it, because you'd never really be able to really grasp the nuances. *"Alors—"*

"And can the French. You're Paulie Donofrio, remember?"

He smiled. "I always remember. Know that and you know me."

"I don't *want* to know you, Paul. Do you get that? What I do want is for you to leave my loft. I was going to write you or have a lawyer do it, but you're here and I'm here, so . . . pack your stuff and leave my loft. Out." I turned away and walked past him to the bedroom. He followed behind me.

"I've taken another look at autumn," he said. "I know there's no reason that matters to you now, but it happens to be true. *'Les sanglots long de violon—'* "

"I told you, knock that off!"

"It's part of a poem, Verlaine, not my usual. In English it's called 'Song of Autumn.' It could have been written for now, for us. 'The long sobbings of the violin of autumn wound my heart with—' "

"Do I have to wound your heart with a kitchen knife to stop you? You work some scam that gets my father killed—don't deny it; I know you must have pulled something. Then you try to sell me on how lucky it was he died fast. And while I'm flat out in a hospital with an oxygen tube in my nose, you steal my money. Now you want to recite about sobbing violins. Next you'll be telling me how dearly you love me. I've heard the riffs. Could we just press the mute button?"

"You are the shortest distance between two points, Grace, the cleanest human I know."

"I don't know what that means, and don't bother to tell me. Just get out of here and let me get dressed."

"Let me ask you this: what if I told you that the money I took out of GraceL went to George—went with him?" His eyes shone like twin rays of hope.

A drum beat crazy rhythm in my chest, throat, ears, knees: I was a big, pounding heart, only that, as I waited.

Paul's lights went out. "I wish I could honestly say that to you, but I can't." He left the bedroom quickly. Minutes later I heard the front door open and close.

The heart, seduced and devastated, revolted. I wept. I banged my head against the wall hard enough to hurt. And then I wept some more. I took a shower, put on a very red dress and hung a new black-and-silver, shield-shaped piece around my neck. By the time I arrived at the Huffman wrapped in Keiko's kimono, the place was pretty well filled with down-towners and uptowners trying to pass as downtowners. I did a bit of kiss kiss with people I knew and some I didn't. I spotted Sheilah across the room and waved. Beside her, turned in the other direction was Marina Beck.

I sipped some champagne, thinking it might calm my raked insides, but it went down like lye so I held onto the half full glass, just so no one would stick another one in my hand. I was looking at a piece called *Party Girl*. The party girl in this painting was a grandmother, gray bun, wrinkles, sags and all. She stood full-length in bright green silk, chin raised and smiling at herself as she primped in a mirror. I did not see Paul come in, did not know he was there until I felt warm lips touch my neck.

I crossed the line before I was aware of feeling rage. Fists swung, feet kicked. With a grunt of surprise he fell back heavily against *Party Girl* and grabbed out at the painting beside it, pulling it from the wall as he hung on to keep himself from falling. And then I ran.

Minutes later, gasping for breath, I double-locked myself inside the studio and huddled on the floor wrapped in a blanket but unable to stop shivering. The phone began to ring after a while, but I did not answer it. It was Sheilah. I'd assumed that and found out later I'd been right.

The following morning I filed for the court order of protection against Paul. It was dangerous for me to be around Paul. That was the truth—except for an omitted footnote: I was frightened of what I might do to him if he came within my reach.

———

The room was dark except for the rectangle of television screen. I'd arrived home from Marina's house cold, wet and played out. After a quick check of the computer had yielded nothing from *allenbirn*, I copied the floppy from the office into my hard drive. Then I warmed myself with a quick scotch, a hot shower and a bowl of canned lentil soup and swaddled inside a large, fluffy afghan on the not-so-comfortable couch. I lay there watching hour after hour of sitcoms that played themselves out in some galaxy different from the one where I had ever lived—which was, of course, their appeal.

The phone rang. Michael I hoped. I'd called him on his cell as soon as I'd gotten home, bursting with the news about Paul and Marina. I'd gotten his voice mail and left a plain vanilla message, with a "love you," I could not resist saying at the end. I rushed to extricate myself from the afghan and instead tangled my legs and went down flat on my butt—while the phone rang and rang once more. My message picked up just as I'd made it to one knee. Then I heard Michael's voice.

"Figured you'd be home by now. Maybe you are and you're sleeping. Poor you, you must be exhausted." I was halfway to my feet when I heard, "Thing is—God, this is so hard to say—I need some time." *Again.* He was running out on me *again.* I couldn't believe it. I *did* believe it. What was not to believe? Michael being Michael. "I'm . . . I don't know what I am except confused. Damn, the last thing you need is some fool who can't even articulate what he means. No, the *last* thing you need is me—unless I can work out my shit and come to you free and clear. I don't know how you're feeling tonight—probably as mixed up as I am." Long pause with background crackles and pops of breath. "It was great. I love you, Grace. That's the one thing I *do* know."

Part of me wanted to make the dash, grab the phone and hold onto him: "I love you too" and "Great doesn't begin to describe it: even the thought of your skin and your mouth and your breath bring me halfway there right now" and "Just let's keep on holding hands. How can we not? We bring each other joy, you asshole. It's worth so much; it's worth whatever we have to do to keep it." But the part that kept me standing in the middle of the room, gooseflesh cold, hands trembling, registering every word, agreed with what he said.

Ultimately, Patty Ann had been dead right. Hapless and hopeless with her own disasters, she had hit a bull's-eye on my core question: Why risk a fall down the rabbit hole with Michael Pyatt and all the old baggage that came with him? Why not a really fresh start? Why indeed?

A lyric from my own childhood, not George's, called freedom another word for nothing left to lose. But it didn't apply to me now. I had something left to lose, not only my actual freedom to walk the streets I wanted, when I wanted, to eat Chinese food and hear opera, to stay up all night if I felt like it, but also the start of something I'd barely dared hope for. I had *allenbirn*. And, yes, baby step though it was, teeny-tiny nothing: I had sketched a picture of a pendant shaped like a wing.

I wrapped the afghan around me and clicked onto AOL on my still open laptop. The message was my lone piece of mail. *"Guy walks into a bakery and orders an S-shaped cake. Next day he comes back and the baker starts to put the thing in a box and the guy says, 'Nah, don't bother to pack it up, I'll eat it here.' Remember that one?"* I laughed; it sounded loud, eerily festive alone in a small room at—I looked at my watch—God, two in the morning. Oh yeah, Michael might be gone but I did have something to lose.

The message hadn't yet been here when I arrived at nine or so. I wondered when he'd sent it, whether he was sitting at his computer now. I wondered where he lived but there'd be no point in asking it again. *"Still funny. I work for Sheilah now. Lucky to have the job. What time is it there? Are you okay? You are 75 after all."* I knew better than to stare at the screen waiting for a response which could take hours or longer than that. I downloaded the exchange into a new file on the hard drive I named *Allen*, went off-line and shut the computer lid, putting this new and precious piece of world to sleep like a caged canary.

I curled back up inside the afghan on the couch. The bed would have been much more comfortable, except that I knew it would smell of Michael still—maybe even bear the faint imprint of his body. I found myself empty of tears. I clicked off the TV and managed an unlikely dive into an apparently dreamless sleep.

———

The morning was clear, last night's rain blown somewhere else. The clouds in my mind were staying put. The edge of surprise about Marina had worn off: seeing her as Paul's mother felt weirdly natural—almost as though it were one more thing I'd known without knowing it. But Michael's cut-and-run, no matter how noble his supposed reasons, had not lost its shock value overnight. God*damn* it! And Goddamn you, Michael!

George's reply waited for me. *"76. I'm okay, I get dizzy lately sometimes, a little unsteady on my pins. Steady was never my strong suit though, right? Maybe the job with Sheilah shouldn't last too long, but who am I to give you advice?"* I typed back, *"My father, that's who."* Though it ran contrary to everything our life together had been, I liked typing those words, liked seeing them up there.

I hung the black suit jacket I'd worn to Sheilah's party in the bathroom and turned on the shower full blast to steam the wrinkles out. When I retrieved it smooth and ready to wear I found in its pocket Danton's business card. I propped it on the kitchen counter, looked at it as I peeled and ate an orange, and I felt something hard to define but which probably belonged under the general heading of good. I wouldn't do anything with that card today: Danton, pocket-sized duke of Soho, was too much for me just now. But one day I would call him—if I managed to keep my nose above water, I would. I put the card away in the dresser drawer with my jewelry, and started to exchange the pin on the black jacket lapel for another piece: a blackened silver circle with a thin bright gold edging. It looked like a solar eclipse.

After a moment of liking its heft in my hand, I put it back. I already was feeling my own inner solar eclipse—and truth to tell, I wasn't quite up to wearing jewelry that day.

Craig and I did another of our good-morning exchanges, neither of us stepping in any closer to the edge of the great divide. Before closing his office door he gave me a wide, sunny smile that came out of nowhere I knew of.

"I spent some time last evening with Gabriel," I said, not sure why I was saying it.

His smile turned thoughtful but did not disappear. "Was this for you or for him?"

"For me. I think I may be rid of him, finally."

"Good."

Craig?" His name hung there in the air, a small kite with no real loft to it.

"Yes?" he said after a few beats, a prompt to what he might have known was coming next.

"He really did play you, didn't he? I mean . . ." I spread my hands out, palms up.

"I *know* what you mean," he said gravely. "Do you need to hear me say it? Again? Will you believe it all the way if I do? I'm not sure you will. I'm not sure you can now." The smile flashed bright again. "Let's just see how it goes."

I spent the day doing odds and ends, intermittently checking for a George message that wasn't forthcoming and trying to hold real thoughts at bay. Maybe reading the word "father" had spooked George into flight. Cynthia came to my rescue with some hours of busywork that I found quite soothing. I doodled no wings nor anything else on a yellow pad that day. I was out for a sandwich and some air when Sheilah called in at midday from London. I tried her back but she was out to dinner. I left at five, walked downtown and ended up on Houston Street, the divide between the Village and Soho. The Angelika was showing an assortment of the offbeat movies that were its trademark, and all news to me. I chose the Italian one and ate a turkey sandwich in the lobby café while I waited for the next showing. I took the subway home feeling that I could do this, day by day, night by night. I could do it and it would get easier—and maybe I'd sketch something else. I would one day.

I poured myself a medium-sized scotch and raised the glass, *"L'chayim."* Then, only then, did I check the computer. *"I don't deserve the word father from you. I guess I never wanted you to call me that so I wouldn't have to try and deserve it. Let's stay with George and Gracie, if we go on with this at all, which maybe we shouldn't."*

I drained the scotch in my glass and fired back. *"If you're too scared to go on, then don't.* I pushed "Send" and felt miserable. I crawled into bed without bothering to brush my teeth.

I imagined some trace of Michael was still there in the bed—two nights had passed, only that, so why wouldn't there be? I could of course change the sheets. Instead, I buried my face in the pillow he'd slept on: that clean, sawn-wood smell of him—just a trace of sex smell too. I put my hand under the covers and found myself wet.

Tomorrow if the weather was nice I'd go for a good, long run. Maybe I'd go up to the Cloisters like Sheilah and I used to do some Saturdays to look at the river from way up high, wander among medieval art and congratulate each other on being unicorns. And then Sunday I'd . . . when tears began to stream down my cheeks I didn't mind them coming. I was free: Sunday I could do anything I wanted. I was free. That was the thing to hang on to.

———

"It's not that I'm scared these days, it's that I've done enough damage to you." That was the message that waited for me when I woke up.

"What about the damage I've done? Maybe underneath you resent me for it."

He answered, *"No, don't ever think that. Hey Gracie, I hear your sister has a new job."*

Okay. I typed back, *"Yeah, that's right, George, she's a diesel fitter in a lingerie factory."*

The expected answer: *"A diesel fitter in a lingerie factory?"*

The punch line: *"That's right. When the pants come off the assembly line, she holds them up and says, 'dese'll fit 'er.' "*

I laughed and filled the coffee maker. It was not a bad way to start the day.

CHAPTER TWENTY-EIGHT

Tuesday morning I showed up for my weekly session with Patty Ann, filled with dread and prepared with *mea culpas*. In the days since her disastrous drop-in visit I'd thought about calling her—several times I'd had the phone in my hand—and chickened out, not knowing any good way to apologize, especially since what I really wanted was to pretend the whole thing had never happened. When I arrived, she was at her desk—pale, worn looking, but composed and on time.

"Hi, Patty Ann. Uh, I'm sorry." Face to face with her, I found I meant every stumbling syllable. "I was out of line—what I said when you came to my place last week. I had no business saying that."

Her eyes narrowed as she looked at me with that frosty gaze blue-eyed people manage best. It stopped me cold. She said, "I have no idea what you're talking about." Her chin lifted, as though for emphasis. "Now, everything's all right on the job?" I nodded. "Anything else you want to discuss? Any problems?" I said a quiet no. "Then you're on your way. I've got a busy morning here."

I virtually skipped my way to the office, I was that relieved. "Sheilah wants to see you," Cynthia said, when I arrived.

Sheilah had a glow to her. She'd flown in from London early last evening as planned and her perfect dinner with Todd Berenstain had come off, also as planned. We sat across from each other on opposite sides of her desk now, each with coffee in a white china cup, a china plate of cheese Danish between us. Sheilah loathed eating and drinking from cardboard, always had. She broke off half a Danish and took a big bite.

"He's so . . . *right*," she said, not quite finished chewing. "Married before, so chances are he's not gay like my last one. No alimony, and no kids, which—well, just between us, I would find kids the pits to deal with—I know it's politically incorrect to say but . . ." She swallowed and refilled her mouth. "When I walked into Gramercy Tavern and he stood up and held out his arms, I just felt this smile from my insides right out through the skin. Know what I mean?"

"Yeah, I do." I guess I sounded dubious.

"Oh, Grace. Clumsy me—Paul and all, I—"

I held my hand up. "Don't be an idiot."

"I know but—"

"The eggshells have to go, Sheil. Everything can't be about Paul and me."

And it wasn't about Paul and me this time; it was about something less personal and more immediate. Sunday morning I'd taken myself down to the Twenty-sixth Street flea market to browse, maybe treat myself to a cheap treasure, if one presented itself. While rummaging through a huge carton of junk, I found a bag of wonderful old odds and ends of glass: greens and reds and ambers—a few Venetian beads thrown in, and couldn't not buy it. As I was paying, I saw a couple, arms flung around each other's shoulders, coming straight at me. Todd Berenstain and Jan Simone. Jan spotted me and waved.

The three of us exchanged the smiles and "heys" and "what did you finds?" that people do in such circumstances. The two of them exchanged the body language of people who'd shared a bed not long ago. Though Todd's manner toward me had been casual verging on friendly, I caught a look in his eye that said, "What's the harm?" "We're all grown-ups." "You're not really going to weigh in on this and upset Sheilah, are you?"

"Stay the hell out of it." Since this was a lengthy set of messages for a pair of eyes to transmit in a quick glance, I suspected that some of the text came from inside my own head. "I found Todd the best magazine rack," Jan had said, "French bentwood thing from the twenties. You won't *believe* how cheap . . ." He'd grinned over at her: a boy having fun.

"You don't know him very well . . . yet, Sheilah," I said now, sounding to my own ears like a prude. I was worse than a prude, though. Never mind about partial truths: I was a liar.

Her eyes rose from the Danish plate, sharp, ready. "What are you trying to say?"

"Uh . . . look, this may give you a laugh and a half coming from me but go slow, be careful."

"Am I hearing you saying that you should've been slow and careful about Paul? Or do you know something you're not wanting to tell me?"

"Hey, I should've been all kinds of things I wasn't about Paul." My chance: I did not take it. Instead, I took a deep breath. "There's nothing I know. I just . . . care about you." There were a dozen different ways to dress this up as principled behavior, but it wasn't that. I didn't want to take responsibility for bursting Sheilah's bubble. Coward was the word.

"Grace," she said, voice turning a fresh page with a new topic heading. "Teresa's not going to be staying. It's official now." I nodded. "Well, I'm going to be needing a different kind of help." I was aware of my hands going cold, while my cheeks warmed. "No, I'm not firing you, just the opposite. There'll be some scheduling to do of course for me, but it won't be a full-time job—oh, maybe it never really was. Here's the point: where I'm going to need help is in the primary recruiting."

A feeble kick of protest tried itself out in my gut. The basic rote work I'd been doing required little of me: persistence, patience, politeness—well, all right, a certain resourcefulness of the jigsaw puzzle variety: satisfying the way some of my prison work had been. But this would be different, something else. It would be a job of persuasion; it would—

"Don't look so alarmed," she said. "What you'll be doing is making that first contact with a potential candidate—getting him on the phone, telling him about the opportunity in a general way, getting some input on the job he does now—and his comp. You'll do it off Craig's research. You know, you've seen what he puts out for me, org charts of functions within target companies, broken out depending on our search: data architecture; development; finance; marketing, like that. You'll have names, titles, phone numbers and background on and off the record he's accumulated about any of the prospects."

I stood up, maybe to somehow physically separate myself. "Sheilah, I . . . this is the meat and potatoes of what you've been doing for the better part of twenty years. I don't know anything about it. Sure I've scheduled candidates for meetings about jobs, but, God, I've never had to talk about those jobs in any real way, or know what they are, let alone convince—"

"Hold on." One of her shiny red-and-white smiles. "*I* will do the convincing. That's what I *do*. I'll also do the assessing. *That's* what I do too. What I will teach you to do is the first step: getting someone to call you back, giving him the basics of the job description and skill set and getting him to give you a few of his basics. If he makes the cut, based on what he says and how he handles himself, you'll schedule a phone meeting for me. If not, one less person I have to spend time pursuing. It will make me so much more efficient. You know, this was an idea my mother had for me years ago—not with you involved of course—and I kept telling her all the reasons it wouldn't work, but for once I think she was right." *Sheilah and her mother.* A bad combination for Sheilah—and not a good one for me.

I was pacing now, and since there was no real room to pace in her office it felt more constraining to walk than to sit back down, which I did. The notion that this arrangement had traveled from Mrs. C-D's head out Sheilah's mouth did not seem a good omen. "I know this is what you do, but I . . . I don't think it's something *I* can do." *Or want to do.* My simple office life was suiting me just fine. George and I were having e-mail conversations daily now—all right, nothing emotionally challenging yet, and maybe never, but we were, in a manner of speaking, together. And I had the feeling that with enough blue-sky tranquillity of the spirit, my occasionally unsteady hands might make more sketches. The last thing I needed was a new challenge that did not interest me. "I'm not going to be able to give you what you need, Sheil."

"Of course you will. You're smart. You think fast. You're assertive. You have this great voice. And—you will have a great teacher. You'll listen to me on the phone; then I'll listen to you. It'll be fun, Gracie. Much more interesting than what you're doing now."

I don't want interesting. I want simple. I said, "I think you're sticking to an exalted—outdated, I should say—idea of how good or fast I might be at picking up anything. Sheil, you've seen how I am now. You just don't *want* to see it."

She bit off a large piece of the Danish in her hand. A small crumb of cheese stuck to her lipstick. "I've gotten compliments on how you've handled yourself. This is a good next step for you. If you were going back to designing, well that would be another story, and I'd be right up there at the front of the line saying go for it, but you say you're not ready to do that."

"No." I looked into the bottom of my coffee cup as though there were something to see.

"You also say that I've seen the way you are now, but I haven't—not much. I've been out of town and during the workday our paths don't cross anyway. And we've spent very little time together out of the office, a few dinners. I feel like you're holding me off. Hell, I'll bet that Craig's seen more of you than I have."

"I wouldn't say that." I could hear how stiff I sounded and didn't like it.

"Come on, lighten up, Gracie. You need to get back into life. I said the new work would be fun and you'll see, it will be. Also, you need to . . . look, maybe this is presumptuous, but you've been spending much too much time alone. I know you're reattaching to the city, to a different life, and you *think* you want to do it alone. I know you have things to figure out and grieving to do. I know all that, but you need *people* too—you do, Gracie.

"So my party bombed for you; that doesn't mean everything will. We're such old friends, you and me. We're going to be working together every day. And after work I'm someone you can relax with. It'll be good for both of us. We can go to the movies together, to a museum, the way we did when we were kids. I bet it would be fine with Todd if you joined us sometimes."

Her face moved closer to mine as she talked, more than halfway across the desk now. I summoned up a crazy picture, not the first time: Sheilah taking a nip off my nose. "Sure," I said, lifting the empty mug to my mouth: a shield, a distance keeper.

I told myself I loved Sheilah warts and all. I told myself that she and she alone in this world gave a damn whether I lived or died, that yeah, we'd had lots of good times and could again. I told myself that I was standing guard over a personal fortress so broken down it wasn't worth her effort to storm it. All these things were true, yet I knew I would not tell her about George or Michael or Marina or anything that lived in the dark bottom of my heart. Here's why: as deeply and honestly as we cared about each other, our souls were—had always been—acquaintances not mates. She would question and she would disapprove. I did not have the words or the will to debate my tangled instincts or defend . . . anything. I stood again and moved toward the door.

"I'll tell you what," Sheilah said, "Teresa's leaving officially a week from Friday, but her stuff ought to be out of that office before that. You'll move into that space as soon as it's free. Only a few steps outside my door—it'll make our new arrangement much smoother, and give Craig back his privacy, which I'm sure will please him a lot. This afternoon I'll put together some material for you to read and absorb and we'll talk later."

I nodded, not having a word nor trusting myself to find one. Also, I knew fresh what I had known my first day out of Bedford Hills: that she signed paychecks which I cashed. Right here, right this minute I was as subject to my boss as I was to my parole officer.

Her smile stretched wide again. "Want to have dinner tonight?"

I didn't want to. Fact was I felt bone dry inside and very quiet. I wanted to work and then go home and e-mail George and go to bed. "Fine," I said, my hand finding the doorknob behind my back.

CHAPTER TWENTY-NINE

The ground rules for George and my communication were tight. They'd always been that, so why would they change, especially now? I wrote that the job at Sheilah's was really okay. He wrote that if she grew to be more like her mother, which was always a danger, she'd be hell to live with. I risked asking what he thought the chances were I'd grow to be like *my* mother, knowing that would get no answer. I didn't ask again, any more than I asked again where he lived—or pushed him to say why he didn't want to see me. Aside from that one brief, exchanged mention of guilty feeling, we had kept off Paul and Michael and Josh. So far, we had. We talked memories (good ones) and music and told each other jokes. What it was, I realized one night as I was falling asleep, was the relationship we'd always had, only less palatable with its liquid flow of the day-to-day extracted: a freeze-dried essence like instant coffee.

"I'm feeling like an island surrounded by Sheilah these days. Her boyfriend's seeing someone else. Should I tell her?" I wrote—and then in a burst, *"Was it really Paul who saved your life? If so, how can you possibly forgive me?"*

The answer was, *"Import some landfill or build a bridge. Maybe a tunnel would be safer. She'll find out soon enough. Keep your spoon out of her soup."* Period.

The week after I began my new job, Teresa Woo left and I moved my gear from the desk outside Craig's door to her former office. "I'll take that for you," Craig said as he saw me lift the computer tower.

"Little gal? I've got half a foot on you, Craig, and I won't even brag about my muscles, since they're going to seed pretty fast. But, hey, leave me my heavy lifting. It may be the only thing I'm good at."

Craig and I had kept a benignly opaque distance between us these days. I made it a point to look for nothing in him and so saw nothing—except that he seemed to be back in his old groove: doing work that gave him a bang and, if he was lucky, not beating himself up for doing it too well. I hoped he still played piano at night. I hoped . . . It was not my business to hope anything about him.

"You shouldn't be recruiting," he said flatly when I came back for the next load. I glanced at him over the top of the monitor now in my arms. His skin was if anything even whiter, more translucent than usual—alabaster rather than marble. Against it his eyes shone like green river stones. Looking at him closely this way reminded me that I had not heard from Gabriel McCail in two weeks now. If my hands had been free I might have found some wood to knock. "The business is not for you, Grace."

"No shit. Hold the door open for me, would you?"

"One, you'll never be good at it. Two, it's a skill that fights with everything you are. Three, doing what you're doing keeps you just where Sheilah wants you." He held up his thumb and brought it down slowly, just in case I might have missed his meaning.

Tell me something I don't know. On second thought, don't. "Thanks for the consultation. It's not covered by my medical insurance though, so I won't take any more. Would you get the Goddamn door?"

He walked past me and held it open with a slight bow. "And a piece of Paul will stick in your craw, as long as you keep trying to do it."

"Go fuck yourself." I marched through the door. The twisty son of a bitch was right. And that gave me a chill. Somehow he knew that Paul's smile, disembodied like the Cheshire cat's, had taken to coming and going as it pleased inside my head, mocking my ineptitude at learning moves as natural to him as breathing itself. A walking, talking haunted house, that was me. One ghost was truly dead, another chose to float disembodied in cyberspace. The third, Michael, was no ghost, but equally beyond my reach, needing to remain so for my sake—never mind what he'd declared about his own sake. He was not always on my mind but when he was, the missing him hurt hard. It would happen when my eye caught a man on the street because he moved in a certain way; it would happen when I thought of a novel he'd admired, like *A Sentimental Education* or a film like *The Producers;* it would happen when I slouched in a chair to watch the eleven o'clock news and found myself suddenly, out of nowhere, horny as hell.

"My hair turned white in prison," I wrote George one night late, *"except I have a black streak in the front, like a reverse skunk. I'm a lot thinner, not like a fashion model but pretty stylish, if I say so myself. What do you look like now? Tell me more about how you're feeling—health I mean. Do you still gamble? I know you won't answer that one but I'm asking anyway."*

The answer bounced back within minutes (atypically), *"I'd recognize you with any color hair but you wouldn't know me. Health? If I take all the pills I'm mostly okay, but sometimes I forget. It's boring to get old, boring and sad. You think too many things. I've spent my life avoiding that and now I'm stuck with it. I am not much of a gambler most of the time. See, I did answer."*

"That time, when Josh tried to give me money and I threw it on the floor. Did you take it?" My finger made little circles above the "Send" button. It came down and brushed it weightlessly. I teased myself with pushing it—and couldn't ask the question. I pushed "Delete" and typed instead, *"I can't imagine not knowing you. It's safe, now that he's locked up, right? Please consider coming to me or letting me come to you."* I added my home phone number, took a deep breath and pushed "Send." I had no answer until the next afternoon at the office.

George's e-mail read, *"It's easier for me to live with myself the way things are. Let's leave it that way, at least for now."*

I looked at the screen a long time and decided for the first time not to respond instantly. I looked down at my yellow pad and saw that I'd been doodling: the beginnings of a bird's head. With a few quick strokes I sharpened the shape and gave it one swoop of wing, intentionally out-sized.

I did my new job and hated it about as much as I'd expected to. My performance on the phone was marginal: I was pretty good at understanding the specs, what the client was looking for, what qualifications were required; I was not bad at all at leaving a voice mail message that got a return call. But when I connected with the potential candidate I was way below grade at countering resistance. I'd hear, "Look, I couldn't be happier at XYZ Corp.," or "My wife and I love it here in Dallas" or "My son's a senior in high school and captain of the football team," and I'd think, "Right, sounds good. Live and be well. Enjoy what you've got"—which would color whatever I said next. If I managed to keep him (it usually was a him) on the phone long enough I was able to progress to asking about the scope of his job, but I'd wince at nosing into how much they paid him, and that would show up in my voice too.

Sheilah would be listening, mute button depressed, on an extension. "Grace," she would start the critique. Sometimes the syllable was exasperated, other times, carefully kind, which was worse. I grew to dislike the sound of my name on her tongue.

"Don't even think about it," I said when after ten days she offered me a small raise because I was handling what she called a more professional function. "Please, Sheil. I feel inept enough as it is. A raise would do me in." It was the truth: taking more money for doing a substandard job at something I loathed would have amounted to a trifecta of arrows to what ego I had left.

Sheilah and I had spent some nice time together, including a fine, blustery afternoon revisiting the Cloisters and a dinner of marvelous sushi at a new hot place she'd heard about. We'd also spent some less nice time: too many evenings when I ached to be alone after an eight-hour day together on the job. I was invited to a Sunday night supper hosted by Todd Berenstain who called Sheilah Pretty Girl a lot and instructed us on the dangers incurred by liberal politics. Sheilah allowed as how his points were really worth a lot of thought and told me by eye signals that she wouldn't appreciate my frank statement of what I thought they were worth. So I asked for more coffee instead. I liked none of the three of us that evening, nor Todd any evening.

"What about Thanksgiving?" Sheilah asked, popping her head into my still new office. I looked up from the computer, feeling a blush rise to my cheeks because I'd been sending an e-mail to George. Her face was large when it beamed the way it was doing now—bigger than life even from yards away.

"Haven't thought about it," I said, which was not true. This was Monday, which made it less than a week away. I'd thought that since George might be on my screen but wouldn't be at my table, I wanted to lose the day: a late sleep in, followed by back-to-back movies and a pizza. Sheilah's own plans were, I knew, in abeyance, resting on whether Todd Berenstain accepted her invitation to dinner, which included her mother. But even this late in the game the prince remained evasive: maybe he would need to be out of town, he'd said, maybe not. On the subject of him I'd kept my teeth together. I had still not been able to bring myself to mention the Jan Simone thing—less and less confident I was doing the right thing.

"I'd really like it if you were with us. Now look, don't answer fast. I know my mother's not your favorite person but it would help me out. I mean if Todd comes I'll cook and I think things will work better if it isn't just a threesome. You know how she gets. And besides, Todd likes you—says he gets a kick out of you." I looked back at her wishing I were anywhere else, even at Bedford Hills, because I knew what was coming next. "Do it for me, okay?"

After all I've done for you. Maybe she wasn't even thinking it. "Could you . . ." I began. "Could I let you know?"

"Sure," she said, her smile gone.

CHAPTER THIRTY

At a little after six the same day Craig appeared at my doorway. "How would you feel about having an early dinner?"

"I kind of thought I'd just head home with a bag of Chinese."

"I'm heading out to Montana tomorrow. Thanksgiving with the family."

"Montana? That where we're from today?"

"Yup." He stuck his hands on his hips, threw back his head and laughed. "Bow-legged cowboy, who could mistake me?"

"Just stick on the right hat to cover the head-shave, lose the earring and you're good to go."

"Take pity on me. Think of it: three days of Mom in my face insisting I love creamed onions and Dad too depressed to threaten to take off his belt and whale somebody, even if there were someone around too weak to fend off a diabetic on three-day-a-week dialysis. Eat Chinese with me. I'll pay—I'll even pay *you*."

He got the laugh he was looking for. I'd seen little of him since my move into Teresa's former office, the day he'd invoked the spirit of Paul in warning me that recruiting was not my game. Somehow his presence now, after the heavy weather of Sheilah, felt like a stiff fresh breeze. I didn't have to trust him to enjoy him. I didn't have to trust him at all.

"Okay," I said. "But no soul-searching talk of reform."

The eyes went joke-wide. "You thinking of reforming?"

"No more than you are. Give me half an hour, okay?"

We stood in front of the building deliberating a destination. "Can I switch you from Chinese to Japanese?" he asked. "I've got a great sushi place with twenty kinds of sake and—"

"Not a chance. Too much of it recently—I'm about sushied out."

"And Sheilahed out?"

"No comment. Hey, how about Sichuan Pavilion over by the U.N.? Providing it's still around. I haven't been there since I got out but it used to be good, pretty cheap." Michael had liked the place a lot, but I didn't say that. Craig shrugged "fine," and we began walking east against a chilly breeze. "She's my oldest friend and she's been damned good to me," I said over some rush hour car honks.

"Aren't we defensive."

"You take her checks to the bank too."

"I do. Earned. Sheilah and I manage fine together. You know why? Because she's *not* my friend, old or new, and I keep it that way."

We should probably stay off friends, mine and his, if we were going to make it through dinner. But somehow it was I who couldn't quite. No sooner was a bit of red wine warming my gullet than I said, "I haven't heard from your former great and good friend in more than two weeks."

He nodded and sipped his bourbon and water. He looked almost sleepily content, kind of like someone who'd just eaten a good meal. The only thing was we'd ordered no food yet. Just then the waiter arrived. "Want to share?" Craig asked, giving me a small smile.

"Sure, whatever." The food was at the moment of not much interest to me. He ordered a lot of it though—and good stuff: steamed dumplings and spring roll; twice-cooked pork and garlic eggplant and General Tso's chicken. As I eyed him across the table something clicked. He reminded me of the way Paul's face would look sometimes—*did* look during the weeks before I learned about the FBI's pursuit of George. It just struck me now how, at the time, I'd thought his sunny face meant that things between us were on an upswing, that our marriage would make it after all.

"What is it, Craig?" I asked. "Cut the cute stuff. Why are we here together—and don't tell me it's about Asian cuisine."

He took a beat and a sip, and put his glass down. "Here's what I'm going to tell you, a few things actually. One, a lover hates being spurned. Two, a scammer hates being suckered. Three, a friend hates being used to hurt a friend. That's hate to the third power—and you're not looking at just *any* scammer here, I'm a very competitive one. Are you following me?"

"You're pissed off about being made a fool of, especially by a twerp way beneath your—shall we say, professional level?"

"Okay, you're following as far as you need to—as far as you want to."

The waiter put down the dumplings and spring rolls and asked about more drinks. Craig said yes for us both, which was quite okay with me.

"What the hell are you planning to do, put out a hit on him? Knock him off? Blow him away?" But my voice strained as it rolled out the old heavy sarcasm, because I knew I could be talking more than forties movie exaggeration. I could be stating a simple fact. After all, somebody had wounded me and I'd shot him dead.

Craig broke into one of his cackling laughs and reached for a dumpling, not bothering with chopsticks. "And you call *me* a drama queen. Remember that first evening you did?" He dipped the dumpling in sauce and popped it into his mouth. "Good," he said. "Try one." I made no move to do that. "Okay, I'll stop teasing. The punishment will fit the crime like a pair of custom shoes. Look, does the name Auguste Gramont mean anything to you?"

I thought about it. "No, not a thing. Should it?"

"No, didn't think it would. But when McCail calls you—and you can expect he will—he'll ask you that question. Don't tell him any lies, just say you're not sure, but you may have heard the name. That's all." He giggled again. "And it happens to be the absolute truth now. You've heard the name." He ate another dumpling.

"You're obviously having a great old time playing whatever you've been playing. I know the signs; I should have spotted them earlier. So what's the fallout for me?"

"How about you just might be rid of him for real. That fallout please you?" He didn't like the look on my face, and he was right not to. "Look, not a hair on his head or a dimple on his butt will be harmed. I punched him out already. It wasn't all that satisfying." He looked at the dumpling plate. "If you won't eat your share I'll just have to eat them all, spring rolls too."

"I'll eat my share," I said, believing—wanting to believe—the eyes, the face, the voice, as well as the words. But this could be Folly talking. Think I didn't know that? I reached for a chunk of spring roll anyway.

"Good. Then let's talk about something else and do some serious eating."

"Just one thing," I said. "I have a question for you. Do you know that Marina Beck is Paul's mother?"

"Yes," he said. "I knew that—or should say I figured it—about a week after I met . . . McCail." He shook his head in a way I can only call rueful. "I'm stuck really: calling him Angel makes me gag or want to cry, but I still find I have to pause a second before saying McCail. Anyway, hints he dropped made me wonder—you know, that silly cunt's downfall will be his need to show off. I started playing with the Paul and Marina elements, just for fun: ages, the funny closeness, even genetics. They didn't look alike of course, but the coloring, the light eyes. . . . And all the clips I pulled up on Marina talked about how she reinvented herself. Once you factor in witness protection—"

"You are one scary dude, you know? Why the hell did it take me so long to even think of the possibility, while you clicked into it like *that?*"

"For the same reason I make my living piecing together puzzles and wheedling information—and you should be making yours designing wonderful things. You want that last half a dumpling?"

We ate a lot, talked a lot, but not about Gabriel McCail or Sheilah—or about anything personal. At one point I felt an absurd impulse to tell Craig about the e-mails from George and my responses to them, just to see what he, with his chambered nautilus of a brain, thought. I stuffed some more eggplant into my mouth instead and waited for the impulse to recede. I wasn't that crazy.

———

I sat at the round dining table sketching the bird's head again—on a real sketch pad, bought last weekend. I'd opened it several times but had not made a mark until now. I redrew the head, bringing it to a crownlike point on top, my hand trembling only the tiniest bit on the curve the first time and not at all the second. Something about tonight's dinner with Craig had energized me—or maybe it wasn't that at all, but making a straight-out bid to see George, offering my phone number. Anyway, I felt good for the first time in a couple of weeks.

Then the phone rang. My "Hello" sounded tight as a crow's caw. Could I really believe it might be George? More likely Sheilah, unwilling to wait until tomorrow to get her Thanksgiving answer, or Gabriel McCail making the call that Craig had warned me about.

"Hey, it's me." A skin ripple of pure surprise: Michael. "Grace? Grace, you there?"

"I'm there. Here. What . . . can I do for you?"

"I don't know. What do you want to do for me?"

Fuck your brains out, as you damned well know. "Nothing, Michael. I thought we were past that, scratched the itch, et cetera. It's not such a good idea, you and me. Didn't you leave a message to that effect a couple of weeks ago?"

"That the way you took it? Shit, well, I can see how you would. I was so . . . so scared of making a wrong move."

"Well, look both ways before you cross and you'll be fine."

"I wanted to spend every second I could with you—every second you'd have me. But it can't be just about what I want."

"Yeah, I know. We've got a past with enough toxins in it to wipe out the tristate area, and then there's the little fact that you live with someone."

"True, absolutely true. Look, I said I needed some time, and I did. For one thing, I'm no longer living with anyone. But if that were the only issue, I'd take your hand, if you'd give it to me, and walk into the sunset, and we could talk and laugh and fight. We could do those any time we weren't making love or fucking each other blind. You know what I'm saying, Grace?"

"No, I don't think I do. But I . . . I have my own doubts about us. I didn't that night, not a doubt in the world. I just felt—never mind what I just felt. But see, while you were still asleep that morning, my PO took it into her head to drop in for a surprise home visit. She took a look in the bedroom and she wanted to know who the guy in the bed was. When I told her, she asked a very elementary question. Now she's not one of the world's subtle people, but then neither am I. The question boiled down to, 'Are you crazy? Why wouldn't you put all that behind you?' And at that moment I was flying high and kind of flipped her off, in not a very good way. But she had a point, didn't she? The same point you had."

"Not exactly," he said slowly. "I said I needed some time. I took the time. I know you must have thought, 'Oh, look, there's Michael ducking out one more time,' but Grace, don't you get it? I ruined your life by being too damned spineless to make you hear me, if I had to bind and gag you to do it, about Paul, what he was. Maybe if I had, you'd've gotten out early enough. So whatever blame you live with, I own a piece of it. What I'm trying to say here is I do not want you hung out there to dry again, especially not by me."

"You know, I don't want to be hung out to dry either and I guess I'll have to begin to watch out better for people coming at me with clothespins in their hand. But that is *my* lookout not yours. How exactly are you afraid you might do me damage?"

"By not being honest with you—or by being more honest than I . . . than it's safe to be."

"Safe?" Did he after all know where George was? "So tell me, is this a call from Michael saying good-bye or hello?"

"Hello. It's Michael saying hello. It's Michael saying I want to see you—and to talk to you for real. Here's the thing—just a second." While I waited, my ear catching muffled dots and dashes of medical jargon, my mind was a rush hour tunnel, headlights zipping through too fast and bright to identify the make or model of the cars. *I want to see you—and to talk to you for real. Cross my heart it's true. Do you believe me?* Then Michael was back. "Sorry. I've got to go now; my kid's going to surgery. But look, I had this idea. Thanksgiving. Could we spend it together? Woodstock: I still have the house. Mine now. Say yes and I'll come pick you up Wednesday night late after I get off shift. Do you . . . will you trust me that far?"

"I don't know. Can I call you tomorrow?"

"Sure," he said after a beat. "You've still got my cell number? You didn't throw it out?"

"I didn't throw it out." I hung up.

I heard George's voice in my ear, hoarse and filled with his kind of humor. *"So you got a full dance card, Gracie. Do you wanna dance with any of them or sit it out? Or do something else?"*

Jesus, George, why couldn't you do something else? I opened the laptop, with some thought of telling him about my current pair of Thanksgiving offers, and realized I couldn't: the mention of Michael and me together would not please him. A message from him, *"I need to stay on the easy road, Gracie. No visits, no phones. But hang in with me, you're the best medicine."*

I answered, *"I'm hanging. You can't get rid of me so fast. Is medicine your way of saying you're not feeling good? I mean in some new way? I may be going away for Thanksgiving with a man I like a lot. I'll take my laptop with me so we can keep talking."*

I collected three phone messages that had come in while I was talking to Michael and e-mailing George. Two were from candidates on whose voice mail I'd left my home number, the other from Sheilah saying she was considering a dynamite recipe for corn pudding to go with the turkey and five other sides, and Yes! Todd had accepted. In fact he'd done so that very evening at the Carlyle, where Bobby Short was beyond fabulous. "And Todd said he'd love you to be with us for Thanksgiving. Come on Gracie, for *me?*"

CHAPTER THIRTY-ONE

atty Ann was a no-show Tuesday morning. No one claimed to have any information about when she might be expected, but I noticed some looks dart back and forth behind the check-in counter when I asked for her. I signed in, waited the better part of an hour and requested the desk officer's permission to leave. The answer was no. Twenty minutes later, a harried PO, a man in a green suit, walked over and asked me about employment, domicile, use of illegal substances and consorting with bad elements. I gave the right answers, he jotted them down, wished me a good holiday. I hightailed it off to work feeling oddly like a kid playing hooky from school.

"Sheilah." I stood at her open office door. She'd just hung up the phone.

"Good morning." Her smile said that those two words were filling her up like honey in the blood. It was a feeling I'd known in a distant past and had tasted again twice. I smiled back at her in a kinship that would make what I was going to say to her easier and also harder.

"Sorry to be late, my PO never showed and I had to wait to see a sub." She gave an accepting nod followed by an impatiently expectant look. *No stalling now.* "Sheil, I'm not going to come to dinner Thanksgiving." She started to say something but was silenced by that chaos of hurt and anger that tends to cause a jam-up in the throat. I'd felt it myself enough times to recognize it when I saw it, especially in someone who mattered to me. "I'm going out of town for those couple of days. I . . . I'm really sorry."

"Out of town? But you're not *allowed* to."

"Well, strictly speaking, I suppose, since I won't be sleeping home. I can fly under the radar on that one, especially with Patty Ann MIA. Leaving the state would be something else but I'm not doing that." Our eyes connected and stuck that way. Her mouth tightened, waiting: it was my move. *Tell her. She'll think you're nuts but tell her anyway.* Was this a test? I guess it was. I could have given her a lie about needing to be alone or . . . God knows what, but I did not want to. I wanted finally to hand her a piece of hard, awkward truth. "Sheil, I'm spending the holiday with Michael Pyatt."

"No." Just the one word, but it was Mrs. C-D speaking out of her daughter's mouth with the same inflection she always used referring to the late, despised Donlan.

"Sheilah, don't do this."

"What's *this?* The fact that I'm rocked and disappointed by your dishonesty and selfishness, not to mention rotten judgment?"

I hadn't sat down—probably some instinct about being trapped. I was standing right behind a chair, and only as I felt my face go hot did I realize I'd been grasping the chair's steel back bar like a subway handrail. I turned it loose and stepped away.

"You don't own me," I said, a bit overloud for the room. Once I'd begun it felt easier, these things overdue for saying. "As good and generous as you've been, you don't get the right to play dolls with me as your doll. We are *friends:* old friends, good friends. Also, I work for you and you pay me—maybe you pay me too much, maybe I'm not good enough at what you need me to do in this office now. If so, fire me. But don't, *don't* . . . presume. I won't take it."

"I want a report by tomorrow morning on *every* candidate on your hit list—the ones you reached, the ones you didn't and how many calls you placed to them and what messages you left. I also need a detailed schedule of the phone meetings you've been able to set up for me. I will be available to speak to them from home over the holiday. I assume you will make yourself available too."

My slap had stung. Her quick dive into the haven of business boss-talk underscored that. I didn't feel much better about our skirmish than she did, but I was relieved to change the subject, no matter to what. My report wasn't going to thrill her: that she knew already, but she'd have it all right. "Yes. Yes, of course I will."

CHAPTER THIRTY-TWO

Wednesday night I waited for Michael to come pick me up. I paced the apartment stealing the odd glance at my packed satchel, fat with sweater and jeans and sneakers, sitting by the door ready to go. *Michael. Woodstock. Joy. Desolation.* I checked my watch. He wasn't even late—yet. Did I really think he wouldn't come? To even ask the question meant that part of me thought he wouldn't, and when the phone rang I was certain that what I'd been trying to brush off as a case of jitters was not that at all, but a premonition rooted in the facts of past behavior.

"Hello," I said. The syllables could have been fuck you.

"Grace. Gabriel McCail." Craig had prepped me. *Okay, Craig, I'm ready. Eager.*

"Yes, Gabriel?" Lots of background noise. He said something but I couldn't make it out. "I can't hear you too well," I said.

"I'm at JFK. They just announced a last boarding call for some damn plane going where people have relatives. Thanksgiving—zoo time here. Look, something's come up and um . . . I'm going to be out of the country for . . . I'm not sure. I need to ask you though: Does the name Auguste Gramont ring a bell with you?"

Pause, not too fast. "Nooo, I don't think so." *Beat, beat.* "The name sounds *kind* of familiar to me, but . . . no I really can't place it."

"Think. Paul. Switzerland. Older guy: stocky, big head of silver hair? Gramont would've surfaced in New York shortly before your dad disappeared?" *Tasty bait.*

"Sorry, Gabriel. I really draw a blank. But, hey, if you find out anything you think might jog my memory, give a call." He grunted a quick goodbye, or something less polite and turned his phone off. Moments later, the downstairs buzzer sounded.

Michael sat like a king in the driver's seat of a low-slung blue Mercedes ragtop, which was more than half as old as we were. "You're kidding," I said as I approached and tossed my satchel and laptop in the back.

"I never told you this was my dream?"

"I thought *I* was your dream," I said deadpan and slid in beside him.

"True. I bought myself this car seven months ago, for my fortieth birthday. A resident doesn't make a hell of a lot so I took out a loan. See, I didn't want to use my father's money; I wanted it to be from me to me. And I guess since I'm saying that to you, it's something I'd like you to know."

I touched his arm but lightly enough that I couldn't tell whether he felt it or not through the leather jacket. We rode through the November wind. For about fifteen minutes it was heaven. "Okay," he said, answering nothing spoken, "I'm gonna pull over and cover this animal's cage."

Maybe half an hour later we were back on the highway weaving our way past the Bronx. The holiday traffic had passed its peak but the roads were still far from empty. With its top up and windows shut the space inside the car was intimate and rather quiet. I think it was this sense of being in a space capsule, removed from any need for context that let me say so easily, "You drove George away that night; you sort of said that but . . . that was one of the *verboten* pieces—things you wouldn't talk about. You *did* drive him, right?"

"I did, yes. That's what I did: I drove him and I left one not too obvious print on the steering wheel—and I made sure that a couple of people on Hudson Street caught sight of me in the area earlier that evening. In other words, I was a cog–a necessary one–small but necessary."

"Where? Will you tell me?"

"Grace, I'm going to tell you everything now. That was one of the reasons I needed to take the time out–to be sure I *could* tell you how things happened without any bad rebound. My daddy's been up in Otisville for four months now, so common sense told me that George was irrelevant to him, but I wanted to ask the question eyeball to eyeball, just to make sure."

My heart was thudding. "You made sure?"

"I went up there to do that over the weekend. Josh said, and I quote, 'George Leshansky could dance naked in Times Square and nobody would give a hot fuck, except the boys who cart crazy old men off to Bellevue.' "

"Thank you," I said quietly. The grin I was talking through started somewhere around my toes. It would have been the time to tell him about George and me–about the e-mails, but I didn't. Perhaps it was because I didn't want to sidetrack him from what he was going to say next. I'd have liked to believe it was only that.

"I drove him up to Dutchess County, the Route 44 exit," he said, his voice constrained, as it had not been a moment ago. "We left the city at five in the morning, got there at about a quarter of seven–designated spot on Route 44 about two miles out of Millbrook. A dark green Ford wagon was supposed to meet him. It did."

I saw the scene in my head. It was as clear as the one I'd seen there so many times, the one of George running, getting gunned down. "And he just got out of your car and into that green wagon? Did you see who was driving? What did he say? I mean George. You were together for what, almost two hours? What did he *say?*"

We hit a clear patch of road and he made an economical move into the fast lane to take advantage of it. "Grace, Jesus I wish I could tell you something that'd make you feel . . . if not good, then better. But I'm not going to lie to you. I didn't want to be in that car and neither did he. It was just the least bad option in a bad bunch. When I picked him up he said, 'Thanks, I think.' Then he said nothing. I didn't either. I don't know who was in the green wagon—even whether it was a man or a woman. When I pulled up to let George out he said, 'Are you gonna be able to help my daughter?' And I said—it sounds so damned callous, but it's what I said. 'It's a little late for you to be thinking about your daughter's welfare.' He said, 'For sure,' and got out of the car."

"He got out of the car," I repeated. Traffic stalled again and he turned to look at me. I saw lines in his face I hadn't noticed. They all pointed down. "Look, Michael, I don't need fairy tales. I know who my father is, and I know how you feel about him, so I wouldn't believe pretty speeches between you two, even if you did decide to make them up. There's more you have to tell me, I can see that."

"Oh yeah, there's more."

"Okay, I'm listening."

And he talked. Eyes on the road ahead the whole time, Michael talked.

"I was as clueless as you were about this FBI thing. And then late one morning—I remember I was working the register at the Strand and we were busy—I had a phone call: Paul, from a street pay phone saying he needed to talk as soon as possible, and could I take a break in two hours and meet him inside the Fifty-ninth Street subway station, uptown side, right by the Bloomingdale's entrance. It was such CIA parody stuff that my first reaction was to laugh, like, 'What's going on, man? Got a surprise *other* wife to introduce?'

"But he didn't laugh back and I think I knew then we were in trouble. What he said was, 'I've got the only wife I want, but sacrifices must be made sometimes.' He sounded so weird, some mix of sad and excited. I don't know, whatever I caught in his voice, it kept me from hassling him for information on the phone.

"When I got there, he was waiting. He grabbed my arm hard and led me down the subway platform. Then the whole time, the two of us marched back and forth like soldiers on sentry duty. Once the talk started, we stopped only when the train noise got so loud you couldn't hear without someone hollering. 'They're going to kill George, it's that simple, no euphemisms.' That was the opening line; he had my attention.

"Then he ran through how the FBI agents had begun closing in a couple of weeks earlier with a kick-ass dossier on the washed money: fake companies, capital improvements, whole damned thing with the name George Leshansky writ large all over it. Seems the Feebs had done their homework, even as far as knowing that the son-in-law was little Paulie Donofrio, not the fancy Harvard boy he occasionally claimed to be. Funny, when Paul said that, he had this satisfied little smile on him, which gave me the idea that his sleeve was no more empty than usual.

"But the next thing he said had no smile about it. 'If George gives up Josh and whoever else is in that package, he's a dead man, just the way my father was. Witness protection for a minnow like George Leshansky amounts to a goldfish bowl hidden behind a chair. He gets to swim around trapped inside the glass waiting to be found, which he will be by anyone with the tracking powers of a ten-year-old. The only question is whether it takes weeks or months. With your father doing the looking, I'd figure it wouldn't take long.'

" 'That little chickenshit plans to rat out my daddy to save his own miserable skin? Maybe he *should* be a dead man.' Sorry Grace, I'm giving you the words, and at the moment I said them I meant them. Then Paul said, 'George is not going to give up Josh, nor is he going to die. We can't let either of those things happen.' And I said, 'What do you mean we?'

"Right about then we reached the end of the platform for a second time and made an about-face. Paul grinned like a man about to announce he'd won the lottery or found God. Christ, even now I can see the damned scene move by move, hear it word for word.

" 'What would you say if I told you I have designed a witness protection program that's going to work—a plan that will keep Grace's father alive and safe and yours out of prison?'

" 'I would say could we skip the sales pitch and get to it? I know whose father we're really talking about and so do you. Come on, Paul, you *know*. You're hooking me into something using Grace as bait that you're sure I'll take. And the something you want from me obviously has to do with my father. But at the bottom of this swamp my X-ray vision spots *your* father. For Chrissake, Paul, you do *not* get to do it over!'

" 'Most people don't get to do it over, that's true. All the more reason . . .' Paul's face got tight looking in a way it usually didn't. 'Are you ready to put away the psych textbook now and listen to me, Michael?'

" 'Talk.'

" 'This is still a work in progress, but here's the first chapter: George is going to tell the Feebs yes to testifying and witness protection, and then he is going to disappear; I mean disappear so nobody'll look for him. And that's the challenge because the Feebs are not as stupid as they look and Josh and his colleagues are fairly efficient when they need to be. So George is going to have to be dead.'

" 'Lost you. I thought that's what you're wanting to prevent here.'

" 'Correct, and to do that, George has got to be dead before he testifies, not after. He has to be credibly, persuasively dead—whacked according to a scenario that everyone will believe. The only thing missing will be a body.'

" 'And I bet you've figured out a way to make that piece of fiction credible—also a way to make sure it remains fiction?'

" 'I have. But I will need two things from you to make any of it work.'

" 'From me? *Through* me is what I think you mean. I assume what you want has to do with convincing my daddy to go along with your master plan.'

" 'That's one part of it, yes.'

" 'Are you smoking bad weed, friend? Why would Josh Pyatt put his own ass on the line to send a time bomb like George Leshansky out to God knows where? That man was ready to give him up! Still is, for all I know.'

" 'No, you're wrong. George is terrified of Josh—so much so that he is ready to go to prison rather than give him up. *That's* the way George is feeling this minute. But it doesn't matter what he feels one minute to the next, because constitutionally scared men are not resolute, they'll cave to the terror of the moment. So once the government gets hold of him, isolates him, softens him up a little more, he becomes a *true* danger to Josh.

Now, here's the alternative: George disappears in the next couple of days, having given up nobody, and is never, ever seen or heard from again. He is in fact a different person: different face, different body, different Social Security number and—well you get the picture. So—if you were in your father's position which way would you pick?'

" 'You've got a point there, Paul. You know my father pretty well, better than I do in some ways. And the two of you have always seemed to have a certain . . . rapport. Why don't you just go lay it out for him yourself?'

" 'Michael, you disappoint me. It's too obvious for you not to see it. I do know Josh—well enough to be sure that if he heard this from me his first thought would be to go me one better and have George hit, really. He's a simple man, your father, a *primal* man, and that would be the primal solution. The only thing is, George would be dead—after pissing his pants in terror for half an hour or an hour or three hours between the time they grabbed him and the time they killed him. And Josh Pyatt would be suspects number one, two and three—the Feebs would never let up on him.'

" 'So you're saying that if *I* approach him with this he'll see it your way. How do you picture the scene, me sitting on his lap? Why the *fuck* would he listen to what I tell him on something like this—or on anything?'

" 'Because you are his son. You *own* him, remember? You told me that when your parents split he said he owned you until you were eighteen and after that you would own him. I take that statement as gospel from an utterly literal man who believes profoundly in blood ties. Hey, I may go by a French name but in my heart where *I* live I am an Italian. Machiavelli and Paulie Donofrio, we understand blood loyalties—and we understand the obligations of the prince.'

" 'In your heart where you live you are a con man.'

" 'Michael, I swear to you that if you give your father the choice of following the plan or losing you permanently, he will cooperate. He will believe you are serious because he knows how you feel about Grace.'

" 'Now I'm gonna tell you something *you* can believe: if you use Grace to twist my arm one more time, I will knock your teeth right through that smile.'

" 'I do believe that. In some distant corner of your soul, you are your father's son, aren't you? You've got a certain tough streak, Michael. You need to find it and I'm going to give you that chance.'

" 'Thanks a bunch. Could we skip the distant corners of my soul on the 6 Train platform and cut to what you mean, Paul?'

" 'As I said, George's kidnapping and death will be an immaculate illusion—as persuasive as the one created to persuade the Nazis that the Allied invasion would be launched from Pas-de-Calais. If you know your World War Two, you know it worked. I'm missing only one crucial element to make mine work.'

" 'What element is that—besides a body of course?'

" 'A suspect.'

" 'Not my father you have in mind, right?'

" 'No. That would be a bad move, even if he'd go along with it—which of course he wouldn't. If George is a minnow then Josh is at best a midsized fish. If he were ever taken into custody the bigger fish he works for would get very nervous about his making a deal and giving them up.'

" 'But he would never give them up. Never. The man has his codes, insane as they are.'

" 'Look, Michael, we're dealing with perception here. This project of mine is a palace built of perceptions, towers of them: glass bricks, mirrors. No, Josh isn't the suspect I have in mind.'

" 'I know that.'

" 'Right. You get it then. I'll take care of planting and cultivating the suspicion, seeing that it closes in around you—but only up to a point. What you need to do is stay away from the loft; stay away from us. After tonight I mean. Tonight I want you to come for dinner with what's her name, the Swede, just as planned. I'm cooking a bouillabaisse.'

" 'And Grace? What's your plan about Grace?'

" 'The plan for Grace: I will tell her nothing yet, and afterward just a few strategic lies. I said when I called you today that sacrifices would have to be made. That is a big one. It breaks my heart.'

" 'As if. You mean to say that this card trick is going to be pulled off on Grace, that you don't trust her with George's best interest? She *loves* that old bastard, she'd never hurt him."

" 'She'd never *mean* to hurt him. But Grace is emotionally unreliable.'

" 'Unlike you? Unlike me?'

" 'Correct. We're totally reliable for different reasons, the two of us—me because this enterprise is the core of my being; you because you know that if you fuck up or go sentimental you will kill that man, and you don't want it on your conscience. Grace would intend to go the distance but she couldn't stay away from him; she'd make an impulsive move and crack it wide open: in effect *she'd* kill him. So you won't say a word about it to her, not tonight, not after.'

" 'And she will think I killed her father.'

" 'Probably she will for a while. Then again, maybe not. For once, I'm not going to debate you, Michael. All I'm going to do is ask you to take a minute to think, or as long as you need—and then tell me whether you're in.'

"It didn't take me very long to tell him, 'Yes, I'm in.' "

I had not said a word, not moved in my seat. A dark little girl with a kaleidoscope pressed to her eye, trying hard to hold still and keep the design from going away—it was like that: if I shifted Michael might just stop talking and the awful, compelling pattern would disappear.

Because of Paul's singular touch with truth I found I had known both more and less than I'd supposed. My shocks of recognition were what you might experience walking through the bombed-out rubble of your own home, identifying bits and pieces of things you had lived with, the debris all the more sinister for its familiarity. Picture for example the surviving fragment of what had been a bright pottery vase. Now it was a long curved dagger-shaped shard, blackened, the shiny red glaze showing through only at its sharp tip.

"Paul was right about me, you know," I said. "I would have fucked it up. I did fuck it up. I killed the best friend George had." *And no matter what he's said about not blaming me, how must George really feel about that?*

"I told you once, and I meant it," Michael said, taking a hand off the wheel and squeezing my shoulder, "Paul was nobody's friend."

"Thanks. I mean . . . Oh, God. Thanks." It came crashing into my brain like surf governed by the tide of an angry moon: lives saved, lives ended, lives crippled by villains who were heroes and heroes who were villains. A sob that had nothing to do with weeping came out of me. "I think I need to be quiet for a while."

CHAPTER THIRTY-THREE

The town of Woodstock, when we passed through it, had been shut up tight—one in the morning; it would be. I remembered driving this route in Josh's car all those years ago, Josh blathering on about "a nigger out of Alabama" owning a house on the site of the summer of love; me sassing back with words like "fuck" to prove I wasn't scared of him, like whistling past a graveyard—and George mute beside me in the backseat, knowing the bargain he was making. Knowing where it would lead? Nonsense, he couldn't have known. But he would have imagined.

I looked out at the trees that lined the long private road into the Pyatt property. They'd grown taller—of course they had. I saw them silhouetted against the slate sky as enormous forged iron sculptures, their naked, skeletal arms reaching desperately skyward—which says everything about my state of mind at that moment.

"Paul was right about something else, a lot of things, actually," I said. "He was right about autumn. He used to say that the wild color everyone makes such a big fuss over every year is nothing but death in fancy dress. Look, late November now: no leaves, all the costumes gone. We can see what's what."

He stopped the car, turned the motor off. The house itself was not yet in view. For the first time in a couple of hours our eyes met. He said, "If you don't want to be here, I'll understand. This place is simple for me; it can't be simple for you. I didn't know I'd be telling you all I did on the drive up, so . . . what I'm saying is maybe it wasn't such a hot idea to come here. We can go somewhere else, anywhere else. It doesn't matter."

"Yeah, it matters. It does. You're right it isn't simple for me here, but hell, it isn't simple anywhere. And some of my memories of this place are pure gold." I reached over and stroked that lower lip of his with my finger. "A bad bargain began here for our fathers, but we began here too." He reached for me now and kissed me quick and hard, then long and almost lazy, as though we had all the time in the world. My head leaned against his when I said, "We're staying. I want to be here with you."

He started the car, but before he hit the gas my hand reached out to cover his. "Wait," I wanted to say, "let me tell you this now, before one more second goes by; I know for sure that George is alive and okay—we've been e-mailing. He found me on the Internet and—" I wanted to say that, wanted to give him truth for truth, but somehow I couldn't get syllable one out.

He turned to me, inquiring. "Nothing," I said. "Just touching your hand. Let's go see the house."

Ourside and inside, the house seemed unchanged, amazingly so: still the Cleaver house, maple American dining room and all, set for the sit-com television cameras to roll. "It's mine now," Michael said. We were standing in the entrance hall, able to glimpse the dining room to the left, living room to the right.

"And?" I asked.

"And, I don't know. He transferred ownership to me a while before the shit hit for him. He's in Otisville for life so . . . the truth is I haven't come up here that much."

"Tell you what," I said, "I want to be in a bed with you—more for the just being than for the sex even, if you can believe it. Could we sleep in your old room? I don't think I can manage Josh's bed."

So we slept in the lower bunk bed in a brown-and-red plaid room with mustard shag carpeting. It was an achievement of sorts for a pair of long people to intertwine themselves to fit the space, kind of like a snug pair of socks in a bureau drawer. That was the sleeping part—the expanse of carpet may have been scratchy against naked skin, but it offered much richer opportunities for the presleep activity.

I awoke with that slightly disoriented feeling of having traveled some long way while I was unconscious. Michael was not beside me. I stretched and found myself a little sore inside and out. I smiled: sex ache; what ache could be better? I called his name a few times but heard no answer. I got up and into a navy flannel robe draped on a chair beside the bed. I'd never seen it before but it smelled slightly, nicely of Michael.

I spotted my satchel in the far corner of the room, and beside it my computer. I remembered vaguely Michael saying before we drifted off, "You brought the machine? Considering spending the weekend working?" and me murmuring back, "You never know." Thinking of that now gave me a twinge with a bad bite to it. No good telling myself that the timing had been wrong for a revelation: half asleep, sated with sex—not the moment to break the news of my e-mail lifeline to George. The fact was that in the place where such decisions are really made I could not summon up the trust.

I trusted no one—hadn't in these eight years. Loneliness lapped at my soul now like cold seawater. I wanted to give trust, wanted specifically to give it to Michael. With half a heart I'd tried and come up empty. But the emptiness was deeper even than that: I wanted something impossible to retrieve: my arrogantly blind optimism. Finally, I had reached the stage of knowing what I knew. *Gotta tell you Paul, it's highly overrated.*

I booted up the computer and plugged it in to my cell phone the way Sheilah had taught me. Such zest she had for the spiffiest, the tastiest, the best: haute technology, haute couture, haute cuisine. I pictured her glossy red lips slightly open, ready to take a bite and knew, with some sadness, that I would always disappoint her, slipping out of her grasp just when she thought . . .

I opened my e-mail to a sweepstakes offer and one for a credit card, but nothing from George. I checked my watch—just past ten, nothing to worry about.

"Happy Thanksgiving," Michael said looking up from his coffee mug with a nice grin as I appeared at the kitchen door, "except for one small glitch."

I wrapped my arms around him from behind and kissed the top of his head. "I'm ready."

"I forgot to buy a turkey—or anything. I can pour you some coffee, orange juice from concentrate and we've got muffins and butter out of the freezer—oh, and jam. Give me a seven-letter word that means idiot and starts with *M*."

I kissed his head again and began to laugh into the soft curl of his hair, and once I'd begun it was hard to stop. Not that his mild joke was all that funny, but the thought of the hapless pair of us was, contrasted with—

"Hey, what is it?" he asked, swiveling around to face me.

"Just that . . . just that . . ." After another gale I got hold of myself. "Just that I was remembering how Paul used to fuss about Thanksgiving. How dare I even say 'used to'—I only had the two Thanksgivings with him, didn't I?" Suddenly, nothing seemed funny. I sat heavily on the chair catty-corner to Michael's and wiped my eyes, which were more than damp. "I'm sorry, it's no big whoop. I was just thinking how, even with food, he produced the show and we applauded. And now, between us, we can't manage to come up with a fucking Thanksgiving turkey—even a frozen one. I mean, you didn't mention it, neither did I, and all the while Sheilah was going on about the corn pudding she was going to make and the . . ." I began to laugh again—out of control and I knew it.

Michael was at my side now, kneeling and holding me. "Maybe it *is* a big whoop. We're a big whoop. Grace, look at me. Come on, look at me." For a second his face was blurred as though I were seeing it through a wet windshield. Then it was sharp and clear, face within face within face: the boy I'd fallen in love with, the father of that boy, the man I loved—might love—now. Was "now" the most or least important word in the language? "You and me. We're just you and me. It's enough."

I laughed again, very quietly this time. "What do you say we scope out the blandest, squarest, most Hallmark restaurant in a twenty-mile radius and go eat turkey with creamed onions and cranberry goop and mashed turnips there?"

"Or a diner for chiliburgers with cheese and fries?"

"Yeah. That'd be good too." I kissed his forehead and then kissed it again. "You know what I'd love to do right now? I love to take a walk with you. I know it's raining but what the hell."

"What the hell." We bundled up in sweaters we'd packed and slickers and yellow rubber boots from the mudroom outside the kitchen and walked the property, holding hands like people who'd been with each other a long time.

"You can't see it in this season but remember my mother's gardens? Choked with weeds, like they never existed. Up till the time the Feds nailed him he kept coming here, tended to the inside of the place like it was a museum exhibit but let the grounds mostly go to hell. You'd have liked my mother."

"I don't know about that. She didn't like me." It was still a sore point for me, evidently.

"She never had the chance to know you. All she knew was that you were the daughter of someone mixed up with *him*. She would've loved *you* to pieces. She had your guts and your openness—you'd have recognized each other. She was out there, the way you are." *And the moral is that women who are out there pick disastrous men to marry?* I knew that wasn't what he meant and I didn't have the heart to throw it back at him.

"What happened to the damn dogs?" The question was my clumsy effort to change the subject, but thinking of the dogs brought back to me vividly how the sight of them had terrified George.

"Died, long time ago. If they hadn't they'd be the longest-lived Dobermans in history. They were really pretty good dogs. My daddy trained them well—and gently, you'd be surprised."

"Next you'll be telling me how Hitler pampered *his* dogs. I'm not interested in good surprises about Josh."

"Subject closed," he said quietly. "For now. Do you dislike all dogs or just those dogs?"

"Don't really know. I never had much to do with any." We were at the top of the ridge now. We stopped walking and stood looking down at the swimming pond. It was gray as smoked glass in the rain but the memory of shining midnight blue under hot sun was sharp. "We began by fighting about our fathers. Maybe we haven't come all that far."

"Yes we have. We just don't know exactly where it is we've landed. Hey, going back to the dogs, remember how you asked me right before we did it that first time was I sure they were locked up, because otherwise they'd go right for your big, naked white ass?" He laughed loud and free—the opposite of my morning bout in the kitchen. I laughed with him now: no pain in this flashback; it was plain funny and plain good.

"If we were closer to seventeen we'd throw off all these clothes and do it now." I pointed ahead slightly to the left. "Right under that second tree, the big one."

"I've got an alternative suggestion. It involves a living room couch that's way more comfortable than yours and smoother than the carpet in my bedroom."

Later, while Michael was in the shower, I checked the e-mail again. No George. The prickle of unease—not fear really, not yet—got through to me though I did try to dodge it. My father was nothing if not elusive, always the opposite of reliable. He'd skipped a day here and there in this correspondence. Maybe he was out having turkey and stuffing around somebody's white-clothed table. When pigs fly, I thought. George was still George inside his skin: the most potent of Paul's magic hadn't altered that.

At a diner that looked like one, we swigged beer and scarfed down chili cheeseburgers as though we were a rural couple, "comfortable" the key descriptive word. I asked Michael more about being a doctor, a pediatrician, and he told me a few stories of sick kids he'd treated: ones who were the victims of bad genes or luck and others who were the victims of mad parents or simply of what comes with relentless poverty. You'd have had to be blind and deaf not to get how much he loved his work. The first time he'd talked about it, weeks ago in my bed, I'd felt envy. Now, as I reached across the Formica table to dab some chili off his chin I was purely happy for him—and, I realized not a split second later, happy for myself.

"I've been sketching," I said. "It's not exactly design yet, and I don't think my hands will ever really work the same way but . . . it feels so *good!*" I held both my hands up and examined them. At that moment they felt almost steady.

Michael nodded and reached across the table and took them in his. "I'd like to take this particular minute and frame it and hang it up for us to look at any time we feel bad. So what've you been designing?"

"Birds, wings—something along those lines, lots of points and angles. I'd have to work with a jeweler, of course. You know, Sheilah said to me on our ride down from Bedford Hills that I'd design jewelry again. And I snarled back at her like some animal. Less than two months ago, hard to believe. She was right—as she often is."

"She was right and you weren't ready to hear it. Happens."

"Not really an excuse." I told him about the rough ride she and I were having at the office—how wrong I was for the new work I'd been assigned. "It's a matter of time, I suppose I always knew that. But it feels like I'm face to the wall. I need the job, not just for money but to keep my PO off my back. Look, she gave me that job out of friendship, and I'm not treating her these days like the friend she is. I mean when I was locked up Sheilah was the best and . . ." I flipped my hands out, palms up to underline.

"Maybe she had you where she wanted you."

"Michael, that's a rotten thing to say!"

"Especially from me, who was nowhere in the vicinity."

"That isn't what I meant. I mean . . . I've blamed you to hell, but after what you told me last night how could I blame you for anything? I owe you."

"Let's don't do blame and owe, because if we get started it's gonna be a toss-up which one of us'll end up feeling worse. It *was* a rotten thing for me to say but in a way it's true. Hey, I've always liked Sheilah, but she's someone who wouldn't mind seeing you trapped in a burning building so she could save you."

"Do you mean 'you' as in me, Grace, or is it people in general Sheilah wants to save?"

"Probably not just you but not people in general either. She picks her targets; I don't know her well enough to know the others." It seemed a bit melodramatic, what he was saying, yet the ring of it hit me as unpleasantly real.

"That's way overstated. Are you comparing Sheilah to Paul?"

"No, no way. Paul would've led you into the building and then set the fire himself."

Into my mind popped something I couldn't believe I'd forgotten to bring up. "Michael, you said you'd never met Paul's mother, right?"

"Right," he said, wary because he'd heard a different note and didn't know what was coming. A little mischief maker crept into my mind to suggest he might be wary because he did know. Doubting: it had developed in me like a tic—like the occasional trembling in my hands. Involuntary.

"You *have* met her," I said. "So have I." As he leaned across the table my spasm of doubt in him passed: he didn't know what the hell I was getting at. "It's Marina. Marina is Paul's mother."

I watched his eyes widen a bit rounder than their normal almondish shape. "What? Why would you think that?"

"It's not a theory, it's a fact, and once you know, it fits like the right jig-saw piece." I told him about my meeting with McCail at Marina's house. "I was getting ready to leave and she came in on her way to some party, looking like . . . like death in fancy dress. I had this brainstorm—unusual for me: I'm not a person of good hunches, as you know. Anyway, after she left, McCail confirmed it. He couldn't keep it back. It's a blockbuster revelation in his book."

"How do you know they weren't playing you to get some response they wanted?"

"You had to be there, Michael. You had to see her face and his: our Gabriel may be obsessed with Paul, but his kind of ego makes him way more transparent. And when you think about Marina and Paul as mother and son, a lot of things make sense. Each of them had the cover of witness protection to become anyone–*anyone*. And they both had the scam genes to carry it off. She married a rich old man and became a rich widow and a patron of the arts. He became . . . Paul. They never separated–just served each other's needs and enjoyed their private joke."

Michael shook his head slowly, likely reviewing his own relationship with the friend who was nobody's friend. "That *motherfucker!*"

"May be literally true," I said. "Paul told me shortly after we met about how he and Marina had sex but never made love. He was very proud of me for not being jealous." I scrubbed at my eyes with my fists like an over-tired kid. "I don't want to talk about him any more right now. It makes me feel like such a stupid shit!"

"I'm with you there." Michael held up his beer bottle. "To two stupid shits." We toasted with the raucous clink of almost empty glass. The bad moment was over–for the moment. There would be others coming, I knew. I wanted this man with me when they did.

"Remind me to tell you I may be in love with you," I said.

"Back at you, with the 'may be' excised," he said.

On the ride back to the house it occurred to me to ask, "Does the name Auguste Gramont mean anything to you?"

"Don't think I ever heard it before. Why?"

"Not important–or maybe it is, in a good way." I told him about Craig's brilliance with computer and phone, and filled him in on the affair gone bad. "I said a little while ago that McCail's no Paul. He may have just done himself in here, taking on the wrong guy to scam, because there *is* a Paul-like side to Craig. I don't know the details of what he's up to but he told me that Gabriel's punishment would fit his crime, so some way or another Auguste Gramont is–ta da–Tarbell's Revenge."

We got back to the house around ten. Michael wanted to switch on the television and see what was up and down in the world. We sat on the couch where we'd made love that afternoon, slumped against each other now, watching CNN. So comfortable it was. There should be no secrets between us. On the other hand, you could say the correspondence was George's secret, not mine alone. Which reminded me that my e-mail had gone unchecked for a full day. I'd ask George, that's what I'd do. I'd tell him about Michael and me, about Josh inviting him to dance naked in Times Square. Then I'd ask his permission to tell Michael. If I explained how things were . . . "I'll be back in a minute," I said.

I wriggled out from under his arm and got myself quickly upstairs. A minute later, secrets stopped mattering. I was hollering Michael's name.

CHAPTER THIRTY-FOUR

R emember *Thanksgiving 1968 in wherever it was? Sometimes these days I can't get my head around a word or name. Your old nam's gold . . . Not what I meant ot right. OK, we were flat out borke in that motel with the running toilet and Minnesota won for me at 8 to akel/...........xeor amlp——————————————*

We huddled together at Michael's schoolboy desk where my computer sat and looked at the weirdly frightening message, my trembling finger pointing at it as though I were about to say something illuminating. Finally, it was Michael who spoke. "George."

"Yeah. I . . . I can't go through the whole thing now. We've been e-mailing—obviously. I've been on the edge of telling you since last night. I'm sorry—I'm *not* sorry. It makes no damned difference whether I'm sorry or not. Have I . . . led someone to him? Did your raising the subject with Josh . . . have I killed him after all?" I felt my body begin to shudder.

Michael surrounded me, arms wrapping tight as ropes. "Sshhh. Sshhh." It sounded like soft waves hitting a calm shore. "I'm not asking you for any long explanation now, okay? You are thinking that somebody's tracked him through e-mails from you and grabbed him right there in the middle of typing?" I nodded, which he couldn't see but could feel against his chest. "I can't rule that out to a certainty," he said slowly, a different sound to him than any I'd heard. "But it makes no sense, and it's at odds with what's on that screen."

I was having a little trouble breathing with my nose squashed against him, yet I didn't want to be turned loose: there was this feeling that without his arms holding me together I'd explode into useless spare parts. Just then, he relaxed his grip but not completely. "No one would have a reason to go after George," he said, "no one we know about. Look, are you up to sitting beside me on the bed there? I have a different idea of what happened. But you're gonna need to talk to me. If you can't yet bring yourself to trust me as Michael, trust me as a doctor."

He walked me the few steps to the bunk bed holding me by the arm: a professional's hand on a patient in shock. I gulped a deep breath and let it out very slowly. "Okay," I said feeling drugged. "Okay, Doctor." Once I was seated he sat too.

"You've got no clue where he is?" he asked.

"No. He's dead now, dead for real. Isn't that what you think?"

"I won't lie to you. Maybe. Here's what I think: I think George had a stroke or some other cardiovascular event in the middle of that e-mail. He needs to get to a hospital." His voice toughened to an interrogator's rasp. "I'm asking you again and I would advise you to be straight about it: *do you know where he lives?*"

Fury shocked through me—echoes of interrogations past. I snapped back, *"No, your honor, I do not."* I sprang off the bed and walked to where the computer was—back to George, I thought idiotically. "God, Michael, forgive me. I'm . . . I'm talking to Michael now, not the doctor. His first e-mail came the day we met at that bar—the night we made love. I wasn't even sure it really was him, but I got sure fairly fast. I didn't tell you about it then because . . ." I responded to the downturn of his mouth. "There was a lot you didn't tell me either until yesterday. I would have told you this weekend—I *think* I would have; I can't say for sure."

"Ah shit. Who the hell do I think I am, coming on like a storm trooper with you?" He walked over to where I was and pointed at the laptop screen. "Look at that pattern, the mixed-up words—where he tries to say, 'your old man's getting old,' and he then knows it's not right but he can't get it right, that could be what's called a TIA: transient ischemic attack. What that is is a ministroke: tiny blood clot blocking tiny artery in the brain. It can be a warning sign of a bigger stroke–a clot in a major artery– either later . . . or sooner. If–and I'm hypothesizing here–if he's had TIAs before or dizzy spells, that could tell us–"

"He has–dizzy spells." I could almost feel my ears sharpen like a dog's, tensed for a signal. "He mentioned that in one of the early e-mails, said he was unsteady on his pins, but that steady hadn't ever been his strong suit. I took it as a joke, the kind of George-Gracie thing we used to bat back and forth between us." For an instant I filled with hope: not a murderous attack but a warning signal for a stroke. If he got to a hospital in time . . . the instant passed. "Even if you're right, there's nothing I can do. Nothing. I don't know where the hell he is."

His arm went around my shoulders, gently this time. "Hey, maybe he's not alone. Maybe he has friends; maybe he lives with someone."

The friends part didn't sound much like my George but the living with someone part . . . George was used to that. They say people seek out what they're used to. I broke away from Michael and clicked Reply. *This is his daughter. My email address is right there, Gracieido@aol. My cell phone number is 917-436-6697. Please call or email at once.*

I looked up and caught his eye. "Couldn't hurt," he said. "Look, do you have the other e-mails? Did you save them?"

"Of course I did. When I'd pick up a message on my office computer, I'd forward it home and then delete it–delete my reply, too. I was being so careful–I thought. Anyway, the whole correspondence is filed in this machine."

"Here's my thought: maybe if we go over them now we'll catch onto a shred that'll give us some idea where he is." I nodded glumly and opened the *Allen* file. A midsummer night's snowflake hunt and we both knew it.

I moved the computer to the floor and we crouched down there with it. Nineteen days, fourteen e-mails, some no longer than a line, others longer–one of them, the one that recalled a last-minute score he'd made on New Year's Eve thirty years ago, how he'd sprung for *Die Fledermaus* tickets at the Met, scalper's price, to treat us, went on for two paragraphs. The one where he mentioned getting dizzy sometimes made my eyes burn with anger at myself for just letting it go by. *He was seventy-six, for Christ's sake. How could I have* . . . useless hindsight. Useless.

We scrolled through, scrutinizing message after message, not for what they said but for a speck of telling lint. I had a flash memory of Michael and me at the Film Forum down on Houston Street, watching a revival of *Blow Up*—how the photographs of a murder, enlarged to reveal a key clue, turned instead into a spread of meaningless dots.

"Looks to me like he's somewhere in our time zone, give or take an hour. What I mean is some of your exchanges were late night or early morning our time. It's a fuzzy indicator, I admit."

"My God, there's no hope at all of getting to him in time is there?"

Michael reached for my hand. "Let me be clear," he said, voice quiet and kind like a good doctor set to deliver bad news. "If it was a TIA, it could've just passed after a while; they do. But if what he had was a massive stroke and he was alone at the time, the chances are he's dead." I nodded my understanding and squeezed his hand back hard. "Now, if he or somebody with him managed to call nine eleven or the equivalent he might've gotten to a hospital in time. If we could home in on location I could start calling hospitals."

"And ask for? We know *allenbirn* is his e-mail address but maybe it's not the name he's using. It could be Birnbaum, which was George Burns's real name: Nathan Birnbaum. Maybe . . . I felt a skin-puckering ripple throughout my body, a visceral reaction to the heat of an idea I knew was right. "Michael, I want to see your father."

"My father." He said nothing more. His face went utterly still, taking on the look of a sculpture carved by a primitive African hand a long time ago. But the dark eyes gave evidence that thoughts were tag-teaming behind them.

"He knows. It just hit me now that he'd have made it his *business* to know. Okay, you and Paul persuaded him to let George disappear, but that crafty old bear would have a plan B; he never trusted anyone in his life."

"Somebody did put him in Otisville," Michael said. Then he added almost to himself, "Not one of his own, though."

"That's my point: he kept tabs on his own. All the years I was growing up, when things got dangerous in New York because George was in too deep and couldn't pay, we'd pack up our stuff and move for a while till things cooled off and he could win or earn enough to pay up. But somehow I always felt that even when we scampered that way, Josh knew where to find us if he wanted to. I mean, after that bad beating we went to Florida—and then one night, there was Josh on the phone offering the devil's bargain. He had the number, not from George, but he had it."

Michael nodded slowly. For a moment he seemed on the edge of tears. "We're some pair, you and me," he said with the bitterness of someone very young, "the clueless couple. Look, this fool will drive you up there tomorrow. It'll take us only a few hours. They won't put a phone call through this time of night, but I'll call him first thing in the morning. Thanksgiving weekend, Friday visits might be on."

"They were at Bedford Hills."

"There wouldn't be a problem anyway," he said sourly. "Josh Pyatt figured pretty quick how to throw his weight around up there just like he did in Harlem and the Heights."

He turned away and went to the bed. I followed and put my hands on his shoulders, kneading what felt like angry knots of muscle. "Michael, are you thinking they played you—both of them, Paul and Josh?"

"I'm thinking I don't want to talk about this now, okay?" He reached back and stopped my hands working on him. "Thanks, feels good, but it's wasted on me right this minute. Only thing that's going to help me is to get unconscious for a couple of hours. Wake me if . . . there's anything."

With the ease that doctors, soldiers and such develop at grabbing chunks of oblivion in the midst of chaos, he was gone in minutes—except for his shoes, fully clothed. I sat cross-legged in front of the computer screen waiting for an e-mail that did not come. First my feet fell asleep and sometime after that the rest of me unfolded onto the shaggy carpet and began to follow suit.

CHAPTER THIRTY-FIVE

When I opened my eyes it was quarter past four. I checked the computer—again nothing. I checked my cell phone even though it lay three feet away from my head and hadn't rung—nothing there either. When I opened my eyes again it was almost seven-thirty. Michael sat on the bed looking down at me as though he'd been doing that for a while.

I felt like I'd been drugged; everything hurt. "Hello," I said with very little sound to it. A gladness at the sight of him cut through the murk.

"Hello yourself. I'll call him and set it up for us to come. He's got it fixed so they put my calls through as quick as they do his lawyer's—doctor-son of seventy-three-year-old diabetic. Did I tell you Josh has diabetes? Pretty bad too."

I shook my head no. My bleary eyes were already on the screen. I dialed up and found no message except a few overnight garbage ads. "Tell him *you're* coming. I'll be a surprise guest."

"I could also lay it all out on the phone, give him some time to reach his lawyer and have him try to look into it—I mean just in case you're wrong and he *doesn't* know."

I swiveled around fast. "He knows. I want to eyeball him and dare him to tell me he doesn't. *You'd* rather risk George dying in some hospital alone than learn for sure that your daddy lied to you."

"That makes me cruel—and it's nothing like the truth. But I have to admit there's a true kernel in there somewhere. What's also true is that I love you. I've been awake here looking at you sleep for the better part of an hour. Here's the thing: I love you enough to take my lumps on this to help you get what you need."

I raised myself up on my knees and got myself over to where I could touch him. "I just have this gut feeling that it'll work better in person. He *does* know, Michael." His tongue ran over his lower lip, like a kid's. I felt a teary burning at the back of my nose. "I love you too."

Otisville Federal Prison is in Orange County New York, south and west of where we were. The drive took a little over an hour and a half. We'd been on the road almost that long when my cell phone rang, causing my heart to stall.

Sheilah said, "I hope it's not too early to call."

The impulse to push the disconnect button showed its nasty face. I slapped it down, but the wish provoked almost as much guilt as the deed. "Michael and I went out for an early breakfast," I said carefully. He threw me a glance and I mouthed "Sheilah." He shook his head, gave my shoulder a pat and turned his attention back to the road. I asked, "How was Thanksgiving?" The beaten tone of her first few words had previewed the answer.

"I needed to talk to you. Grace, it was—well, not awful—but in some way it would have been better if it had been. Awful, I mean. He came, he was . . . correct: complimentary about everything—how I looked, the food; nice to my mother, but . . . Grace, I caught him looking at his watch. Twice. And he left before seven. I mean, he came at three but he didn't even suggest that we might, I don't know, go out to a movie or . . . He wanted to go," her voice shook, "and he went."

"Oh, Sheilah, I'm so damn sorry. But he isn't worth—"

"Maybe it would've been different if you were there."

"It wouldn't have been different. Sheilah, listen, *hear* me: Todd Berenstain is not worth the sweat off your left boob. He's a—"

"Come *on,* he's great—he *is* in so many ways. You didn't like him from the beginning, I could tell—urging me to take it slow. You know, I think he just felt claustrophobic yesterday with my mother being grande dame all over him, that's what I think. That's why I say if you'd been here—"

"Now he's *my* fault? Let me tell you something, friend, he is a creep, and no, I didn't like him. I think he's a self-absorbed phony who—"

"And when did you become the big authority on picking men?"

I took a very deep breath. "Not yet," I said, each of the words a little hard pellet into her ear. "Sheilah, I'm sorry you're hurting but I can't have this conversation now. Don't call me back today because I won't answer. I'm hurting too—and I can't take . . . you on." I pushed End, cutting her off a few words into an eloquent, wounded response. "Shitshit*shit*." It wasn't sufficiently under my breath that Michael didn't hear.

"Girlfriend stuff?" The first two words out of him in a while.

"You could say. Jesus, I hung up on her. What does that make me?"

"Human—and on a short fuse. You'll explain to her later. It'll be okay."

"How much longer to Otisville?"

"Ten minutes, maybe less . . ."

Michael and I sat beside each other at a rectangular table, metal legged, Formica topped, prison issue. "Feels weird being on the visitor side of things," I said. "It'll feel weirder to see him—here or anywhere." I cleared my throat. I was dry and frog-voiced. Josh Pyatt would walk through that door any minute, escorted by a guard and wearing whatever was regulation here. I hadn't seen him since I was seventeen, the day he tried to hand me money, pay me for the loss of Michael. No, that was not quite true, I had seen him once.

Twenty years ago, I'd seen him coming out the door of our Washington Heights apartment building just as I was rounding the corner of our block on my way home from Cooper Union, a bulky portfolio of industrial de-

sign drawings under my arm. In my racing heart and brain, I let the portfolio fall to the sidewalk and rushed him—scratched long bloody lines
down his face, then kicked his big balls from Broadway to Fort Washington Avenue. But my gut was the ruling organ that day and it was a coward.
I turned back the way I'd come, ducked into a shadowed doorway and
waited a timed five minutes before making my run to see whether George
was okay or beaten to a pulp. He was in fact drinking a Dr Pepper and
watching news on Channel 2.

Was my bent for sudden violence already in place back then: a wild
seed, ready to burst into quick, thick growth, given the right watering?

Though I had pushed for it, I was scared of being face to face with
Josh—not scared I'd fly at him but scared he'd stonewall me, scared I'd re-
vert to being a child who, it seemed to me now, had been too frightened
sometimes to do anything but pretend. Also, following the phone fight
with Sheilah, I couldn't help pondering my spectacular failure as a chooser
of men, and what bearing that might have on my love for this one. As we
waited together in a prison meeting room, I didn't doubt that we loved
each other, but wondered whether we did for reasons that had the health
and muscle to survive in rough terrain.

"I'm scared, you know?" I said to Michael, needing to clear my throat yet
again. I said it because I had an urge to tell him something absolutely true.

He reached for my hand and held it firmly, down below tabletop level
where no one could see. "I know you are. How wouldn't you be?"

The door opened. A large man padded with more hard fat than I'd remembered marched in: an African king making a public appearance. His
now dark gray hair was close cropped, shiny black skull showing through.
The orange jumpsuit seemed not the garment of a prisoner but kind of a
royal leisure suit. Michael had said his father was a bad diabetic, but he
did not look sick. The accompanying guard walked a step and a half behind like an equerry and quickly sat himself in the corner chair farthest
from the meeting table. Josh gave him a quick nod of approval.

Josh had registered my presence fast. I was a surprise, but not one that
knocked him sideways, or any way at all. Josh Pyatt looked as invulnerable

as ever. I don't know what level of humbling I'd expected but Josh was Josh, and whatever tower of hope I'd built up in my head was kicked to the ground as easily as a pileup of kindergarten blocks.

"Well, good morning, Miz Grace." It was the same thick, sanded honey voice, more sand now. He smiled wide and I saw the teeth: gleaming white choppers—not the subtle porcelain perfection of Sheilah's cosmetic dentistry, but old-time dazzlers, false and proud *of* it. They were ridiculous, and yet, oddly, they made him look more, not less menacing.

"Hello Josh." I managed this without clearing my throat again—barely.

He was still standing at what you'd have to call the head of the table, looking at us like a proper patriarch. "Glad to see you two together. I always favored that idea, from the time you were a girl—always said you were a pisser just like my boy." He reviewed Michael's angry face. "No hug for your daddy?"

"Don't think so," Michael said.

Josh sat across the table from us. The chair was small for the width of him. "Ah, Grace, you're not gonna believe this, but I am sorry it turned out the way it did for you. And I mean for *you.*"

"How about for Paul? Not sorry how it turned out for him? Well you wouldn't be, would you? Part of a day's work in—" Michael's hand still held mine. It felt so completely like part of me that I'd forgotten it was there until his fingers tightened, reminding me why I'd come here. I took a deep breath, preparing to start over. Josh watched me, not smiling. "Josh—"

"You still a good lookin' woman," he said, "skinnier—little too skinny for my taste now—but fahn lookin'." I heard an echo in my head of a seventeen-year-old boy, skinny when I was not, saying those words, trying to imitate his daddy. "Can't a beauty parlor do something about that hair?"

Improbably, I laughed. "If I asked them to, I suppose." The laugh did it for me. "Josh, I came here to ask for your help—beg for it if I need to."

Now he laughed, that rich phlegmy sound. "Hell you'd hold a gun to my head to get what you want. Maybe you'd fire—at least this time you'd mean it."

"What in hell do you know about what I mean or not?"

My last few words were lost under Michael's louder, "You're out of line, Josh."

"Josh?" Josh asked softly. "Not wanting me for your daddy just now?"

"Our sorry family drama can wait its turn," Michael said. "Let's get back to what Grace was saying." Josh flashed those teeth again, but didn't mean it, and looked at me, waiting.

"I need to go to George and I need to do it now. You know where he is. Don't even bother to tell me otherwise."

"And don't you be tellin' me what to bother to do." There was that calculated slowness in the bear's tone. I found myself bracing—remembering the times he'd sounded that way, like lightning before thunder. Those preludes, often ending in a chummy *Georgie,* would be followed by the business end of an *or else* order. This time he just said, "Catch more flies with honey, girl."

"Please," I said, meaning it. "I know you know because Paul would've figured it was safer to tell you than not."

He nodded, slow, heavy, approving. "Smart girl. You heard from your daddy at all?"

I didn't even take a beat—no point. "Yes. Just a few weeks ago," I added quickly, as it struck me, in the light of what I knew now, how big a risk it had been for George to send me the anonymous birthday *love you* notes.

"So how come you don't just ask him where he is?"

"I did. He didn't want to tell me." It hurt to say it; I was surprised at that. I took my hand out of Michael's and put it in my lap—a need to pull back even from him, I suppose.

"Why do you suppose he don't want to tell you?"

"He's afraid, you know that damned well. Are you enjoying playing with me, Josh?"

"Afraid of who? Me? You think Georgie's afraid of me now." He laughed and I ground my teeth together. "I guess I *am* havin' a little fun playin' with you. Not much fun available here abouts. Okay, Miz Grace, your daddy is a scared man. I didn't make him a scared man; God did that—and part of the way God made that man turned out to be a favor to me, though I'm sure it wasn't God's intention. I'm not one of his favorites."

Josh's big head moved toward me. Only inches, but it seemed to bring him much closer. I wanted to draw away and didn't. "Eight years ago George would've been crappin' his drawers if he knew that I could've put out my paw like a big cat and grabbed him off any time I wanted. But that's over. I'm locked up here; anybody else his testimony could've hurt is locked up too—or dead, so Fibbies got no interest in him. Way it is now, I'm gonna wanna guess George is afraid to eyeball you."

Never mind all the God talk, the substance of what Josh had just said rang painfully true.

Michael's voice cut in, tight with tension. "Get off Grace's back, because I'm about to get on yours. I've been figuring out a few things on the drive here—things I never really looked at before. It was very important to Paul that *I* drive George away. He pressed me into service knowing I'd do it for Grace's sake, but the more important reason he needed it to be me, not some plain vanilla recruit from Detroit or somewhere, was so he could hold that fact over your head. Oh yeah, I had a safety net alibi, which did help save my dumb ass." Rapt as I was, I did sneak a reflexive look at the guard, slouched in his chair in the corner—a look Josh caught me taking.

"Don't be nervous 'bout Gordon here, good man. Besides, nobody committed no crime in what we're discussing—not that I'm aware of. Where were we now, Michael? Paulie wanted you to give George a lift and you did. That about it?"

"Except that if *you* had decided at the last minute to change the deal, and George had ended up really dead, my alibi would've evaporated. We all know how alibis can do that if you expose them to the right chemical agent. *You didn't know I was going to be the driver.* Paul never told you that in advance, did he?" Josh's face was dead still and shining with sweat that had not been there minutes ago. He was not having fun now. "You only found that out when I got arrested."

Michael stood up, eight feet tall as the bottled outrage geysered out. "All that crap Paul fed me about how *I* and only *I* could force my father to go along with the plan was fucking window dressing—steaming bullshit for my benefit. You'd've gone along with Paul without a syllable from me, because it was the smart thing for you to do. But Paul had to take out that piece of insurance—putting me at the wheel—because finally he didn't trust you. Hurt your pride? That why you never told me, once you knew what he'd done?" Josh's lips tightened themselves. "It would've meant something to me to hear that from you, that you'd been played too. But you couldn't admit it. Josh Pyatt doesn't *get* played."

I thought for a second that Josh was going to apologize; he looked that troubled. But what he said was, "Warranty on the father you got's expired, long time now. You don't get to order a replacement."

"Thanks, I don't have use for one any more," Michael said. Judging by the tones of voice and sets of face as they glared at each other, a newcomer to the room would have called Michael a chip off the old block.

"Talking about fathers," I said, "could we get back to mine? His typing went berserk in the middle of an e-mail. That's why Michael thinks he's had a stroke. Now where exactly is he?"

Josh looked down at the table for a moment and shook his big head. His eyes then met mine. "Bad luck. Georgie's luck . . ." He motioned me to lean across the table closer to him. "Okay now," he said softly. We all knew that any notes taken in a prison interview room are subject to examination. Josh mouthed an address. The guard in the corner (good man though he might be) was not in position to see his lips. "You got that? It's in the Jew section of Montreal, Saint Urbain, they call it," he added very quietly. "Thought was he'd blend right in there."

Michael stood. "I'm headed back to the car to get on the damn cell phone. You got a name for him?"

"Allen Birnbaum," he mouthed.

"Phone number?" Michael asked. Josh mouthed one. "One more time, please?" Josh complied.

"Come on, Grace, we're outa here. You concentrate on remembering the address. I'll remember the phone."

"Ain't anybody gonna compliment me on *my* memory?" Josh wanted to know. He was having a good time for himself again. "Seventy-three years old with the diabetes, not so bad."

"I'll meet you in the car in a few minutes," I said. "I have a couple of more things here."

Michael and I locked eyes briefly. He nodded. The guard called someone to escort him out. He left without another word to his father.

"To scam the FBI, I lost my father and my business," I said to Josh, "and I ended up killing someone. George was in no danger from you once they really believed he was dead. Is that correct?"

"It's correct. But be clear here, if they *didn't* believe it, your daddy would've been in plenty of danger from me. Paulie knew that better than anyone."

"You'd have had George killed?"

"Yes I would—with no second thought. He'd've spilled his guts to them, whether he meant to or not. Think *I* couldn't buy my ticket outa here by givin' up some folk? Never happen. You are who you are. I always liked your daddy, but I went along with Paulie's plan because it was safer for *me*. Why would I risk bein' tied to some shooter who could turn on me later— unless I had no better choice?"

"I see." If I felt any emotion just now except a consuming curiosity I was not aware of it. "Let me ask you, did Paul watch you kill his father?"

"No."

"So that's something you didn't do."

"Didn't say that. Paulie wasn't there that day, didn't see nobody do nuthin'. His mama took him up to Montreal to visit her relatives."

"You are a monster."

"Who you callin' a monster, me or your late husband? You think he didn't know what was what? He knew, and he knew it was necessary. Jojo Donofrio was a chickenshit thief—understood the rules and he broke them. Paulie understood the rules too. He broke them with you. I don't blame what you ended up doing."

"If you expect me to say thanks, forget it."

"I don't expect thanks for sayin' a plain fact. I knew Paulie pretty well. I was the best friend he had back then—kid with no daddy and a mama who couldn't wait to get movin' on her own ambition. 'Course they turned out two of a kind."

"You *know*." I stared at him across the table, astonished.

"Know what?" But his smile said he was teasing me again.

I said it anyway. "That Marina Beck is his mother."

"I know a lot of things, Grace. I pick which ones I talk about."

"It was Marina, right? She made the call, gave up her husband."

"No," he said simply, no smile now, his eyes searching my face for something he seemed not to find. He sighed. "It was Paulie made the call. You never thought of that?" I was too stunned to respond. "He wouldn't talk to nobody but me personally. He just said, 'Mr. Pyatt, get me out of here,' and he told me where. I could hear he was cryin'. I told him to have his mama take him on a trip and I'd take care of it—and of him." He paused, giving me a chance to express . . . what? "People do what they got to do," he said.

"I . . . I think I have to leave now." What I thought was that if I didn't get away quickly, I might burst into crazy tears. The shock and pity that filled me had no place to go. If Paul had been here I might have held him close, as I used to, uncomprehending, while he cried about it. "Good-bye, Josh." I got up and put my bag on my shoulder.

"Just a second," Josh said sharply. "How you planning on gettin' into Canada with no passport?"

"Dunno," I mumbled, embarrassed. I hadn't thought. "I'll . . . work something out." *What? A dash across the border with armed patrollers chasing your ass? Be sensible.* Sensible: I imagined trying to reach Patty Ann and explaining. That was a nonstarter.

"Listen to me, Grace. I could get you a good passport but the guy I have in mind, it'd take a day or two, and going by what Michael thinks, you got no time for that. *Do not* go official. Red tape with your PO about compassionate grounds'll take even longer than fake papers. And do not try to deal with strangers who say they'll sneak you in for money: they'll give you up soon as look at you.

"Here's what you do. Tell Michael to call . . ." He mouthed a name, "Tully Jamison" and added "Plattsburgh." He said, "Don't know that phone number but you'll find it. The man has," again just the lips formed, "an orchard." Sound back on: "A commercial one. Now Michael and . . . this man know each other from years ago. Michael should make the call and tell him what you need and that I said to do it for you. When you meet him, tell him, 'apple for the teacher.' *You* say that to him."

"Thanks," I said, making my eyes meet his.

"Well, just like this man owes me, I owe *you*. And I don't mean for anything about your daddy or Paulie. I owe you for that time I tried to give you money and you threw it back in my face. But see, my boy had broke your heart and money was what I knew how to do."

I nodded, not trusting myself to say anything. Jesus, next I'd be kissing him.

"You don't need to tell Michael any of this stuff about Paulie we talked about," he said.

"I think I want to tell Michael everything. I think he plans on sticking around this time."

"I hope he has the brains. And I'm'na tell him that next time he comes up."

"Next time? What makes you think there'll be a next time?"

A loud, deep laugh. " *'Course* there will. He owns me, he knows that. You don't turn your back on someone you own."

"You'd've killed George, and you owned him."

"Different. That was business."

CHAPTER THIRTY-SIX

Michael stuck a thumbs-up out the car window as soon as he spotted me in the parking lot. I ran toward him like a kid ready to shout, "Home, free all." He left the car and held out his arms for me.

"Got him!" he said into my hair. When he stepped back I saw that his victory smile was gone. "He's in intensive care over at McGill. He's alive and in a top hospital, that's the good news. Not comatose, that's good news too. Grace, there's also some bad news. I was able to get hold of a neurology resident who's on the case. George's left side's paralyzed and his swallow reflex isn't working well, which means IV feeding tubes until it comes back—if it does. He's fragile but his mind seems to be working okay. He does go in and out of time, and falls into deep sleeps.

"It's too early yet to tell what functions can be brought back, what's gone." He drew me closer, his hands on my shoulders. "But that'd be presuming he makes it, Grace." I felt suddenly watery in the knees, shaky enough to be glad Michael still had hold of me. "My darling, I am so sorry."

"No, no. Thanks for putting it into straight English for me instead of medical gobbledygook. So . . . he's probably *not* going to make it?"

"Maybe not," he said quietly. "But he's still with us and we have to get you to him."

"Let's get in the car, okay? I need to sit down." The minute I did and the passenger door shut beside me, some inner control that had been clenching tight since this morning slackened and my floodgates opened wide. By the time Michael had walked around to the driver's side and gotten in, the relatively composed woman he'd left seconds ago was washing out to sea. "T . . . timing. The . . . the wo . . . orst timing. And timing's *everything*," I got out between sobs. "We never . . . so many missed chances, so many . . ." I was aware of him stroking my head like a mother bear might its cub. "Under . . . stand? *Do* you?"

"Yeah, I do. I do—starting with me ever letting go of you, dropping you like I did. I think we'd be married, married a long time now, have our own kids." He went on, his voice a shade darker. "And the worst things would never have happened. Paul would've been this crazy friend from when I was a kid, nothing more to us than that. And George would not be stroked out up in mother-fucking Montreal."

"Oh, God, Michael, oh, God. And . . . and Josh just told me the worst thing about Paul. *He* . . . he was the one who called . . . who betrayed his fa . . . father. That little boy who . . ." My face burrowed into the warm wool of Michael's sweater and I cried some more, while his hand stroked my head very gently.

"Explains a lot," he said quietly, after a while, "all of it so damned . . . pathetic. I love you so much."

"Soul mate," I murmured and rubbed my slick, wet cheek against his. I wondered whether I could sustain a mating of souls; I was forty and hadn't yet, not really. "Kleenex, please." He got me one. "I think I've got the genie back in his bottle."

"Genies do good stuff, I thought—three wishes and all."

"Mine must've been a rogue genie." I gave a long satisfying honk into the Kleenex. "Anyway, we don't have the time for him now. We have to get moving. Let's get out of here; we've got a long drive, straight north." He started the car. "Any idea how he happened to get to the hospital in time?"

"I don't. I did call George's apartment first, got his voice mail. When I started on the hospitals McGill was first on my list because of its location and size. Got lucky. I was zeroed in on talking to the doc about his condition—didn't think to ask who called the ambulance or if anyone came with him. I said Mr. Birnbaum's daughter was on her way—and to tell him to hang in."

"Well I am on my way, thanks to your daddy."

"Leave it to him," he said sourly. "I've been wracking my brain for an excuse to come up with a quick way to get you into Canada with no paper. Only damned thing that occurred to me was driving back to New York and trying to twist my ex-girlfriend's arm into lending you her passport—presuming she's not out of town for Thanksgiving weekend."

"That is a really stupid idea, Michael." Yet I couldn't resist asking the question that would pop into any female head. "She looks enough like me so I could use her passport?"

He laughed. "Not if you look real close, but say you got a black wig about shoulder length and put on a darkish makeup base . . . she's part . . . ah, fuck it, never mind. Stupid idea."

I reached over and ruffled his hair. "Maybe it would've worked, we'll never know. But here's what your father said to do . . ." I told him about the apple farmer in Plattsburgh who owed Josh—told him he was supposed to make the phone call. "Josh said you know the guy from years ago. Tully Jamison?"

"Tully Jamison. They used to call him Apple Jam. Yeah, I remember him. Low-level crew guy for a while, wasn't very good at the work and he had no heart for it. Only reason he got the job, and the only reason he came up to Woodstock, where I met him, was because he came from the same little town near Mobile as my daddy. You know, you're right: I'm gonna have to stop calling that scum my daddy."

"Maybe, but today I'd vote for calling him Jesus Christ and all the apostles. So what about Apple Jam?"

"He got the nickname because he was crazy for apples. From the minute the man came north he loved apples. He'd come to Woodstock occasionally and always bring a bag of them from some orchard or another way upstate. I haven't seen or thought of him for years, but I think my . . . Josh ultimately loaned or gave him a grubstake a few years back to buy himself one of those orchards. Those properties go begging you know—the farther north, the cheaper, I guess. Kids of these farmers go to college and . . ." he held his hands out, "become doctors." He smiled, but quickly it was gone. "The grubstake obviously has long strings attached and we're going to bust in on Apple Jam's life and yank them."

"Plattsburgh, right up there near the border. That's where he is. Josh said you should call him and tell him what I need and that Josh says for him to do it. 'Apple for the teacher,' I'm supposed to say that to him."

"My God, that's what he'd always say when he walked into the house. He'd have the sack of apples and he'd be carrying a big one in his hand. He'd hold it out. 'Apple fo' de teachah.' Tully had an Alabama accent made my daddy sound like an Oxford don."

I laughed. "Bottom line that's who he is, your daddy, for better and worse. You know, after you went out to the car, I said something about how he might never see you again, because you were so mad at him in there. And he laughed and said that would never happen because you own him and you don't walk out on what you own."

"We'll see about that. I might donate him to charity—take a tax deduction. Okay, Apple Jam, I am about to shake your poor tree." He fished the cell phone out of his pocket and dialed 411.

Which was how I came to be crossing the Canadian border at five-thirty in the morning in the flatbed of a produce truck, giving a silent scream of prayer that an overdiligent customs inspector would not decide to remove, one by one, the sacks of apples that covered my body.

The farm in Plattsburgh had been no trouble to locate: it was in fact called Apple Jam Farm. The drive had taken the better part of eight hours. Twice along the way, Michael phoned the hospital. George's condition remained critical but stable. "Stable's the word we want to keep hearing," he'd said to me. "Just hold that thought."

The Jamisons had put a good face on the welcome. Apple Jam, his wiry body as agile and pliant as a Gumby, did the talking. He asked after Josh and gave a hearty, "Look at *you*, a doctah!" to Michael, whom he hadn't seen in close to twenty years. Mrs. Jamison, a light-eyed redhead with some orange still brightening the white of her hair, stood behind him trying to smile. But they were far from pleased to see us, and who could blame them for that? This was a marker Josh had called in, suddenly out of the blue, and the Jamisons were stuck with paying up. Tully Jamison, respectable, law-abiding small upstate businessman-farmer had to smuggle a woman across the border to visit her sick father. No identities and no details about George's identity or mine were disclosed to him or his wife.

They owed Josh and they were scared to refuse him, no matter what. As Gabriel McCail had put it, Josh Pyatt had never cared for being stiffed. Apple Jam, who had worked for him, but had lacked the heart for the bone-breaking business, would know that as well as anyone.

While Michael was on the phone checking in again with George's doctors and Mrs. Jamison—Shirley—was putting out sandwiches and coffee for us on the large kitchen table, I'd taken Apple Jam aside. "Josh said for me to say, 'Apple for the teacher,' but what I really want to say to you is, I understand. I grew up under Josh's thumb. My father was a dumb gambler who used to get beaten when he couldn't pay up. I know you're helping me out because you have no choice and I can't honestly be sorry about that because I need the help so badly, but . . . I am sorry for how you have to feel."

He patted my arm. "I wouldn' have my spread here, 'cept for Josh. Once ya take whut's in the hand, ya got the obligation. Hell, I knew that. Hard on Shirley though: I only met her after I got up here. She live in Plattsburgh all her life. She don' know the other side of the world." He grinned at me, long piano-key teeth a bright ivory against twine-colored skin, dry as old barn board: a farmer's skin. "But she don' be sweet to y'all, I'm'na hafta kick her butt for her. Only kiddin', she the best, Shirley. An' I never was much of a butt kicker. Josh'll tell you dat. Josh Pyatt, he is somethin' *else*. He was a legend in our li'l town, I tell you—big, black Paul Bunyan."

Michael walked in. "He's stable still, for now. I'll follow your truck, Apple Jam. How soon can we leave?" I heard the tension and knew what "for now" meant.

Tully looked past Michael and paused. I turned and I saw Shirley, hands on hips, at the kitchen doorway, willing him not to compromise himself into greater risk. He nodded and said, "We're gonna hafta wait a bit, Michael. What is it, 'leven o'clock? If I take you crost now, it'll look fishy. I usually load up the truck and go 'bout five in the morning—get to the markets in plenny a time. Inspectors know dat—know *me*."

"This is a holiday weekend, Tully," Shirley said. "Who knows what inspectors will be on duty? You don't. Be honest."

"Darlin', we gonna hafta take dat chance. I'm a pretty good talker." He smiled again, but he was as nervous as she.

"Not until five," she said, slow and cold. Nobody opposed her. "Sandwiches are laid out, and coffee. Let's go into the kitchen."

On our way there, I took Michael aside and said, "I want to go up there alone."

He looked stunned—slapped. "Why?"

"Not because I don't trust you. I do, with my life or . . . with anything. And I love you so much. I said that I wanted to go alone. It's more like I need to. This is George and me. I can't explain it better than that. But will *you* trust *me* and go back to the city? I'll call every—"

He put his hand very lightly over my mouth. "Shh. Yeah, I'll trust you. But I won't go back to the city without you. I'll be here however long I need to be. You call in and let me know what's going on."

The ride to the border took fifty minutes. For the first half hour I rode up front with Apple Jam; for the last ten I rode beneath the sacks, a length of slim copper pipe clutched in my fist, ready to stick into my mouth just in case we hit a bump and the load shifted to a position where I couldn't breathe at all.

George lay trussed up in a hospital bed, hooked to four, five flashing, beeping machines that kept his body alive. He was in and out of deep sleep, the doctor had told Michael—back and forth in time. *Stable for now.*

As I lay in the total darkness, taking rationed half breaths of apple air, I visualized it for the first time: his dead face, waxy white against the white-white hospital linen, absolutely still. I broke discipline and gasped and then coughed, or started to, before realizing that the apples were too heavy on my chest to allow any emotional eruption, and I could fuck up the whole deal if I didn't get hold of myself.

I turned the kaleidoscope and remembered myself in a hospital bed. God, I hadn't thought of that time in years. I was seven. My stomach had started to hurt at school, hurt bad—the kind of ache I'd never felt before. The nurse had gotten me over to Columbia Presbyterian where they removed my appendix. Nobody could find George beforehand and the doctors and nurses told me that we couldn't wait—that I shouldn't be scared, I was going to be fine, and my father would be there when I woke up. The last thing I recalled thinking before I fell asleep was, no he wouldn't be: I knew him and they didn't—he'd be there sometime but not when I woke up.

But he was. He was. "Hey, Gracie, you sure know how to surprise a guy . . ."

The truck stopped, not actually a lurch but it felt like one. I grabbed the copper pipe tighter and drew an experimental breath. It was okay—just—but better to stay still than to risk using the pipe and moving apples under the eyes of an inspector: the pipe was only for an emergency. The truck was still, no motor vibrations. It seemed like a long time. I strained to hear voices, steps. I thought I felt the apples move above me and held my breath entirely as long as I could. Finally, I did hear something: Apple Jam's nice belly laugh, and then his Alabama drawl, "Here you go. Apple fo de teachah. Y'all have a nice day now." Then the motor revved and we crossed into Montreal.

"Allen Birnbaum," I said to the ICU nurse. "I'm his daughter."

The nurse nodded and led me through the doors and toward his cubicle. She pulled aside the curtain to reveal the scene I'd pictured less than an hour ago, lying under the apple bags, except . . . "This . . . it isn't him."

I stared down at the waxy face against the white linens and didn't recognize it. "Not *him!*"

The nurse took my arm and began to lead me away: the crazy lady's raised voice had no place in an intensive care unit. After going along for a step or two on legs that couldn't be mine I stopped, and remembered. "Oh, my God," I mouthed. He'd said in one of the e-mails that I wouldn't recognize him. I'd passed that off to myself as, I dunno, overstatement. "Wait, I'm sorry, Nurse. I, um, haven't seen my father in almost eight years and . . ." I held my hand out toward the bed, "he . . . looks very different."

"I understand," she said quietly but her gaze at me was speculative. Suspicious?

"He was in an accident about that time and his face needed a great deal of reconstruction."

"Ah." Suspicious no longer. "I was wondering about the plastic surgery. Pretty extensive."

"It was a bad accident." We were back at his bedside now. The stranger who was George gave no sign of awareness. I looked hard, ingesting the face with my eyes: taller forehead, wider cheekbones, short chunky nose, squared-off chin. "Is he still . . . stable?"

She hesitated and then tipped her hand left to right. *"Comme ci, comme ça,"* she said. "He is surprising though, Mr. Birnbaum. When he wakes up and talks, he's not so hard to understand, despite the slur from the damage on the left side. You're Gracie?"

My body, head to toe, tingled with something I can only call pleasure. "I'm Gracie."

"If . . . when he wakes, he'll be glad you're here. Is there a . . . Dolly?" I shook my head. "Josh?"

"Oh yes, there's a Josh, but he won't be coming. Do you suppose you could find the doctor for me while I stay here with my father?"

Once she'd left the cubicle, I pulled the single chair over to him, close as I could get with all the machinery. "George," I said quietly, close to his ear, "I'm here. I came in an apple truck under bags and bags of them. Can you smell apple on me? I can. And the guy, the guy who brought me over the border like that insisted on giving me a big one to take along—like that was just what I needed! 'Apple for the teacher,' he said." I was babbling on, sure, but I had the desperate idea that if I kept talking that, sooner or later, he'd respond. Or maybe that was something I'd seen in a movie, and it was total bullshit. I took hold of his one accessible hand—very lightly so as not to disturb the IV needles in that arm. The hand, to my relief, felt only a little cold. And it looked like George's hand.

"So, George, open your eyes, okay? Open your eyes just for a second and then you can go back to sleep." The eyelids were shut and still, but his face—this new face—didn't look dead, not really. Something in it, something let me think he might be hearing me. "You had a stroke. You know that, right? And look at you, you're still here. A blood clot stopped the traffic in your brain but it didn't kill you. Not my George." I thought I saw a smile play at the corner of his mouth.

"Ms. Birnbaum?" I turned my head and saw a medium-sized blond guy of about my age, dressed in green scrubs. I nodded, not wanting to get into name games just now. "I'm Doctor Hayes, chief resident neurology? Your friend, Doctor Pyatt, and I spoke—we spoke a few times. You want to come out into the hall with me for just a minute? Then you can go back, be with your dad."

"I'll be right back," I said to George's closed eyes, and turned to follow the doctor.

He told me how unpredictable the aftermath of a stroke could be. George's, it seemed, had occurred a fraction of an inch from his cerebral cortex—a kind of Command Central for the brain. But for that fractional distance, he would have died almost instantly. "Treatment is hard to calculate," Hayes said, "a catch-22, kind of. If you aggressively try busting the clot, you risk a bleed, which would be fatal. If you don't, another clot can form and do more damage. Or not." He held out his hands, palms up, to underscore the point.

"By the time he got here, it was a little late to initiate heroic measures. Not that we would have taken that chance anyway. His heart isn't in the best shape. We've introduced some meds to try and stabilize heart function and to thin his blood but . . . he's seventy-six, I understand from Doctor Pyatt?"

I nodded. "Do you know how much time passed between the stroke and his getting here—or who it was that called the ambulance?"

"I don't know offhand who called it in. The name will be in his chart—one of the nurses can check it. As to lapsed time? An hour, possibly closer to two. I'm sorry not to have better news for you, Ms. Birnbaum. We're doing what we can to keep him going. I wish I had something more definitive to tell you. He could wake up again any time. I noticed when I came in you were talking to him. That's good; keep at it." He glanced at his watch. "I'm due in surgery. I'll check back with you later. And . . . good luck."

I went back to my chair near George's head and lightly touched his cheek, which looked cold and felt warm. "I'm back. The nurse said you'd been asking for me—also for someone called Dolly? Who's Dolly, or did she hear you wrong?" I saw his mouth move again, maybe not a smile, but something. And the eyelids, while they didn't open, twitched slightly—I thought they did. I brought my mouth closer to his ear. "I love you, love you, love you, dear, I cross my heart it's true," I sang in a soft quaver. "Do you believe me?" I took his hand in mine and concentrated on delivering every drop of will and prayer in me. "Wake up," I said silently. "Do you believe me?" I sang again.

And damn, his mouth made the words, "I do."

CHAPTER THIRTY-SEVEN

His eyes fluttered for a second and then opened. They can change everything, but they can't change the eyes, I thought. Well, maybe they can, but they didn't. Bleary, yet remarkably clear, even the left one that drooped a bit, they were smart, wary tobacco brown eyes—ready to laugh, ready to cut and run: George's eyes.

"Hello," I said. "Long time."

"Sing it again," he croaked. "My line, but *you* sing. I can't . . . not so good."

So I did, and he managed his "I do." As the nurse had told me, despite the slur his speech was not very hard to understand. "Your throat must be sore as hell, it sounds dry. Want some water?"

"Can't swallow. They have these sticks with a damp sponge thing on the end . . . one to suck if you can find it." It was there on a side table. I unwrapped it and put it gently between his lips, having patted them first with a cloth I'd dipped in the water carafe. "Mmmm." I held the cloth to his forehead. "Better. 'Member when they took your appendix out, Gracie?"

"Funny, I was thinking of that on the way up here. They told me you'd be there when I woke up."

"And I was. Now, name me one other time I came through for you. Beep, time's up." He tried a laugh and it hurt his throat enough to make him groan in pain. "Sit back down and hold my hand again. Talk to me." His eyes closed themselves but his hand squeezed back; I knew he was there.

I talked about what I thought he'd want to hear: George and Gracie-like telling fairy tales to us both. I was in the middle of some anecdote about Sheilah's mother, when he said without opening his eyes, "Not Dolly."

"What?" I leaned in closer. The syllables were blurrier now, would have been more so but I knew his speech—remembered it so well.

"Not Dolly, Dalit. It was your mother's name." It hung out there. I couldn't think of a thing to say and so I said nothing. "Funny you always said Indian princess. Almost right."

"She was Indian—like from Arizona or like from India?"

"India." His face, the half that was able to move, contorted with effort.

"It's okay, George. You don't have to say more. Hey look, I've gone forty years not knowing. What . . . what's the difference, right?" But if that were true my voice would not have been bobbing and weaving the way it was: I'd had no stroke. "I've got you."

"Not for long."

"Now. We're in the *now*," I said.

"No, won't work—too much of the *then* pushing at us, too little *now* left. Tell you . . . she was at Columbia, studying physics—Dalit. Tall like you. Twenty-two. Good Indian Muslim family—no chador for her but still . . . see, she gambled, couldn't stop . . . was how we met. She thought your old man was exotic—said that. A laugh, no?" *No, not a laugh; something else, but not a laugh.* "Wrong, all wrong: her father shoulda come and shot me dead, cut my head off, whatever those people do. She was . . . she tried to stay but . . ." I could see beads of sweat dotting his big forehead. I wet the cloth again and lay it across. His face relaxed a bit. "I gotta finish this. Important. I set up . . . abortion. Begged her to go. Hollered, cried, tried every way I could to make her. But she was stubborn, case you ever wondered where you got it from, and you got born."

"What happened?"

"Now that part I always told you the truth about. Remember? She had to go back to her tribe. She *did* have to—couldn't take you, wouldna worked back there. School was over; she graduated; you were four months old. Promised her I wouldn't give you away—promised you'd be fine."

"And I am. I *am.*" The nurse walked in with a pair of doctors and told me I'd have to wait outside for a while. "Don't go away," I whispered into George's ear. "They're kicking me out for a few minutes but I'll be right back."

He'd kept me. What kind of a singleton gambler, thirty-six years old would regard such a promise to a foreign student sex fling as binding? Hell, I'd always known—prima facie evidence—that he'd decided to keep me. But things were somehow changed. I walked into the small ICU waiting area feeling about to burst with new feelings for him, love and pride tussling inside me to see which could expand fastest.

"Hello, excuse me." I turned to see a small, chubby woman with a chapped ruddy face. She was wearing a heavy tweed coat that hung to the top of her sturdy boots and a woolly cap over gray curls.

"Yes?"

"You just came out of the ICU with Mr. Birnbaum?"

"I did. I'm his daughter, Grace. Who are you?"

"Oh, a daughter!" She peered at me through little round horn-rims. "I'm his neighbor, Mrs. Turtletaub. I was the one found him. I came to see how he was doing." She gave me an expectant smile, the kind you might give in hope it'll make the news good.

"Not too great, Mrs. Turtletaub. But if not for you, I think he'd be dead. 'Thank you' sounds so inadequate."

"You don't have to with the thanks. I only wish I could've been there for him when it happened. See, I was taking your father some borscht I just made. Too much, I always make too much—and now I'm a widow, a *lot* too much. So, a daughter—I didn't know that." I can't swear that her glance held a reproach along the lines of, What kind of daughter never shows up to see her father in eight years? It occurred to me that from what George had just said, my mother would be about Mrs. Turtle-taub's age.

Maybe that's what prompted me to say, "I've been living overseas. Australia. I'm a widow too." Shameless: I shut up.

"Your father, he's such a nice man, always with the joke. He keeps himself very private, but sometimes we'd have a beer and a bite, listen to a little music—opera he loved. But you must know that. Well, I rang the bell, you know, with the borscht in my hands . . ." She told the story tasting each detail the way people unaccustomed to being heroes do—which was fine with me. I was as eager to hear, as she was to tell. "And just on the other side of it, I hear this banging around and funny noise like, you should excuse me, a dog whimpering—no words, just the whimpering. I jiggled the doorknob. The door opened, but only a crack. I was so surprised I almost dropped the borscht. Your father was lying straight across in front of it. Thank God he got himself as far as unlocking before he fell down. Otherwise . . ."

I walked closer, leaned down and kissed the woman's forehead. I think she was as surprised as I. Just then, the nurse motioned that I could go back inside. "You did a wonderful thing for us, Mrs. Turtletaub. I can't even tell you how wonderful. I'll tell him you came."

"Wait just a second, I'll give you my number—in case you need anything or . . . you know."

Hospital time, I found out, is like prison time in that it has little relation to any other kind of time. The hours spent on hospital vigil leave you exhausted as they creep by. That's the way it was during the hours I sat in the waiting room: each check of my watch showed the same time as the previous one. When I was in the cubicle with George I didn't check my watch, even though most of the time he slept. Occasionally, I'd go down to the lobby where I could pick up a sandwich and coffee and use my cell phone to give Michael, who waited at the Jamisons, updates about George—and tell Tully I was not ready for him to come and take me back across, and didn't know when I would be. Michael needed to be back at the hospital Monday, which meant that he'd have to start the drive down sometime tomorrow, Sunday. I was expected back at work Monday too, and for my PO visit Tuesday.

He and I didn't get into any of this on the phone, but we both knew that I was going nowhere as long as my father lay in that ICU bed. If George was here, I would be here, no matter what.

I sat talking to an unconscious George, hoping something would get through, feeling okay with his hand in mine, even if it didn't. I told him how I'd stalked his father, Dr. Junius Lester, when I was sixteen—how surprised, and not altogether displeased, I'd been to see that my grandfather's eyes were the same shape and color as my own. I told him he was safe from Josh, nothing to fear from that quarter ever. Then I told him about Michael. "I love him, George. Whatever else, I never did get over that. He's a good man though, so don't worry—not that you need to worry about me anyway." I saw the eye flutter that meant he was surfacing again.

His hand squeezed mine. ". . . 'Member the next line?"

"Of . . . of what?"

"Burns's song."

"I love you, love you, love you, dear?"

"Ummm, yeah. After, *I do*." My mind stalled. His mouth started to work, soundlessly at first. Then, though I had to strain to hear, I did. *"And you're the one and only girl I ever said that to. Do you believe me?"*

I sang back, *"I do."* With a full heart.

"Gracie, that time . . . that time when Josh came, money on the floor. I . . . I took it. Short . . . needed to cover. Money's only money but . . . it was yours and . . ."

He fell back into wherever he went when his eyes closed.

Sometime after midnight, he woke once more—woke me too: I'd been dozing in the chair beside him, dreaming something I forgot the instant I opened my eyes.

His eyes were open very wide. "What? What, George? Shall I call the doctor?"

"No." His voice was stronger but had a strangled sound to it. "Money . . . Yours."

"I know, George, I know." I stood over him now, my hand on his paralyzed cheek. It felt eerily cool. "You told me—Josh's money on the floor. I don't blame you. It's . . . okay. I love . . ."

"Not that money! Password . . . computer is Dalit. File . . . your money." His mouth was wide as a gasping fish's. I pushed the call buzzer. They came in seconds but he had fallen back asleep, this time snoring in occasional loud bursts of sound that seemed to come not from inside him but from a great distance away.

My father lived through the night, into the next morning, but he didn't wake up again.

CHAPTER THIRTY-EIGHT

Sometime a little before daybreak on Sunday morning, I left the hospital and took a cab to the apartment where George had lived for the past eight years: third floor back in the St. Urbain section—kind of what the Lower East Side was to New York before it began turning chic. Mrs. Turtletaub buzzed me in and was waiting in the third floor hall, when I reached the top of the stairs.

"I'm so sorry, Grace darling," she said. "But at least his flesh and blood was with him at the end. I say that as someone who has no children. Here's your father's door, this one. I'm the door right across the hall. His door still isn't locked. I couldn't find the key and I didn't want to, you know, go through his things. It's a safe building here, and I keep an eye out. Do you want me to go in there with you?"

Surprising myself, I said yes. I didn't know how I would feel about being there with a stranger—or being there at all—but as it happened, the instinct to accept her offer was wise. Her presence seemed to give weight to these years of George's life, make them real. He'd had someone to say good morning to, someone to laugh at his jokes. Someone to place his bets? It was a question I would not ask. If so, and it had given this lonely, nice woman a small taste of adventure to spice her borscht, it was fine with me. I didn't need to speculate on what gambling gave George: it gave him nothing; it was just what he had to do. I bit my lip hard. "So you listened to opera together," I said. "We used to do that a lot."

She showed me his CDs—opera and old, old songs. "I like *Tosca*," she said proudly, "and *La Bohéme*—and some of those crazy twenties songs: things I never heard before but he knew all the words."

"You keep the CDs, Mrs. Turtletaub, okay. I want you to have them—a gift from him. I've got the old records we used to play and . . ." It burst out before I could edit. "Did Geo—my father ever talk about his past? About me?"

"No," she said, sad to be hurting my feelings, "he never did. But he was such a private man."

"He was, Mrs. Turtletaub. He always was. I . . . I think I'd like to spend some time alone here now."

I walked George's apartment the way I had my own that first day out of prison—taking its measure, learning its shape, pondering the things that furnished it. Very few things: my father always did travel light. The place was not unlike the apartment in Washington Heights: grayish walls, brown functional sofa, a few chairs and tables of various sizes. Nothing on the walls: he hadn't hung up even opera posters to look at. Sitting on a desk was his open laptop computer. I'd seen it as soon as I walked in, but even after Mrs. Turtletaub had left I'd resisted its pull. I wanted to jiggle that black screen back into life and find George, what was left of him, and yet I stalled and paced a while before I did. I'm still not sure why.

Finally, I sat at the desk and worked the mouse control. The Internet connection had broken itself off. I dialed it back up, opened e-mail. His inbox was empty. Apparently, he'd deleted all mail after reading it. After some searching around, I saw he'd done with our correspondence the same thing I had—downloaded it into a hard drive file called, straightforwardly, *Gracie*. The only thing still on e-mail was his last incomplete message to me. I looked at it a long time and wept a little before closing the computer down and unplugging it to take with me.

I stood near his door, ready to leave. I was finished here. Earlier, from the hospital, I'd told the crematorium to send Allen Birnbaum's ashes to Grace Birnbaum, care of Grace Leshansky in New York. They would be an urn of ashes, not him. Ashes meant nothing to me, but still . . .

Suddenly, I was seized with a yearning to have something of his besides the computer and the ashes that were to come. The desk drawers and kitchen cabinets yielded nothing that wasn't utilitarian and impersonal. I opened his clothes closet and saw three ties on a rack: two of them were thin, constrained striped things, ties George would never choose to wear. The third was wide and yellow with large deep red squares scattered at random angles all over it. Maybe he'd bought it just to keep here in the closet to look at sometimes—to remember. I ran my hand over its satin finish before putting it in my bag.

I crossed the U.S. border a few hours later in Apple Jam's flatbed truck, this time under bags of fertilizer. The fragrance was no treat but I didn't much mind it. After he'd pulled over into a secluded lay-by and I'd transferred to the passenger seat, I turned to him. "You gave me the most important gift anyone could have." And he said, "I'm sorry your daddy passed, glad you got to see him. But if you're thinkin' of feelin' grateful to me, don't. I didn' give you no gift. I paid off a debt with my arm twisted 'hind my back. A person don't deserve no credit for that. Just count yourself lucky that Josh Pyatt was on your side."

By noon, Michael and I were on the highway heading south to New York. I'd taken time for a quick shower at the Jamisons', despite the fact that Shirley—and Apple Jam himself—had a hard time containing their eagerness to have us gone. I couldn't blame them. At the moment, I'd have been hard put to blame anyone in the world for anything. Tully Jamison had been right on the mark. I'd been lucky to have Josh Pyatt on my side.

Michael pulled up in front of my apartment at nine-thirty. I'd told him a lot on the long ride down—the way it had been those hours in the hospital; things George said; things I said; Mrs. Turtletaub; the yellow tie; Dalit, my mother. Not many cohesive sets of sentences, but a bushel of fragments spaced out with long easy silences, short frequent touches of skin to skin and exchanged grunts of displeasure over the world news on the car radio. We were learning a new language together and becoming increasingly fluent. Once we hit the Upper West Side, I asked Michael to double-park for a moment while I ran into the Grand Union. When I came out my brown bag included a turkey sandwich and a Coke for him and the same for me.

"Happy Thanksgiving," I said, handing him his makeshift supper. "You'd better gobble it down while you hustle uptown. You're on shift pretty soon, no?"

"Eleven. But I'm a bonus for them today. I called in saying I might be stuck upstate in a family emergency. You gonna be okay tonight?"

"I am, you know. I feel blessed—in a state of grace: some way I've never felt before. It wasn't in the cards that I'd ever see George again. Enough to make you believe in luck or God or—"

"Or the power of Josh Pyatt," he said dryly.

I laughed. "That too."

"You're a believer though," he said. "Maybe state of grace was what George had in mind when he named you."

Gracie. You're Gracie. What else would a Jawge name his girl? "I don't *think* so," I said with a grin.

"It's what *I* have in mind, Amazing Grace. I'm a believer too, in my way." We held each other very tightly for a bit. Then I opened the car door. "Hey, your satchel and two laptops and a grocery bag. Need a hand?"

"Nah. Scoot. When do you get off?"

"I dunno, sometime tomorrow—when I'm done is when."

"Tell you what. Just show up here. I'll have food and drink, and a set of keys for you."

My cell phone, which I'd kept turned off while I was in the ICU had, I now noticed, seven messages on it: three of them from Sheilah, four from prospective candidates who had expected calls from me over the holiday weekend. The apartment voice mail held duplicates of almost all of them—except for one: a message received on Friday morning from a crisp-voiced woman saying that Patricia Carlson had resigned from the parole office and that she, Tanya Riggins, had been assigned my case and looked forward to meeting me Tuesday. *Thank you, God,* rang in my head, followed quickly by, *Second chance, Grace. Do not fuck this one up.*

I emptied my Grand Union bag and stood for a moment holding the extra thing I'd bought there, a *yahrzeit* candle, looking around to decide where it should go. I placed it in the center of the round dining table and lit the wick. I uncorked a fresh bottle of red wine, unwrapped my turkey sandwich and put Callas's *Tosca* on the old record player. It was a good memorial ceremony. George would have thought so too.

I was at the office early the next morning, not bright eyed and bushy tailed exactly, but fairly calm and quite determined. I'd stayed up a good part of the night with George's computer. I'd found the money file he'd named Dalit easily enough: all the information I needed to tap a certain account in Cayman Islands bank. Who knew how much there'd be in it? The file didn't say and at the moment I didn't care. I'd found many Internet sites he frequented under Favorites: they ranged from puzzles and games to show business lore and music—opera, of course. And I did find the single piece of e-mail he had probably forgotten to delete. It was not in the in-box but under Sent Mail. I was astonished to the point of not comprehending what I saw—but only very briefly: only until I thought, well, of *course.*

What I did not find, could not find, was a Letter to My Daughter, or anything of the kind. Christ, in any novel, any movie about long-lost parents and children there's always one of those, isn't there?

"Morning Cynthia," I waved. "Good Thanksgiving?"

"I had the whole family, both sides—take us till Christmas to get the house back together, but yeah, it was good." Her eyes looked past me at the hall. "Sheilah's in her office," she said carefully. I nodded and sailed into the wind.

Her door was open. The look she gave me made words superfluous, not that that would keep her from saying them. "You have betrayed everything about our friendship. As far as I'm concerned, you are beneath not only contempt, but—"

"George died," I said.

"*What?* But I thought—are you telling me he wasn't dead all along?"

"That's what I'm telling you. Everybody assumed he was but I . . . began to hope it wasn't so."

"Oh, Gracie. Come on in, sit down." She waited until I did. "Now *tell* me."

I did, with some heavy editing that cut out McCail and any mention of Craig, not to mention a few other items.

"He was in Montreal? How did you get across the Canadian border with no passport, especially in times like these? That's what I want to know."

"No, you really don't want to know." She got my meaning and did not, for once, push. "But I did get there in time. I was with him when he died. We talked . . ."

"I'm so glad for you on that. You found him on the Internet? You're a quick study."

"Other way around. I opened an AOL account with a screen name he'd recognize and he found me," I answered blandly. "Who knows better than you what a wondrous thing technology is? You've told me how it's transformed your business."

"Are you mocking me? You *do* that, you know."

She wasn't wrong. "Sorry, just my kind of humor—maybe it's sharp tongued but I never mean it to hurt, certainly not to hurt you. I love you, Sheilah." Her eyes welled up and mine were about to. I knew I'd have to say the rest. "I can't go on working here, we both know that. It's not good for either of us." Her eyebrows went up, but she didn't say I was talking nonsense.

"What would you do instead? What about your parole?"

"Sheilah, I've started to sketch—to design, just the way you said I would—remember, in the car? I damn near bit your head off but you were right. I think I can do it on paper and find jewelers who'll make the piece. I'm not saying I won't miss doing the do, but—"

She grinned. "Nothing's perfect. Who knows that better than thee and me? You always used to say that when we were kids and I was down about something. Remember?"

My throat lumped up. "How could I forget? Suppose you consider this notice—three weeks? I promise I will bust my chops on the work here during that time. As far as a paycheck afterward, Danton and I had a few words at your party. I haven't called him yet, but I have an idea something might work out with his gallery. Also, believe it or not, George left me some money in a Cayman Islands account. Now I have no idea how much, but . . . and another piece of news: there was voice mail while I was gone from a new PO. She sounds mellow, at least on the phone. It's a fresh start and I'm lucky to have it. My first one was a pretty fucked-up chick, but the chip on my shoulder didn't help."

"Grace, can I bring up Michael without you flaring up?"

"You can. In fact, I want to. Let me tell you for starters, I'm gonna marry that man if he'll have me. And I *do* know what I'm doing . . ."

I began busting my chops on the phone trying to hook up with the people I'd skipped out on over the weekend, plus the ones I'd had on my list for today. It's amazing the verve you can bring to something you don't like doing once you know you won't be doing it much longer. It was near the end of the day before I crossed the office and went through the door to Craig's area. I found him sitting at his desk working the keyboard.

"You are a virtuoso at that thing, aren't you?" I asked. "I take it you survived Montana?"

"Didn't even break a sweat."

"My father died over the weekend."

He looked up, giving me wide-eyed innocent surprise. "I thought he *was* dead."

"Knock it off, you lying swine." His face went back to neutral, dark neutral. "And thanks, friend." My voice trembled on that. I took a deep breath and waited a second. He made no move, said no word. "Come on, Craig, I found it in his computer, on his sent e-mail. I guess he forgot to delete it." I stopped but he still didn't jump in. "You are one tough case. Okay, it was George's reply to ctarbell@Lelandconsulting.com. It read, 'What makes you think she's my daughter?' I'm assuming you gave him an answer that satisfied him enough that he risked an e-mail to me. I guess you found my AOL address one day when I was out at lunch or something. God only knows how you found him."

"Through George Burns; it wasn't all that hard. Shit, child's play for me. This is part of what I do for a living. Okay: your first day here you were pretty curious about how to find someone on the Internet. Then as we became friends I got curious and researched your case and the background to it, which included your father who was MIA, presumed dead. The day we went to Ellis Island together you talked about him a little, how crazy he was about George Burns.

"Burns, Allen, George, Gracie, Nathan, Birnbaum—there was also Pee Wee in my mix, because Burns began as one of a bunch of kids calling themselves the Pee Wee Quartet, and there were Ethel, Cecile and Rosalie—those were Gracie's middle names—and . . . well, you get the idea. After that, it's Rubik's Cube, code-breaking: match possible screen names with possible Internet providers. allenbirn@hotmail wasn't brain surgery—call it three hours."

Suddenly his king-of-the-hill look morphed into scared kid. "How did he die? Did it have anything to do with my—"

"No, no. He had a stroke." I'd been standing just inside the doorway. Now I perched on the corner of his desk. "I was there when it happened. I wouldn't have been but for you. I . . . ." I leaned far over and kissed his bald forehead. "You are one dangerous son of a bitch. Remind me never to turn my back. And wipe the lipstick off your pate. Someone might get the wrong idea."

CHAPTER THIRTY-NINE

'T was the week before Christmas. The world was a nervous place where real fears over terrorism blended seamlessly with paranoia in its full spectrum of colors. But personally, I'd been having a fine time. My turn perhaps: a random shift of the kaleidoscope and the glass bits had settled in my favor—for the moment.

Michael had moved into the apartment with me. It was our place now, just as Woodstock was where we went weekends when he was off duty: all those "we's" and "our's" tended to send a shiver through my gut. The thing was, it all felt so natural. Not that we saw everything refracted the same way. Late at night, Michael sleeping beside me, I'd get one of those shivers and wonder: was it pure pleasure, or was I scared it would be taken away?

"What about Dalit?" Michael asked one evening when we'd been talking about something else entirely. "Do you want to try and find her?"

"No. No, I don't. See, for me Dalit is *not* unfinished business. I've thought about her. A lot, and mostly what I feel is sympathy for the twenty-two-year-old girl who couldn't leave her tribe. From what George said, she might have thought she could, but in the end she couldn't.

People do what they need to. *Your* mother went out and married Josh, broke with her tribe on purpose. I guess what I'm saying is that, knowing about Dalit—hearing about her from George—finished the business for me. He gave me the girl who gave birth to me, who maybe in those first couple of months thought she could hack it—and couldn't. I'm happy to have her. I don't want to go on the hunt for some stranger in her sixties."

Less than two weeks ago, when I left Carpenter-Donlan, Sheilah was almost as happy for me as I was for myself. Danton offered me the job of running and expanding the "wearable art" section of his gallery and hooked me up with a young jeweler, a silversmith, he thought might be a good match for the future.

And then the shit hit: Jan worked for Danton too; Todd Berenstain showed up at the gallery regularly, giving me a cheery wave. This time I couldn't *not* tell Sheilah, who had reached the point of hanging on every phone call she did or didn't get from him, parsing it later for tone and content, twisting logic into a shape that would add the flavor she craved, squeezing out whatever juice she could. As it turned out, she would have shortly found out the painful news for herself: Jan and Todd ran off to some damned Caribbean island too exclusive for most people to have heard of it and got married.

"Liar. Yes, liar! You *lied* to me; that's why they *call* it a lie of omission. You listened to me go on like a moron about him and you . . . just get out of my life, okay?"

"*Not* okay, Sheil. I don't want out of your life—or to have you out of mine. It's a tough thing to tell someone you care about something she desperately doesn't want to hear. I'm sorry if I took too long about it. Maybe I was hoping it would all go away and solve itself. Shit, I don't know. We're friends. I'm gonna try to be a better one."

"What is that?" Michael asked softly. We'd just finished eating a pizza in bed—eating in bed was a nasty habit we enjoyed sharing.

"What's what?"

"You know damned well what. We could go around where I say, 'You hardly ate a whole slice,' and you say, 'I dunno, I wasn't that hungry,' but could we skip that useless part?"

A long sigh came out of me—relief maybe. I didn't begin speaking though, maybe because I didn't know *how* to begin.

"Come on, darling," Michael said—he called me darling sometimes these days; I found I liked it. "I could give this more of a kick start, but it's better if you do."

I nodded and sat up fully in the bed. This was not talk for lolling around on pillows. "I can't seem to keep my mind clear of it and I don't know where to put it, Michael." He needed no road map and I knew it. I watched him sit up beside me, chin resting on his bent knees as he waited. "I . . . never told you about the night I killed him," I said looking down at my own knees. "You never asked and I never said. I mean, my story was that I kind of blanked out in rage, and when I came to, there he was, dead—and me with the hot gun. I wish it had gone that way."

I felt his hand touch my bare back but I didn't turn to look at him. "You're right, I never asked. I'm still not asking. I knew Paul; I know you. I don't need to know this. I love you and that's not gonna change. So tell me, if you want, but only if you want, okay?"

"I want." So, naked in the touring dancer's bed, Michael's palm, warm against my skin, anchoring me in the now, I told him.

———

Paul let himself into the loft that night with a key—strange in itself because I'd had the locks changed when he moved out. He found me sitting on the couch reading that morning's *Times:* unimportant that my mind was absorbing little from the columns of type, since it was already yesterday's news. The sight of him was a dull kind of shock—like the way it must feel to get hit on the head when you expect to get hit on the head. I did not get up, just looked at him.

"I'd ask about how you got in here, but the answer would be boring: either you scammed the locksmith or know how to pick the damn things."

"Or you left the door unlocked."

For a shaved second he had me—dropped jaw and all. Then I said, "Of course I didn't."

He laughed. "No, you didn't."

"What do you want? I'll have the order of protection pretty soon, so this is your last chance. What do you want, Paul? There's nothing I have to give you that you haven't already taken from me."

" 'There is nothing you can take from me, sir, that I would not the more willingly part withal—except my life. Except my life.' Hamlet," he explained.

"Is that what you're here for? To kill me? I tell you, just keep throwing quotes at me in my apartment in the middle of the night and I'll kill you. I swear, Paul. One word of Nietzsche and you're history. I wish you'd just go, so I don't have to go." His smile began and widened as I talked. I put the *Times* aside and got up. "I'm out of here." I walked past him toward the coat closet.

"I don't think so." Something steely in his voice made me turn around. He had the gun in his hand—not pointed at me, but in his hand, and that Paulie Donofrio set to his face. Time hung there, nothing moved. I did not want to die but couldn't say so. I couldn't seem to say anything. "Sit down," he said, "over there." The gun pointed at one of the chairs that flanked the coffee table. I did what it said. "Now, I'll sit on this other one and I'll put this right here on the table." He sat and placed the gun dead center between us. "I have some things to talk over with you."

He began by telling me something I sort of knew already, that he'd married me for my father—for the kind of father I had and for the kind of bond I had with him. "Don't mistake this, Grace. I did do a lot of research and I had my criteria. But I loved you when I met you and I love you now. You won't believe this, but I have never loved you more than I do right this minute."

It wasn't just the words but the light in his crystal eyes as he said them that made me think—for the first time, incredibly—he's crazy. I looked at the gun between us, wondered whether I could make a successful grab for it. *But what would I do then?*

He caught my train of thought and reached for it himself. *Too late, Grace. Stupid you.* He didn't pick it up but slid it in my direction. "I want you to feel secure, *chère*. The gun is at your disposal. Pick it up. Hold it. Go ahead."

So what harm in just having it in my lap, instead of in his easy reach? He is crazy. I did take it. It felt heavy and cold on my thighs through my jeans— and I had the unreasoning fear it would fire itself and blow me to pieces. "So talk," I said. "You've inoculated me against so many varieties of your shit I'm immune to it all. Would you agree to, say, fifteen minutes and then you go?"

"Half an hour," he said. "By the way, that gun is called a Sig Sauer. It's cocked and ready. All you need to do is squeeze the trigger."

"Shut the fuck up about the gun and start talking." I checked my watch. "You're eating into your own time: twenty-nine minutes and counting."

"That's my girl," he said and laughed. "I'm going to lay out some possibilities for you, like a hand of cards. Remember how George used to lay out a hand of cards. Those stubby fingers could really move . . ."

In my pumped-up bravado, I'd claimed immunity. I was far from immune. As he began to lay out his cards face up, I began to fold. One scenario had George, with a new face and identity, living blocks away from here, Chelsea perhaps, Tribeca, passing me on the street, forced by his fear to look away. "It's possible," he said. Another had him home free, almost— only to be robbed and killed by random thieves, walking away from his bookie with an unprecedented big win in his pocket. There were other cards, ones he'd shown me early on: ones with Josh's face or Michael's on them.

It is hard to convey without the Paulness of Paul there in the room doing this talking how vivid was the effect of each new tale. In spite of all I knew, I found myself in a chilly sweat, looking down at the gun instead of at my watch.

Out of nowhere he broke the tension and said, "I love how big you are. You're wide open, heart, mind and body. You are the sea and the sky."

I took a ragged breath and checked the time. "Is that someone's quote? No, I don't even want to know. You're out of time, Paul." I took hold of the gun and stood up. "I'll give you this when you go out my door."

He stood too and walked a few steps toward me. He looked me straight in the eye. "Ever think about who put the FBI on George's tail in the first place?" His smile told me the answer.

I shot him, squeezed the trigger, felt my finger do it. *I am killing you now.* I mustn't have hit his heart directly because he said something as he went down. He said, "Thank you. I knew you could."

It seemed very cold in the little bedroom; Michael's hand on my back was hot. I began to shiver. He wrapped the quilt around my shoulders and then his arms around the quilt. "He played you one last time, Grace. He'd pulled off the big one: changed history, saved his father, after all—expiated that sin he'd lived with most of his life. He couldn't top that, not ever. Except maybe by making you kill him."

"So we'd both be killers? He didn't make me, Michael. He set me up, sure. He played me. He fucked me over. Say it any way you choose. But he didn't make me. Nobody can *make* you do that. *I* did it. *I* own it."

After some time of not saying anything, Michael said, "I know it won't go away for you, but you will find some place to put it. *We* will. No matter what you say, to some degree it's community property. I now pronounce us man and wife."

AFTER

T hat night in bed Michael and I talked until it wasn't night any more. And we imagined how life might be . . .

Here's how some of it has been: Michael and I got married December 31, at five in the afternoon by a justice of the peace in Woodstock. We did not know at the time that I was three weeks pregnant with the golden brown miracle who would enter the world with the name Naomi George Pyatt.

I've led with the best. But pretty good was the three hundred twenty-four thousand dollars George had left in the Cayman Islands bank. It's been a bit of trouble getting hold of it, but my father-in-law happens to have a Ph.D. in money laundering and I've taken the short course with him. No guilt about that: it is, after all, my money, so there's a certain symmetry in its being used to start up my new business. I still can't weld or be what I'd call a proper jeweler, but Danton's steady-handed young silversmith—a superb craftsman—and I have collaborated on some good work and things look promising. It's too early to use words like "success." We'll see.

Michael, Naomi and I still live on the Upper West Side, though not in the touring dancer's apartment. We bought a place of our own on

Riverside Drive. It's an easy subway trip to Washington Heights for Michael, not bad getting downtown to Soho for me, and it's lovely having the park right there for Naomi, who's beginning to walk.

Naomi adores her aunt Sheilah who brings her outrageously great toys and loves getting down on the floor and helping her play with them. Our friendship hits the same bumps it always has, and gets past them one way or another. That's the thing about friendship.

Speaking of friendship, I also see a fair amount of Craig. Yes, he still does the same work, and he still cries alone after he's pulled off a good one. He also still plays wonderful piano in his off-hours. So far there is no lover in his life—not that I know about. No, I don't trust him three feet away, but we kind of love each other and I will never forget that he gave me back George.

Craig's Paulist tendencies do not sit easily in Michael's head or heart, but even he feels a certain gratitude: Gabriel McCail's book was yanked from his publisher's list at the last minute in a scandal that made hot media gossip for a few days. It seems there was an anonymous tip to the media that major sections describing Paul's elaborate scams, pulled off in partnership with one Auguste Gramont, were bogus, invented by the author to add excitement. Investigative reporting proved that no shady Swiss venture capitalist by that name existed. McCail protested loud and long through any media that would have him; Marina Beck, Paul Boudreau's longtime patron and client, let it be known that she was incensed by the author's unprofessional conduct and publicly repudiated the book and everything in it—especially the notion that she might be Paul's mother—as nothing but "a filthy lie." McCail was able to come up with no proof to refute her.

Paul still visits me. He always will, I know, but it happens less—sometimes for days in a row, not at all. Maybe this means I'm coming closer to finding places to put things, but I don't know about that. I wonder sometimes as I hold Naomi in my lap what way I will find to tell her that her mother killed. How? When? Can there be a right time? What place inside herself will she find to put this knowledge? I will tell her the truth—all of it. But it's likely to come in pieces.

And George . . . sometimes I catch myself humming and Naomi looks up at me with my own amber eyes—my grandfather's eyes—and I sing louder: *I love you, love you dear, I cross my heart it's true. Do you believe me?* I'm just teaching her to call out, *I do.* She's a comic in her bones and it makes her laugh.

I do, George. I do.

ML

7/03